10 -

COLORADO RIVER COUNTRY

ALSO BY DAVID LAVENDER

Los Angeles Two Hundred

The Southwest

Winner Take All:
The TransCanada Canoe Trail

California:
A Bicentennial History

Nothing Seemed Impossible:
William Ralston and Early San Francisco

David Lavender's Colorado

California, Land of New Beginnings

The Rockies

The American Heritage History of the Great West

Climax at Buena Vista:
American Campaigns in Northeastern Mexico, 1846–47

The Fist in the Wilderness

Red Mountain

Westward Vision:
The Story of the Oregon Trail

Story of Cyprus Mines Corporation

Bent's Fort

Land of Giants

Trail to Santa Fe

The Big Divide

Golden Trek

Andy Claybourne

Mike Maroney, Raider

Trouble at Tamarack

One Man's West

COLORADO RIVER COUNTRY

DAVID LAVENDER

E.P. DUTTON, INC.   NEW YORK

The photographs used as headnotes for each chapter have been reproduced here with the permission of the following:

Chapters 1, 2, 3, 5, 6, 7, 9, 11, 13, 14, 15—Department of Special Collections, University of California, Santa Barbara
Chapters 4, 10—Henry E. Huntington Library
Chapter 8—Utah Historical Society
Chapter 12—Stan Rasmussen, Bureau of Reclamation

Portions of this book have appeared in slightly different form in *American Heritage* and *The American West*.

Published in the United States by
E. P. Dutton, Inc., 2 Park Avenue, New York, N.Y. 10016

Library of Congress Cataloging in Publication Data

Lavender, David Sievert,
Colorado River country.

Bibliography: p.
Includes index.
1. Colorado River (Colo.-Mexico)—History. 2. Colorado River Valley (Colo.-Mexico)—History. I. Title.
F788.L38   1982   978.8'1   82-5190
AACR2

ISBN: 0-525-24151-5

Published simultaneously in Canada by Clarke, Irwin & Company Limited, Toronto and Vancouver

10 9 8 7 6 5 4 3 2 1
First Edition

To all those with whom I've run the rivers,
especially Mildred

Contents

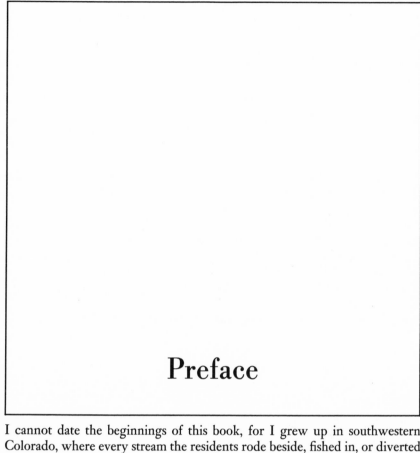

Preface

I cannot date the beginnings of this book, for I grew up in southwestern Colorado, where every stream the residents rode beside, fished in, or diverted water from ran toward the river that gave the state its name. Plus this: in the La Plata Mountains, overlooking the distant escarpment of Mesa Verde, is Lavender Peak, 13,160 feet high, named for my brother; and about one hundred miles to the northwest, running through the sandstone at the southeastern edge of Canyonlands National Park, Utah, is Lavender Canyon, named either for the color that suffuses the rock at sunset or, oldtimers say, for my stepfather. One part of the basin and what its water means to the people who live there has always been ingrained in me. Even so, a full awareness of the river's scope waited until one day in 1938 when I rode with some of Al Scorup's cowboys—you'll get to know him later on in the book—to a canyon rim fifteen hundred feet high, looked down, and saw the Green and Colorado rivers mingle. That image and some of the questions it aroused have never lost their vividness.

More images and more questions have come since then from roaming most parts of the basin by foot, horse, and jeep, and from running many

xii   COLORADO RIVER COUNTRY

sections of the main river and its major tributaries by boat. Why did people come here at all, to this stark, angular land, its bones clearly visible in the bare walls of giant canyons? It was their insistence on coming, and staying— exploring, trapping, mining, farming, testing each resource they found according to their own lights—that finally aroused the interest of the federal government in a region it had tended to ignore. Once the U.S. Reclamation Service, later renamed the Bureau of Reclamation, went into the business of storing and transporting water, the history of the Colorado River Basin changed radically. Although the region embraces one-twelfth of the area of the nation's contiguous states, its history up until then had been mainly that of men and women of many different persuasions trying to get along with arid nature as best they could. Afterward, as the river was being harnessed, the struggle with nature was replaced by conflicts between antagonistic groups. Water users in one region were set against those in another. Environmentalists battled water and electrical-power brokers. Recreationists quarreled with all of them and with each other over what kinds of development, in and around artificial bodies of water or beside majestic natural wonders, were most to be desired. In the midst of those confrontations the drama of the often desperate earlier struggles was forgotten.

It is not my intention to write about the controversial present—that subject has been well covered in several recent volumes, both scholarly and popular (for instance, Philip Fradkin's *A River No More*)—but to recover the story of the river's long past. About the time I was laying plans to do so, Otis "Dock" Marston died. That indefatigable collector of Colorado River memorabilia had bequeathed his papers on the subject to the Huntington Library, San Marino, California. After the hundreds of file boxes had been fumigated against paper-chewing insects and blight (and permeated with a most dreadful odor), I received a grant-in-aid from the library for a preliminary investigation of the collection's resources. That done, I went ahead on my own among Marston's assemblage of diaries, rare books, pictures, and reminiscences.

Another valuable hoard, gathered by that quintessential river rat, Harry Aleson, is now part of the holdings of the Utah Historical Society, Salt Lake City, where I skimmed as much of it as my time allowed. And, as usual, the staffs of the Western History Department, Denver Public Library; the Colorado Historical Society; the Museum of Northern Arizona; the special collections library at Northern Arizona University; and the Arizona Historical Society were helpful. So, too, were the people in the Bureau of Land Management offices at St. George and Kanab, Utah; those at Arches / Canyonlands, Zion Canyon, Mesa Verde, and Grand Canyon national parks; and those connected with the Bureau of Reclamation in Phoenix, Boulder City (Nevada), and Salt Lake City. Equally courteous were the public relations officials at the Lake Mead and Glen Canyon recreational areas. Meanwhile, home base, so to speak, remained the Wyles Collection and the Special Collections of the University of California, Santa Barbara—with a special nod to Denise Miller and Dodie Anderson, resourceful librarians at the Thatcher School, Ojai, California. To all of them, my thanks.

Finally, any author treating a subject that tempts him to discursiveness needs an editor such as mine, John Macrae III. He roused my ire at times, but much of the book as it now stands bears his imprint.

COLORADO
RIVER
COUNTRY

Grand Canyon from the north

1

The Land

The region drained by the Colorado River is vast—some 244,000 square miles altogether. In a normal year, as much as 70 percent of the water carried by the river originates in the Rockies, which form the region's eastern boundary. In spring, as snowdrifts deposited by winter storms begin to shrink, water gurgles among the interstices of millions of gray talus boulders that litter the mountain slopes above timberline. Glittering streamlets slide into alpine lakes half blue with sky reflection, half gray with sludge ice, then leap over waterfalls and escape into spruce-filled valleys. More rills dash in from the sides. The swelling streams grow turbid; their caroling turns into a roar.

As the Colorado's northern tributaries gather force, and the elevation drops, the look of the land changes. Thick stands of spruce, fir, and aspen give way to stately groves of ponderosa pine. These are followed, lower down, by forests of twisted junipers and piñon pines, then by thickets of Gambel oak, and still lower by vast flats thinly covered with sagebrush and occasional clumps of prickly pear cactus. No trees grow here except for narrow bands of willows and cottonwoods along the streambanks and around an occasional ranch house. Beyond the Uinta Mountains, which run roughly parallel to the

Wyoming-Utah border, lies the most spectacular part of the entire river basin. This is the Colorado Plateau—or more properly the Colorado Plateaus, for the entire expanse is cut through by numerous canyons anywhere from fifty to five thousand feet deep: sudden precipices where the world drops away without warning. The Utah segment of the plateaus was known by native Americans as "the land of frozen rainbows" because of the magnificently colored and banded sedimentary rock that has been carved by the action of wind and water into arches, pinnacles, vast winding escarpments, and sheer canyon walls.

Just north of the Arizona border, the high plateaus of Utah drop abruptly through a series of huge, variegated steps—pink, white, red—to what is known as the Arizona Strip. The Strip itself, a dismal, isolated oblong of broad, parched terraces, is moated on the south by the Grand Canyon. Beyond the canyon are the pine-cloaked Central Highlands of Arizona, which extend toward the Continental Divide in southwestern New Mexico and form the Colorado Basin's southern boundary. Here the Gila, the river's main southern tributary, has its tenuous beginnings. What is left of it after passing through the southwestern desert joins the Colorado itself at Yuma, Arizona, where precipitation averages three inches a year and summer temperatures may reach 120°. Below Yuma, the river meanders through a vast, sluggish delta before finally emptying into the Gulf of California. Its career has brought it a distance of fourteen hundred miles or more from the high slopes of the Rockies, at elevations of more than ten thousand feet, where its northern tributaries—the Green, the Yampa, the Dolores and the San Juan, the Eagle, the Roaring Fork and the Gunnison—have their origin. Near the end of that career, the river's perennially shifting course used to spill over occasionally, before Boulder Dam was built, into the Salton Trough, whose lowest point is 235 feet below sea level.

The plateau region, midway between these extremes, is a mile or more above sea level. But it is generally believed that the entire expanse more than once lay under water—that it has been submerged at least seven times over, by oceans that later withdrew. Each of these epochs left behind a massive layer of sediment—sometimes several layers—which through eons of pressure and chemical action were altered and solidified into rock. Whenever the land was exposed, the forces of erosion stripped away accumulations that had been gathering over many millions of years.

In addition, changes have occurred because of shifts within the earth's unstable crust. According to current thinking, that crust is made up of huge natural rafts or plates that float on the semiplastic layer known as the mantle. Any bumping or scraping of one plate against another produces shock waves and cause the edges to hump into ridges or, more frequently, to produce fractures known as faults. Somewhere between sixty-five and seventy million years ago, the plate on which the North American continent rides is thought to have received a tremendous shove from the west—a continuing, massive pressure that lasted for perhaps twenty million years. As a result of that protracted collision—geologists call it the Laramide Revolution or Orogeny —vast areas that had been under water were raised and the sea that covered them retreated. It has not returned since—which does not mean that it is gone forever.

According to current geologic thinking, the Laramide Revolution was the event that raised what we know as the Rocky Mountains and sent what we know as the Colorado River toward the sea. The process was a repetitive one: periods during which the forces of erosion smoothed down the uplifted rocks were followed by new pulsations, often accompanied by furious volcanic activity, during which fresh mountains appeared, to be attacked by erosion in their turn. Changes in climate were a part of the process. During a sequence of Ice Ages that ended about ten thousand years ago, glaciers accumulated on the upper slopes, and it is their work that accounts for most of the scenic rock carving in the high peaks of Wyoming and Colorado: the open-ended gouges known as cirque basins, the horn peaks, knife-edged arêtes and splintered crags, and also the broad, rolling tops and great rounded slopes where soil clings and short-stemmed alpine flowers meet summer with a blaze of color.

By and large, the geologic period of which we are a part has been one of erosion. The landscape it has produced in the Colorado River Basin may even now be at the peak of its grandeur. If so, the grandeur is a fragile one. It is threatened on many fronts, and from many quarters; but the most urgent of those threats has to do with water supply. For water is precious here. Much of the land drained by the Colorado is seared by heat, wind, and desert glare. According to measurements kept for nearly a century, the total amount of water carried down from the Rockies and the high plateaus of Utah to the Gulf of California averages a meager 13.8 million acre-feet a year. By comparison, the Columbia River, with a drainage area only slightly larger, carries thirteen times as much. Nevertheless, for tens of thousands of years, undeterred by a harsh climate and a contorted topography, people have insisted on living here. This book is an account of how they fared. (A more detailed explanation of the geology of the Colorado Basin is contained in the appendix, The Geology of the Colorado Basin, p. 192.)

Mohave (Mojave) Indians

2
───────

The Ancient Ones

Tens of thousands of years ago, cold air radiating southward from the ice sheets that stretched from the Arctic into the northeastern and north-central parts of the present United States created, in the Southwest, an ideal environment for big, grass-eating mammals and the predators that hunted them. Precipitation was frequent, and the Colorado River Basin and adjacent areas held many streams, ponds, and marshes; grassy savannas spread over the valleys and mesas. East of the Rockies—or so it is believed—vast herds of mammoths, tapirs, sloths, and big-horned bison roamed, and some crossed the Continental Divide to graze on the meadows of the Colorado River Basin. By 12,000 B.C., human hunters were tracking those animals into the Southwest.

Not much is known of these people, whom archeologists refer to as Paleo-Indians. Like the hunters of the Great Plains, they knew the uses of fire and had learned to chip stone into thin, fluted spear points, three or four inches long, and to attach these points to wooden shafts for spearing animals. When occasion offered, several bands of hunters might join forces to ambush a mammoth at a water hole, or to separate young animals from a herd. After slaughtering the quarry, they were able to skin the carcass with stone knives;

perhaps women did this work. The Paleo-Indians may have draped hides over a framework of brush, bone, and antlers as a temporary shelter, and they also took refuge in caves and under overhanging cliffs. They kept their bodies warm with the skins of large animals and the fur of small ones. Women aided in food procurement by gathering seeds, berries, and nuts.

As the ice sheets retreated northward—slowly at first, then with increasing momentum—the local glaciers in the Rockies poured howling floods into the Colorado River, and the sandstone sides of the laccolithic peaks above the plateau were deeply scoured by erosion. By around 10,000 B.C., all the ice caps had vanished from the mountain peaks of the Southwest. Increasing warmth was attended by increasing aridity. As the great savannas disappeared, the herds of mammals thinned out. Desperate for food, the hunters congregated around the survivors and hastened their extinction. Whether the Paleo-Indians then migrated eastward to the less desiccated plains east of the Rockies, adapted themselves to the Basin's changing climate, or died out entirely is unknown. In any event, a new culture arose in the Southwest. Known to archeologists as the Western Archaic or Desert Culture, by around 5500 B.C. it had become widespread throughout the region between the Rockies and the Sierra Nevada.

Instead of depending primarily on meat, the Desert People lived mainly on plant foods, supplemented occasionally by rabbits, ground squirrels, birds, fish, lizards, desert turtles, large insects, or—on lucky days—deer or bighorn sheep. Extended family groups of twenty to fifty people foraged on the plateaus in the fall, when pine nuts were ripe and deer were fat; in spring they moved into the foothills and canyons to harvest cactus and yucca fruit, or to dig up bulbous roots with pointed sticks. Often they found shelter in caves, as the Paleo-Indians had done, or heaped brush into what later people called wickiups. Seeds were ground into flour with a cylindrical stone (later known in Spanish as the *mano*), rolled endlessly back and forth over a concave slab of rock (the *metate*). Some Desert People made crude vessels of clay, but they had not learned the art of firing them for durability. They cooked their food in baskets so tightly woven that they held water, which the cooks brought to a boil by dropping in hot stones; fragments of their basketry dating as far back as 7500 B.C. have been found in Utah. The Desert People showed great artistic skill, using colored earth and plant juices applied with fingers or brushes, or sprayed from the mouth, on protected cliff faces. A notable example, showing a procession of cloaked, ghostly beings, is still to be seen on a wall of Horseshoe Canyon in Utah (now part of Canyonlands National Park). Petroglyphs were pecked or incised into the dark patina of desert varnish in such a way that the lighter-colored stone beneath showed strongly through.[1] Animal figurines made of split willow twigs, dating back four thousand years, have been found in caves along the Grand Canyon.

The summer clothing of the Desert People amounted to little more than breechclouts for men, short aprons for the women, and crude fiber sandals; they made robes for winter use by winding and tying together strips of rabbit fur. They hunted with spears, hurling them with the *atlatl,* a device made of wood and sinew, and also caught rabbits by driving them into defiles across which long fiber nets had been stretched. The difficulties of food procurement discouraged the melding of family groups into bands or tribes. Only two or three times a year did a few of the wandering groups come together for ceremonies and the marriages that helped cement their fragile alliances. Primitive though this society was, it was maintained by the Southern Paiutes with little change for ten thousand years, and was not finally shattered by white intrusion until late in the nineteenth century.[2]

Agriculture, which had been practiced in central Mexico since about 5000 B.C., caught on slowly farther north. Although primitive varieties of maize had been carried north by 2000 B.C., as discoveries of tiny cobs in Bat Cave, New Mexico, indicate, cultivation was not carried on extensively until new migrants equipped with hardier kinds of seed reached the Gila River in about 300 B.C. Those newcomers are known to us as Hohokam, with the accent on the final syllable. (The name is the plural form of a modern Pima Indian word, *hokam,* meaning any item, such as an empty jar, abandoned hut, or race of people, that is "used up.") The region was already occupied by a group we know as the Cochise—nomads who preferred the mesquite-saguaro foothills, whereas the Hohokam settled close to the river.[3] The largest of the Hohokam villages—called Snaketown by Pima Indians who occupied the site many centuries later—sprawled across 250 acres on the north bank of the Gila, near present-day Chandler, Arizona. The town proper occupied the higher of two wide terraces; the lower one was planted with corn, beans, squash, and cotton, and was watered from a canal three miles long that fed a series of precisely engineered irrigation ditches. By 1000 A.D., Snaketown housed about two thousand inhabitants. Eventually a complex of ditches aggregating more than 150 miles in length nurtured several satellite villages in the area.

Dwellings were pit houses, consisting of a depression about two feet deep, topped by a timber-supported dome of earth with a smoke hole at its apex. The earthen walls served to keep out the cold in winter and the heat in summer. Interspersed among the houses were well-trampled work and play areas, trash mounds, and cremation sites—the Hohokam disposed of their dead by burning the corpses on beds of mesquite coals. They dug slanting, walk-in wells that reached water at ten feet underground; when these became fouled with use, they were turned into trash pits. The villagers also constructed big, bowl-shaped depressions, walled with stone, in which they played games with hard rubber balls, and they erected, evidently for religious purposes, flat-topped earthen pyramids. Artists pecked designs into boulders, carved figurines from stone, and produced the first etchings ever made, using seashells and an acid derived from cactus juice.

At some time between 600 and 900 A.D., overflow population from the Hohokam towns drifted north to the Verde Valley and west to the lower Colorado. In the latter region the migrants mingled with a Desert Culture group, ancestors of the modern Yuman tribes. Not all of the ideas the newcomers brought with them were accepted by the river people. In the fiery climate of the lower Colorado, brush huts rather than pit houses continued to be used for shelter. Nor did the river people build irrigation ditches. Instead, they waited for the annual spring rise of the Colorado to recede, and then planted corn, beans, squash, melons, and gourds in the mudflats left by the retreating water. The summer solstice was by then at hand, and the intense heat brought the crops to maturity before the soil dried out. Stored carefully and supplemented with mesquite beans, saguaro fruit, agave roots, and small game, the harvest normally provided a year's food supply. The chief drawback was that an occasional drought in the distant Rockies meant that the river did not rise; in such a year, since there could be no planting, there might be hunger to the point of starvation.

While the Hohokam were spreading their culture throughout much of what is now southern Arizona, another vigorous group, the Anasazi (from a Navajo word meaning "the ancient ones"), was developing new ways of life in the Four Corners country—the region surrounding the point where Utah, Colorado, New Mexico, and Arizona come together. As nearly as archeologists can deduce, the ancestors of the Anasazi were Desert Culture people who left their original homes west of the Colorado River a little more than two thousand years ago and, after traveling east in small groups over many years, at last put down roots in the high canyon country creased by the tributaries of the San Juan River. From roughly 1 A.D. to 550 A.D. they lived mostly in caves and under overhanging cliffs; these shelters and the area's dry climate have preserved their artifacts and have mummified their corpses so remarkably that archeologists have been able to reconstruct many details of their appearance and their customs.

Until about 500 A.D. they remained gatherers of plant food and hunters of small game. Like other Desert People in the Southwest, they used milling stones, *atlatls*, nets, and baskets. They also produced necklaces and pendants of highly polished, colored stone and of seashells that must have been traded from group to group across the long trails from the ocean. Other ornaments were made of acorn cups, juniper berries, and feathers. Their early rock art displayed big trapezoidal figures bedecked with elaborate headgear and fringed belts.

Slowly, beginning in about 500 A.D., the Anasazi exchanged their cave dwellings for pit houses and took to supplementing their hunting and gathering of wild plant food by the raising of corn, squash, and beans—practices that probably reached them from the Mogollon people, who lived south of them along both slopes of the Continental Divide and were in contact with the farmers of Mexico. They acquired the bow and arrow, and succeeded in domesticating the wild turkeys of the high mesas, apparently for their feathers rather than for their flesh. Hair clinging to mummified skulls indicates that the men wore theirs elaborately coifed; the women, on the other hand, periodically cut their hair short. The strands may have gone into the making of the pouches and belts, woven of both dog and human hair, that have been retrieved from the ruins.

Stable food supplies brought about increased birth rates and attracted immigrants from the outside, forcing later generations to spread farther and farther out through the San Juan Basin, where they developed an extraordinary ability to utilize every bit of available moisture. The women, who had been the chief foragers for wild plants, took over the role of cultivators. On the high mesas, where elevations ranged from sixty-five hundred to seventy-five hundred feet, they cleared away sagebrush with heavy hoes made from the scapular bones of large animals and indented the ground for seed with pointed sticks while it was still moist from melting snow. At these altitudes, enough rain would generally fall to bring the crops to maturity. At lower elevations, they searched out spots where storm water percolating down through porous sandstone emerged in springs or seeps at the base of cliffs, and there they planted their seeds. They cleared fields in the alluvial fans where narrow side canyons break out onto more open country. Storm water rushing out of those funnel mouths spread naturally (or was guided in its spreading by low rock walls built by the farmers) across the alluvium, and thus new areas were made ready for the expanding population.

Other short rock walls were spread in parallel rows—a sort of stepladder effect—across small, shallow gullies dropping down out of areas of relatively high precipitation. The walls trapped sediment and built up small terraces of moist, fertile topsoil. No single terrace was big enough to harbor many plants, but several utilized together would feed an extended family. Favorable places —the north slope of Navajo Mountain, near the Arizona-Utah border, for one —were checkered with them, and more than a thousand have been counted in the Wetherill Mesa section of Mesa Verde National Park alone.[4] In only a few places were irrigation ditches built.

Meanwhile, other home-seekers were carrying their experiments with agriculture into the deep, twisting side canyons of the San Juan, into the Glen Canyon section of the Colorado, and, to a lesser extent, into the upper part of the Grand Canyon itself. On high ledges in these canyons, and wherever else deep defiles were available, they built miniature stone huts as storage places for the grain they harvested. Whether this was mainly out of concern with hiding their caches from wild animals or from human sneak thieves is a matter of speculation. But since these small granaries survived (thanks to their high location) long after the bottomland houses had vanished, the first white explorers concluded that they must have been built as dwellings by a race of dwarfs. John Wesley Powell, noting their structural resemblance to the more imposing ruins still to be found in the Four Corners area, suggested that they had been built by ancient progenitors of the Aztecs.[5] (In fact, during the later nineteenth century the words "Aztec" and "Montezuma" were attached to ancient ruins in both New Mexico and Arizona.)

Beginning around 750 A.D., some of the Anasazi—but not all of them—began moving from pit houses to surface dwellings. At first, the new towns consisted of only half a dozen or so living and storage rooms arranged either in a straight line, a shallow arc, or an L-shape. Then, as the villages grew, the lines of houses bent inward to enclose central plazas where trading took place and ceremonial dances were held. If additional space was needed after that, it was found in one of two ways. Either a new village was built near the original—there were sixteen clusters within a radius of a quarter of a mile at the Farview section of Mesa Verde National Park—or a town expanded upward. Pueblo Bonito in Chaco Canyon, New Mexico, reached the then-extraordinary height of five stories.

Pit houses were not forgotten. Back-country farmers (and they may well have constituted the bulk of the population) still utilized them near their fields. And even after city people had moved into surface houses, they recalled the intimacies of the former sunken living quarters and of the simple religious ceremonies that had been held there. Accordingly, they transformed the old quarters into new underground structures known to us now by the Hopi word *kiva.* * What had been the hearth became an altar. Near it was the *sipapu,* a small hole symbolic of the passage through which the first people were believed to have emerged from the underworld. The side entrance became a ventilator shaft, and a ladder protruding through what had once been a smoke hole furnished ingress and egress. Each clan had its own kiva, which, as village life became more complex, constituted the exclusive domain of the males. Since the women, who tended the crops, returned each season to the same field and thus established usufructory rights to it, Anasazi society became matrilinear: that is, when a man married he went to live with his wife's family, and the family name and ownership of property passed down through her. The males retained their importance as shamans and as leaders of increasingly complex religious ceremonies; the sacred objects connected with these were kept in the kivas.

Increasingly, there was trade, some of it over long distances. Turquoise

*A few kivas, notably those at today's pueblo of Zuñi, were built aboveground.

mined along the canyons was exchanged for parrot feathers brought from Mexico. Salt was another valuable article of commerce; one vein in the Virgin River canyon was tunneled out to a depth of three hundred feet with the most primitive of tools. In the warmer valleys, cotton-growing took hold, and with it came spinning, weaving, and the production of more comfortable clothing —occupations carried on by men, as in Pueblo society today. Pottery, made by women, took on exquisite shapes and distinctive designs.

By 1000 A.D. or so, the Anasazi cultural tradition had spread from southwestern Colorado across southern Utah into the lower valleys of the Virgin and Muddy rivers in Nevada; it extended along both sides of the Continental Divide in northwestern New Mexico, into Monument Valley, and along the eastern part of the Grand Canyon's south rim. During periods of favorable precipitation some farmers even occupied choice spots in the gorge's bottom, as they did in the bottom of Glen Canyon and its tributaries.*

A little after 1100 A.D., the Anasazi of the Virgin and Muddy rivers had begun to drift away from their homes. By 1150, none remained. Paiute raiders may have been one cause of their departure. Drought and exhausted soil may have played a part, as they did later at Sunset Crater and also in forcing the abandonment of Anasazi farms in the bottom of the Grand Canyon and along its southern rim.

The displaced Anasazi may have traveled east to join the communities in what is now the Four Corners area. There, in such centers as Mesa Verde and Chaco Canyon, and along the banks of the San Juan River, a burst of city-building and an opening of new farmlands took place. But soon thereafter, as though swept by a sudden frenzy, the people of Mesa Verde moved into spectacular cliff dwellings along the sides of the region's deep, tawny gorges. Throughout the southeastern part of the Colorado River Basin, other groups did the same—the Sinaguas, south of what is now Flagstaff; the Salados, near Tonto Creek and the Salt River, not far from present-day Phoenix; and the Mogollons of New Mexico. They usually chose cliffside caves with a southern exposure that caught the sun in winter, and that contained seeps of water. But these must have been dangerous places for the old and the very young. Fields and firewood were hard to reach, and even a cave with a southern exposure must have been oppressive compared with the airy sites on the mesa tops and in the valleys that had been left behind.

Where there were no caves, as at Aztec and Chaco canyons, multi-storied dwellings were turned into fortresses. Kivas were moved inside the towns,

*Enough regional differences developed here and there, especially in pottery and rock art, that archeologists have given individual names to the main sub-provinces of the Anasazi culture. A brief description of them, and of the Fremont and Cohonina people, who occupied adjacent territories and were influenced by the Anasazi, appears in Note 6 on page 199.

and the entrances everywhere were now reachable only by ladders that could be pulled up at will. At the same time, however, it would appear that the pit-house dwellers went on living in the same exposed way as before. And though the ladders suggest fear of outsiders, no conclusive evidence of warfare has been discovered.

In any event, few of the cliff dwellings lasted more than a century. Drought is the explanation most commonly offered for their having been abandoned. But although Mesa Verde tree rings do show that from 1273 to 1299 precipitation was considerably below normal, tree rings also show that the Anasazi of the region had already lived through six acutely dry periods without any significant change in their way of living.[7] A more likely conjecture is that the builders may have brought on their own doom through abuse of the environment. During the course of several centuries they might have cut too many trees for use as firewood and in construction, opening the way for widespread erosion of land already overused for planting—a conjecture supported on a local scale by the series of population dispersals that occurred in the Kayenta area of northwestern Arizona between the years 1250 and 1300.

Before 1250, small settlements were numerous in broad Monument Valley, north of today's Kayenta, and in Kletha Valley, to the west. Between the two valleys is a rugged area of red mesas stacked one on top of each other. They drain through a trellis of side canyons into Tsegi Creek, whose sandstone walls rise in some places to a height of a thousand feet. Although Tsegi was (and is) well watered by its side canyons and by several seeps and springs, close archeological study has revealed that only a few families lived there before 1260 or so. On the other hand, the more open lands of Monument and Kletha valleys sustained several hundred people—until about 1250, when families began, one by one, to abandon their dwellings. In the 1260's small parties started entering Tsegi Canyon. Evidence based on ceramic types, details of construction, and dates established from tree rings in logs used for building strongly suggests that the newcomers were from the Monument-Kletha area; the assumption is that they had left because erosion was lowering the water tables near their former homes so much that springs were running dry. The fact that after arriving in Tsegi these newcomers cut and stacked more timber for construction use than they themselves needed has been taken to mean that they were scouts for a future migration.

If so, they found what they wanted where two side streams enter upper Tsegi Canyon from opposite directions, creating a large hollow filled with fine loam where the water table was shallow and the stream meandered gently. The hollow could be devoted entirely to agriculture, and homes could be built in the western tributary, which is unique to this day for the aspens that flourish there in the heart of the red desert. A little above the tops of the trees a great arching cave breaks the smooth face of the gulch's towering wall, and there, in about 1272, a burst of construction began. Within a decade, Betatakin, as the town is now called, contained 130 stone rooms of varying sizes. Some were two or three stories high. Others were tucked deep into the recesses of the cave. Others perched almost at the brink, overlooking the shimmer of the aspens.

A few years later, building of the same sort began in the upper reaches of Keet Seel Canyon, which enters the Tsegi opposite the mouth of Betatakin gulch. The cave here was a long, low-roofed slit, its walls streaked by a tapestry of desert varnish—a phenomenon believed to be produced by manganese and iron oxide carried in water seeping downward along the rock face. By the time the buildings at Keet Seel were finished, in the year 1287, the total population of the two cliff dwellings plus a few huts on the canyon bottom came to seven hundred or more. Three years later, everyone had departed—no one knows where.[8] During the period from 1290 to 1300, the entire Four Corners area was likewise abandoned: Mesa Verde, Chaco Canyon, Aztec, Hovenweep, the settlements in the tributaries of Glen Canyon, the cliff houses of Canyon de Chelly, the towns of central Utah and northwestern Utah, all fell silent.

At Betatakin and Keet Steel, the reason for the exodus seems fairly clear: erosion, eating upstream as it invariably does, lowered water tables until farms on the canyon floor dried out and were no longer productive. But for the others, just what combination of factors—worn-out soil, religious upheaval, discord between villages, attacks by nomads, drought—may have been responsible is still undetermined.

It is known that some of the refugees settled on the mesas where the Hopis now live, and as far south as the Gila, where the Hohokam were by then living in surface dwellings rather than pit houses. Others, ancestors of the eastern Pueblo Indians of modern times, crossed the Continental Divide to the valley of the Rio Grande and its tributaries. One group perched itself on top of Acoma Mesa, in New Mexico. The Mogollons may have assembled in the six cities of Háwikuh, whose remains we known today as the village of Zuñi. The widespread cultural unit known to archeologists as the Fremont people are believed to have lost their own identity by mingling with the Utes.

The Hohokam, as their energy waned, had been allowing their canals to go to pieces. By around the year 1400, they had regressed to the desert style of living that had prevailed in the region a millennium before. It is believed that their descendants are the Pima and Papago Indians of today. The southern Paiutes, still following their ancient ways, drifted into the Virgin River valley and eastward along the north rim of the Grand Canyon. The Utes spread through the mountains of Utah and Colorado. Apaches and Navajos, once members of the same tribe, came down from the north in about 1500 and split into two groups as they gradually moved westward—the Navajos toward the San Juan, the Apaches (or some of them) toward the Gila. Then the Spaniards arrived, and a new era of intrusion had begun.

Zuñi pueblo in New Mexico

3

The Spanish *Entradas*

The first foreign eyes to see any part of the Colorado River Basin would seem to have been those of Alvar Núñez Cabeza de Vaca and three companions: Alonso del Castillo, Andrés Dorantes, and Dorantes's black slave, Esteban. In 1528, after their ship, bearing several hundred would-be colonists, was stranded near Tampa Bay (today's Florida), they had improvised boats out of horsehide and timbers and crept west toward Mexico. Storms swamped the last eighty of the wayfarers off the Texas coast, where those who did not drown were enslaved by Indians.

The four men escaped and again headed west, escorted by crowds of natives, who took them for great healers. It is possible that they touched the headwaters of the Gila River before veering southwest into what is now Mexican Sonora. In any event, they had heard of the Colorado Basin and brought tales of it to Mexico City in the summer of 1536—marvelous tales picked up from Indian sign-talk and a smattering of words learned from their fellow travelers, tales of cities far in the north where people wore clothes made not of animal skins but of cotton, lived in buildings many stories tall, and had turquoises, copper, and emeralds. The tellers could prove the existence of "emeralds" for in Sonora an Indian trader had given Dorantes five lovely green arrowheads that he had acquired in the north in exchange for parrots' feathers. Probably the stone was malachite, a mineral of copper, but no one thought so. For it was a standard article of Spanish faith that materials rare in the Old World were common in the new.

Emeralds for feathers! Antonio de Mendoza, the king's new viceroy in Mexico City, listened rapt. At once credulous and cautious, he wrote the king suggesting a reconaissance of the rumored cities and asked the three white wanderers to take charge of the exploration. Each refused. The viceroy then purchased Esteban and gave him as a guide to a Franciscan priest, Fray Marcos de Niza. The black man, who was illiterate, was to send Indian couriers back from time to time with reports of what lay ahead. To overcome language barriers, communication was to be by symbol. If the messenger carried a small cross, the land was ordinary, "and if there were something greater and better than New Spain, he should send a large cross."[1] But Esteban was to wait for his superior before going on to the cities.

Soon a cross as tall as a man came back—presumably a sign that by then Esteban had made contact with the regular trade route between northern Sonora and the six Zuñi pueblos in western New Mexico. A little later, from traders who had seen the terraced villages, Marcos himself began to hear impressive reports of them and of the kingdom, Cíbola, in which they stood.

The friar began to hurry. But then fugitives from the retinue that Esteban had gathered as he passed through Sonora stopped him and gasped out their story: at a place called Háwikuh, the black man had been killed, some young boys with him had been made captives, and the rest of the escort had fled in panic.

Marcos later told the viceroy that, notwithstanding the fugitives' story, he had moved on north until he could see, from a little hilltop, a glorious city spread across the plains in front of him. He had erected a cairn to mark the spot where he took possession of the land in the viceroy's name. He added that the trail was good, and that on the last stretch, for a man on horseback, the ocean was less than a day's ride away.

None of this was true.[2] And yet Marcos probably did not think he was lying. Esteban had sent back word of a stupendous city; the friar had heard similar reports; he had seen Peru and knew of the splendor of the Aztecs. And no doubt it was judicious to let it be supposed that he had laid eyes on the great city. Powerful rivals were in the field. Hernán Cortés, who claimed the sole right to explore the north, had already sent three ships under Francisco de Ulloa up the Gulf of California, which was not then recognized as a gulf, to see whether Cíbola could be reached by water. Hernando de Soto was moving westward from Florida, and Mendoza feared that he might reach Cíbola first. So the viceroy put together, under the supreme command of young Francisco Vázquez de Coronado, an expedition big enough to outface all Háwkiuh.

The core of the force was cavalry—275 soldiers of fortune, each owning one or more mounts, in a land where horses were still uncommon. Sixty-two others joined as infantrymen. Likewise on foot were five missionary priests, with Marcos as their leader, and close to a thousand Indian auxiliaries, a few accompanied by their wives. More than fifteen hundred head of cattle, sheep, and goats were driven along to be butchered as food during the march. Finally, there was a fleet. Another of Mendoza's protégés, Hernando de Alarcón, agreed to outfit two supply ships in Acapulco and pick up a third that would be waiting for him at a harbor near Culiacán.

When the ponderous land column reached Culiacán in late April, 1540, Coronado received a discouraging report. The town's *alcalde* (mayor), Melchior Díaz, who had done a little scouting on his own, said that the land ahead was rough and that the army should be divided for greater maneuverability. Agreeing, Coronado decided to push ahead with a vanguard of eighty cavalrymen, thirty foot-soldiers, all the priests (they were insistent on reaching the heathen as soon as possible), a few Indians, and a minimum of edible livestock. Melchior Díaz was ordered to come along as an additional guide and pacifier of strange Indians. The main army was to follow slowly to the Sonora River and wait there for instructions.

A hard march followed. The road Marcos had said was good was wretched. Highborn cavalrymen had to walk much of the way, leading their leg-weary, underfed mounts. Often they had to build trail. Each day they packed and unpacked their own beasts of burden, and cooked their own meals. Coronado grew more and more worried about supplies. Food was dwindling at an alarming rate, and the Indians they met along the way repeatedly told them that they were moving farther and farther inland. How, then, was he going to make contact with Alarcón's three vital ships?

They dragged out of Sonora to the Gila River. Crossing it, they angled northeast among a maze of dry, flat valleys and soaring mountains known as the *Despoblado*, the Uninhabited Place. From then on they found no Indian villages where food could be requisitioned. Tightening their belts, they struggled through heavy forests of pine, and into and out of difficult canyons. At length, half starved and exhausted, they dropped down from the Mogollon Rim onto the vast red and gray plains bordering the Little Colorado River.

The Indians of Cíbola had observed their approach. When the gaunt Spaniards drew up in front of terraced Háwikuh, all women and children had been removed, and the pueblo was defended by warriors recruited from throughout the district. It seemed a meager place quite without opulence. Scores of men stood armed with bows and arrows between them and the walls, while Indian shamans drew lines of cornmeal on the ground, marking a symbolic barrier. Behind them on the terraces, the defenders' bows were augmented by heaps of throwing stones.

A ritualist to the end, Coronado made signs of peace and had his heralds call for a bloodless surrender. The Zuñi on the ground, who had probably understood none of this, advanced with drawn bows. A sudden charge by the hungry Spaniards killed a dozen of them. The survivors scuttled back onto the terraces, pulled the ladders up behind them, and resumed their threatening attitudes. An assault was then launched, with Friar Marcos's blessing.

For a little while the defenders held out, as the cavalrymen whirled back their horses to avoid the storm of arrows. But then Coronado led the infantry against the walls, and the Zuñi were overwhelmed. Their arrows could not penetrate the armor of the Spanish officers or the heavy leather jackets of the soldiers. Coronado himself was knocked unconscious by a stone; otherwise there were no serious injuries. In less than an hour the Indians were begging, by means of signs, to be allowed to withdraw without further bloodshed.

Having recovered from his concussion, Coronado dutifully took note of the pueblo, its people, and the flora and fauna of the surrounding land, writing frankly to Mendoza: "There wasn't much here." Yet he kept looking for encouragement. Within a week of Háwikuh's fall he heard of seven more pueblos in a "province" called Tusayán, 120 miles to the northwest—we call it Hopi country today—and sent Captain Pedro de Tovar to investigate. Later a party led by another of his captains, Hernando de Alvarado, rode toward the Rio Grande.

By now it was evident that, with the expedition so far from the ocean, supplies would have to be brought overland from the nearest port on the Sonora shore and a station built halfway between to keep the Indians under control. That job Coronado turned over to Melchior Díaz, who was also to send word to Alarcón to have the matériel in his ships forwarded by trail. In addition, Díaz carried a letter in which Coronado asked Mendoza to send still more matériel from Mexico City. Friar Marcos de Niza, his usefulness ended, went with Díaz.

The group had scarcely left when Pedro de Tovar returned from Tusayán. The pueblos there were not impressive; but Tovar, through sign language and the stumbling efforts of an interpreter from Háwikuh, had picked up the information that there was a great river several days' ride to the west.

Coronado's mind jumped. A river! Where did it go? Could supply ships use it? Was Alarcón even then trying to navigate his way upstream? He ordered Cárdenas to take twenty-five men to the Hopi towns, enlist guides, ride to the river, learn as much about it as he could, and return in no more than eighty days.

A journal-keeper went with the party, but his account is now lost.

According to the summaries that have come down to us, the explorers rode west from the Hopi towns for twenty days. In that length of time they could easily have followed the south rim of the Grand Canyon westward, for scores of miles; but it would appear that they went very little distance, if any, past the point where the old Hopi trail first strikes the canyon, at today's Desert View.

How long Cárdenas sat there on his tired horse, gaping at a spectacle for which he was unprepared, is unknown. We do know that he estimated the distance from rim to rim correctly—ten to fifteen miles. But as his gaze dropped across those great bands of cliffs, the crumpled slopes and terraces, the profusion of inner buttes, and then reached the chocolate-colored river coiling through the bottom of the abyss—he guessed its width to be six feet! The Indians tried to set him straight. They are said to have told him that it was half a league across—a figure that must be the result of faulty translation, since half a league is a mile and a half. We know that Cárdenas spent three days riding along the rim looking for a trail into the canyon, though whether he went upriver or down is not clear. Nor has it been explained why the Hopi guides failed to take him to one of the trails they used in reaching the bottom.

At any rate, the three nimblest members of the party finally sought to scramble down on foot. After covering about a third of the distance they were forced to turn back, perhaps by the massive precipices of the Redwall. But they were able to determine that the river, even during the low-water stage of autumn, was considerably wider than six feet.

Another four days of riding added nothing to this slim store of knowledge. Pinched by shortages of water, Cárdenas gave up and returned to Háwikuh. His report to Coronado must have been pessimistic; even if Alarcón succeeded in pushing boats into the gorge, a most unlikely event, it was clear that the goods in them could not be packed out.

Díaz, meanwhile, was riding south to deliver his messages to the main army in Sonora, and Alarcón was edging northward along the coast. He found no signs of Coronado, but he did realize (as Cortés's ship's captain, Francisco de Ulloa, had done the year before) that he was in a gulf. The shores curved in on him; the water shoaled and took on a reddish tinge. Ahead he saw a tumult of foam filling what might be a river mouth. It was caused by the Colorado's awesome tidal bore.[3] The sight had halted Ulloa, but Alarcón was bolder. On August 26, 1540, during a pause in the churning, he led his three vessels into the delta—and was promptly grounded. The bore caught him, washing completely across the deck of his flagship. It was a miracle that his sailors were not all drowned. But then the tide lifted the vessels and all three managed to whirl with it into the estuary, where they now confronted a stream whose current was too swift to be withstood.

In spite of the sailors' protests, Alarcón moored the vessels behind a point where he thought they would be safe. Some of the men were delegated to clean the ships' bottoms and otherwise patch them up. The rest he directed to load supplies and a small cannon into two launches. They tried to row upstream, but the oars failed. Alarcón brought out tow ropes. The sucking mud and soft banks caving in underfoot resisted those efforts, too. It was then that hundreds of tall, naked, curious Cocopa Indians, their skins garishly painted, appeared out of the thickets of delta brush. In response to gifts of trinkets and urgent sign language by the group's Indian interpreter, they agreed to help with the pulling. For the next fifteen days the flotilla moved slowly ahead, one tribe giving way to the next, in debilitating heat, past endless sandy wastes and barren, fin-backed mountains. Their interpreter had somehow picked up a few words of the Yuman tongue that was widespread in the area, and through him Alarcón kept asking for news of Coronado. On about September 10 he learned of the battle of Háwikuh, fought the preceding July. His plea for volunteers to carry word across the desert to the land column evoked no response. Utterly frustrated, Alarcón decided to return to his ships. After reassuring the sailors there about his safety, he stocked up on provisions, recruited fresh soldiers, and started back up the river.

This second effort carried him only one day's journey farther upstream than he had gone before. There he encountered "some very high mountains through which the river flowed in a narrow canyon, where the boats passed with difficulty because there was no one to pull them"—almost certainly the vicinity of Pilot Knob, a few miles below the junction of the Colorado and Gila rivers.

By now the Indians near the river junction had also heard of the attack on Háwikuh, and had grown suspicious of these bearded newcomers. One of their shamans is reported to have thrown magic wands into the water, in the hope of bringing evil to the boats. No disaster ensued; still, it was not a good place to be stranded in. Alarcón halted, reasoning that since he had heard of Coronado, the expedition's commander might also learn of him. He had a tall cross erected, with letters in a container at its foot. Then he turned south and in mid-October, 1540, began his retreat through the gulf. The name he gave the river—Buen Guía (Good Guide)—came from Viceroy Mendoza's coat of arms.

Díaz, Coronado's lieutenant, just missed him. Once again, our knowledge of his trip depends on vague summaries set down at second hand. We do know that after launching work on the halfway station, Díaz headed west with twenty-five Spaniards and several Indian servants, guides, and interpreters—presumably at a slow pace, since they drove a herd of sheep with them for food.

It is believed that he moved directly west to the Gulf of California and then swung north across the terrible wastes of the Sonoran coast to the river's mouth.[4] There was no sign of Alarcón, but the group did find Indians who told them that white men in boats had been on the river recently and had left papers at the foot of a tree no great distance away—a glaring inconsistency in the narratives, for Alarcón had reported depositing his messages at the foot of a cross.

Deciding to make the best of the situation, Díaz set about exploring areas that Alarcón could not have reached. According to the summaries, Díaz was impressed by the awesome physical strength of the naked Yuma Indians. He exaggerated the size of their pit houses and remarked that on cold mornings they took torches from their campfires and carried them in front of their bellies for warmth, a custom that led him to name the stream Rio del Tízon (Firebrand River).

Where the men went, after somehow crossing the Tízon with their sheep, no one really knows. What finally happened, at any rate, was anti-climactic but terrible. Seeing a grayhound torment a sheep, Díaz ran at the dog with a lance. The weapon's point caught in the ground and the butt drove itself into his groin. The men got him across the river and started back for the halfway station in Sonora. He died in agony somewhere along the way and was buried in an unmarked grave.

The entire expedition was a failure. No jewels and no gold were found, although Coronado pursued rumors of them as far as the plains of central Kansas. Ailing and despondent, he turned back toward Mexico in April, 1542.

Nevertheless, both he and Alarcón had made an opening into the un-known. The "island" of California was now known to be the western edge of a long gulf into whose head a mighty river flowed—the same river, it was accurately surmised, that Cárdenas had glimpsed in the bottom of the Grand Canyon.[5] The Continental Divide had been recognized for what it was, and the Hopi, Zuñi, and Rio Grande pueblos had been clearly described. But this dry knowledge was unprofitable, and so it was forgotten.

Shortly after Coronado's return to Mexico, silver was discovered on the country's bleak central plateau. Prospectors and missionaries poured into what is now Chihuahua, on the eastern side of the Continental Divide. Tales of the prosperous cities of Cíbola were revived, and the valley of the Rio Grande became the target of the next *entradas*. Again there was disappoint-ment. It was as a last resort that the principal search turned to the Colorado River Basin.

Antonio de Espejo began it late in 1582, when he got permission to try to rescue three friars who had been stranded in the Rio Grande valley several months before.[6] On finding that the priests had been slain by Indians, some members of Espejo's party turned back. But the captain, with nine others, chose to cross the Continental Divide and see what lay to the west. They came back in the spring of 1583, after obtaining four thousand cotton blankets, some colored and some white, from the Hopi Indians—items for which there was a market in the Chihuahua mining towns. Hoping to be appointed governor of a new province to be called New Mexico, Espejo claimed, in addition, to have found silver ore, somewhere near what is now Jerome, Arizona, and estimated that in those wide wastes a quarter of a million Indians waited for the word of God.

By the time the king's council acted on his petition, Espejo was dead. It was Juan de Oñate who, in 1598, took upward of five hundred people and seven thousand head of livestock to a point near the junction of the Chama and Rio Grande valleys, and formed a settlement there.[8]

Though some of his scouts found signs of ore in central Arizona and heard Indian tales of a great river farther to the west, Oñate himself stayed in the east, plagued by Indian revolts and by discontent among his colonists. When he finally did break away, he went into Kansas, looking for the golden city of Quívara as Coronado had done sixty years before. He found no more than Coronado had, and on his return he learned that most of his colonists had fled back to Mexico, bearing tales of his mismanagement.

It was then that he ventured on a trip of discovery into the Basin. With thirty soldiers and two friars he followed the trail through the Zuñi and Hopi pueblos, and then turned southwest past the San Francisco Peaks until he encountered a stream we know as the Bill Williams River. This led him, not without trouble, to the Colorado. He named it Buena Esperanza (Good Hope).

As the explorers drifted south, they added to their repertoire of fables— Indians who lived on the odor of food alone; Indians whose ears were big enough to shade half a dozen people; Indians who slept underwater; Indians wearing golden bracelets and pendants, who had migrated south from a lake called Copalla. Aztecs! Oñate thought, and his tale of the golden ones would persist in the Southwest until the latter part of the nineteenth century.

On January 25, 1605, the party appears to have reached the Gulf of California. Oñate, however, did not recognize it as a gulf. The slant of the naked mountains and the yarns of the Cocopa Indians made him think that he was looking at an arm of the ocean. The mouth of the river, he added (did he see no tidal bore?), formed a marvelous natural harbor where galleons sailing from the Philippine Islands could find refuge from English freebooters. Moreover, the Indians had told him of fisheries nearby where they had found pearls as big as hazelnuts.

Ignoring the voyages of Ulloa and Alarcón, the authorities accepted Oñate's geographical report, and for another hundred years California was shown on the maps of the world as an island. But since his stories of wealth were unaccompanied by evidence, Oñate was recalled in 1608.

His New Mexican colonies remained. And it had been he who offhandly gave the river its name: of what we know as Little Colorado, he observed that "the water was nearly red [*Colorado*]."

He made one other observation. Between Zuñi and the shaggy western foothills of the Continental Divide is a mesa girt by pale sandstone cliffs two hundred feet high, known to us as El Morro, from its fancied resemblance to a castle. On top were two deserted pueblos. Below them, in a recess in the cliffs, was a deep pool from which Indians had once drawn water. While his group rested their horses, watching the reflected flicker of sunlight playing across the stone with its Indian petroglyphs, Oñate drew his dagger and carved into the rock, in curling script, a record beginning with the words *Paso por aquí*. Translated, they read: "There passed by here the Adelantado Don Juan de Oñate, from the discovery of the Sea of the South, the 16th of April of 1605."

Paso por aquí is a folksaying in the Southwest now. Since Oñate's time, many Spaniards and, afterwards, many Anglos have left their brief records there where Indians had incised the rocks long before. To preserve them while the stone itself lasts, the government set El Morro aside as a National Monument in 1906.

For nearly a hundred years after Oñate's removal, the only entrepreneurs along the edges of the Colorado River Basin were Franciscan missionaries eager to bring the Zuñi and Hopi pueblos into the fold. The process was slow, dangerous, and, where the Hopi were concerned, ultimately futile. What little progress had been made ended abruptly during the widespread Pueblo revolt of 1680. Having killed the missionaries, the Hopi opened their doors to refugees from the Rio Grande, enough newcomers to justify two new villages.

Fearful of Spanish reprisals, the refugees built their new villages atop mesas that would be hard to storm. The Hopi followed suit. When Diego de Vargas visited them during his reconquest of New Mexico in 1692, they went through the forms of submission, but with little or no intention of keeping their promises. In 1700, when a pro-Spanish faction in the village of Awatovi seemd disposed to accept missionaries, it was razed by warriors from the other villages, who killed all the males and made captives of the women and children.

Such intransigence infuriated the whites, but distances were enormous, the land was as resistant as the people, and Spanish energies were dwindling. Occasional military expeditions succeeded only in burning a few cornfields, and after the attackers had gone the Hopi returned from their hiding places as defiant and independent as ever.[8]

By 1700, the year of Awatovi's destruction, Jesuit missionaries were advancing north from Sonora toward the Gila River. Their leader was Eusebio Francisco Kino.[9] In addition to planting missions in Arizona's Santa Cruz valley, Kino made repeated journeys westward to the Colorado River and proved once again that Baja California is a peninsula, not an island, and that the river debouches into a gulf nearly eight hundred miles long.

The journeys fired his imagination. A great city, hub of many trails, could be planted at the junction of the Gila and the Colorado—El Río Colorado del Norte, he called it on his triumphant map of 1701. One trail could lead into Baja California. Another could cut through the sand dunes of southeastern Alta California to the Pacific. A third could avoid the Apaches, who had moved into the erstwhile Despoblado of southeastern Arizona, by following the Colorado River north and east—a clear indication that the Grand Canyon had been forgotten—and give access to the land of the recalcitrant Hopi. For rumor from Santa Fe said that though the Hopi had rejected the Franciscans, they might listen to the Jesuits.

Nothing came of these imaginings. Although two of Kino's successors, Jacobo Sedelmayr and Ignacio Keller, did receive permission to try to reach the Hopis during the 1740's, both failed.[10]

Years later, fearful of the English in Canada and the Russians in Alaska, the authorities in Madrid ordered the occupation of Alta California, and during 1769–70 settlements were planted at San Diego and Monterey by ships and parties originating from Baja California. But since that desolate region offered few supplies and no people for additional expansion, and since travel by the tiny ships of the time had proved to be a ghastly ordeal, the search for a usable trail from the mainland began.

The task fell to a small squad of professional soldiers under Captain Juan Bautista de Anza and Fray Francisco Garcés, a Franciscan missionary. (The Jesuits had been expelled from Mexico for political reasons in 1767.) Guided by an Indian named Sebastian Tarabal, the men proved that it was possible to ford the Colorado River just below its junction with the Gila, push across the Imperial Valley and its bordering mountains, and thus reach the coastal plains near the new mission of San Gabriel, nine miles east of what would one day be Los Angeles. Next the viceroy in Mexico City authorized Anza to recruit a body of settlers and take them to Monterey during the winter of 1775–76. Garcés, another friar named Tomás Eixarch, and the Indian Tarabel were directed to accompany the column as far as the junction of the Gila and the Colorado and to start working among the Yuma Indians with a view to establishing a way station at the crucial river ford.

And yet doubts about the Yuma route lingered. The Apaches were troublesome—they had caused turmoil by stealing several of the settlers' horses, and would probably continue to harry travelers on the trail to the river. Also, the deserts west of the Yuma crossing were difficult to traverse, especially in summer. Accordingly, an alternate route from Santa Fe was proposed. Crossing the river two hundred miles north of the Yuma ford, it would avoid the Apaches and pass near the towns of the Hopis, who could then be brought back into the Christian fold. Thus Garcés was directed to get Eixarch started among the Yumans and afterwards ride north along the river with Tarabel until they found a suitable crossing at about the latitude of Santa Fe. He was then to explore the country *west* of the river for trails to the coast.

Work between the river and Santa Fe was to be initiated by another Franciscan padre, Silvestre Vélez de Escalante. He was a native of Spain, in his late twenties (his exact birth date is unknown), easily shocked, and not particularly robust, but he was a talented observer. On reaching New Mexico in 1774 he was stationed at Zuñi, which by 1774 had acquired a veneer of Spanish civilization. Its mission church had been functioning for nearly a century and a half, having re-opened a dozen years or so after the 1680 revolt of the Pueblo Indians. The blanketed Indians attended mass dutifully. They had peach trees in their garden plots, and they herded sheep and cattle along the edges of the mountains, keeping alert for raiding Apaches and Navajos. A few Hispanic ranchers and soldiers mingled with the natives. In 1774 their *alcalde*, appointed for life, was Don Juan Cisneros, a native of Spain. Don Juan's position was symbolized by a black cane tipped with silver. He received no salary but collected small fees for preparing documents, and presumably had a land grant outside of town.

Behind the veneer, Zuñi remained an Indian pueblo. Tame eagles roosted on the roofs, each restrained with a cord around one leg. The men still assembled in the kivas, people still placed feathered prayer sticks *(pahos)* in sacred places, and grotesque kachina masks were still produced to educate children concerning the various spirits that were bound up with the people's lives.

In the spring of 1775, when the peach trees were fully leafed, a few Hopi arrived at the village to trade for such Spanish artifacts as knives, hoes, kettles, glass beads, and mirrors. Mindful of his assignment to learn what he could of the country to the west, Vélez de Escalante somehow persuaded them to guide him to their pueblos, 120 miles to the northwest. Don Juan Cisneros, on the scent of trade, was among the party. At the Hopi towns, perched almost invisibly along the edges of dull gray mesas, the chiefs rebuffed Escalante. But then he met a visiting Cosnina; probably he was a member of the tribe we now call Havasupai. Escalante questioned him for two hours through a Zuñi interpreter. While they rolled cigarettes and passed them back and forth, drawing the bitter smoke slowly into their lungs, the Cosnina drew a map of the regions to the west on a piece of saddle leather. But he spoke discouragingly of the dry country, the canyons, and the bestial Jamajabas, who lived near the crossing of the great river and ate the corpses of their enemies.

While Escalante digested this information, he had to watch a Hopi ceremonial dance performed by men stark naked except for bizarre masks over their faces and with "a small, delicate feather, subtly attached . . . to the end of the member it is not modest to name." The abandon of Escalante's fellow spectators at the performance, he wrote, "saddened me so that I arranged for my departure the next day."[11]

Back at Zuñi he wrote a report for his superiors, setting forth alternative proposals. One was to conquer the Hopi by force, establish a *presidio* among them to keep order, and from that base acquire control over the Indians south of the great canyon, or, as he called it, the Río Grande de los Cosninas.

Given the physical difficulties of a southern trail, he went on, it might be well to consider the north side of the canyon, in the territory of friendly Yutas (today's Utes). New maps showed Monterey to be at approximately the same latitude as New Mexico's northernmost settlements, Taos and Abiquiu. For the past several years, Ute Indians had been coming to those towns to trade buckskin, dried meat, and kidnapped Indian children (who were in demand as household servants) for guns, cloth, and other manufactured items. More recently, footloose New Mexicans had been reversing the flow, inching northwest across the Continental Divide into the Ute lands of southwestern Colorado in quest of ore, stolen horses, and pelts. Thus it would be easy to find guides and interpreters for the first part of the journey, and after the trailblazers had flanked the great canyon they could swing west to the coast.

In the spring of 1776, Escalante's superior, Fray Francisco Atanasio Domínguez, arrived from the south to review the condition of the New Mexico missions and summoned Escalante to Santa Fe for consultations. The upshot was a decision that the two friars go into the field with a party of experienced frontiersmen, to look both for a trail and for possible mission sites.

While they considered the problem of which route to follow—among the Cosninas, south of the canyon, or the equally pagan Utes, to the north—an Indian runner brought them a letter. It was dated July 3, at Oraibi, the principal town of the Hopi, and was addressed simply to the missionary at Zuñi. The writer was Francisco Garcés.

Although the letter was incomprehensible in parts, its purpose was clear. Garcés had not only gone west from the river as instructed but had found a way east as well.

What had happened was this: After settling Eixarch in a mouse-infested hut just west of the Yuma crossing, Garcés and Tarabal had ridden two hundred miles north to a river-bisected valley.[12] Fifteen miles wide and twice that long, it was the home of the Mojave Indians—sturdily built, garishly painted males who went around entirely naked, and plump women, also naked, except for tiny aprons fore and aft. Three cheerful males volunteered to show the explorers the trade route by which the Mojaves traveled to the coast.

A grueling eighty-mile ride into the desert provided the key: a dying stream, to which the Mojave River, born in the San Bernardino Mountains to the southwest, had been reduced by the scorching heat. That rivulet showed the way to a pass over the San Bernardino Mountains to Mission San Gabriel—and to another that opened into the broad San Joaquin Valley.

The explorers returned to an ecstatic welcome in the Mojave towns. "From the running about, the yelling, and the general hubbub, and from the great heat [it was late May then] I thought I should fall ill." By then Anza was on his way back to Mexico City, having settled his colonists in California. He had sent Indian runners north to learn whether Garcés was still alive and, if he was, to order him to return straightaway to the Yuma crossing. But now Garcés learned from visiting Hualapais of an extension of the trade route he had followed along the Mojave River which would take him east to the land of the Hopis. The orders notwithstanding, how could he ignore the opportunity?

The Mojaves warned Garcés that the Hopi would murder him, and Tarabal balked. But the missionary heeded neither. Putting Tarabal in charge of the little gear he could not take with him, he headed joyously toward the rising sun with his new friends the Hualapais.

The Indians passed him along like a baton, one group of villagers to the next, until at last he fell in with some Cosninas from the "Jabesua" River— our Havasu Creek—and left the main trail to visit their settlement. After a heart-stopping ride along a thin ledge on one of the sandstone precipices, he dismounted for a shortcut down a rickety ladder, while his guides led his mule into the canyon by a longer route.

He reached the bottom safely and was enthralled—as visitors have been ever since. Supai red: geologists searching for a type name with which to label the topmost crimson band of the Grand Canyon, the one that has spread its vivid stain to the giant Redwall cliffs beneath, found it here in the ledgy slopes cupping the creek. As a shield against sunlight lancing off that red, there was green shade: massive-trunked cottonwoods, each heart-shaped leaf shimmering in the faintest breeze. And the water! The tourist catch-phrase for Havasupai, "Land of the Sky-Blue Water," conveys the color, but not the luminous dip and glide, the whispering effervescence, or the compulsion to roll up one's sleeve, lie flat, and reach for the gleaming bottom of that stream.

Garcés stayed in Havasu Canyon for six days. Thirty-four families lived there. They farmed their irrigated fields with digging sticks and metal hoes traded from the Hopi. They had horses and a few cows, which he supposed they had stolen from the Spanish settlements and had driven across the thin-soiled Coconino Plateau. So the way could not be too difficult.

He resumed his search with a few Yavapai who chanced by. As they moved across the plateau he saw in the distance the deep gash hewn by the Colorado River through the Kaibab Plateau. Possibly—though the side trip would have been out of the Indians' way—he went to the rim and looked down a full mile past alternating bands of cliffs and slopes and terraces into the canyon's dark inner gorge. If so, he was not impressed by beauty. The terrain there struck him, he wrote, as "a prison of cliffs and canyons."[13]

On July 2, with only one old man and a boy left to guide him, he reached Oraibi, the principal Hopi town. After their rudeness failed to halt his proselytizing, the townspeople drove him off the mesa at dawn on July 4, 1776. All he had accomplished had been to find an Indian from the Zuñi pueblo who agreed to take a letter to the missionary there.

Alone, he mounted his leg-weary mule and turned back toward Havasupai, growing confused among the washes and arroyos of the Painted Desert. He might have perished, but the two Yavapai who had taken him to the Hopi towns caught up with him and put him straight again.

At first it had seemed to Domínguez and Escalante that Garcés's letter left them with nothing to do. Then they decided to search the north for a friendlier route west.[14] The governor, Fermín de Mendinuetta, gave his approval, but suggested that they compare the two trails by returning from California along Garcés's tracks. He gave them permission to take only eight men, instead of the twenty Escalante had recommended.

The priest chose three volunteers from Zuñi—the *alcalde* Cisneros; his servant, Simon Lucerno; and another man. Mendinuetta had provided an interpreter, Andrés Muñiz, who the year before had traded and prospected north into what is now Colorado; and a map-maker, Don Bernardo de Miera y Pacheco, a seasoned military engineer. The remaining four members, one of whom had also been north into Ute country, were to help pack and unpack the cavalcade's supply train each day, gather firewood, cook, and care for the horses at each stop.

After a late start, they crossed into the Colorado River Basin just south of the present New Mexico–Colorado border. They skirted the high, snow-streaked peaks of the La Plata Mountains and on August 12 camped beside an Indian ruin overlooking the Dolores River, so named by earlier adventurers. There Domínguez fell ill, and the party had to lie over until his health improved. During the pause two tame Indians from Abiquiu, New Mexico, appeared out of the brush. Thinking that this was a trading trip, they had left the town without permission and skulked behind the expedition until they thought it safe to show themselves. Escalante was nonplussed. There was no use ordering the pair back. Since they were unlikely to go home for fear of being punished, and might fall in with local Utes and perhaps stir up mischief if dismissed, he let them stay—sadly, for this meant two more mouths to feed from supplies already closely calculated.

As soon as Domínguez could travel, the party, augmented to twelve, followed the Dolores northward, close to the Utah line. Forests thinned out; red sandstone cliffs closed in. The guide, Andrés Muñiz, grew confused. Faced with an impasse, "We put our trust in God and our will in that of His most Holy Majesty." They cast lots. The outcome directed them toward the northeast, though Monterey lay west.

Indians they met showed them the way to the top of the heavy-shouldered, aspen-cloaked Uncompahgre Plateau. Where meadows opened viewpoints through the forest they could see the snow-creased helmet of what later received the name Mount Sneffels, 14,150 feet high, and farther on, blued by distance, the rearing parallelogram of Uncompahgre Peak, 14,309 feet. Out of an elbow formed by the cornering of the peaks rushed the Uncompahgre River. This was the water trap: the higher one went, the damper the ground, the colder the air. Miera noted on his map what was to him a significant detail: these uplands were so wet that cranes nested there.[15]

Muñiz knew where he was. And now he led the party down the Uncompahgre until it was swallowed by a larger river sliding in from the right—the Gunnison of today. He turned up it and found a camp of Sabuagana Utes. Visiting with them by chance were two Laguna Utes from a big lake far to the west. The pair agreed to lead the explorers there. One was an adult male whom they named Silvestre, after Escalante. The other, a stripling boy, they named Joaquín, after one of the party's soldiers, Joaquín Laín. Because no manageable saddle horse was available for young Joaquín, he was assigned to ride double behind his namesake. Now there were fourteen to feed.

Leaving the Gunnison, the party turned north again, struggled over Battlement Mesa, and at last encountered the surging Colorado River, across which they splashed near today's town of Grand Valley. They looked up with dismay at the long talus slopes and deeply embayed, laminated gray cliffs, tinged here with red, there with brown, which the Indian Silvestre said they must now surmount.

A ragged canyon gave them ingress. Oil-shale country now, it was pure hell then. They had to dismount and claw their way on foot up the brushy, rock-strewn slopes, dragging the reluctant animals behind. Two pack mules tumbled down the slope, fortunately without serious injury.

Topping out, they entered Piceance Basin: outcrops of shale, black patches of piñon trees, long reaches of velvety sage, and miles of tall brown grass rippling in the sunlight. The horses were happy again. So too were the men, after they left the lead-colored mesas behind and entered a wide basin bisected by a south-flowing river; there, after a wild chase, the soldiers killed a buffalo.

They had just crossed a sizable divide, riven by a west-flowing stream —our White River—and they thought, with reason, that they had entered a new watershed. They hadn't. The Colorado Basin was far larger than they had imagined and the southbound river was the Green. They named it San Buenaventura and speculated a little on how near to Monterey it might flow into the sea.

But they did not follow it. Instead, Silvestre struck west up a broad, well-watered valley that ran parallel to the Uinta Mountains, looming high on their right. They left the Colorado watershed by way of an easy pass, and on September 23 they emerged onto the bountiful flatlands of the Utah Valley, near the southeast corner of Utah Lake. A favorite hunting ground of the Laguna Utes, it was a delicious spot. Men and horses rested three days, the priests taking advantage of the occasion to extol, to the Indians camped there, the advantages of Christianity. If the Utes would receive a mission, the padres who came to supervise it would bring not only the hope of heaven but also wheat, cattle, cloth, and hardware.

The Indians agreed, and the priests, although they had heard of a bigger, briny lake farther north, saw no gain in riding there just to look at it. The season was late, Monterey far to the west and south. They would have to hurry.

They wanted to take some of the Laguna Utes with them, to train them as helpers for whatever padres were assigned to the mission they hoped to build. Young Joaquín promptly volunteered. Silvestre preferred to stay at home and was replaced by an Indian whom the friars rechristened José María.

A relentless north wind pushed the party south. High plateaus were on their left, a grim desert to the right. After four days they encountered a small river flowing through a gap in the mountains into the desert. Miera at once decided that they had re-encountered the San Buenaventura, on its way to the Pacific, and he so showed it, with dotted lines representing the unknown stretches, on the map he was compiling. Actually, the stream was the Sevier River, and it died in a salty lake in western Utah; but such is the force of recorded error that as late as the 1840's men would be searching for the San Buenaventura's outlet to the sea.

After being confined to their camp for two days by a roaring October blizzard, the friars decided not to follow the stream. Supplies were short, and the Indians they met professed no knowledge of a big sea or of Spanish-speaking people anywhere to the west. It would be better, they argued, to drop south into the land of the Cosninas, follow Garcés's trail to Oraibi, and from there press toward Santa Fe. It might also be that this new cast would open a shorter route between New Mexico and the land of the Laguna Utes, now awaiting a mission, than the roundabout road the party had followed on its outward journey.

The decision enraged Miera, who had envisioned great honor and mercantile profit from blazing a trail to California. For two days he rode along
in a black fury, mocking the cowardice of the friars. After Laín and Muñiz
sided with him, the priests decided to cast lots, with Miera to take command
if the decision favored him.

But it did not. "And it was decided in favor of Cosnina. And now, thank
God, we all agreeably and gladly accept the result."

They now returned to the Colorado Basin by crossing a little divide at
the head of Ash Creek and dropping down that to the Virgin River. There
they met Paiute Indians who warned them that they could not cross the
Grand Canyon if they continued south—although, they said, there was a
usable ford far to the east. Hastily recruited Paiute guides then took them,
perhaps deliberately, into a blind pocket in the ragged walls of the Hurricane
Fault. It was only after enduring a waterless, foodless camp that they were
able to backtrack and fight their own hard way up onto the Arizona Strip.
There thirst became a recurrent ordeal for men and animals, with hunger
adding its torments. But again and again a pool or seep would appear. They
were sometimes able to purchase a little food from the wary Indians they met,
and when there was nothing else they would butcher and devour one of their
gaunt horses.

After dropping down the steep eastern side of the Kaibab Plateau, they
found themselves on a platform of almost naked stone, pinched between the
converging Vermilion Cliffs, three thousand feet high, and the ragged wound
of the Colorado River's Marble Gorge. A small stream, the Paria, let them
reach the river, but what gain was that? Across the way another wall of red
rock bent back in a sharp V before striking south as far as they could see, a
stupendous barrier known today as the Echo Cliffs.

They were in a cul-de-sac. Escalante's name for it was San Benito Sal-
sipuedes, the last word meaning "Get out if you can." It was October 26.
Nights were cold; the only food was horsemeat and piñon nuts. But surely,
though the river's far bank looked frightening, this must be the ford the
Indians had told them about. If so, then somewhere to the south there must
be a trail through the cliffs.

Nearly a century later, John D. Lee, a Mormon fugitive from the law,
would establish a famous ferry at the spot. But there is a vast difference
between a ferry and a boatless ford. After five days of trying futilely to cross
the stream, the Spaniards decided that they had gone astray: this could not
be the place the Indians had told them about.

During the layover, Juan Cisneros had pushed his way three miles up the
rugged canyon of Paria Creek and had spotted a slope by which he thought
the group might be able to escape.[16] On the morning of November 2 they
tackled it, leading the horses up a series of diagonal ledges onto a steep terrace

carpeted with loose sand. They floundered up the treacherous path to rimrock wrinkled just enough to be passable. Three hours to cover two thousand feet —and they still had to go down the other side through tight gorges and over red sand—"very troublesome for the animals," Escalante noted in his journal.

For four more days, drenched once by a heavy rain, they slowly made their way upcountry, into a heartbreaking succession of side gullies and then out again. Their food was still horseflesh, supplemented, now that the piñon nuts were gone, by toasted cactus leaves with an insipid sauce boiled from hackberries. Each day scouts probed downward through the slickrock, hunting not only for a way to reach the river but for a usable ford that led to a negotiable route on the far side.

On the seventh they found that they could drop into a passable tributary canyon by using their axes to chop a few steps into the worst part of the drop. They led the horses down unencumbered by packs or saddles, lowered their gear with lariat ropes, repacked, and, angling across a wide shallows, reached the opposite bank, "praising God our Lord and firing off a few muskets as a sign of the great joy we felt." A terrible place. But it was the one the Indians used. Until the end of the nineteenth century it was known as the Ute Crossing—whereupon the romanticists took over and retitled it the Crossing of the Fathers.

After another rocky struggle, this one with the water-clawed breaks on the slopes of Navajo Mountain, the party reached Oraibi. There they managed to buy food from the insolent Hopis and rode on to Santa Fe, arriving January 2, 1777.

After all this, no mission was sent to the Laguna Utes. In 1780 two nondescript settlements that fell far short of the expectations of the Yuma Indians were placed on the west side of the Colorado River, along the road Anza had opened between Sonora and California.

The explorers fared no better. The long circular trip around the Colorado Plateau must have undermined Escalante's already frail health; he died three years later, en route to Mexico City. Meanwhile frictions had developed at the Yuma Crossing. During a wild uprising on July 17, 1781, fifty Spanish males were massacred by the Indians and the women and children taken captive. Later the prisoners were ransomed and permission gained to remove some of the bodies for burial in Sonora. Among them was the corpse of Francisco Garcés, who had been beaten to death with war clubs. The two stations beside the river where he and the others died were never reopened.

A fur trader's rock art

4

The Americans Arrive

During the nearly three centuries that Spain controlled Mexico, the northern frontiers were closed to foreign entrepreneurs. On gaining independence in 1821, Mexico, hungry for imported merchandise, reversed the policy and invited American traders in. Beaver trappers immediately took advantage of the opening, often posing as merchants in order to reach the streams that attracted them.

Where the Colorado River Basin was concerned, two men were primarily responsible for leading the way: William Ashley and Étienne Provost. Ashley, born in Virginia about 1776, reached Missouri before the territory was annexed by the United States; Provost, born in Canada about 1782, does not appear in the records until 1815, though he may have arrived in St. Louis before then.[1] Ashley was educated, articulate, and socially and politically ambitious. About five feet nine inches tall, he was thin, with a jutting nose and prominent chin. Provost, fat and illiterate, was at home in riverfront saloons, and had had long experience in the fur business. Ashley was the tyro when the two men met, yet it had been his plan to revolutionize the western fur trade that had brought them together.

In 1821 Ashley's wife had just died, and he was at loose ends. He had recently been elected lieutenant-governor of the new state of Missouri, but the job did not fill his time. So he joined Andrew Henry, a longtime friend and experienced mountaineer, in putting together a crew of trappers whom Henry led, in the spring of 1822, to the headwaters of the Missouri, with plans for Ashley to reinforce him the next year. After the second party was attacked by Arikara Indians, with heavy loss of life, the partners decided to leave the Missouri and to send their trappers overland to the Continental Divide, in what is now Wyoming.

The first group to set out numbered a dozen and was led by a man who has become an American folk hero, the lank, grim, imperturbable Jedediah Smith. On learning from Crow Indians that a big stream rich in beaver flowed southward on the far side of the Divide, he headed that way before winter had relaxed its grip. On March 19, 1824, after fighting gales, thirst, and near starvation, his party reached the wide sagebrush plains through which coiled a stream that the Crows called Seedskedee Agie (Prairie Chicken River). Today it is known as the Green. To their dismay, they discovered clear evidence that other trappers had been there before them.

Still, it was too big a valley to have been stripped yet. To increase their range, they split into two parties. Smith took five men south toward (but not to) the crenellated peaks of the Uinta Mountains. Thomas Fitzpatrick and four other men went upstream to the vicinity of what is now Daniel, Wyoming. Taking advantage of a blinding snowstorm, Shoshoni Indians swooped in and made off with all of Fitzpatrick's horses. The event gave a nearby stream the name Horse Creek. Undeterred, the men hoisted their riding gear and pack saddles out of sight among the limbs of a big cottonwood tree and proceeded to trap on foot. Staggering under as many pelts as they could carry, they chanced upon the horsethieves, outbluffed them, and recovered the animals. When they rejoined Smith's group at an appointed rendezvous to the east of South Pass, they were laden with riches.

Tom Fitzpatrick and three others were delegated to take the furs to Ashley, along with word that the Seedskedee was still a paradise of beaver, that more of Henry's men would be coming in at any moment from their camps on the upper Missouri, and that a packtrain loaded with supplies would be needed as soon as possible. Meanwhile, Jedediah Smith and the rest of his crew would spend the summer, when furs were not prime, looking for fresh beaver grounds, as well as for some clue to the identity of the people who had trapped the region ahead of them. (They were, he soon found, Hudson's Bay Company employees who had reached the Green from a post in western Montana during the winter of 1821–22 and again in 1823.[2] What was more, they planned to return in 1825.)

After a series of misadventures, Fitzpatrick's people reached Fort Atkinson, located beside the Missouri River just north of what is today Omaha. He dispatched a letter to Ashley in St. Louis, recounting the year's events and asking urgently for supplies. Next he rented several horses and hired helpers, finally turning back toward South Pass to retrieve the bales of furs he had been forced to cache on the way down.

That was to be the only good news Ashley received that fall. Andrew Henry appeared in St. Louis at about the same time as Fitzpatrick's letter did. He was gray with discouragement. Blackfeet had killed so many of his men, and had stolen so many of his horses and furs on the upper Missouri, that he saw no point in risking life and fortune any further. His defection simply hardened Ashley's determination. A few weeks before, he had failed by only a handful of votes in his campaign for the governorship of Missouri, and he was grimly bent on recouping his fortune.

Legalities presented the first problem. American law forbade trapping by whites on Indian land and allowed trading only if the merchant took out a license that stated where the trade was to be conducted. Fur companies ostensibly met these requirements by carrying a few goods to their assigned locations and then trapping as they pleased far from the government's not very watchful eyes—and often to the annoyance of Indians who regarded the game on the land as theirs.

What location was Ashley to ask for? In search of more definite geographical terms than the local Indian word Seedskedee Agie, he turned to John King Robinson's 1817 map of *Mexico, Louisiana & the Missouri Territory &c.*, much of it plagiarized from Miera y Pacheco of the Domínguez-Escalante expedition.[3] Two streams caught his eye—the San Buenaventura, purportedly flowing from the central Rockies to the Pacific near Monterey Bay, and the Colorado, shown flowing into the Gulf of California. That gave him two solid names to use; the license he asked for and obtained authorized him to trade with the Snake (Shoshoni) Indians west of the Rocky Mountains "at the junction of two large rivers, supposed to be branches of [as some clerk spelled the words] the Buonventure and Coloredo of the West, within the territory of the United States." Although it was clear, from what Fitzpatrick had told him, that the Seedskedee Agie flowed south into Mexican territory, he did not apply for a passport, perhaps because of the delay it might cause.

He started west from St. Louis late in September, 1824, leading a caravan of twenty-five men and fifty horses laden with supplies, and reached Fort Atkinson on October 21. There he halted, waiting for the Indian agent, Benjamin O'Fallon, to patch up a peace with the Pawnees, who were harrying travelers bound across the plain toward New Mexico. During the pause he asked so many questions about the New Mexican commerce that the people at the fort became convinced that he meant to enter the territory.[4]

Impatient to get his supplies to his men, he went recklessly ahead into the teeth of a Rocky Mountain winter. The party suffered acutely and lost seventeen horses to Crow Indians before reaching the barrens surrounding the Seedskedee River on April 19, 1825. There was no sign of Jedediah Smith and his men. Presumably they were trapping; spring was the best season, and already Ashley was late.

Hurriedly he split his crew into four groups. Since not enough horses remained for everyone to ride, he decided to float south down the river with six men. It is not likely that he knew where he was in relation to the Mexican border. In fact, since the river runners took to the water a few miles above the junction of Big Sandy Creek with the Seedskedee, they were already south of the forty-second parallel and everything they were doing was technically unlawful.[5]

Using rawhide for lashings, the boatmen shaped from cottonwood poles and willows a frame sixteen feet long and seven feet wide. Hunters meanwhile killed and skinned six buffalo. The boatmen stitched the skins together with sinew and fitted the leather over the frame. Lacking resin and tar, they waterproofed the seams with a mixture of buffalo tallow and ashes, an extra supply of which they put into skin bags to take with them. The result was a flat-bottomed "bull-boat," the first American-built craft definitely known to have navigated any considerable part of the Colorado River system. Ashley, it is worth noting, could not swim a stroke.[6]

Before taking off he pointed toward the Uinta Mountains, their snowy summits shining in the south. Somewhere along the northern foothills, he told the others, he would select and conspicuously mark a site where they were all to reassemble "on or before 10th July next." At that rendezvous point he would cache most of the knives, cloth, powder, traps, and other items he had brought west for buying the men's personal share of the beaver they had caught. The rest he would take with him to trade for horses, if the opportunity arose, and to use as samples for luring to the rendezvous any New Mexican trappers he met.

Shortly after launching the craft on April 22, they discovered that seven men huddled in it with the cargo were too many. Halting, they killed four more buffalo and constructed a smaller, supplemental bull-boat. The stop was almost fatal for Ashley. Dodging the charge of a wounded bull, he fell over a small cliff into jagged rocks and was cut and bruised so painfully that for the next few days he could hardly travel.

At Henry's Fork, named for the partner who had forsaken him, he cached the bulk of his goods. Then on they went, still in two boats, driving straight toward the mountains, until suddenly the river bent east as if searching for a chink in the barrier ahead. As they entered the foothills, the walls steepened. Dotted with pine and cedar, they took on a reddish hue—Precambrian quartzite, more than a billion years old. "Gloomy," Ashley called the stretch as gusty winds swooped down, laden with sleet. The water turned thunderous. Years later John Wesley Powell would call that stretch of canyon the Flaming Gorge. Still later, dam builders would smother it and its neighboring chasms under the waters of a reservoir. Among the losses would be a wall in the dramatic Red Canyon on which Ashley had inscribed his name and the year, 1825, with vermilion paint.

A respite from portaging goods and boats around the boulder-fanged rapids came in the long oval of Brown's Hole, known today as Brown's Park. Ashley noted that as many as a thousand Indians had recently been camped there, with a still larger number of horses. From a relatively flat bottom, gentle swales rise to timber-covered mountains.

But the peacefulness of this winter haven ends abruptly as the river twists sharply south toward the dark slit of Lodore Canyon, to descend between walls two thousand feet high and less than a musket shot apart. It was, one viewer said, "a great stone mouth, drinking a river."[7]

For the trappers the descent was an ordeal: bad weather, the constant din from raging rapids, backbreaking portages, long halts to patch the boats, and, toward the end, when they ran out of provisions, the gnawings of hunger. Near the mouth of the Yampa River, which enters from the east, the dark red rock that had engulfed them for so long gave way to vast cliffs of pale yellow Weber sandstone, streaked in startling perpendiculars with black desert varnish.

Below the river junction, the stream made a hairpin curve around the monumental prow of Steamboat Rock and then tore through a canyon whose once-horizontal strata have been twisted into vertical upthrusts. In that weird district Ashley killed a buffalo, ending a two-day fast. Rejoicing was premature, however. The small boat capsized in a rapid and was refloated with difficulty. A short distance farther downstream, thundering billows washed completely over Ashley's larger craft. None of its crew had life preservers, but two of the men jumped overboard with ropes and managed to check the bull-boat's floundering tumble.

When the journey was resumed, after a day spent drying the cargo and repairing damage, hope rose at last. The weather had turned fine and, to use Ashley's word, the mountains were "declining." Late on May 17 they broke out of Split Mountain—as it is known today—saw a tempting creek mouth to the right, and paddled over to land. Ever since then the stream has been called Ashley Creek. There, Ashley noted in his diary with no sign of surprise, they encountered two Frenchmen from Missouri.

The employer of those two Frenchmen, Étienne Provost, was an old hand in the Rockies. In 1815, when he was about thirty-three, he had joined a trapping party that Auguste Chouteau and Jules de Mun of St. Louis proposed to lead into the mountains north and east of the Arkansas River. It was a risky venture. Although the United States considered the Arkansas the boundary line with New Mexico, Spanish authorities, resentful of Napoleon's sale of the Louisiana Territory to the United States, had not yet agreed. It was well known, moreover, that trespassers on Spanish land faced grim punishments.

In spite of the uncertainty, Chouteau, de Mun, and their men roamed through the area for a year and a half. It was good beaver country. The Arkansas opened a spectacular gate through the Front Range of the Rockies —the chasm is known today as the Royal Gorge—and then bent northward into a broad valley lined on either side by tall, round-shouldered gray peaks. Having to limit their trapping to one side of a stream was frustrating, and the leaders of the party had sought permission from officials in Santa Fe to cross to the mountains on the Spanish side. The requests had already been turned down when a patrol suddenly appeared, arrested the trappers on the presumed American side of the river, and hauled them off to jail in New Mexico. Six weeks later they learned their sentence: they were to forfeit thirty thousand dollars' worth of furs and all of their horses except one riding animal each, and were to leave the territory.

The question arises whether all of those pelts had been trapped on the American side of the Arkansas River. Certainly there had been time enough to cross into Mexico. And at least some of the men had gone far enough into the mountains to learn where the Divide was.

When independent Mexico opened its borders to traders, Provost traveled west again with a partner about whom we know only that his surname was Leclerc and that his Christian name may have been François.

The pair seem to have spent the winter of 1822–23 scouting prospects. Since the Mexicans knew nothing of the craft of making beaver hats, the backcountry streams were untouched. Yet guides were available, for ever since the days of Domínquez and Escalante traders from Santa Fe and Taos had been following their trail into the Green River Basin to swap bits of cloth, hardware, food, and other knickknacks to the Utes for pelts and child slaves. Encouraged by what they learned, Provost and Leclerc left New Mexico in the summer of 1823 and hurried back to a trading post near Fort Atkinson to pick up men and supplies. Among the crew they hired were several Iroquois Indians who had deserted from a Hudson's Bay Company trapping brigade in Idaho in 1822 and now wanted to return west.[8]

During the winter hunt of 1823–24, Provost's brigade probably had little competition. Not so the following season. On July 28, 1824, the largest wagon caravan yet assembled in Missouri reached Santa Fe. On being released, many of its bullwhackers, guided by Mexicans, headed for the intricate watershed of the Gunnison and there fanned out in small groups wherever they could.

Provost and Leclerc, however, sternly held together their group of twenty or thirty, including Anglos, Frenchmen, Mexicans, and several Iroquois, as they pushed into the deserts of northeastern Utah. Ahead of them rose the east-west Uinta Range (whose far side Jedediah Smith was currently approaching), and beyond it, about forty miles to the south, the vast bulk of Tavaputs Plateau. Between the two lay the Uinta Basin, the bed of an extinct inland sea, which was then a favorite range of Ute Indians. Cutting straight through the Uinta Range and then through Tavaputs is the Green River. In 1824 Provost sent trappers along the northern and southern fronts of the great plateau, and it may be that some of them also followed the Green through its heart.[9] If so, they would have been the pioneer navigators of the upper river.

Provost himself reached the Green some miles below the point where Escalante had crossed it in 1776. There, where the east-flowing White River joins the parent stream, he set up a base camp. Leaving part of his crew to scour the adjoining regions, he continued with the rest into the Uinta Basin and followed it westward across the Wasatch Mountains out of the Green's drainage system. Eventually he went into camp on the bank of the stream (which Mormon settlers would later call the Jordan) linking Utah Lake, to the south, with Great Salt Lake, to the north. There they met with catastrophe.

The year before, a band of Shoshoni Indians had lost their chief during a set-to in southern Idaho with Iroquois Indians working for the Hudson's Bay Company. When some members of that band encountered Provost's Iroquois, they retaliated against them and their associates. Eight men died. Provost and one or two others—the number is uncertain—escaped and made their way back across the Wasatch Mountains to the camp at the confluence of the White and Green Rivers.[10]

In spite of the disaster, Provost stayed in the field while four of his men returned to Taos to sell pelts and pick up supplies for the spring of 1825. On their return Provost again sent out his crew among the streams of the Uinta Basin. He himself went back to the Wasatches. It was during his absence that Ashley's soggy leather boats emerged from Split Mountain close to the camp of the two Frenchmen who have already been mentioned.

They told him that they didn't need supplies, having just received a consignment from Taos, only fifteen days away by pack train.

So Ashley buried the goods in a cache near the river bank for safekeeping while he searched for horses to carry his party to its rendezvous around the western end of the Uintas. During the next three weeks, the bull-boats no longer being serviceable, he hollowed a canoe out of a cottonwood log and floated down the river to the upper end of what is now called Desolation Canyon. His hunters searched far and wide for game but found little to eat except a few fish. Having finally obtained from various trappers and Utes a riding horse apiece (but none for carrying merchandise), they started up through the Uinta Basin on their roundabout way to the rendezvous on Henry's Fork. Along the way they met Provost coming down-country with twelve men, a mediocre catch, and a few spare horses. He would not sell the animals but did agree, for a price, to haul Ashley's cached goods back to Henry's Fork. As they jogged along together, Ashley picked up a few bits of geographical information. According to Provost, the Spanish name for the lower reaches of the Seedskedee was Verde. From then on Ashley referred to the river as the Green, though some trappers went on calling it the Seedskedee.[11] Provost also confirmed what Ashley had already surmised, that the Green was part of the Colorado River system. If the San Buenventura existed at all, it lay farther west.

When Ashley reached the rendezvous early in July, he found more than a hundred men waiting for him, including several deserters from the Hudson's Bay Company. He collected the fur owed him for outfits furnished on credit and then gathered in the surplus by swapping merchandise for it at astronomical markups. He reaped another small fortune the next year, and then sold out to three of his former employees: Jedediah Smith, William Sublette, and David Jackson.

In an effort to learn whether there might be a stream flowing into the Pacific up which supplies could be brought easily and cheaply, Jedediah Smith made two heroic trips through the southwestern deserts to the coasts. On the second of these, ten of his companions were killed by Mohave Indians at a ford across the Colorado River not far from present-day Needles, California. And he found no usable river. Throughout the next dozen years the fur trade of the northern Rockies depended on supplies delivered each summer to a predesignated rendezvous by an Ashley-style horse caravan. Of those rendezvous, seven were held in the broad valley of the Seedskedee River.

Ashley, meanwhile, had acquired a beautiful young second wife. In 1831 he was elected to Congress, where he served until 1837. Provost seems to have trapped for him for awhile, and after that roamed back and forth across the dangerous lands between the upper Missouri and the Green for various other employers. But no one could lure him back to the Southwest.

Records of the Southwestern fur trade tend to be scanty. Much of what we know of it is derived from a piece of literary hackwork concerning the career of one James Ohio Pattie, who spent the years 1825–28 in the area and two more in Mexican California. The hack was named Timothy Flint, and he depicted Pattie as a slayer of grizzlies, vanquisher of savages, and rescuer of maidens. Although exasperatingly confused about geography, the book is not all fiction.

From it we learn how James Pattie, with his father, Sylvester Pattie, reached New Mexico in the fall of 1825 with a caravan led by a St. Louis Frenchman who had the improbably similar name Sylvestre Pratte. Young

Pattie was then twenty years old. In Santa Fe, Sylvestre Pratte was granted a trapping license by Governor Antonio Narbona of New Mexico, after agreeing to take on a few Mexican citizens as apprentices. He led most of the party off to Utah Lake, where Étienne Provost had recently hunted. Seven others, including both Patties, were delegated to investigate the headwaters of the Gila River. On the way they were joined by another group of seven trappers bound for the same destination.[12]

Just east of the Continental Divide, in Apache country, they passed the Santa Rita copper mine, whose adjuncts included a small fort, corrals for safeguarding horses, a blacksmith shop, and a canteen where fiery drinks could be purchased.

Here the Gila-bound trappers hired two Mexican roustabouts, presumably to fulfill the licensing requirements, before proceeding across the Divide to the Gila. Afterward, according to Timothy Flint's narrative, dissension split the group; Indians whooped down, "arrows falling around us like hail," and made off with their horses and mules, as well as, eventually, the furs they cached. The Patties now decided to lease the Santa Rita copper mine, and settled down there for a time.

As the autumn of 1826 approached, scores of would-be trappers, turning away from the overcrowded Gunnison, Grand, and Green areas, passed through Taos and Santa Fe on their way to the Gila. The activity aroused the ire of James Baird, who had reached Spanish New Mexico with a few companions in 1812 and had been arrested for the trespass. Freed when Mexico became independent, he had taken out citizenship papers and had settled in El Paso as a trader. The influx of latecomers, many of whom did not have either passports or licenses, threatened his plans to exploit the Gila area, and he wrote an angry letter of protest to Governor Antonio Narbona in Santa Fe.[13] The complaint reached Narbona after he had issued trading licenses to several Americans. He now proceeded to revoke the licenses, unbeknownst to the recipients, and sent a dispatch to the governor of Sonora warning him to be on the lookout for unlicensed trappers pretending to be traders. The Sonoran forwarded the message to the commander of the small Mexican garrison at Tucson.

Meanwhile the younger Pattie had grown weary of mining, and when a group of French-speaking trappers came by Santa Rita he joined them. Their leader (whom academic detective work by Joseph Hill several years ago identified) was Michel Robidoux, youngest son of a powerful St. Louis fur-trading family.

At a Papago Indian village a little below what is now Phoenix, the natives greeted them so cordially, with promises of a pumpkin feast, that Pattie grew suspicious. But only one of his companions heeded his warning and withdrew along with him. Shots and shrieks, almost before they had their horses saddled and their mules packed, told them that a massacre was taking place. They hid out in the mountains, and the next day they were astonished to see a lone, badly wounded survivor, Michel Robidoux, staggering across the desert below them.[14]

Some historians have suggested that the commander of the Tucson garrison, prompted by Narbona's message, had urged the Papagos to scare off any intruders, and that the massacre was their response. Actually, no one knows what their motives were, but in any event the Indians paid for what they had done. A few evenings later Pattie and his companions spotted camp-fires in the dusk, and discovered thirty or so Americans under Ewing Young and Thomas L. Smith. This group had been attacked some weeks before. Eager for retaliation, they swooped down on the Papagos. According to Pattie, 110 of them were annihilated, though Kit Carson, a friend of many of those involved, later put the figure at fifteen.

More hunters fell in with the party, until there was a small army of trappers along the Gila. On reaching the Colorado they turned upstream. Several of them launched dugout canoes, becoming the first Americans to float that section of the river. They clashed with Mojave Indians and, according to Pattie, hoisted several corpses into some handy trees, "to dangle in terror to the rest, and as a proof, how we retaliated aggression."

The hunters now veered east, parallel to the Grand Canyon. Quarrels led to a split. Ewing Young, with some of the men, struck across central Arizona toward Santa Fe. The others, eager for more beaver, found a way onto the Hualapai Plateau and descended what is now called Spencer Canyon into the lower section of the Grand Canyon. They were the first non-Indians known to have reached the bottom of that profound gorge. Three trappers who wandered off by themselves were killed and roasted by Indians who—again according to Pattie—were on the point of devouring their victims when the main body of hunters arrived and drove them off.

It would appear that, unable to work upstream through the Grand Canyon, the men climbed out of Spencer and drifted back west to a point opposite the mouth of the Virgin. Here they managed to cross the Colorado, perhaps by building a raft. Apparently they followed the Virgin northeast toward Zion Park. In the neighborhood of today's St. George, Utah, another quarrel erupted and the party divided once more. Tom Smith and a few companions went north. They crossed the high plateaus of central Utah, found trails left by Mexican slave traders, and followed the tracks to Taos. Pattie's group may have chosen to climb the Hurricane cliffs in hope of finding a way back to the Colorado River, hating every inch of "these horrid mountains, which so cage it [the river] up, as to deprive all human beings of the ability to descend to its banks and make use of its waters."

On they labored, by untraceable routes, until they reached what Pattie says were the headwaters of the Yellowstone and Columbia rivers. They could not possibly have gotten that far. Pattie wasn't necessarily lying, of course; he and his men simply did not know where they were, and in talking to his ghost-writer years afterward, Pattie may have tried to orient himself by studying the inaccurate maps of the time—all of which followed Zebulon Pike in drastically shortening north-south distances in the Rocky Mountains.[15]

When the adventurers reached Santa Fe in the summer of 1827, a new governor, Manuel Armijo, confiscated their furs on the grounds that they had no licenses. Unwilling to create an international incident, according to Pattie, they decided against forcibly retaking the pelts. Ewing Young's men resisted, but they too lost their furs, and Young served a term in jail.

The official hostility prompted two different bands of trappers, one led by Richard Campbell and the other by a Dr. Alexander, to find, early in 1827, a safer market for their furs among the American ship traders who by then were regularly visiting San Diego, California. Meanwhile the Patties were suffering further setbacks. A trusted clerk embezzled thirty thousand dollars in gold bullion from the Santa Rita mine and it went bankrupt. Hoping to recoup their fortunes by gathering furs and marketing them in San Diego, as Campbell and Alexander had done, father and son managed, with six friends, to scrape together an outfit. On their way west during the fall of 1827, they fell in with a second group of trappers under George Yount, until recently an apprentice of Ewing Young's.

About the time the combined groups reached the junction of the Gila and Colorado rivers, another quarrel split them. The Pattie campany built canoes and floated south to the Gulf, stripping the river ahead of Yount's party, who tried to thresh out a passage through the dense thickets on horseback. In the "sober sullen stillness" (Yount's words), the Patties caught many beaver. Yount's people did not, and returned to New Mexico.[16]

Again the Patties' luck changed. Brought to a halt by the Colorado's notorious tidal bore, they tried to retreat upstream and were hit by a flood. Abandoning their canoes, they cached the furs and set out overland for the coast, which they assumed could not be far distant. After a dreadful trip they reached San Diego—an event confirmed by the town's official records. For now they were jailed as American spies, and Sylvester Pattie died a prisoner. Four of the party were allowed to return to the Colorado delta to retrieve the pelts—and found that they had been ruined by flood water.

Now that travel overland to California by way of the Colorado's lower basin was known to be possible, commerce by that route was inevitable. Soon there was a brisk trade in California horses and mules, many of them stolen from the coastal missions, that were driven across the desert for sale to

American traders in Santa Fe—a commerce that also included Paiute children taken along the way from their parents.

To escape raiding Apaches, the traders in horses and mules worked out a new route far north of the Gila. Shaped like a huge, inverted U, the trail slanted through northwestern New Mexico, nicked the southwest corner of Colorado, and slipped through a break in the Grand's crimson walls where Moab, Utah, now stands. Still angling northwest, it vaulted the Green at the site of the present town of Green River, Utah, flattened out on its way through the rumpled deserts to Castle Dale, and at last dropped south along the edges of the Utah plateaus. It touched the Virgin and eventually reached the Mojave River. The route soon attracted Mexican and Anglo families seeking new homes in California. Since for much of the way they were following tracks left by such predecessors as Garcés and Escalante, the route was known from the beginning as the Old Spanish Trail.

Farther north, meanwhile, fur traders were erecting, as trading posts, the first American habitations in the upper basin. In 1832, Captain Benjamin Louis Eulalie de Bonneville, on leave from the United States Army, brought twenty wagons over South Pass to the Green. In the V between the river and Horse Creek he built a stockade whose upright pickets, fifteen feet tall, were protected by blockhouses set into diagonally opposite corners. Winters were harsh in the wide, treeless valley, competition was intense, and Bonneville lacked experience as a fur man; he failed, and the post was soon abandoned, apparently justifying the name Fort Nonsense, which rival traders had given it. But another trader—Antoine Robidoux, an elder brother of James Pattie's occasional associate—had already proved that less elaborate establishments had a place in the western trade. In 1828 he had built near the Gunnison River, on the trail between Taos and the Green, two or three small, dirt-roofed cabins protected by a rude stockade; the town of Delta, Colorado, occupies the site now. Later he purchased from an uncle and nephew named Reed a small post, Fort Winty or Uinta, that they had constructed where Whiterocks Creek flows into the Uinta River—an area Etienne Provost had opened—and became the region's leading entrepreneur. Robideaux's customers were mostly Ute Indians who bought knives, hatchets, awls, tobacco, and ammunition, or small groups of individualistic white trappers, not bound to any company, who bought ribbons, armbands, metal pots, and vermilion for their Indian women, and whiskey for themselves. One of those largely anonymous hunters, by name Denis Julien—he had also been associated with the Reeds —became the first river runner to use the upper Colorado system as a highway. On canyon walls from Desolation in Tavaputs Plateau, in what is now Arches National Park, and southward to below the junction of the Green and Grand he carved his initials (and occasionally his name) and dates between

44 COLORADO RIVER COUNTRY

1831 and 1844. What he intended to convey by once incising the outline of a rowboat in the rock, above what looks like a winged sun, remains a mystery.

As the fur trade disintegrated, increasing numbers of derelicts hung around Robidoux's little posts. Whiskey and flagrant offenses against Indian women led to quarrels, and the Utes eventually destroyed both places. When Fort Winty fell, in 1844, five or six Mexicans and one American were slain, and their consorts were made captives. Robidoux himself survived, having been away at the time.

Before then, other posts had been built. On the north side of the Uinta Mountains, where Vermilion Creek runs into the Green River near the lower end of Brown's Park, was Fort Davy Crockett, sometimes called Fort Misery. Built in 1836, it consisted of a low building of mud-chinked logs with three sway-backed wings extending from it.

In 1839 an Oregon-bound pioneer, Thomas Jefferson Farnham, saw it by moonlight and wrote eloquently of its site, "in the shade of wild and dark cliffs, while the light of the moon shone on the western peaks and cast a deeper darkness into the inaccessible gorges." Later, in 1840, the year of the trade's last meager rendezvous, Fort Davy Crockett was abandoned.

Many men preferred to stay in the mountains, trapping on their own, and there were traders who undertook to supply their needs and those of their women and mixed-blood children.

Among the entrepreneurs were Jim Bridger and a longtime sidekick, Henry Fraeb (presumably an immigrant from Germany, though nothing is known of his early years). Having made a tenuous connection with a fur-trade supply house in St. Louis, in August, 1841, they started building a post on the west bank of the Green, a few miles below the point where the trail from South Pass dropped down to the main stream.

The venture was short-lived. Needing meat for the work crew and for the coming winter, Fraeb took a band of hunters east and south to a camp he used off and on, beside the Little Snake River. There a war party of Sioux and Cheyenne Indians fell on them, and Fraeb was one of the five whites slain.

Bridger now reconsidered the site they had chosen for their trading post, first moving it farther down the Green, then abandoning that site as well. He formed a new partnership with one Louis Vásquez, and at Black's Fork of the Green they chose a magnificent new site with a soaring view of the Uintas to the south, where a cold stream divided to form a tree-studded island.

Later that year, 1843, Bridger explained his choice of the site in a letter (dictated rather than written, since he was illiterate) to Pierre Chouteau, Jr., head of a firm of St. Louis wholesalers: "I have established a small store with a Black Smith Shop, and a supply of iron in the road of the Emigrants, on Black's Fork, Green River, which promises fairly. They, in coming out are generally well supplied with money, but by the time they get there, are in want of all kinds of supplies. Horses, Provisions, Smith work, &c, brings ready cash from them; and should I receive the goods hereby ordered, will do a considerable business in that way with them!"[17]

High up in the Colorado River Basin, Jim Bridger had seen the wave of the future.

General Kearney's supply train

5

Rediscovery

When General Stephen Watts Kearny started out from conquered Santa Fe on September 25, 1846, to participate in the American attack on Mexican California, he took with him, in addition to his three hundred dragoons, a fourteen-man unit of the Army's élite Corps of Topographical Engineers. Guiding it were two mountain men we have met before, Antoine Robidoux and Thomas Fitzpatrick. Neither had actually been in the regions they were to cross, but years of wilderness experience gave them confidence. They could talk Indian sign language; they understood Indian psychology. They could smell on the night wind the coming of danger.

Probing for more exact information had been the job, since 1838, of the Corps of Topographical Engineers. They constituted a rare breed—there were just thirty-six of them altogether, and they reported only to their own colonel, who was responsible only to the Secretary of War. Most of these men were graduates of West Point, soundly trained in engineering, topographic sketching, and natural philosophy (physics). They were required to know French, which in those days was the language of science.

They generally took artists and scientists with them into the field, the better to understand what they saw. They made precise maps, searched out sites for army camps, studied harbors, estimated the navigability of rivers, and made inventories of natural resources. The idea of a transcontinental railroad was by then much talked of, and they paid particular attention to potential routes.

Commanding Kearny's topographic unit was First Lieutenant William Hemsley Emory, whose chief assistant was First Lieutenant William H. Warner. With them as a compiler of data was a civilian, Norman Bestor. Their artist was John Mix Stanley. The rest of the party consisted of camp tenders, survey assistants, and mule herders.

Kearny planned to follow the old trapper trail past the Santa Rita copper mines to the Gila. As a concession to the rugged terrain he mounted his command on mules. His orders directed him to blaze a wagon road, and accordingly he loaded part of his supplies on vehicles pulled by worn-out oxen, the only animals he had been able to requisition in New Mexico.

Just short of where the trail to the Gila swung away from the Rio Grande, the party encountered Kit Carson and fifteen other riders, hurrying east with dispatches for President Polk: California had succumbed virtually without resistance. It was Carson's intention to catch a few moments in Taos with his young wife, Josefa, with whom he had had very little time since their marriage three and a half years before. On reaching Washington, he intended to deliver his dispatches personally to President Polk. For a man who had run away from home as a youth and still could not sign his own name, all this was something to think about.

Kearny turned the hope upside down. Since there was no need to fight in California, he sent two hundred of his dragoons back to Santa Fe, thus reducing his supply problems by two-thirds. He then ordered Carson to hand his dispatches over to Fitzpatrick and guide the remnants of the column back over the Gila trail. Carson certainly knew it well, having covered it in 1829 and 1831 when he had been a trapper with Ewing Young.

Two days later, fearful that the faltering supply train would prove unable to negotiate the rough Gila trail—a judgment in which Carson concurred— Kearny decided to assign the job of finding a wagon road to a belated part of his command, the Mormon Battalion. Its members, just then approaching Santa Fe, had enlisted in Iowa at the beginning of the conflict with the understanding that their pay and clothing allowances would be turned over to their church, thus helping to defray the cost of the Mormons' migration to Utah. The enlistees were hardy if cantankerous. To command them Kearny sent back Philip St. George Cooke, whom he elevated from captain to the brevet rank of lieutenant-colonel.

As Kearny's shrunken command followed Carson and Ribidoux across the Continental Divide into the narrow defiles of the upper Gila, nobody had enough to eat. Even so, the men held out better than the animals. Eventually, most of the command were afoot, dragging their glassy-eyed mounts behind them by the reins.

In spite of such difficulties, the topographers took several hundred astronomical and barometric observations, from which Emory would later prepare the first relatively accurate map of any part of the Lower Colorado River Basin. He marveled at giant saguaro cactus fifty feet tall, yucca spikes rising above rosettes of bladed leaves, and grotesquely twisted Joshua trees. He theorized about the ancient ruins they passed, concluding against the still widespread opinion that the original builders had been Aztecs. He noted the cotton that Pima and Maricopa Indians were raising on their irrigated farms near the big bend of the Gila River, and predicted that any farming in the region would demand irrigation—which in turn would require strict regulation of water use, and would thus be "repugnant to the habits of our people."[1] It is a repugnance that the people of central Arizona have learned to overcome.

On reaching the Colorado, the column captured several Mexicans who were driving military horses from California to Sonora and obtained from them twenty-five or so mounts a little better than their own. Less pleasing was the news that fighting had broken out in California. After hastily loading every animal in the command with grass and mesquite beans for use as fodder beyond the river, they rode ten miles downstream to a crossing fifteen hundred yards wide yet only four feet deep. It was a time of low water, however, and Emory was sure that for most of the year the Colorado would be navigable as far as Gila. Such a surmise, coming from a topographical engineer, was certain to be remembered.

After they had splashed through the long ford, the dragoons and engineers endured a week of scorching desert travel, followed by cold rains. Sodden and miserable, they encountered Mexican lancers several miles short of San Diego. A third of the command were either killed or injured; Kearny was painfully wounded, and so was William Warner. Without the help summoned by Carson and a naval lieutenant, Edward Fitzgerald Beale, who had ridden out earlier from San Diego to meet them, the outcome might have been total disaster. As it was, at least a small segment of American regulars had reached the coast by land. Now it remained to be seen whether Cooke's Mormons and their wagons could do so as well.

By October 19, 1846, Cooke was on his way down the Rio Grande with twenty wagons, 340 unmounted Mormons, and five women—all wives of enlistees, enrolled as laundresses.[2] Like Kearny, the new lieutenant-colonel had employed two mountain men as guides. One, Paulino Weaver, whose associates insisted on calling Pauline, was a part Cherokee Indian from Tennessee. Like Carson, he was illiterate.

The other, Antoine Leroux, part French and part Mexican, had trapped extensively throughout the Southwest and in his time was well known as a pathfinder.[3]

Because Leroux feared water might be hard to find along trails in New Mexico that were otherwise suitable for wagons, Cooke headed farther southward, beyond the thirty-second parallel, onto what is still Mexican territory. The walking was hard, and the Mormons continually complained as they crossed the Continental Divide at Guadalupe Pass. Part of the way here was so narrow that they had to disassemble the wagons and carry them in pieces. Descending toward the north-flowing San Pedro River, they were charged again and again by wild Mexican bulls, escapees from an abandoned ranch, as they chopped their way through sixty miles of sharp-thorned mesquite. The small garrison at Tucson offered no resistance. They dragged on for another eighty miles through barren country, to the Gila, where they again picked up Kearny's tracks.

To lighten the loads of the faltering draft animals, Cooke improvised a barge by lashing two wagon-beds together. He attached dry cottonwood logs for extra buoyancy, piled in twenty-five hundred pounds of supplies, and ordered a few of his men to test the Gila as a boatway. After a seventy-five-mile battle with snags and sandbars the crew profanely declared that the river was not navigable. Their effort was nevertheless to prove historic. When the command reached Colorado, the wagon-beds functioned well, becoming the first ferryboat, other than the Indians' reed rafts, ever to carry men and equipment across the lower river.

The battalion reached San Diego with only five of its original twenty wagons. But Cooke was delighted, and on January 30, 1847, he declared in an extravagant order of the day: "History may be searched in vain for an equal march of infantry. . . . With crowbar and pick and axe in hand, we have worked out a way over mountains which seemed to defy aught save the wild goat, and hewed a passage through a chasm of living rock more narrow than our wagons. . . . Thus, marching half naked and half fed, and living upon wild animals [he meant the Mexican bulls of the San Pedro], we have discovered and made a road of great value to our country."

After reflecting on his own experiences with Kearny and digesting Cooke's official reports, Lieutenant Emory, with possible railroad routes still in mind, wrote Secretary of State James Buchanan that when peace came between the United States and Mexico, the boundary should be drawn as far south as the thirty-second parallel.[4] During the actual negotiations, however, the U.S. envoy agreed with his Mexican counterpart that the boundary should continue up the Rio Grande beyond the thirty-second parallel and then run westward, with some jogs, to the Gila, which would then form the boundary as far as the Colorado. From the junction of the two streams the dividing line would then continue west along a line one maritime league south of San Diego.

The California gold rush that began in 1849 soon showed how impractical the boundary was. Thousands of emigrants headed with their pack trains through lands that, according to the treaty of Guadalupe-Hidalgo, were Mexican territory. Some went as far south as Cooke had; more followed Kearny's trail; others used alternates in between. All eventually reached the south side of the Gila, which also, according to treaty, was Mexican territory. Meanwhile the boundary surveyors, often quarreling bitterly among themselves, struggled to mark the ignored line with precision—only to have to discard the work and begin again, this time to accommodate the Gadsden Purchase of 1853, which gave potential American railroads the room they needed.

During the year 1849, some twelve thousand Anglo-American and Mexican gold-seekers converged in a stifling bottomland on the California side of the Colorado River.[5] The journey had been long, monotonous—"distance, mere blue, naked distance," in the words of one diarist—difficult, and, toward the end, horrifying. Perpetually ravenous livestock ate and trampled out the grass along the Gila, and before summer was over the trail was fetid with the carcasses of dead animals. People were hungry, too. The American flag over the tent of a young cavalry lieutenant, improbably named Cave J. Couts, whose unit was stationed there, brought them swarming. In answer to their pleas for sugar, flour, molasses, salt pork, and, most desirable of all, fresh beef, there was little he could do.

A warlike faction of the Yuma Indians who lived in the vicinity increased the feeling of menace.

After Couts bought a wagon and made it into a ferry, he won thanks from those he helped across the chocolate-colored torrent. On being reassigned to more congenial duty in California, he sold the makeshift boat to Able B. Lincoln, a doctor from Tennessee. Word got around somehow that during the first three months of 1850 Lincoln had already grossed sixty thousand dollars from his new acquisition. This was unlikely, but when the leader of a gang of roughnecks, one John Glanton, got wind of it, there was real trouble.

Sizing up the situation, Glanton told Lincoln that his men would protect the ferry in return for a share of the operation. By that time the troops were gone, and some of the Indians were growing obstreperous again. Lincoln consented, and did not protest when the gang hiked rates and began seizing Mexican women and carrying them off for their private amusement.

Their monopoly was finally challenged when a party of Americans refused to pay Glanton's prices, built a boat, and crossed the river some miles downstream. They gave the craft to the Yuma Indians who had helped them, and who now decided to go into the ferry business themselves. They hired an army deserter named Callaghan to help them operate the boat, and from then on it was preferred by Mexicans traveling to and from California—until the day when the Glanton gang arrived, picked a fight with Callaghan, killed him, beat up the local Yuma chief, and set the Indians' ferryboat adrift. For this last outrage, on April 21, 1850, the Indians killed eleven whites, including both Glanton and Able Lincoln.

Three men who had happened to be out cutting willow poles escaped and carried news of the killings to San Diego. The report swept northward to San Francisco, and from there eleven entrepreneurs decided to go to Yuma and risk reopening the ferry. A leader among them was twenty-four-year-old George Alonzo Johnson, his thin face adorned with a jib-boom nose. Traveling fast, they reached the river in July, 1850, erected stockades on either side of the crossing, and were open for business as the year's migration reached full flood.

Close behind the ferrymen came 142 volunteer militia troops under an Army officer named Morehead, with the intent of at once avenging the "massacre" and collecting pay for their time and effort, as well as for the horses, guns, ammunition, camp equipment, and food they had brought with them. Untrained, undisciplined, and stunned by the summer heat, they were bested in their only skirmish with the Indians, and ran up bills totaling $76,588.26, which would take the troubled state of California four years to pay.[6] Needless to say, the Yumans grew bolder than ever.

Convinced at last that emigrants on the Gila route needed help, the Army's Department of the Pacific authorized a post at the crossing. When teamsters demanded five hundred dollars a ton for hauling freight to the Colorado from San Diego, someone in the quartermaster's office recalled Emory's surmise that the river was probably navigable as high as the Gila. Another guidebook was *Travels in Mexico*, written by R. W. H. Hardy, an officer of Britain's Royal Navy who, on leave from active service, had sailed a small schooner into the river in 1826 while searching for pearls. According to a map in Hardy's book, the Gila joined the Colorado only twenty-five miles above the delta.

On the strength of those bits of information, Captain Alfred H. Wilcox of the 120-ton schooner *Invincible* was ordered to transport ten thousand rations to the river junction by way of the Gulf of California. Accompanying Wilcox was Second Lieutenant George W. Derby of the Corps of Topographical Engineers, who was to map the river, take soundings, and record any useful information.

Meanwhile, Brevet Major Samuel Peter Heintzelman was to march three companies of infantry, equipped with a minimum of supplies, to the same junction and there make contact with the mariners. He reached the river without incident on December 1, 1850, and went into camp on the California bank, a mile or so below the northern stockade of the San Francisco ferrymen.

When the Indians told him that salt water was far away, however, Heintzelman grew nervous. Christmas passed, then New Year's Day. Still no schooner. Scurvy had appeared among the troops, when, on January 11, a Cocopa runner appeared with a note from Derby saying that the *Invincible* was stalled below a promontory twenty miles or so above the delta. Exploration several miles upstream in the ship's boat revealed no sign of the Gila.

The next morning Heintzelman and five oarsmen started downstream in what the major called, in his report, a "surf boat," conducting a rough survey along the way. In two days of rowing they covered approximately eighty miles before they came to a widening in the river that amounted almost to a lake. Near it they met Derby, and between them they established that there were two channels entering the head of the lake. Heintzelman, following the main river, had arrived by the eastern one. The western one was little more than a slough. When Hardy had mapped the lake a quarter of a century earlier, the bulk of the red water—the Colorado—had been pouring down the western channel. He had assumed, accordingly, that the smaller eastern flow was the Gila. Since then the Colorado had shifted its course from one side of its elevated bed of silt to the other. Having deduced this, George Derby was able to make an important adjustment in the existing maps. He struck out Hardy's version of the Gila and moved the Colorado eastward into its new position. He then renamed the western channel, shrunken now to a mere overflow stream, "Hardy's Colorado."[7] Adding Heintzelman's figures to his own, he computed the distance from the river junction to the delta at 104 miles.

Straightening out the map did nothing to move the *Invincible*. The schooner drew nine feet of water and could not negotiate the crooked channel of the river above the lake. The only way to deliver the stores was to unload them on the open Sonora bank, in the hope that Heintzelman's teamsters could reach them with wagons. To start the wheels turning the major and his oarsmen began their laborious ascent of the river on January 15.

The next day, a thundering tidal bore snapped the schooner's anchor chains and carried it headlong up the stream. Seizing the wheel, Captain Wilcox turned the prow toward the bank and had his seamen jump precariously from the jib-boom to the shore with kedge anchors. The ship caught and held. Dragging up driftwood, the men constructed a stout mooring and unloaded the cargo. In due time the first wagon appeared. Assured that the transfer could be effected, the mariners happily left the river to which they had now been confined for a month.

Back at the river junction, Heintzelman moved his camp from the water's edge onto a low bluff directly opposite the mouth of the Gila. There, among the ruins of one of the two mission-presidios the Spanish had built to defend the crossing at that same spot eighty years earlier, he established Fort Yuma. For living quarters the men erected little huts made of mesquite stakes daubed with mud and roofed with bundles of arrowweed. The officers occupied some of the Spanish mission's roofless cubicles, cutting away the sun with canvas from their tents.

Heintzelman laid out his military reservation in such a way that it embraced the California landing of the ferry. When the operators objected, he blandly advised them to sell their holdings to him. Since the ferry was not earning enough to support all eleven owners, Alonzo Johnson and eight of his partners complied. Heintzelman then went into the ferry business with the remaining two.

Hard times followed. Although both Derby and Heintzelman suggested that an attempt be made to ascend the Colorado with shallow-draft steamboats instead of sailing vessels, the Army was unwilling to risk the experiment. In May Heintzelman was advised to withdraw from Fort Yuma until some other solution to the supply problem could be found. In June he obeyed, leaving Lieutenant Thomas Sweeny and ten men behind to guard the fort—and the ferry. Passing squadrons of hungry troops drained away the few rations that did reach Fort Yuma by wagon. In December, 1851, Sweeny's guard was also forced to withdraw.

To the rescue came the erstwhile ferryman, Alonzo Johnson, who, early in 1852, managed to unload supplies from an ocean-going steamer onto flatboats and to have them poled and pulled upstream from the delta. Heintzelman, who had just reoccupied the hilltop at the crossing, sent forty soldiers overland to help with the operation. Two hundred Yumas now struck. During an all-night battle nine men were killed and the rest withdrew to the fort. In retaliation Heintzelman took to the field, burning the Indian towns and destroying crops. Preoccupied just then by one of their intermittent wars with the Cocopas, the Yumas withdrew from the river, and Johnson was able to get the flatboats moving—though just barely. One sank with a full cargo, and the others (nine, eventually) could scarcely keep up with the appetites of the five hundred men at the post.

Early in 1854, Johnson, ever persistent, brought in a sidewheeler 104 feet long, and was soon grossing twenty thousand dollars a month.[8]

Few soldiers liked Fort Yuma's stifling heat and dullness. Desertions were frequent, and there probably would have been more except for the Great Western, nickname of Sarah Bowman, a redheaded Amazon six feet two inches tall. She had been following the Army since the days of the Mexican War, ministering to the troops as laundress, nurse, cook, prostitute, and, later on, procurer. The Colorado crossing marked the end of her wanderings. She ran the officers' mess at Fort Yuma for a time and in 1853, aged forty, built a small adobe house near the ferry's Arizona landing. There she sold odds and ends of merchandise to travelers, served meals, and housed stray girls, mostly Indians and Mexicans. She offered the willing ones to the soldiers and stoutly succored those who were not. What grew into the town of Yuma absorbed her building—she soon leased it to a grocery keeper—but she lived on in the neighborhood until her death in 1866.[9]

By the end of 1853, the crossing was relatively safe, but the search for swifter, surer means of travel by railroad continued.

The sectional rivalry over whether Chicago or St. Louis—or, alternatively, Memphis or New Orleans—was to become the terminus of the road went on for longer than is generally remembered. The first proposals appeared in eastern newspapers in the 1830s.

In 1848, before news of the California gold discoveries had reached the East, private capitalists in St. Louis asked John Charles Frémont, son-in-law of Senator Thomas Hart Benton of Missouri, to prove the practicality of the thirty-eighth parallel as a year-round route. To Frémont that meant tackling the Colorado Rockies in the dead of winter. The upshot was the grisly loss of ten men to starvation and freezing.

After the gold rush began, the search intensified. Among the many private contenders was Francis Xavier Aubry, a Santa Fe trader who took to the field to prove his point as an advocate of a roadbed along the thirty-fifth parallel through northern Arizona.[10]

In June, 1853, he had just driven thirty-five hundred sheep from Santa Fe to San Francisco by way of Fort Yuma and Los Angeles, and he decided that on his way home he would show the world that a railroad could easily run farther north than the Gila. His exploring party consisted of eighteen men; his closest approach to a scientific instrument was a compass. His sheep venture having prospered, the party drove with it a fine herd of newly purchased horses and mules.

The men followed the Mojave River to its deathbed in Soda Lake and then struck northeast across the simmering desert to the Colorado, which they intersected a few miles south of where Boulder Dam now stands, perhaps at El Dorado Canyon.[11] After crossing the stream on a raft contrived of driftwood, they rested their animals for five days and then slanted southeast to the vicinity of present-day Peach Springs, Arizona. For the next several-score miles their route coincided approximately with U.S. Highway 66.

In mid-August, high on a shoulder of the San Francisco Peaks, the party camped near an Indian village whose inhabitants seemed friendly. About fifty men, women, and children thronged about them. No arms were in evidence, and many of the women carried babies with them on cradle boards. But at a prearranged signal the women produced clubs they had hidden in their blankets, the males rushed at the explorers, and two hundred more attackers came screaming out of hiding places in the brush.

Some of Aubry's men broke loose before they were immobilized, however, and poured bullets into the throng with new, rapid-fire Colt revolvers. Demoralized, the Indians fled. Many of the women unburdened themselves by throwing their babies into a nearby gulch. Presumably they had hoped to return to them later—though most of the children were almost surely killed or maimed by the fall. The victors counted twenty-five adult corpses, and in their fury over the attack they scalped several. But sixteen of the eighteen-man party were wounded, twelve of them severely. Aubry was one of these. They limped into Zuñi, and within a few months Aubry put together another, larger band of sheep and repeated the trip. This time he returned along the same parallel with a wagon in which he carried a boat for crossing the Colorado. His party this time was larger than before, and the Indians avoided it.

After reaching Albuquerque, Aubry announced publicly, "I am satisfied that a railroad may be run almost mathematically direct from Zuñi to Colorado"—he meant the river—"and from thence to the Tejon Pass in California."

Richard Weightman, the editor of an Albuquerque newspaper that supported a route along the thirty-second parallel, as well as New Mexico's delegate to Congress, printed an unfavorable account of Aubry's investigations. When the two chanced to meet in an Albuquerque saloon, a quarrel erupted. Weightman threw a glass of whiskey in Aubry's face. Half-blinded, Aubry spasmodically drew his revolver. It misfired into the ceiling. Weightman then stabbed him to death with a bowie knife and escaped penalty by pleading self-defense.

In 1853, when the national debate about routes had begun to sound nearly as vehement as the dispute between Aubry and Weightman, Congress instructed Secretary of War Jefferson Davis to initiate surveys of all principal strips under consideration, with the exception of the central overland trail through southern Wyoming, northern Utah, and Nevada, and of the Gila Trail, which had already been surveyed at least in part.* Davis was granted four hundred thousand dollars for the work, which was to be completed in ten months.

So far as the Colorado River Basin was concerned, the thirty-eighth parallel through central Colorado and Utah received the most consideration. The official party there was led by a topographical engineer, Lieutenant John

*Late in 1853, reconsideration of proposals to use the thirty-second parallel led the War Department to order Lieutenant John G. Parke of the Corps of Topographical Engineers to make a fresh evaluation of the intricate geography of the Gila's headwaters.

Gunnison, assisted by Lieutenant E. G. Beckwith. Their guide as far as the
Grand River was Antoine Leroux. With a train of eighteen wagons, the party
crawled into the Basin by way of Cochetopa Pass and then followed the left
bank of the river, which now has the name of the expedition's leader. It was
tough going. With relief they at last veered off into the Uncompahgre Valley
and picked up Robidoux's old trail to Utah. At the crossing over the Grand,
Leroux left them.

In Utah they paralleled the Old Spanish Trail through Castle Valley and
over the Wasatch Mountains to the vicinity of Sevier Lake. There a band of
Pahvant Utes caught them offguard, and Gunnison was killed, along with
seven of his men. The next year Beckwith reorganized the party and finished
the work.

Anticipating that Gunnison's and Beckwith's official reports about the
central route might be unfavorable, Senator Benton and his St. Louis support-
ers sent out two private parties to gather material that could be used in
rebuttal. One, led by a former naval lieutenant, Edward Fitzgerald Beale, was
equipped with a press agent, Gwin Heap. Traveling light in fine summer
weather, the party had no trouble and sent back laudatory accounts. The
second was led by Frémont—who, eager to redeem his 1848 fiasco, again
tackled the trail in the dead of winter. Blizzards engulfed his party as it
plodded across the deserts that bracket the Green River in Utah; horses gave
out and some of the riders had to walk. When they, too, began to droop,
Frémont unloaded the pack mules, cached the equipment, and mounted his
party on them. Huge drifts all but swallowed them as they toiled out of the
Basin over the Wasatches. By the time they straggled into the Mormon
outpost town of Parowan, one man had died of exposure and two were so
weak that they stayed behind when Frémont went on to California two weeks
later. One of the pair, Solomon Carvalho, was the first official photographer
ever to see any part of the Colorado River Basin. The other, once grossly fat
but wasted almost to a skeleton when he reached Parowan, was Baron F. W.
Von Egloffstein, a topographer from Germany. Both recovered after being
nursed by the Mormons. Unwilling to risk more exploring, Carvalho went
to Salt Lake City and became something of a social lion before continuing to
San Francisco. Egloffstein, his girth regained, made contact with Lieutenant
Beckwith—who was about to continue with the Gunnison survey—and
signed on to replace a topographer who had been killed by the Utes the year
before. We shall meet him again.

The last of the surveyors to be considered is Lieutenant Amiel W. Whipple,[12]
who was put in charge of the official reconnaissance of the thirty-fifth parallel.
Though he had his difficulties, a feeling of lightheartedness attaches to his
adventure, as recounted in the *Diary of a Journey from the Mississippi to the*

Coasts of the Pacific, originally written in German by Whipple's artist-naturalist, Heinrich Baldwin Möllhausen. He told how, out on the plains, the party suddenly decided to build a huge bonfire, and, enthroning a teamster who owned a fiddle on a high wagon seat, proceeded to hold a wild, all-male dance, attended by several Mexican traders and wandering Indians who happened to be in the vicinity. At another ball, this time in the little adobe town of Anton Chico, beside the Pecos River, dark-eyed Mexican girls and whiskey punch added to the hilarity.

In Albuquerque Whipple's party gleaned information about the trail from Francis Aubry, who was still recovering from the wounds he had incurred near the San Francisco Peaks. Fortunately for Whipple's own peace of mind, his military escort was augmented by the arrival of more troops under the command of Lieutenant Joseph Christmas Ives, recently graduated from West Point. In Albuquerque Whipple also picked up two new guides, José Saavedra and the ubiquitous Antoine Leroux. When the party continued its march in November, it consisted of about 120 men with two hundred mules, a few horses, and sixteen wagons. Just after crossing the Continental Divide, they paused to note the register of names that travelers for nearly two and a half centuries—beginning with Oñate in 1606—had been carving into the sandstone walls of Inscription Rock.

On Christmas Eve the party camped near the spot where Aubry had been attacked. The men warmed themselves by setting some pine trees afire and held yet another drunken celebration. Fortunately, though Leroux was edgy, the Indians stayed away.

Moving west, the party followed approximately the route of today's Highway 66 for a ways, then dropped south to the Bill Williams River, and at length greeted the Colorado, with cheers and gunfire, at what is today the site of Parker Dam. Unable to cross there, they turned back upstream to the north. More wagons fell by the wayside, until only the little carriage that held the party's surveying instruments was left. After skirting the naked pinnacles known as the Needles, they entered, in Whipple's words, "the magnificent valley of the Mojaves."

Here they got on well with the Indians, made friends with two chiefs —Cairook and Ireteba—and, aided by the natives, began the laborious crossing of the river, which Whipple estimated to be five hundred feet wide. As the column straggled along beside the Mojave River, Paiutes caught a lagging herder and killed him, later devouring the three mules whose stubbornness had caused his delay.

Although the reconnaissance touched unexplored land only occasionally, the Corps of Topographical Engineers added measurably to what was known of the Colorado River Basin. They catalogued its flora and fauna, related its geology to what was known about other parts of the earth, and made painstaking inquiries into the languages and customs of the Indians. They drew the first scientific, astronomically coordinated maps of the region, determining its high and low spots by barometric observation. Their findings were made available in thirteen massive volumes, profusely illustrated though poorly organized and poorly indexed—the *Reports of Explorations and Surveys to Ascertain the Most Practical and Economical Route for a Railroad from the Mississippi River to the Pacific Coast.*[13]

The imposing title was already anachronistic, as tension between North and South precluded any hope of a prompt decision. Californians accordingly began calling for federal help in building wagon roads, on which work began in 1857. In general, the road-builders in the Colorado Basin followed paths already laid down by their predecessors. Stage lines, mail contractors, and emigrants quickly took advantage of their efforts. But a few miles away, the great river that had shaped the land remained hardly better known than when Cárdenas had first peered at it from the rim of the Grand Canyon.

Junction of the Gila and
Colorado Rivers, 1851

6

The Mythic River

William Manly, born in Vermont in 1820 and raised on the Michigan frontier, was just the sort to catch the California gold fever. He had been earning his own living since he was sixteen or so by chopping wood, working in lead mines, hunting deer, and trapping. He could build and handle rafts and canoes; he was adept at Indian sign language. Deciding abruptly in the summer of 1849 to go to the gold-fields, he hired out with six other teamsters to a migrant named Charles Dallas.

The small company started late. Troops they encountered in Wyoming warned Dallas to winter in Salt Lake City rather than try to cross the Sierra Nevada after snow fell. Dallas accepted the advice but said that he would not support his hired hands in idleness during the layover. Itching to reach California and reluctant to winter almost without funds among the Mormons, of whom they had heard hair-raising tales, Manly and his companions were ready for any alternative.

At the ford over the Green they found an abandoned ferryboat twelve feet long and six wide, half filled with drifted sand. One of the officers traveling with the company had an old map that showed the Green flowing into the Pacific. Although he warned of cascades along the way, the gold-seekers decided to try the route. They dug the ferryboat out of the sand and patched it up.

Although the defection put Dallas in a difficult position with his wagons, he helped the adventurer by accepting Manly's pony in exchange for grocer-ies and ropes. They had their own guns and fishing lines, the boat was sturdy, and they were in high spirits as they skimmed along toward the distant Uinta Mountains.

The first of the canyons' rapids forced them to land, portage their goods, and then line the heavy craft down among the boulders. At rapid after rapid they repeated the process, until finally the current wrenched the ropes from their grasp and the barge upended against a massive rock. There the surging water kept it pinned so tight "we could no more move it than we could move the boulder itself."

From tall, straight pines that grew nearby they hollowed out canoes. Two were fifteen feet long; one was twenty-five. They lashed the fifteen-footers together for greater stability, and off they went again. As their skills increased, they began risking rough water in preference to portaging their burdens along the boulder-strewn banks. In time, overconfidence led them into a rapid that flipped the smaller boats; one of the crew nearly drowned.

Hungrily, for they had lost most of their guns and ammunition in the wreck, they coursed Desolation and Gray canyons and at last broke into the open near the site of today's Green River, Utah.[1] There they met a camp of Ute Indians under famed Chief Wakara. When Manly inquired in sign lan-guage about the river below, Wakara drew a map of the part of the stream they had just run, lined it with stones to represent canyon walls, and raised his hands with a cry of "E-e-e-e!" Assured that Manly understood, the chief made a map of the country farther down, piled up two or three tiers of stones, raised his fists as high as he could, and shouted "E-e-e-e-e-e!" at the top of his voice, all the while shaking his head "No! No!"

That was enough for the crew. Leaving the river, they hiked nine days west, short of food, until they found, near Utah Lake, a wagon train they could join.

A more ambitious attempt to test the unknown river was initiated by Lieutenant James H. Simpson of the Corps of Topographical Engineers, who had been sent west in 1849 and attached to a punitive expedition against the Navajos. He thoroughly disliked the country's "*naked, barren* wastes" (his emphasis) and "sickening colors." But he was dutiful. He described the pue-blo of Zuñi more thoroughly than anyone else had done since its discovery. He also conducted the first Anglo investigation of the great Anasazi ruins of Chaco Canyon, which he thought were of Aztec origin. He listened with interest to campfire talks about shorter routes from Santa Fe to Los Angeles than those provided by either the Gila Trail to the south or the Old Spanish Trail to the north. Back in Santa Fe, he talked to Richard Campbell, a trapper, who told him that building a road down Zuñi Creek to the Colorado of the West would present no trouble.

This was a misunderstanding, since, as Campbell must surely have known, Zuñi Creek runs into the Little Colorado, not into the main Colorado. Although other trappers spoke of ferocious gorges, Simpson felt duty-bound to recommend an investigation[2]—and probably was relieved when the assignment went not to him but to Lieutenant Lorenzo Sitgreaves, who was ordered to "pursue the Zuñi to its junction with the Colorado, determine its course and character, particularly in reference to its navigability. . . . You will then pursue the Colorado to its junction with the Gulf of California" with the same ends in view. Counting himself, he was to have four scientists in his party, an escort of thirty soldiers, thirty pack mules tended by fifteen roustabouts, and a flock of sheep for food. As guide he hired—who else?—Antoine Leroux. Rendezvous point was Zuñi, from which the company departed on September 24, 1851.[3]

Leroux must have been amazed. The navigability of Zuñi creek? During the dry fall of the year it would scarcely float a stick. The Little Colorado was no better. Although late-summer rains had given the stream more body than it sometimes possessed at that season, the overflow had created bogs that the expedition's mules could scarcely negotiate—certainly a rowboat couldn't. Nevertheless, Sitgreaves was determined to follow instructions. Northwest he went, downstream past the point where modern Holbrook now stands, and on among the multicolored hills of the Painted Desert. After miles of that, the command came in sight of the tall, gray-headed San Francisco Peaks, rising dramatically above black cloaks of timber. Closer by, as they advanced, was the black volcanic cone that would eventually be named Sunset Crater because of its yellow rim. But where the trail wound there was only lava, black sand, and an occasional stunted cottonwood tree shading a sparse patch of dry grass—"the most desert lukking plase," one disgusted Mormon wrote twenty-two years later, "that I ever saw, Amen."[4]

The stream-bed fell away over a double-tiered wall of black rock 125 feet high. During rare flash floods, liquid mud pours thunderously over the drop, now called Grand Falls, but Sitgreaves arrived at a time when only three thin ribbons of water were sliding down the cliff. At the bottom the stream made a right-angle bend and drove on between lava walls to another broad but shallower plunge, today's Black Falls. At last Sitgreaves gave in and agreed with Leroux's insistent advice that they skirt the vast gorges that lay ahead and gain the main Colorado near the Mohave villages. From there the command could reverse direction and push as far back as possible upstream into the big canyon. That plan should at least let Sitgreaves determine where the head of navigation lay.

Off they veered into the lava wastes surrounding Sunset Crater. Indian ruins abounded, and the sharp lava cut the animals' feet. Halts had to be made so that the mules could be reshod and pine gum be put into the cracked hooves of the sheep. Water was scarce, dry camps frequent. Yet as the command straggled westward over the north shoulder of the San Francisco Peaks (today's main east-west highway goes south of them), Sitgreaves was able to marvel at the brilliant fall gold of the aspens and to write, "There was much of beauty in some of the glades and mountain glens we passed." But as they dropped lower, the land turned bleak, and the Cosnina (Havasupai) Indians were hostile. At first casualties were limited to mules, but later, as Leroux was riding ahead to scout for a pass through a mountain barrier, he was ambushed and received three wounds, one of them in the head, that disabled him for the rest of the trip.

By the time the party had at last crossed the Black Mountains, at what is still called Sitgreaves Pass, and had dropped down to the river, the men were in no shape to fight the Mojave Indians in order to carry out upstream explorations. Hoping for succor at Fort Yuma, Sitgreaves turned the company downstream, unaware that Heintzelman had abandoned the place in June, leaving only an undernourished guard of eleven men behind.

En route, the hungry engineer tried to salvage what he could of his trip by estimating the navigability of the stream. He had expected more than he saw, for Leroux had regaled him with bright tales about the river. In 1837, the guide said, he and some other trappers had built boats out of horsehide at the point where the Virgin River flows into the Colorado and had floated along until they had come to an island covered with cottonwood trees. Hewing dugout canoes from the trees, they had sailed high and free to the gulf. There was no question that the river could carry traffic, lots of it. But as Sitgreaves studied the sandbars that showed through the low water, he was doubtful.

He was also under considerable stress. First the Mojave and then the Yuma Indians kept sniping at the party. A packer was killed, and the expedition's doctor was wounded in the leg. Rations gave out, but at least when a mule died of starvation, the carcass furnished tough, stringy steaks for the ravenous men.

At Fort Yuma they found sixteen soldiers had already preceded them there. When yet another party appeared on Sitgreaves's heels, the combined forces gathered up what food remained in the commisary, and on December 6, turning their backs on the Colorado, headed for San Diego.

In the late spring of 1854, Lieutenant Sylvester Mowry, who had graduated from West Point two years before and who is known to have picked up a venereal disease from an Indian girl during his first assignment, a railroad survey in Oregon, was transferred to the command of Edward J. Steptoe, then stationed in Salt Lake City. Tempers were close to the edge there. Steptoe was convinced that Mormon missionaries were seeking to convert the neighboring Indians not only to save their souls but also to build up alliances in case of trouble with the United States—an opinion strengthened when the Saints arrested only three of the many Utes who had been involved in the killing of Lieutenant John Gunnison and eight soldiers the year before, charged them with manslaughter rather than murder, and sentenced each to three years in prison.[5] And, as is true wherever troops are stationed, there was the problem of local girls. Those in Salt Lake City were enjoined from the pulpit in the Tabernacle to keep themselves pure, and the soldiers were warned to keep their hands off.

A fiction of cordiality was maintained where officers were concerned, however, and at one of several formal parties Mowry met Mary Young, a daughter-in-law of Brigham Young himself and, according to the lieutenant, "the prettiest woman I have seen yet." The discovery that her husband was away on a mission and that she was rebellious against Mormon polygamy produced a situation that was made to order for intrigue. Mowry boasted in a letter, "She is as hot a thing as you could wish. I am going to make the attempt and if I succeed and don't get my head blown off by being caught shall esteem myself some."[6]

Rumors of the affair soon circulated in Salt Lake City, and Colonel Steptoe felt compelled to get rid of the philanderer. He did so by putting Mowry in command of a detachment to report on the road from Salt Lake City to Los Angeles—the so-called Mormon Corridor to Southern California, already heavily used each fall by wagon trains bent on avoiding the Sierra Nevada—as a highway for troop movements. Though, according to Mowry, Mary wanted to go with him, "Brigham sent me word that if I took her away he would have me killed before I could get out of the Territory. He is a man of his word in little matters of this sort. . . ." On April 30, 1855, the lieutenant rode off at the head of thirty-two dragoons, thirty civilian quartermaster employees, eighty horses, and seven wagons each drawn by six mules.

Controlled development of the road he was following was of fundamental importance to the Mormon hierarchy, who on the one hand would have preferred complete isolation from the rest of the nation, but on the other hand recognized that it was not only physically but also economically impossible.

To resolve the dilemma, the Mormons had begun entrenching their own people in strategic spots alongside all the trails leading into the territory. In 1853, they squeezed Jim Bridger out of his post on Black's Fork of the Green

River by accusing him of selling guns to the Indians. By legal legerdemain they had taken the Green River ferry from the mountain men who were operating it and turned the business over to Mormon entrepreneurs.[7] They had also placed stations in western Nevada, where the California Trail started climbing over the Sierra Nevada, but their main concern was with the trail that Mowry had been sent to examine.

Key settlements had been established astride the corridor as early as 1851. One of these was at San Bernardino, in southern California. Another was at Parowan, in southwestern Utah. A third was projected for the four big, gushing springs that created in the middle of the desert a green stopping-place known as Las Vegas (The Meadows). Only days after Mowry set out, Mormon missionaries designated to make peace with the Indians so that Mormons could take over Las Vegas started off down the same route.

Mowry had heard that the Saints had discovered iron ore at Cedar City, south of Parowan; had erected smelters and foundries; and were casting cannons. (In fact, they weren't doing anything of the kind; the Cedar City iron works would not begin operating until years later.) But Mowry conjectured that the guns he saw in Indian hands came from Mormon traders—as is likely—and that the hostility he had encountered along the way was the result of Mormon propaganda. Accordingly, he warned in his report: "I have no desire to predict an intestine war [between the United States and Utah] but it is, in the minds of all intelligent men who have lived among the God forsaken people of Utah, only a question of time."[8]

His march was successful, notwithstanding the terrain's heat, sand, and wind, and he lost no men. Having suggested a few improvements in the route, he was rewarded by being transferred in August, 1855, to Fort Yuma. "A hell of a place," he wrote his friend, but went on to speak of compensations available through the Great Western: Yuma girls "entirely naked except for a little fringe of bark," and charming Mexicans. "I have just got a Sonoranian ... seventeen, very pretty, dark hair, black eyes, and clear olive complexion."[9]

Mowry and Major Heintzelman became involved in mining ventures in the newly opened Gadsden Purchase. He argued for separate territorial status for Arizona, at that time a part of New Mexico, in the hope of becoming its delegate to Congress. And he wrote his superiors at the Department of the Pacific proposing that he head an expedition to discover the upper limits of navigation on the Colorado River, from which point he would survey a wagon road to Salt Lake City. From San Francisco his suggestion was passed on favorably to headquarters in the East. But now a competitor entered the field. This was Alonzo Johnson, who by now had two steamboats, the *General Jesup* and the newer, larger *Colorado*, plying between the delta and Fort Yuma. Needing additional business to keep his craft busy, he had dropped suggestions that led to a joint resolution by the California legislature calling on the Army to authorize the same thing Mowry had asked for—a full-scale examination of the river. With this backing, and with California's senator, John B. Weller, smoothing the way, Johnson carried his lobbying to Secretary of War Jefferson Davis.

Weller, who favored having private contractors do the kind of work that normally fell to the Corps of Topographical Engineers, proposed that Johnson command the expedition. An Army appropriation bill for 1856–57 carried an item of seventy thousand dollars for the exploration of the lower Colorado River.

In March, 1857, however, a new administration took over in Washington. Jefferson Davis was replaced as secretary of war by John B. Floyd, who asked Captain A. A. Humphreys, chief of the new Office of Western Explorations and a former member of the Corps of Topographical Engineers, to review the river proposals and make suggestions. As a result, the plan proposed originally by Sylvester Mowry was expanded to cover not only the lower river but also the great canyon about which so many marvelous tales had been told. Floyd placed Lieutenant Joseph Christmas Ives in charge of the survey. By then Mowry, evidently putting aside all thought of Mary Young, had inveigled a sick leave from the Army—from which he would soon resign altogether— to further his political ambitions.

Following his graduation from West Point, Ives had advanced himself by marrying John Floyd's socially prominent niece. Alonzo Johnson, on learning of the connection, was sure that he had lost his own bid to lead the Colorado River survey because of it.[10] Though possibly Johnson was right to some degree, the young lieutenant had other qualifications, notably his experience in 1853–54 as a member of the Whipple survey team.

In the spring of 1857 the "intestine" war between Utah and the United States that Sylvester Mowry had predicted broke out. The roots of the trouble were political as well as religious. Although Brigham Young, president of the Mormon Church, had been governor of the territory since its establishment in 1850, most of its Indian agents, land surveyors, mail contractors, and, above all, federal judges, were incompetent, arrogant, and non-Mormon—hacks appointed as a reward for party loyalty. The Mormons retaliated in a number of ways, until President Buchanan became persuaded that Brigham Young must be replaced as governor and directed the Army of the United States to escort the new, non-Mormon appointee west with twenty-five hundred men.

The mouth of
Diamond Creek

7

The Big
One

While the Utah-bound troops were assembling at Fort Leavenworth, Kansas,
Ives methodically supervised the construction of an iron boat in the Philadelphia yards of Reaney, Neafie & Company—a very special craft, designed to
be shipped in pieces to Panama, carried to the Pacific on the new trans-
isthmus railroad, reloaded on shipboard for the journey to San Francisco, and
then transferred to a schooner for the final run through the Gulf of California
to the delta.

Before this journey began, however, Ives put his ship together for test
runs on the Delaware River. It measured fifty-four feet from the tip of its
prow to the farthest blade of its stern-mounted paddlewheel. There was a
four-foot platform in the bow on which the pilot and a man who took
soundings could stand. In the rear was a tiny cabin eight feet by seven. The
rest of the hull was open like a rowboat's. Crowded into that space was the
cylindrical boiler—smokestack at its front, firebox at its rear—that activated
the piston rods leading back to the paddlewheel. It was painted bright red,
and its name, EXPLORER, U.S., was printed in big black letters on the housing
that covered the upper part of the paddlewheel. Ives eyed it with a creator's

pride, fully believing that it would help bring enough fame to his name to make him and his children worthy of his wife's high connections.

Between stints with the boat, Ives wrote letters to prospective members of the expedition: Heinrich Baldwin Möllhausen, the artist and naturalist, whose abilities he had admired during the Whipple survey; the corpulent Baron F. W. von Egloffstein as topographer; and John Strong Newberry, a physician by training, as geologist. They were to make their rendezvous with the mule tenders needed for the canyon part of the survey, at Fort Yuma in January, 1858.

In the meantime, Ives shepherded the pieces of his boat to San Francisco and there saw them stacked onto the deck of a two-masted schooner, the *Monterey*, whose hold was already crammed with cargo consigned to Fort Yuma. The lieutenant traveled with it, accompanied by a man named Carroll who was to serve as the *Explorer*'s engineer, and the eight enlisted men who were to act as the boat's crew. On December 1, 1857, after a miserable, month-long trip, the overcrowded schooner crept into the delta, where the fluctuation between high and low tide was so great that the schooner's captain could not bring it close enough to the soft mud banks so that the parts of the *Explorer* could be moved ashore and reassembled. Ives suggested sailing the schooner through a shallow gully in the river bank and into a kind of bay in the mudflats beyond, at the next high tide.

It was a risky procedure, but the captain reluctantly agreed to try.

The *Monterey* easily rode the rush of water into the basin. As soon as the surrounding gumbo had dried enough to sustain their weight, four of Ives's eight soldiers and some of the schooner's crew began digging out a pit in which the *Explorer* could be assembled. The other men were ordered to harness themselves to logs of driftwood and drag them to the pit for use as derricks and ways.

Slowly the pieces were unloaded. The men hammered the bent sections straight, drilled sixty holes by hand into the iron plates in order to affix reinforcing beams to the hull, erected pulleys, and lowered the ponderous boiler into place. When the next spring tide arrived, they successfully maneuvered the *Monterey* back through the opening.

While the *Explorer* was being assembled, Alonzo Johnson's steamboats arrived from Fort Yuma to pick up supplies brought in by the *Monterey*. Johnson himself brought letters to Ives from Washington, telling him what everyone at Fort Yuma already knew: that the Utah war, to which the lieutenant had thus far paid little attention, had taken a disastrous turn.

Word that troops were on the march had reached Salt Lake City on July 24, 1857, as 2,587 Saints were gathered to celebrate the tenth anniversary of the arrival of the first Mormons in Utah.[1]

With a fanaticism worthy of Brigham Young—who in 1847 had reputedly said, "If the people of the United States let the Saints alone for ten years, all hell cannot prevail against us"[2]—the Mormons prepared to fight back. Militia units began to drill and prepare fortifications. The colonists stationed beside the principal trails in Nevada and at San Bernardino, California— places that were practically indefensible—were ordered to return to Utah with as many guns and as much ammunition as they could obtain. Skillfully led militia units burned the grass off the meadows bordering the Overland Trail so that Army draft animals would starve, and early in October they attacked and put to the torch seventy-two wagons of three U.S. Army supply trains camped beside the Green River. When an early snowstorm added its fury on October 17, the entire invading force had to creep for shelter into the remnants of Fort Bridger and nearby Fort Supply, both of which had been deliberately gutted by their erstwhile Mormon occupants. So many Army draft animals died that Captain Randolph Marcy was sent on a months-long trip to Fort Union in eastern New Mexico to round up more. Meanwhile, the glum commander of the would-be occupation force sent an express east with word that no further action would be possible until spring—unless an attack could be mounted from the south.

The letters Alonzo Johnson had brought from Fort Yuma ordered Ives to push at least as high as the mouth of the Virgin and then return to Fort Yuma with his assessment of the possibility in eight or ten days. And the *Explorer* wasn't yet afloat!

Sniffing an opportunity, Johnson offered to save the expedition by renting it one of his own steamboats. When Ives declined, Johnson's wrath surged again, and he vowed to explore the river himself. "If I find the river navigable," he declared, "I will have it published to the world before you can launch your boat and leave tidewater."[3] But since he made his living from Army freight contracts, he could not afford to be too antagonistic, and in the end he lent Ives one of his employees, the hulking David Robinson, as pilot for the *Explorer*.

Back at Fort Yuma, Johnson asked the commanding officer for an escort, just in case the Mormons were stirring up trouble among the Indians, and was granted sixteen men under Lieutenant J. L. White. He fleshed out this force with an equal number of armed civilians (the old trapper Paulino Weaver was one of them) who could double as roustabouts and woodcutters. On December 31, 1857, off the party steamed on the *General Jesup*. Watching it go were Ives's scientist and the men in charge of the mules for the canyon expedition, who had just arrived at the Fort Yuma rendezvous.

Ives proceeded with assembling the *Explorer* as though nothing had happened. It was finally eased into the river on the moonlit night of December 30, when the tides were at their fullest. The river itself was very low, however.

After a continual struggle with sandbars and snags, interrupted by frequent stops to cut wood for the boiler, the craft reached Fort Yuma on January 9, 1858. When it took off again two nights later, after a drunken farewell party, the workers and enlisted men aboard had to perch wherever they could among stacks of firewood and sacks of provisions. The officers and scientists took turns sitting inside the small cabin, on its roof, or on the forward-facing section of the paddlewheel's curved housing. There they had to endure hot cinders spewing from the smokestack and sand-laden winds roaring out of the desert.

The Indians along its course, who knew where the worst sandbars were, would gather near each one to watch as the incomprehensible white men came ashore in a skiff, and harnessed themselves to tow ropes, to assist the *Explorer*'s groaning sternwheel. But at least the crawling pace gave Egloff-stein time to draw, Möllhausen to collect specimens (he passed out trinkets to Indian children who brought him rats, kangaroo mice, horned toads, lizards, and insects, which they supposed he ate), and Newberry to study the naked, granite mountains that in some places crowded close to the stream.

On January 30 they met the *General Jesup* returning downstream. Having won the race, as he supposed, Johnson was all affability and paused to exchange information.[4] He said that he had gone to the valley above Pyramid Canyon, more than three hundred miles from Fort Yuma. On his way back he had seen the camels.

Camels? Ives was immediately interested. As he knew, plans for a trans-continental railroad had collapsed, and as a substitute the government was building wagon roads across the West. A reconnaissance of the one designed to follow the thirty-fifth parallel—a route that Ives had helped survey in 1853–54—had been assigned to a former Navy lieutenant, Edward Fitzgerald Beale. Experimenting with a camel train in place of mules had been part of his job. The exotic beasts—Beale called them "the noblest brutes alive"—had marched to California without a hitch. Beale was now testing their adaptabil-ity to winter by marching them back east. They had been approaching the Colorado near a big chunk of water-sculptured stone called Bullhead Rock when they sighted the *General Jesup*. Johnson had paused long enough to ferry the noble brutes across the river, even though they had swum it without trouble on the outward journey.[5]

And yes, Johnson would be glad to take Lieutenant John Tipton of the Ives survey back to Fort Yuma so that Tipton, who had come along this far just for the ride, could round up pack stock and rations for the survey of the Big Canyon. Off he steamed, confident that Lieutenant White of the escort would be able to send a navigation report to Washington (and to the San Francisco newspapers, where Johnson was eager for publicity) long before Ives had anything useful to say.

The Mojaves turned out to be as friendly as Ives remembered from his trip with Whipple, and he was able to employ Chief Ireteba as a "guide" for the remainder of the ascent of the river—and, more important, as a visible assurance to the Indians farther upstream that they had nothing to fear from the soldiers. The boat churned and snorted on. Early in March, well above the point where Johnson had turned back, the party reached the mouth of the Black Canyon. Its thousand-foot walls dwarfed those of the other gorges through which they had labored. As they were craning their necks in amazement, the *Explorer* struck a submerged rock with a crash that made Ives think for an instant that the canyon had fallen in. Three days of repair work, engineer Carroll said after inspecting the damage, would be necessary before the steamboat could move again.

Refusing to sit idle for that long, Ives decided to try to take the skiff to the mouth of the Virgin, the high point suggested in the instructions he had received. With him went the mate of the *Explorer* and his pilot-on-loan, David Robinson. For most of the way they were forced by rapids to land and to tow the skiff from the bank. This was Ives's first encounter with one of the Colorado's major canyons, and he wrote of it: "Majestic grandeur . . . cyclopean masses. . . . The solitude, the stillness, the subdued light, the vastness of every surrounding object, produce an impression of awe that ultimately becomes almost painful."

Just as their time was running out, they reached a tiny side stream that Ives persuaded himself was the mouth of the Virgin. (Actually, it was Las Vegas Wash, thirty-eight miles downstream from the Virgin.) Exultantly he dipped his hand in the tepid water. Assignment completed! Back they sped, whooping in the rapids as they covered in six or seven hours the stretch it had taken them three days to ascend.

Those rapids convinced the explorers that the lower end of Black Canyon marked the practical limit of steamboat navigation—a convenient limit, for a quick scouting trip by a detachment of soldiers revealed that a road could easily be built from that point up through the volcanic rocks to the Mormon Corridor, less than thirty miles away.

A little later the edges of the war brushed them. A man pretending to be a lost emigrant on his way to California spent a night in their camp. He was a Mormon, clearly, and anxious to know whether Johnson's boat, Ives's boat, and Lieutenant Tipton's mule train, on its way north from Fort Yuma, were forerunners of a full-scale attack on Utah. The explorers treated him frostily, gave him food but little information, and went on. Later, when they met Tipton's mule train hurrying upstream to meet them, they learned that the Mojave Indians, presumably incited by the Mormons, had tried to stampede the livestock by setting fire to the grass. Ives wrote in his diary, "I feel reluctant to believe that any white man could be guilty of such unprovoked rascality."

At Beale's Crossing, take-off point for the Big Canyon, the whites were surrounded—according to Möllhausen's nervous estimate—by two thousand or more Mojave warriors, frightfully painted and stirred to fever pitch by Mormon spies. When a tall brave insolently killed one of Tipton's mules with an arrow, the whites ignored the challenge. They made camp in the shelter of a grove of cottonwood trees and began a lavish distribution of presents.[6] Ireteba came to their aid, as did another chief, Cairook, whom Ives, in 1854 and again on the *Explorer's* slow journey upstream, had gone out of his way to flatter. The peace offensive had its effect. The belligerents became indecisive, and when a few women and children drifted in to collect their share of the visitors' gifts of beads and mirrors, the immediate crisis was over.

But who could say for how long? Acting swiftly, Ives sent downstream on the *Explorer* the men he would not need in the canyon. The next day, March 24, guided by Ireteba and three other Mojaves, the land party—twenty-two officers and soldiers, three scientists, seventeen packers and trail builders, and 150 mules—struck east along the fading tracks of Beale's camels. The commander was lighthearted again. Although his boat expedition had been partly upstaged by Johnson's, a successful penetration of the river's fabled red gorge might still bring him the fame he desired.

For a week the command moved north and east, crossing a sequence of sharp mountain ranges and long valleys, each a little higher than the one before it. Travel was unpleasant. Months on shipboard had left the men susceptible to saddle galls. Tipton's mules, inadequately fed at Fort Yuma and on the march up the riverbank to Beale's crossing, were gaunt and intractable. Dragging them along, Möllhausen said, was like "pulling the *Explorer* through shallow water."[7]

At Peach Springs, which they named after a single peach tree they found growing there, they turned off Beale's road toward the canyon. Additional guidance came from two timid, ill-favored Hualapai Indians that Ireteba had managed to produce. The pair led them through a forest of big junipers onto the broad top of what today is called Hualapai Plateau. As the adventurers topped its summit, the view halted them in their tracks: row after row of broad mesas cut through by profound gorges whose walls were banded with buff, red, and orange. Along the bottom of one of those openings, invisible from where they stood, rolled the Colorado itself.

On April 4 they started hauling the reluctant mules down among the boulders of a steadily narrowing tributary canyon. On either hand the cliffs soared higher; vegetation was nonexistent. And yet, Möllhausen wrote, the rifts and hollows in this forbidding place furnished a home to "human beings [Hualapais] who in deep solitude seem to have lost all human inclinations." That is, they humiliated the passing parade by paying no attention to it.[8]

Eventually the side canyon brought the wayfarers to a sparkling creek that they named the Diamond. Dr. Newberry was beside himself with excitement, stopping here and there to gouge fossils out of the stone and then running and gasping to catch up. By his count the party passed down through fifteen layers of limestone, shale, and many kinds of sandstone—"perhaps the most splendid exposure of stratified rock," Ives wrote, "that there is in the world."* Below the bottom layer was a greater wonder: dark, ancient, metamorphic rock that had been so heated, compressed, and twisted by unimaginable forces that its original constituents Newberry could not identify.

They camped just upstream from a point where the walls of Diamond Creek pinched tighter than ever on the brawling water. Casually the Hualapai guides indicated that the main river lay a short distance beyond. Because of the lateness of the hour, Ives chose to stay where he was; but the scientists plunged on through the gorge, which soon opened into a broad, sandy-bottomed pocket, fearfully deep. There, Möllhausen wrote, "a wild thundering struck our ears like the repeated stamping of countless ponderous hoofs." It was the river, "roaring in eternal struggle with the lifeless rocks." Towering above the pocket and the stream that rushed through it were mile-high buttes, the crimson glow of sunset on their tops already dimming in the canyon's violet haze. Silent with awe, the explorers drank in the darkening scene, unaware that they were not the first whites to stand in the bottom of the Grand Canyon. It was now thirty years since James Ohio Pattie's fur trappers had worked a way down Spencer Canyon into the inner gorge, just twenty miles downstream.

When Ives reached the pocket the next morning, his response was curiously subdued. The canyon here, he wrote, "was similar in character to those already mentioned but on a larger scale and thus far unrivaled in grandeur." He felt hemmed in and baffled. From where he stood he could see only a few hundred yards of the river whose secrets he was supposed to lay bare. But how? To travel very far along the banks with 150 mules was manifestly impossible. In order to obtain a broader view he would have to take the party back onto the plateaus and find another way into the canyon farther east.

Frustration dogged the search. One day Ireteba and his Mojave companions dropped out, eager to get home. On the next day the Hualapais decamped, taking stolen food and blankets with them. On their own, the whites struggled to the top of a gigantic mesa, where a late spring blizzard pinned

*Today's geologists have recognized and named many more than fifteen layers, the exact count depending on the locale.

them behind a windbreak of small trees. The woebegone mules shivered out the night beside fires that the men built for them in a shallow ravine.

As the weather cleared and the temperature shot up, the cavalcade wound down from the mesa-top onto a broad terrace of almost naked stone. Where now? As an objective Ives selected "a line of magnificent bluffs" that he supposed marked the course of the Little Colorado, whose upper reaches he had crossed with Whipple. That tributary, he decided, must join the main river inside an extraordinary fissure, a superlative spot for exploration—if he could reach it.

They started toward their goal along an Indian trail that followed the bottom of a steeply pitching canyon as far as the brink of a hundred-foot drop. In avoiding the precipice the trail swung abruptly across the bluffs to the right —the same dizzy path, canyon experts believe, that the Spanish missionary Francisco Garcés had used eighty-two years before on his way to visit the Havasupai Indians. Single-file, Ives in the lead, the Americans rode along the scratch "like a row of insects crawling upon the side of a building." Finally the way grew so pinched and the precipice under their left-foot stirrups so profound that the men dismounted and crawled along, some of them, on hands and knees, sweating with acrophobia. Wasted effort. They came up against a set of zigzags that the mules could not negotiate. Utilizing a dangerous little flat that afforded space for maneuvering, they eased the pack train around and crept back.

Sunlight on the naked rock generated almost intolerable heat. The mules had had no water for two days. "With glassy eyes and protruding tongues [they] plodded slowly along, uttering the most melancholy cries." To save as many as possible, the men unpacked them at a wide spot in the canyon, and Ives ordered the Mexican roustabouts to saddle the strongest animals and drive the rest to a pond that they had passed thirty miles back on the mesa.

Subsisting on tiny seeps at the base of the canyon walls, the men of the expedition scattered out to explore while awaiting the animals' return. Möllhausen and Newberry climbed to the top of a commanding butte, where the artist could sketch the vast panoramic arc in front of him. Lounging beside him, Newberry tried to comprehend the geology of the scene. Millions upon millions of years ago, he concluded, the broad expanse that reached from the San Francisco Peaks to the high plateaus on the northern horizon had been a shallow valley. Since then the valley had been scooped out into a sequence of high cliffs, long slopes, and wide, hanging terraces. The deepest part was the Big Canyon, as he and Ives continued to call the Grand. A maze of lateral canyons worked toward it like the veins of a dry red leaf in autumn. Each canyon's striped walls mirrored the formations opposite it. No wonder some geologists believed that this astonishing symmetry was the result of a single cataclysm that had almost instantaneously cloven the earth's crust, much as an ax blow might bite into a tree trunk without altering the essential structure of the wood.

Later Newberry would write passionately that only one element was missing from that logic: *truth.* He underlined the word harshly. The real explanation was simpler, yet far more profound, than catastrophism. Not just the canyons but all the neighboring buttes, deep bays, ribbed slopes, and soaring precipices "are wholly due to the action of water."[9] It was the first statement by a qualified scientist of what came to be called "the great denudation" of the Colorado Plateau by the processes of erosion.

And yet . . . and yet: On that day John Strong Newberry was weary from contemplating too much. His crossing of the wastes of southeastern California, his studies of the barren mountains beside which the *Explorer* had fought its way, and now this enormity. . . . For a moment he recoiled. The death-like sterility that had surrounded him for months, he wrote with uncharacteristic somberness, "had ceased to excite a pleasurable scientific interest and had even produced a positive thirst for *life*—a longing to reach some region where nature's fires had not all burned out."[10]

Meanwhile Ives, Tipton, Egloffstein, and a few soldiers were again creeping along the trail that had turned them back the day before. Unhampered by the mules, they edged down the zigzags and encountered a small stream that soon disappeared over a forty-foot precipice. The explorers sat back, baffled. A trail that ended in air? Actually, it was the Havasupai Indians' *Ii gesbéva* (place of the ladder).[11] Egloffstein discovered this when he chanced to peer over the edge, and saw the uprights and rungs.

In spite of his weight he started down. The first rung broke. Down he slid, breaking rung after rung as he frantically embraced one of the quivering uprights like a fireman in a firehouse. Reaching the bottom chafed but uninjured, he hurried on to the turquoise water flowing through the canyon farther down and followed it around a bend.

Unwilling to risk duplicating the plunge, the others waited apprehensively. In time Egloffstein reappeared with an Indian, a Supai. The soldiers buckled their rifle slings together; the topographer tied the improvised hoist under his arms and with the soldiers' help managed to heave his bulk up the pole. The Indian refused to follow. Perhaps he had come along only to make sure that the intruders left.

Egloffstein said that he had reached the Supai village just around the bend but had been blocked from going farther by a series of thundering waterfalls. He had, however, clearly seen (he said) the point where the Big Colorado, the Little Colorado, and Havasu Creek all joined.* The "discovery" exacted

---

*Ives, Newberry, and Egloffstein customarily referred to the present-day Havasu Creek as Cataract or Cascade Creek because of its waterfalls. The upper part of Havasu is still called Cataract.

its price, however. Darkness caught the party on the trail, and they had to spend the night on a tiny flat, alternating sitting and standing among jagged rocks and prickly-pear cactus.

Further exploration brought them no nearer the river, and in the end Ives had to be content with the single glimpse of the stream that he had caught at the mouth of Diamond Creek. But at least, he thought, their month's hard work had shown them the shape of the land, and he had Egloffstein set about recording it on his map.

From his sighting of the Little Colorado four years before, Ives knew that it flowed southwest, and, as we have seen, he jumped to the conclusion that the prominent cliffs, trending southwest, that he saw beyond Havasu Creek delineated the stream's lower reaches. He was wrong. The main Colorado, which at Diamond Creek surges out of the northeast, bends eastward near the point where Havasu Creek enters it. Thus the cliffs Ives saw actually bordered the main river, not the Little Colorado. That tributary enters the main Colorado 95.5 miles above the point where Ives and the others thought it did. The only stream course Egloffstein laid down with approximate correctness on his otherwise beautifully executed map was Havasu (Cataract) Creek.[12]

They had no chance to rectify the mistake. After lining out the rehabilitated mules, they tried again and again to find a way into Cataract Canyon's terrifying depths but could not. Eventually its network of subsidiary canyons forced them far south into the heavy forests where the town of Williams now stands. There they found themselves once more on the well-marked thirty-fifth parallel route, which they followed disconsolately east to the familiar upper stretches of the Little Colorado.

At the crossing Ives divided the party. He ordered the bulk of the men to take the feeblest mules straight to Fort Defiance, in Navajo country. The remainder, mounted on the best of the animals, followed Ives north through the Painted Desert to the Hopi villages. No one there would help guide him. Around the middle of May, 1858, he tried to push on to the river without help, but he missed vital springs of which he had been told and had to beat a dry, hard way back to the Indian towns, the engorged Colorado still unseen.

That was Ives's last encounter with the canyon country. On returning east he was named engineer in charge of a tidier project, the erection of the Washington Monument. He learned, too, that the Utah war had been ended by negotiations in the spring and that no troops had been, or would be, sent against the Mormons by the river route. Nevertheless, his and Johnson's contest to learn the river did bear fruit for the Army—and for Johnson. Late in the summer of 1858, Havasupai and Mojave Indians made a series of bloody attacks on emigrants bound for California. After some bumbling, the Army located a protective post, Fort Mojave, on the east bank of the Colorado River, a little below what was to become the site of Davis Dam. Contracts for

76   COLORADO RIVER COUNTRY

supplying the installation, which lay some three hundred river miles above
Fort Yuma, fell to Alonzo Johnson, who immediately ordered a new thirty-
five-thousand-dollar steamboat, the *Cocopah*, and put it in charge of David
Robinson, the pilot who had nursed Ives's *Explorer* up to Black Canyon and
back again.

Even before Fort Mojave took shape, Egloffstein and Newberry were in
the West again, probing once more for the river. Although the strife in Utah
was over, the War Department continued to worry over the difficulty of
reaching the southern part of the territory by either the lower Colorado or
the Mormon Corridor. Could an easier route be found from New Mexico?
Captain John Macomb of the Corps of Topographical Engineers, who had
spent the last several years building military roads in New Mexico, was
ordered to find out. He was also to survey the course of the San Juan River
and then locate, if possible, the exact spot where the Green and Grand rivers
came together to form the still-mysterious Colorado.

Macomb began in July, 1859, by pushing north up the Old Spanish Trail
to the southern foothills of the San Juan Mountains, in Colorado. Veering
west, he crossed the streams that finger south out of those mountains to form
the San Juan River, skirting Mesa Verde, where he noted the abundance of
Indian ruins.[13] His main goal lay northwest across a broad, monotonous plain
of sagebrush lapping up toward the piñon forests that girdle southeastern
Utah's isolated, laccolithic Abajo Mountains.

At a spring called Ojo Verde, the party's Indian guide halted. The rest
of the way to the junction of the rivers, he said, was too rough and too short
of pasturage to accommodate a big party. Macomb accordingly left most of
his people in camp. With Newberry, Egloffstein, and five others, he worked
downward into Indian Creek (he called it Canyon Colorado) where it plunges
off the northern slope of the Abajos. Its rough bottom, a tangle of boulders
and brush, took them past vast prows of red rock to a suddenly opening plain
of red sand and stunted bushes bordered by distant cliffs and punctuated by
two high, lonesome pinnacles now called the Sixshooter Peaks. After plod-
ding past those soaring monoliths, the party entered another canyon, twisting
fantastically between shattered walls and grotesque columns; they named it
the Labyrinth. As nearly as can be determined, it was what is known today
as Salt Creek, in Canyonlands National Park.

Forcing a way down it was a contant struggle with dense willows, canes,
boulders, salt brush, rock, and quicksand. Finally the going grew so rough
that Macomb and four others left the livestock with the packers and continued
afoot toward the Green River. A yawning drop halted them. There was no
way they could reach the river, but perhaps they could glimpse it from some
high point. Climbing out of the canyon, they made their way to a chocolate-
colored butte one thousand feet high, "curiously ornamented," Newberry

wrote, "with columns and pilasters, porticoes and colonnades, cornices and battlements . . . crowned with spires so slender that it seemed as though a breath of air could topple them."

The day—August 23—was crystal clear and blisteringly hot. They peeled off most of their clothing and labored upward for two arduous hours. Their recompense came on the summit, with a view, Newberry said, that "baffles description." Nevertheless he tried to give visual reality to those miles of naked rock "of rich and varied colors shimmering in the sunlight . . . a forest of Gothic spires . . . innumerable canyons . . . deep, dark, and ragged, impassable to everything but winged birds."[14] Of those canyons, the most stupendous was the one formed by the Grand River, a gorge fifteen hundred feet deep, curling around two sides of the butte on which the explorers stood. Four miles south another chasm joined the Grand, "said by Indians to be that of Green River."

Guesswork again. But this time it was correct. Egloffstein's map, lovely as usual, shaded and cross-hatched in order to give a three-dimensional effect to his rendering of the land's tormented topography, placed the river junction where it really was.

After picking up the rest of the party at Ojo Verde, Macomb struck south to the San Juan River. This time he halted fifty miles short of the stream's junction with the Colorado. Once again, guesswork from a high point proved sufficient, and the maps had a fair degree of accuracy.

Macomb had long since concluded that there was no possibility of building a wagon road from northeastern New Mexico into southern Utah. And what else, other than scenery, was there to report on?

"A profitless locality," Ives called the southern borders of the Grand Canyon. Macomb was even more negative about the canyon country farther upstream: "Perhaps no portion of the earth's surface is more irredemiably sterile, more hopelessly lost to human habitation."

A Mormon Missionary
in southwestern Utah

8
———

Utah's
Dixie

In August, 1857, Brigham Young wrote to Jacob Hamblin, telling him of his own removal as governor of Utah and of the approach of twenty-five hundred United States soldiers. That same letter appointed Hamblin to the directorship of the Southern Indian Mission, to which he had been attached as an ordinary worker for the past four years, and added pointedly, ". . . [The Indians] must learn that they have either got to help us, or the United States will kill us both."[1]

Hamblin, often referred to in Mormon lore as the Apostle in Buckskin, had arrived in Utah with his family in 1850, aged thirty-two, and had settled at Toole, forty miles southwest of Salt Lake City. Three years later he had received a summons to be one of twenty-three missionaries assigned to convert the Southern Paiutes dwelling beside the Virgin River and its tributaries.[2]

To pioneering Mormons the concept of mission included, in addition to the propagation of the faith, such activities as the searching out of arable lands and establishing new communities.[3] The settlements were invariably laid out foursquare to the compass, with plots—each large enough for a house, a barn, a vegetable garden, and a small orchard—assigned by lottery. The early communities were often surrounded by a stockade, with a stone fort inside for refuge in the event of attack. Outside the stockade were farm plots for raising hay and grain. Still farther out were communal grazing lands. The building and maintenance of fences, roads, dams, and canals, and the distribution of water, were supervised by local church officials. Everyone contributed labor, work animals, and tools as directed from the pulpit of the local church.

According to the Book of Mormon, in about 600 B.C. certain Israelites had come to the New World and had founded a great civilization. Some, however, had lost sight of God's commandments and as punishment had been cursed with dark skins. Unrepentant, these Lamanites, as they were called, had exterminated their devout neighbors but in the process had been reduced to the benighted Indians familiar to the later settlers of America. Since the Lamanites were of the blood of Israel, it was the duty of the Mormons to return them to the fold.

In any event, settlement would proceed more smoothly if the Indians did not resist. Thus the Mormons' missionary zeal tended to rise in direct proportion to their desire to acquire Indian land.[4] Furthermore, converted Indians could help hew wood, draw water, and build houses. Thus it was well to feed them when necessary, teach them to farm and manage water as white men did, set them good examples, and bring them the messages of peace found in the Mormon gospels. If the process of civilization could be quickened by adopting some of their children or marrying their women, well and good.

The staffing of a mission was carefully planned. First the Church decided how many persons should be sent to a designated spot. After consulting with community leaders in existing towns, the officials in charge of colonizing prepared a draft roll of settlers—so many farmers, harness-makers, carpenters, blacksmiths, and the like.

Having been chosen without their knowledge or consent, the draftees were "called." The summons might be delivered during a friendly visit by a local bishop. More often the names were simply announced at a Salt Lake City conference, as Jacob Hamblin's was, or were read aloud from the pulpit. Although the head of every household in Utah knew that he was subject to being called, the actual occurrence could come as a shock. He, his wife (or wives), and children had to abandon homes, orchards, and businesses, sell whatever possessions could not be carried in a wagon or two, say farewell to friends and relatives, and begin life afresh in a forbidding wilderness. Although public-spirited citizens assisted the movers with donations of food and material goods, the missionaries in the main were expected to support themselves.

Community pressure and a conviction that this was the Lord's will generally brought acquiescence. For the early Mormons believed that they were preparing the way for Christ's second coming and that the Lamanites

could be redeemed. They were convinced, too, that cultivation would en-
hance the fertility of the soil and mitigate the inclemency of the weather.[5]

The Southern Paiutes, to whom Hamblin was to minister, were among the
most poverty-stricken Indian groups in the United States. They ate whatever
they could lay hands on—grass seed, roots, rats, rabbits, ground squirrels,
lizards, and crickets. Because they were constantly on the move they could
carry little with them and were content to live in caves, under overhanging
rocks, or in shelters that were little more than hollowed-out heaps of brush.

They were a frequent prey of white, Mexican, and Ute entrepreneurs on
the prowl for children to be sold as slaves in New Mexico. Whenever theft
was convenient the dealers seized the young boys and girls by violence.
Otherwise they acquried them from their parents in exchange for a horse or
two, a gun, cloth, or a sack of dry corn. The parents wept over the transaction
but preferred the gain of barter to loss by theft.

Wherever their country's erratic streams coincided with patches of level
ground, a few Paiutes gathered to scratch out small, pathetic, ill-tended gardens. One such place, occupied by a subgroup called Piedes, lay cupped in
flame-colored hills about five miles up Santa Clara Creek from its junction
with the Virgin River. After a period of exploratory work, Hamblin and some
of his associates—their wives had not yet joined them—settled nearby. Others
of the Southern Indian Mission continued southwest across the Beaver Dam
Mountains to the valley of the Moapa (Muddy) River, where the tules of the
soggy bottom lands harbored malaria-carrying mosquitoes.

Aided by the Indians, the Santa Clara men erected during the next
several months a stone wall eight feet high around a cluster of tiny cabins built
of cottonwood logs. They quarried and lugged by hand enough sandstone to
dam the creek with a structure eighty feet wide and fourteen high. They
grubbed out brush, softened the earth with water, plowed, and planted.

Because they offered protection from slave-hunters, the Piedes clustered
around them, inquisitive, dirty, crawling with lice. Hamblin punished petty
thievery with thrashings, lectured the men for abusing the women, and, like
his fellow missionaries, purchased young children, mostly girls, to help
around the house while they learned the gospel. According to a nimble
sophistry, this wasn't slave-dealing, which had been outlawed by both the
Mormon Church and Utah's territorial government, but a purchase for freedom.[6]

To his discouragement, most of the Indians around the mission stayed
lazy and filthy, disinclined to give up their superstitious beliefs in exchange
for enlightened ones. Still, they were peaceful, and late in the summer of 1855
Hamblin and his fellow missionaries brought their families to Santa Clara, or

Fort Clara, as they called the walled establishment. Because summer heat was intense there, Jacob in 1856 obtained permission to move the mission's cattle, and his own summer home, to cooler lands near the headwaters of Santa Clara creek, in Pine Mountain Valley and in Mountain Meadows, beside the California Trail.

Also in 1855, other missionaries in the Santa Clara area discovered that cotton could be grown there. To Church officials, eager to make Utah as self-sufficient as possible, this was important. In their enthusiasm they called the region Utah's Dixie—the name still persists in St. George's Dixie College, nearby Dixie Mountain, and Dixie National Forest—and in the spring of 1857 they sent additional families south to the Virgin River to experiment further with cotton and also with sorghum and grapes.

They were just beginning to clear home sites near the junction of Santa Clara Creek and the Virgin when Hamblin received word from Brigham Young about the threat of war and his appointment as head of the Southern Indian Mission. Promptly he and a co-worker, Thales Haskell, took twelve Paiute chiefs to Salt Lake City to confer with Young. In the capital, guerilla units were being mustered. Belligerent sermons thundered in the churches. Militant songs shook the meeting halls:

> Up, awake, ye defenders of Zion,
> The foe's at the door of your homes.
> Let each heart be the heart of a lion,
> Unyielding and proud as he roams.

After the Paiutes of the party had gone home, Hamblin and Haskell both went in quest of second wives. In his old home town of Toole, Hamblin courted a seventeen-year-old girl, Priscilla Leavitt, and married her on September 11. With Haskell and his bride the pair started south a few days later, two honeymoon couples in one wagon. But when they were only one day along the way a messenger intercepted them. Hamblin was ordered to speed ahead on horseback to the Basin rim, where the first wagon train of the season to follow the southern route to California—rather than risk meeting with snow in the Sierra—had just stirred up a commotion.

The Mormon settlers had refused to sell them supplies; at Parowan they were denied entrance to the town. A few of the travelers responded by giving the name Brigham to their oxen; they rained obscenities on passing Mormons, shouted "whore" at the women, and made little effort to keep their livestock out of Mormon fields.

A gathering of Saints in Cedar City came up with the notion of using the Paiutes—including some of the chiefs Hamblin had taken to Salt Lake City[7]—to strike a blow for Zion in the coming war with the United States.

It is alleged that the Mormons told them that Merikats—non-Mormon Americans—had poisoned Indian waterholes and the meat of a dead ox. In any event, there were promises of booty.

The emigrants were now camped at Mountain Meadows, resting themselves and their livestock for the journey into the desert. It was there that the Indians had attacked, on the morning of September 8, 1857, killing a number of whites. The survivors hurriedly pulled their wagons into a circle, piled up earth between the wheels, and fired from behind those embankments. They inflicted heavy casualties on the Indians, most of whom were fighting on foot, as was Paiute custom.

During the siege that followed, three emigrants tried to slip through the lines to summon help. One was killed by a Mormon and the other two by Indians. Meanwhile, however, the Paiutes were angry at the Mormons for instigating an attack that had proved so costly. As the days went by, the Mormons became hysterical with fear that the emigrants might realize that whites had directed the attack, and concluded that everyone in the party old enough to bear witness would have to be killed—in such a way that the Indians would win their share of the booty without suffering more casualties. Accordingly, on September 13, a Mormon named John D. Lee, with a white companion, entered the emigrants' camp under a white flag and somehow persuaded them to return to Parowan and stand trial for wrongs that they had supposedly committed along the trail—perhaps on the Mormons' promise to protect them from the Indians. At any rate, they laid aside their arms and marched out single-file with their guardians.

Except for seventeen small children, everyone in the party was killed. Including those slain during the earlier skirmishes, the total came to at least 123. The corpses were tumbled into convenient arroyos or buried en masse in shallow graves. The emigrants' cattle and horses were driven to Lee's ranch to be distributed, and the wailing children were taken to Hamblin's summer ranch nearby, where, in the words of Utah's Superintendent of Indian Affairs, Jacob Forney, who later investigated the massacre, they were "sold out to different persons."[8] Hamblin's wife Rachel took three small girls, including one whose arm had been torn off by a bullet. Because Hamblin had paused along the way to pick up what information he could about the massacre, he did not reach the ranch until September 18. After a brief stay at home he went, so he wrote in his diary, to "the place of slaughter. . . . Oh! horrible! . . . language fails to picture the scene of blood and carnage. . . . At one place I noticed nineteen wolves pulling out the bodies and eating the flesh."

Horrors of such magnitude could not be concealed. Rumors and demands for an investigation reached Washington. The Mormons suddenly turned cooperative; two missionaries were stationed at the crossing of the Muddy to keep the Paiutes there in check, for they had already robbed a second train of its cattle, almost surely with Hamblin's connivance.⁹ Now, abruptly, he began helpfully joining Merikat trains and leading them safely past the Indians. But when rumors of the Ives expedition reached him, and he suspected that invaders were moving up the Colorado, he prepared to unleash the natives once again. It was then, in March, 1858, that with Thales Haskell, Dudley Leavitt, and Samuel Knight he worked his way down from Las Vegas to the lower river valley, to spy on the *Explorer*, and urged the Mojaves to attack it—an effort which the engineers, helped by Chief Ireteba, successfully thwarted.*

Once the Utah war had been ended by negotiation, the non-Mormon governor, Alfred Cumming, took over. Jacob Forney, Utah's new superintendent of Indian affairs, appointed Hamblin sub-agent for Southern Utah, and ordered him to recover "at any sacrifice" the children who had survived the massacre, so that they could be returned to their nearest relatives.

Hamblin told Forney of rumors among the Paiutes of a child being held by Indians east of the Colorado River and proposed an expedition to investigate the tale.¹⁰ To Brigham Young, as head of the Mormon Church, he wrote that this might be the time to investigate the possibility of establishing a mission among the Moquis—as the Mormons, who had picked up the word from Spanish sources, invariably called the Hopis.

Young agreed, and in order to raise the necessary manpower Hamblin closed the beleaguered Paiute missions west of Santa Clara. "If ever I rejoiced in this work," he wrote exultantly on September 16, 1858, to Apostle George A. Smith, head of the Utah Indian missions, "it is now!"¹¹

Six weeks later, on October 28, he started south toward the Arizona border. With him went a Paiute guide, Thales Haskell, Dudley Leavitt, and several others. Turning their horses up Mokiac Wash, they climbed out of mesquite country into a scattering of junipers and piñons, and from there passed through a saddle in the rough hills onto a northern extension of Shivwits Plateau. Turning east, they jogged through broad meadows where pronghorn antelope grazed and then spurred their reluctant horses up a boulder-littered break in the sixteen-hundred-foot wall of the Hurricane Cliffs. On top was yet another plateau, the Uinkaret.

Sweeping out of the north and then curving east as far as the eye could see was the deeply bayed, canyon-cracked, wrinkle-fronted line of the aptly named Vermilion Cliffs, some of their Gothic spires towering two thousand feet high. What the members of the party noticed, however, was the enormous expanse of winter-dry grass rolling from the cliffs south to a line of blue mountains in the distance. Marvelous cattle country, that prairie—and it could be easily held against outsiders, for water was rare. But a few strategic

*Thales Haskell was the spy who actually boarded the *Explorer*. See page 70, above.

84   COLORADO RIVER COUNTRY

springs did exist. The Paiute guide, Naraguts, led the explorers to one that
gushed up through a geologic fault line to create a rustling oasis near the base
of the red cliffs. Here they camped on their third night out from Fort Clara.
During the evening, so a widely accepted story goes, Jacob's brother William
displayed his skill with a rifle by setting up a pipe fifty strides away and
shooting a hole in the bottom of its bowl—whence the name Pipe Spring,
which the oasis still bears.

East of Pipe Spring, the travelers met a company of Paiute Indians who
were returning from a successful rabbit drive and who offered them a share
of the feast. When the Mormons rode on the next morning, nineteen Paiutes
went with them, trotting effortlessly on foot beside the horses. They splashed
across Kanab Creek and entered another twisting slit—they named it Jacob
Canyon—which enabled them to scramble onto the final huge upwarp that
barred their way to the place where Naraguts said they could cross the
Colorado. The name of the plateau in the Paiute tongue was Kaibab (Mountain Lying Down). But the Mormons called it Buckskin Mountain, because
Naraguts said deer abounded there. It was seventy miles long and thirty
across. In traveling to its top from Santa Clara, the missionaries had ascended
from one terrace to another in a series of gigantic steps and were now more
than a mile higher than they had been at their starting place.

The views were splendid, but they felt no urge to linger. The November
days were short and cold; wind thrummed in the evergreens. Hurrying on,
they descended precipitously into sandy-soiled House Rock Valley, lying like
a wedge between Kaibab Plateau on the west and Paria Plateau on the east.
(For the sake of pronunciation, Paria ought to be spelled as the early Mormons
spelled it, Pahreah or sometimes Pahrear.)

Ahead of them stretched the steel-gray wastes of the Marble Platform,
and for the first time they could see the upper section of the Grand Canyon
—Marble Gorge—zigging like a raw wound in the earth's limestone skin. The
thrust of the Vermilion Cliffs, rising there nearly three thousand feet high,
squeezed them down to the chocolate-colored river at the base of Paria Valley,
just as it had squeezed Domínguez and Escalante eighty-two years before.
Unlike the Spanish missionaries, however, the Mormons made no effort to
cross the river there. Instead they dragged their pack mules up the same
hair-raising set of ledges and sand that the Spaniards had used in escaping
from the cul-de-sac and then wound through thirty-five miles of convoluted
pink slickrock to the Crossing of the Fathers, or, as the Mormons called it,
Ute Crossing. There the Paiutes came in handy. Holding hands (or, as some
accounts have it, linking themselves together by grasping the ends of short
willow withes), the nearly naked Indians inched into the cold water, then at
its winter low, found the shallowest area, and so furnished a living guideline
for the riders and pack stock.

From there on, their route was more nearly south than east: over Kaibito Plateau and down among piñons and junipers into wide Kletha Valley, across it to Moenkopi Wash and on through the fantasies of Blue Canyon. They came finally to Oraibi, its ragged stone houses arranged in lines along the edges of a tan mesa overlooking Jeddito Basin, pale red sand slipping endlessly toward the Little Colorado.

The Moqui were in a sorry state. Over the past six years, war with the Navajos and an epidemic of smallpox had cut their population in half.[12] But although they were civil to the visitors and fed them from their scanty stores, they declined to let emissaries return across the river with Hamblin's group to study the advantages of mingling with the Mormons. A minor chief named Tuba gave them a tour of the other Hopi villages, where Hamblin went through the motions of asking for information about a lost white child. Having learned nothing, he at last turned his party home, leaving four men behind to learn the Moquis' language and prostelytize them as diligently as circumstances allowed.

Heavy snow made the return journey arduous, and before the men reached home after an absence of fifty-two days, they were forced to devour one of their horses. (Presumably its price was included in the $318 that Hamblin eventually received from Jacob Forney for his efforts.)[13] Within two weeks the proselytizers followed. The Hopis had refused to support them, and for ten days they'd had to pack wood to the top of the mesa in exchange for pittances of food.[14] Unwilling to work like that for Indians, although they did not mind having Indians work for them, they had swapped guns and ammunitions for supplies and, after bucking floating ice in the Colorado and heavy snowdrifts on the plateaus, had dragged home thoroughly disgruntled by the experience.

Undeterred by the setback, Young ordered the work continued during the fall of 1859. The effort failed again. A third expedition in 1860 was even more disastrous. On that trip Hamblin and Thales Haskell took along their Paiute wives to prove to the Moquis that whites and Indians could unite. (The women had probably been purchased years before, when very young, as part of the conversion process.)[15] Another innovation was a sixteen-foot skiff that Hamblin hoped to use for crossing the Colorado at the mouth of the Paria, so as to avoid the difficult miles of slickrock between that point and Ute Crossing. He hired a Paiute guide, Enos, to find a route suitable for the wagon that carried the boat and then, at the request of Apostle George A. Smith, added Smith's teen-age son, George, Jr., to the party.[16] All told, the group consisted of three Indians and seven whites.

After dragging the wagon and its load up the Hurricane Cliffs and across Kaibab Plateau, the adventurers had to leave it in the deep sand of House Rock Valley. On reaching the Colorado, they built a substitute raft of driftwood.

Three men plying the skiff's oars managed to reach the far shore, but the teetering craft floated so low in the water that Hamblin was unwilling to risk their supplies to it. At Ute Crossing they forded the river on horseback while the Indian women keened their fears. After the usual hard battle with the canyons on the opposite side, they emerged onto open ground—and into real trouble.

Navajos surrounded them and demanded the two women. Hamblin and Haskell countered with an offer to trade supplies they could ill afford to give up. When young George Smith saw an Indian leading away his horse and went after it, he was shot and mortally wounded. Some of his companions held off the Navajos while the others boosted him into the saddle. With one man riding behind to steady him they fled back toward the river. He begged them to let him die in peace, so they wrapped him in a blanket and laid him under a ledge of rock. In that he may have rendered his last service. Content with his scalp, the Navajos followed the living Mormons no farther.

When, early in 1861, in the dead of winter, Brigham Young ordered Hamblin to retrieve the body, he was obliged to ride to Parowan for volunteers. Glare ice on the slickrock leading to Ute ford made each step hazardous —frequently the men had to use hatchets for chopping out footing for their animals—and the river was choked with grinding floes. At the place where Smith's body had been abandoned they found his skull and a few larger bones from which predators had stripped the flesh. They placed the remains in a box brought for the purpose, inched back down the ice-sheathed cliffs and through the slush-filled river, and, on reaching St. George, delivered the box to the boy's father.

The experience chilled further interest in visiting the Hopis. Besides, there were distractions. Late in May, 1861, Brigham Young and a large retinue arrived in Dixie to inspect the 250 acres of fruit trees, vineyards, and hay and cotton fields that bore testimony to the Saints' labor during the past half-dozen years. Pausing in the triangle formed by the junction of Santa Clara Creek and the Virgin River, Brigham prophesied, "There will yet be built [on this spot] a city with spires, towers, and steeples, with homes containing many people."

Following the outbreak of the Civil War, with the expectation that cotton prices would rise as a consequence, a call went out to 309 men (plus their families, bringing the total to 748 persons altogether) to settle in Dixie and raise cotton. During the early weeks of October four hundred wagons, traveling in groups, headed south. Some pushed up into the jaws of Zion Canyon; a larger number went to the locale of Young's prophecy and created a town named St. George, after Apostle George Smith. In addition to the draftees, thirty families newly arrived from Switzerland settled near Fort Clara.

While the newcomers were still living in their wagons, a Biblical flood engulfed them. For forty days rain sluiced the land. Streams rampaged; embryo town sites vanished and had to be relocated. Part of Fort Clara disintegrated, and, except for a friend's lucky throw with a lariat rope, Jacob Hamblin would have gone downstream with it. Nathan Tenney's pregnant wife, near Zion Canyon, felt her pains beginning as the flood waters rose. Neighbors helped the frantic husband carry the canvas-covered wagon box in which they were living to higher ground. While rain drummed on the canvas top, a baby son was born and named Marvelous Flood Tenney.[17]

The land dried, the sun hammered, sandstorms swirled. Like other pioneers everywhere, the settlers of Dixie sought to make discomfort endurable by mocking it with tall tales. Sheep wore their noses off reaching down between rocks for grass. Housewives avoided overheating their cabins by putting pans of dishwater outside on the red rocks; it boiled there in a hurry. And songs:

> The wind like fury here does blow
> That when we plant or sow, sir,
> We place one foot upon the seed
> And hold it till it grows, sir.

Raising cotton demanded exorbitant amounts of water and was a dawn-to-dark struggle that left no time for anything else. No gins were available; to get rid of the seeds the women ran the lint through a contraption that looked like an old-fashioned clothes wringer. Transportation costs, both for materials and for people, were fantastic, which led the Church hierarchy to consider once again the feasibility of using the Colorado River as a freight route. Meanwhile, cotton prices were soaring, and in the fall of 1862 another 250 families were called to reinforce Dixie.

Hamblin did not see them arrive. The Church, obsessed still with gaining a foothold beyond the Colorado, had ordered him and twenty others whose names were read out from the pulpit in St. George to develop a new, safer route to Moqui land by crossing the river below the Grand Canyon. In addition, the explorers were to persuade several leaders of the tribe to visit Utah, the hope being that the Indians would be so impressed with the number and strength of the whites that they would at last receive missionaries and also let settlers cross their country to the Little Colorado River. To the group of trailblazers Hamblin added his adopted Indian son, Alfred, and his Indian wife, Eliza.[18] Loading a rowboat onto the running gears of a wagon, the party cut from the Virgin south across a divide into Grand Wash, a gravelly channel spotted with thorny bushes that opens a way to the river three miles west of the massive Grand Wash Cliffs at the lower end of the Grand Canyon. After shuttling everyone and everything but the wagon across the river in the boat,

the travelers fought their way up the south bank and followed sandy Grapevine Wash to its head. There they swung east toward the San Francisco Peaks.
Along the way eight horses died for want of water. The people and the rest
of the animals survived, thanks to a snowstorm that Hamblin regarded as
providential.

And at Oraibi he at last struck a deal with the Moqui. If three whites
stayed at the village as hostages, four Indians would go with him to Utah for
a short visit. Hamblin led the group back over the Crossing of the Fathers and
the snow-heaped Kaibab Plateau, thus making the first known circuit of the
Grand Canyon.

From St. George he continued with the Hopi to Salt Lake City to confer
with Brigham Young, who was encouraged enough by the meeting to lay
plans for sending a hundred men beyond the Colorado—"brave, generous,
high-minded missionaries . . . such as are willing to work for Israel and do
not worship the almighty dollar." Hamblin was to start the work by developing way stations beside his new route. A place to begin might be Cataract
Canyon, among the Havasu Indians whom Lieutenant Ives had mentioned
in his report, recently issued by the government. First, though, the visiting
Moqui had to be returned home and the Mormon hostages retrieved.

Recruiting three Mormons as helpers, Hamblin crossed the Colorado on
a raft of driftwood, retrieved the skiff he had left there, and rowed laboriously
upward in search of a better crossing than the one he had used before. Almost
at the mouth of the Grand Canyon he found it. Pearce's Ferry would be
established there in time; river runners still use its old south exit as a take-out
point for their craft.

After crossing Hualapai Plateau, the little group followed dizzy trails
down into Cataract Canyon (Hamblin does not mention a ladder) and entered
the Havasupai village. In spite of the presence of the Hopis—the tribes were
longtime friends—the Havasus repulsed the whites. Hamblin later recalled
that the canyon Indians simply asked him not to lead other whites to their
hiding place. But according to Havasu tradition he was told that if any
Mormons returned they would be killed.[19]

After only two days of rest at Oraibi the emissaries started home, carefully avoiding Cataract Canyon on the way. After Hualapai Indians stole most
of their horses, all but three of the animals that remained had to be packed.
For one stretch of fifty-six hours the men of the party were without water,
and they arrived back at St. George with blistered feet.

Distracted by problems in the north, the Church did not follow through
with the plan to send missionaries beyond the Colorado, and for the next ten
months Hamblin stayed close to home, working with his brothers and older
sons in the fields and putting the finishing touches on his new two-story
sandstone house in Santa Clara. But in the fall of 1863 the cotton economy,

of which so much had been expected, collapsed, largely because of high transportation costs.[20] Shortly thereafter, during the winter of 1863–64, the United States Army's relentless campaign against the Navajos in northwestern New Mexico drove thousands of them into what we know as Monument Valley, south of the San Juan River, and onto the rough slopes of Navajo Mountain, west of the valley. Hungry and angry and disposed by their culture to secret, slashing raids, they began crossing the Colorado River to prey on the Mormons of southern Utah. To deal with the threat, Hamblin was instructed, in March, 1864, to lead fifteen peacemakers to the Navajo strongholds, to treat with them as children of God, and tell them "not to let their thieves visit us again . . . lest some of our angry men slay them."[21] He was also to strengthen ties with the Hopis by persuading another pair of them to return to Dixie with him to learn white customs and the crafts of blacksmithing and woodworking.

The group rode along familiar trails to the mouth of the Paria, where they built a large craft of driftwood on which they made several successful crossings of the stream, then very low. This was the first time whites had ever done so at what would soon become well known as Lee's Ferry.

To their surprise, the Moquis met them with hostility. They refused to let any more members of their tribe visit the Mormons, and when they also declined to furnish a guide to the Navajo country, Hamblin abandoned the assignment. In twenty-six days the party was back home again.

In 1865 there was an explosion farther north, where other settlers were endeavoring to confine the once far-ranging Utes to a dreary reservation in the Uinta Valley of northeastern Utah. Promises of annuities won over part of the tribe, but not all. A series of attacks led by Chief Black Hawk killed seventy people, did more than a million dollars' worth of damage, and sent terrified settlers fleeing from dozens of small towns to protection inside the stockades of the larger villages.

The Paiutes, too, were divided. Although many of the older men refused to attack the whites, some renegades, as the Mormons described them, joined the Navajo raiders. When whites were caught in a helpless position, they were killed. Mostly, though, the combined war parties wanted animals. To avoid the difficulty of taking sheep and cattle across the river, the raiders butchered them in secluded spots where the meat could be dried into jerky. The horses that were the Navajos' share of the booty, however, were swum across the stream at the mouth of the Paria or forded at Ute Crossing during times of low water.

In the early months of 1866, five settlers, one of them a woman, were slain in two separate attacks near the foot of the Vermilion Cliffs, and hundreds of head of livestock were stolen. To check the panic that followed, the Church ordered all people and livestock to be relocated, for the time being, in desig-

nated villages in safer areas—a crowding that created other kinds of exaspera-
tion. Then, in August, 1866, a group of sixty-five militiamen under James
Andrus began a reconnaissance, hoping to find every trail the Indians used
to cross the Colorado between the mouth of the Paria and the junction of the
Green and Grand Rivers. On their ride around the high, rough slopes of the
Paunsaugunt and Table Cliff plateaus they scuffled once with Navajos; one
man was killed and another wounded. They also discovered arable lands
where the towns of Escalante and Boulder now stand. And they were probably the first white men to look eastward from the top of Boulder Mountain
toward the distant chasm of the Colorado—a stunning view of "a naked,
barren plain of red and white Sandstone crossed in all directions by innumerable gorges. . . . The Sun shining down on this vast red plain almost dazzled
our eyes by the reflection as it was thrown back by the firey surface." It was
a notable feat of exploration, though we know now that it fell far short of
reaching the junction of the Grand and Green.[22]

        Their finding of several trails that led far back into central Utah led the
Indian raiders to shift to new routes south of the Grand Canyon. They
crossed the Colorado at Hamblin's lower ford and made off with more animals, some from as far away as Pine Valley Mountain, beside the California
Road. But in 1868 Black Hawk died, and his followers reluctantly joined the
Utes who were living on the Uinta Reservation. That same year several
thousand Navajos, who four years before had been confined to a reservation
at Bosque Redondo in eastern New Mexico, were allowed, on their promise
to fight no more, to return to the lands from which they had been driven, and
from then on raids by members of the tribe slowly diminished. Settlers drifted
back to the grasslands south of the Vermilion Cliffs. Jacob Hamblin moved
his family to Kanab, where he worked with the Paiutes and kept community
gardens flourishing while others carried on the labor of town-building. When
the winters of 1868–69 and 1869–70 brought threats of renewed Indian strikes,
he and others manned guard stations beside the icy trails leading to the
crossings, and the last stubborn warrior bands of Paiutes and Navajos ceased
their raids, though at the time no one could tell when they might be resumed.

        The Indian raids—losses in livestock alone were estimated at three thou-
sand head—came at a time when the economy of Utah's Dixie was already
suffering from bad weather, low farm prices, and high transportation costs.
Inability to sell the full cotton crop of 1863 had so discouraged the settlers that
in the spring of 1864 many made no plantings at all. Several abandoned the
lands that had been assigned them by lot and spent weeks on end wandering
along the streams in their covered wagons, searching, generally in vain, for
better situations. Some even abjured their missions and left the country.

        To relieve the suffering the Church began the construction of a red
sandstone tabernacle in St. George, doled out food, and took to watching with

interest the efforts of various entrepreneurs to develop steamboat transportation on the lower Colorado River. Ever since the spring of 1861, when John Moss, a former trapper, had discovered rich silver lodes in El Dorado Canyon, which enters the Colorado from the west near the mouth of Black Canyon, a stampede had been in progress: to placer mines beside the river at Ehrenberg and La Paz, and to deep lode mines farther inland near Wickenberg and Prescott.

Whatever its drawbacks, the Colorado River was still the most economical way of bringing in supplies from the coast, both to the mines and to Fort Yuma and Fort Mojave. Alonzo Johnson, who owned the region's only two steamboats, having grown rich from his shipping monopoly, had by now acquired a large cattle ranch near San Diego and been elected to the California state assembly. That left affairs on the river in the hands of Isaac Polhemus and David Robinson, the respective captains of Johnson's two boats. Robinson, it will be remembered, had piloted Lieutenant Ives's *Explorer* into the Black Canyon in 1858. After moving whatever freight best suited their interests, the pair tended to leave the rest sitting on the wharves, exposed to the weather, and then blamed low water for the pile-up.

The situation caught the eye of young Sam Adams, a fast-talking Pennsylvanian who had come west with the express purpose of being elected congressional delegate of the newly created Arizona Territory. He called a mass meeting of miners at La Paz, got up petitions, and traveled to San Francisco; there he persuaded Captain Thomas Trueworthy, owner of a small sternwheeler, the *Esmeralda*, then plying the Sacramento River, to join him in forming the Union Line. Trueworthy's price was control of the company, but Adams, whose main concern was to be remembered at the polls, was agreeable.[23]

As the river began its annual rise in May, Trueworthy pointed the *Esmeralda* upstream. It was a powerful little boat, and he was able to more than double its carrying capacity by towing along, at the end of a one-hundred-foot cable, a narrow barge—128 feet long, with a twenty-eight-foot beam—an innovation for the Colorado. Alonzo Johnson, on learning of the new company's threat, rushed a hull, engines, and other materials to the river's estuary, and put together a third boat, the *Mohave*. It began service in July, 1864, also dragging a barge. In September the *Nina Tilden*, with its own barge, was put into operation by an El Dorado mining company that was eager to recover its investment by hauling freight for other mines in addition to its own.

As for Steamboat Adams (as he came to be called), although he had precipitated the rush, the election in July found him running last in a field of five, with only 31 votes out of 885. Moreover, thanks to the competition it had stimulated, the Union Line was now teetering on the edge of failure.

The search for ways to fill the boats drew attention to the California Road, where long lines of wagons toiled across the desert, carrying three million dollars' worth of merchandise every year from Los Angeles to military installations and wholesale business houses throughout northern Utah. If that freight were sent instead by ship through the Gulf of California and up the Colorado River to wagons waiting at the head of navigation, the distance of the land haul would be cut in half and (so the steamboaters argued) expenses would drop by a third. Nor would their boats have to go back downstream empty. The ore-reducing mills along the river needed salt, which could be obtained in abundance from deposits beside the Virgin River. The miners needed meat and garden produce that the farms in southern Utah could provide. And, of great importance to Dixie, cotton could be shipped cheaply by river and ocean to textile mills in California.

In his bid for the Salt Lake business, Johnson promised delivery to wagon trains at two different landing points: the mouth of El Dorado Canyon during the season of high water, and Hardyville, nine miles above Fort Mojave, when it was low. Steamboat Adams declared, on the other hand, that even in winter Trueworthy and he would take the *Esmeralda*, loaded with freight, through the Black Canyon and on around the river's great bend to the mouth of Las Vegas Wash.

How did he know the river was navigable that high? According to his own undocumented story, which he submitted to Congress in 1870, he had built a raft of driftwood at the mouth of the Wash and floated it downstream for three hundred miles, studying navigational possibilities.[24]

The competing bids reached Salt Lake City in October, 1864. The Saints promptly formed the Deseret Mercantile Company to deal with them. Adams's statements about the river's navigability led to stern conditions. Whichever steamboat company hauled goods—neither received an exclusive contract—would have to deliver them somewhere near the mouth of Las Vegas Wash. The job of finding a suitable warehouse site, where food for workers and livestock could be grown with water from the river, and of linking the place to the California Road, with a branch highway to St. George, was assigned to a vigorous pioneer named Anson Call. When the news reached St. George, excitement soared so high that one man even built a hotel to care for the anticipated throngs.[25]

Anson Call arrived at St. George in mid-November and recruited five men, including Jacob Hamblin and Hamblin's son Lyman, to help him with his scouting. Six miles upstream from Las Vegas Wash they staked out a choice spot, and the head of the expedition assigned to the unbuilt town the name Callville. It never occurred to them to inquire whether anyone had already filed a pre-emption claim there. Expert stonemasons were at work on the warehouse and adjacent corrals—their fences had to be made of rock since no timber was available—when a man named Cowan presented an adverse claim. Call promptly filed another claim a mile away.²⁶ But Cowan, who had the better site, finished the warehouse there. Thus Mormons could not control the commerce, and, besides, the Central Pacific and Union Pacific by now were moving toward a junction in northern Utah. Accordingly the Deseret Mercantile Company allowed talks with the rival steamboat companies to lapse.

Undeterred, Thomas Trueworthy, Samuel Adams, and the mining company that owned the *Nina Tilden* amalgamated their resources as the Pacific and Colorado Steam Navigation Company and, in the fall of 1865, resumed their search for business.²⁷ A San Francisco wholesaler arranged to send one hundred tons of assorted merchandise up the spring flood aboard the *Esmeralda* to Callville, where a few independent merchants from Salt Lake City were to pick it up in March, 1866. When Steamboat Adams arrived in the Utah capital around July 10 to check on the shipment and arrange for more business, he learned to his dismay that the *Esmeralda* had not reached Callville. Heading south to learn what was wrong, he finally found the steamboat at La Paz, no more than one hundred miles above Fort Yuma.

According to its first mate, Robert Rodgers, the main problem was overloading. Both the *Esmeralda* and the barge it towed had been stuffed so full of mine freight in addition to the Utah supplies that they could not buck the unseasonably late floods, and he had lain over at Yuma waiting for the river to drop. After that there had been crippling battles with sandbars and frequent stops to cut wood for the laboring engines. Adams boarded the craft. In the middle of the Black Canyon an ominous stretch known as the Roaring Rapids brought it to a dead halt. By setting a ring bolt in the canyon wall at the head of the white water and then running a line through the ring to his capstan, Rogers winched his way through. With triumphant blasts of its whistle the sternwheeler churned up at the Callville landing on October 8, 1866.

Utah merchants were unwilling to tie their business to such undependable service, however, and with the approach of the transcontinental railroad there were few orders. Partly out of desperation, Samuel Adams decided to expand the scope of Colorado River navigation a few more hundred miles in order to supply inland Army posts. On March 29, 1867, he wrote a letter to Secretary of War Edwin M. Stanton offering to prove that boats could ascend the river that far.

He knew, he said, that it was possible because of a preliminary investigation of his own. Before starting south to find the long-delayed *Esmeralda*, he had traveled upstream from Callville through Boulder Canyon, which he declared was the biggest gorge in the river system, and had clambered to the top of its walls. Looking upstream, he had seen a placid stream winding through open valleys that finally dwindled gently from sight. He had then built another raft and had floated without difficulty through Boulder and Black canyons to La Paz.

Captain Randolph B. Marcy had already proposed to explore the same section of the river in 1853, when he had offered to lead thirty soldiers supported by a pack train of fifty mules downstream along the canyon rim. The War Department had turned him down. In 1866 he had made a new suggestion, this time to reverse the direction, using small boats to go upstream. Nature, he argued, had surely exposed many veins of gold and silver in the canyon walls, which, he said, were reported to be three miles high. A boat speeding down the current, he added, might be swept to disaster in giant whirlpools and waterfalls, whereas explorers going upstream could skirt such obstructions on foot, hauling their boats up behind them.[28] And then in November, 1866, Colonel James Rusling had written his superiors that he could think of "no better duty than to ascend the Colorado upward and explore all these rivers [the Green, Grand, and San Juan] to the head of navigation."*[29]

Secretary Stanton had no money for such explorations. Adams received a polite note, the Pacific and Colorado Steam Navigation Company quietly expired, and its assets went to Alonzo Johnson. Thereafter only local freight —salt, farm produce, and a little cotton—would be carried down the Colorado by boat.

Still, Dixie survived. In the early 1870's, silver deposits were found in a tilted sandstone formation, afterwards called Silver Reef, about seventeen miles northwest of St. George. Gentiles swarmed into the vicinity—more of them than the Mormons would have preferred had they been able to choose —and the boom was on. It lasted until the collapse of metal prices at the beginning of 1893. By then a tall-steepled temple had risen not far from the tabernacle at St. George, its whiteness vivid against the red cliffs, just as Brigham Young had prophesied.

*Adams, it is worth noting, had conferred with Rusling in Salt Lake City, in the fall of 1866, about the problem of supplying Army posts in the interior of the West. It is quite possible that Steamboat stole the idea of upriver navigation straight from the Colonel.

*William Bell's
Grand Canyon fantasy*

9

First Man Through?

During the first week of September, 1867, several Paiute Indians, hired by a mine supplier, poled a barge up the river to Callville for a consignment of salt. While the craft was being loaded, one of them suddenly pointed toward midstream and shouted the Paiute equivalent of: "White man! White man!" There, waving feebly from the surface of a small raft, was a half-naked Caucasian.

Spectators hauled him ashore. He was incoherent and dreadfully emaciated, his skin partly puckered from long immersion in water and partly blistered by the sun. As his wits returned, James White told how Indians had attacked him and two other prospectors in a side canyon somewhere above the mouth of the San Juan River. One man had died. White and the other survivor had built a raft of driftwood and launched it in a desperate attempt to escape. On the third day White's companion had been swept into the current and drowned. Eleven days of battling with giant whirlpools had passed when White reached Callville.[1]

His story was reported by newspapers in San Bernardino, California, and Prescott, Arizona, and thence traveled to San Francisco, Salt Lake City,

Denver, and New York. A respected naturalist, Dr. C. C. Parry, learned of White's adventure while he was on a survey for the Kansas Pacific Railroad and interviewed him at the behest of its chief engineer.

By that time the erstwhile prospector had recovered from his ordeal and was carrying mail, on horseback, between Callville and Fort Mojave. Parry caught up with him at Hardyville. Whereas White, who was barely literate, had no clear idea of where he had been, Parry had studied every available report on the Southwest and had covered much of it, though not the river, in person. As he tried to put White's wandering tale into coherent order, he gave the ignorant prospector notions of geography that he might otherwise not have had.

Parry's report of the interview was read aloud at the annual meeting of the St. Louis Academy of Science and printed in its *Transactions,* and soon afterward it was submitted to Congress as part of the Kansas Pacific's request for government subsidies. The railroad received no subsidies, however, and was never extended past Denver.

Nevertheless, the tale had an effect. For anyone who doubted it, the circumstantial evidence was too strong to be refuted at first. Moreover, people *wanted* it to have happened.

Born at Rome, New York, November 19, 1837, James White had had very little education and evidently no home ties. When he was twenty-two or twenty-three, he followed the Colorado gold rush to Denver, ended up empty-handed, and drifted on to Virginia City, Nevada. There, on November 1, 1861, he enlisted in the Army for three years and was mustered into Company H, Fifth Infantry, as a carpenter. In January, 1863, he had marched with his company through the desert to Franklin, Texas (the present El Paso). After serving as a cattle herder and teamster, he was shifted to the Quartermaster's Department. In September, 1864, less than two months before his enlistment expired, he was arrested for buying whiskey with goods stolen from the Quartermaster's store. Though sentenced to a year's hard labor, he was freed in the spring of 1865 under a general amnesty declared at the end of the Civil War. Drifting on to Kansas, he landed a job as a stagecoach driver on the Santa Fe Trail. There he fell in with a veteran of the Confederate Army, Charles Baker, who in the spring of 1867 talked White, along with two other drivers, into quitting his job and prospecting with him in Colorado. Apparently Baker masterminded the coup by which they raised money for the trip —stealing fourteen horses from some nearby Indians.

Somewhere along the upper reaches of the Arkansas River, White quarreled with Joseph Goodfellow, one of his fellow prospectors. Both men, as White later recalled, reached for their guns. Goodfellow, wounded, was left to recover at a nearby ranch. The others cut southwest across rugged mountains to the Mancos River, which they followed to the San Juan. According to a letter White wrote his brother Josh from Callville on September 26, 1867, less than three weeks after his rescue,

> . . . we store [started] down the San Won river we travel down a bout 200 miles than we cross over on Calorrado and camp we lad over one day we found out that we could not travel down the river . . . and we made up our mines to turn back when wee was attacked by 15 or 20 ute indis they kill Baker [,] and George Strole and myself took fore ropes off our hourse and a ax ten pounds of flour and our gunns wee had 15 miles to woak to Colorado we got to the river just at night we bilt a raft that night wee got it bilt abot teen o clock tha night. wee saile all that night wee good sailing from three days and the fore [fourth day] George Strole was wash of from the raft and drown that left me aline.

In interviews with reporters White added a few details. They had crossed back to the north side of the San Juan, he said, because Baker wanted to try mining along the lower reaches of the Grand River. Under Dr. Parry's prompting he conceded that, yes, they might well have reached their goal before the Indians attacked.

He described the raft: three cottonwood logs eight inches in diameter and ten feet long. Even under good sailing conditions, however, the craft proved inadequate, and the next morning they reinforced it with more wood. But not long after they hit the first rough water, a companion named George Strole had been washed away, along with the soaked, glutinous flour that had been their only food.

Alone in the bottom of the howling canyon, White lashed himself to the raft. He traveled twelve or fourteen hours a day. At night he tied the raft to streamside rocks and slept on it, since he would have been doomed if he had lost it. He did not try to leave the river for fear of encountering hostile Indians. He nibbled on a few mesquite beans and lizards, and when those ran out he cut a leather knife scabbard into pieces and choked the fragments down.

He pried the craft off rocks, spun through whirlpools, fought to keep from being trapped by eddies. Again and again, rough water washed completely over his raft. But only one rapid stayed in his mind as exceptionally violent, a waterfall "from ten to fifteen feet hie." His narrowest escape came when the raft broke apart. Spread-eagled and clawing, tangled in a loose lariat rope, he managed to hold the logs together until they lodged against some boulders. From there he floundered to an island, found new logs, and built a new raft—the one on which he had floated down the canyon. Some Indians he encountered along the way had pulled him ashore but had driven a hard bargain for food, he said—his revolver and vest for a dog's hindquarters, which he roasted over a bed of mesquite coals.

The trouble with this stirring tale was that it did not fit the geography described by later explorers. Five hundred miles from the Grand River to Callville in fourteen days of low water? Through the exposed rock fangs of Cataract Canyon; over the clutching sandbars in Glen Canyon; into the Grand Canyon's long stretches of slack water punctuated not by one but by many rapids of exceptional violence? No matter now many hours a day a lone man thrust ahead with poles and makeshift oars, no matter how hard he prayed (White said he prayed his way out of one eddy), could he have succeeded?

Defenders pointed to the obvious. He had been so dazed that he had lost track of time. He had not known the country. He had said "Grand River" because it had been suggested to him. More probably, defenders said, the party reached the river well below the junction of the Grand and Green, at Glen Canyon near the mouth of White Canyon.[2] This convenient revision not only eliminated several days' travel time but also got rid of the big drops in Cataract.

Even that shrinkage did not suit some commentators. They decided that the party had not recrossed the San Juan but had approached the main river to the south—thereby entailing an almost impossible horseback ride along the gulch-torn northern slope of Navajo Mountain. Besides, White was stubborn about having gone north from the San Juan and admitted a more southerly route only under pressure from those who were trying to help him.

But perhaps the party had never intended to go to the Grand River. Perhaps White had persuaded them to give up the unrewarding lands where they had been and strike for the lower river, where he knew from his months at Fort Yuma that gold had been found. According to this theory, the trio would have ridden past the San Francisco Peaks and then, seeking ground that had not been overrun by miners, cut for the river through Peach Springs Canyon and Diamond Creek.[3] It would then have been Hualapai, not Ute, Indians who attacked them (the Hualapai were on the warpath during those years), and the flight down the Colorado would have taken place from there.

An entry at Diamond Creek reduced the run to manageable proportions but raised other problems. Not one but several violent stretches of rapids still lay ahead, and they began almost immediately, not after three days of "good sailing." Another problem—and it applied to every supposed entry from the Grand Wash Cliffs to Glen Canyon and beyond—revolves around color. The castaway insisted that throughout the first several days of his run he had passed between walls of whitish sandstone before coming finally to a deep slit of black rock. Could he have been that dazed? Although there is somber black rock in sections of the Grand Canyon's inner gorge, the prevailing tone is inescapably red.

Suppose, however, that the party entered the river at Grapevine Wash, just below the Grand Wash Cliffs. From there on to Boulder Canyon, where the rock is nearly black, the sandstone is indeed almost white. On that stretch, moreover, the water starts placidly and then grows rough enough to be troublesome. Yet it contains only a single rapid that, at low water, is really wicked.

A logical stretch for White to have traveled? Many think so. But again there are problems. The distance now is too short—only sixty-four miles to Callville. Just a few months before White's raft appeared there, Jacob Hamblin and two others, searching for improved road access to the river from St. George, negotiated the stretch in two days. True, Hamblin and his companions were in better physical condition than White and had a good boat with oars. The only time they slowed down was when they lined their skiff down the one big rapid with lariat ropes.[4] Yet White clung doggedly to a time lapse of fourteen days, all spent fighting the river. Even in a stupor, half starved, caught in eddies and whipped by crosscurrents, could so short a stretch have taken so long?

The most terrible question remains. If James White rode horseback scores of miles from the San Juan River across Monument Valley, through Kletha, over the Little Colorado, and on past the San Francisco Peaks to a lower entry, he would certainly have known it, no matter how dazed he later became. Why, then, was he insistent on placing the Indian attack so far up the river that his subsequent adventures became implausible?

A circumstantial accusation has been raised in answer to the query: He did not know the river well enough to realize the implausibility, and yet he had to disassociate himself from the lower area. Why? Because it had been George Strole and he, not Indians, who killed Baker and then fled down the river. Some detractors would have it that White had killed both men and then staggered down Grapevine Wash to the stream. On being rescued, he had improvised his adventure and thereafter found himself stuck with it.

When White was an old man, leading a humble, respectable life in Trinidad, Colorado, the most relentless of his doubters, Robert Brewster Stanton, told him of these suspicions. White denied the charge of murder in tones of such shock and grief that Stanton decided he was innocent.[5]

One would like to think so. But if the motive of murder is ruled out of his story, we are back where we started, chasing fragmentary clues into nowhere—though in whatever version, no one who has heard the tale and then run the river can forget it.

John Wesley Powell's arm chair

10

Testing the River

John Wesley Powell, as the oldest son of a Methodist circuit-rider with strong antislavery views, got into so many fist fights in defense of those views that his father withdrew him from public school and sent him, reluctantly, to a private tutor. It was from that tutor, George Crookham, that young Powell acquired a taste for laboratory experiments and field trips in the physical sciences. Having refused his father's offer to finance a college education if he would agree to enter the ministry, he began his career at the age of eighteen, as a teacher in a one-room schoolhouse at a salary of fourteen dollars a month.

For the next nine years he taught in various schools, taking college courses in science during his vacations. He never received a degree. His education came mainly from long, self-guided field trips, some in small boats along the Illinois, Ohio, and Mississippi rivers. At the end of a hike across Michigan he met and fell in love with a cousin, Emma Dean. His parents objected, even though he was by now twenty-seven and had been elected secretary of the newly founded Illinois State Natural History Society. Before the pair could be married, the Civil War broke out, and Powell enlisted at once. He studied engineering, built fortifications, and joined the staff of

Ulysses S. Grant, with the rank of second lieutenant. He was given a special furlough so that he could marry Emma on November 28, 1861. On April 6, 1862, at the Battle of Shiloh, his right forearm was shattered by a minié ball. Two days later it was amputated just below the shoulder. Emma was on hand, thanks to a special pass from General Grant, and from then on throughout the war she managed to stay close to him.

Despite the pain of the mutilation and of two subsequent operations on the stump, Powell stayed stubbornly with the Army. Appointed a major in command of an artillery battery, he fought often and well. At Atlanta he watched helplessly as his younger brother Walter was taken prisoner by Confederates. Finally, on January 2, 1865, he resigned his commission. He was three months short of his thirty-first birthday, and utterly exhausted: he weighed just 110 pounds.

On recovering his health, he obtained a position teaching geology at Illinois Weslyan University and then shifted to Illinois State Normal University; at both places he followed George Crookham's practice of taking his students on field trips. In the summer of 1867 he gathered together a volunteer expedition for the Dakota Badlands with the announced purpose of collecting samples of Indian artifacts, along with geologic and botanic specimens. Joining the college students on the trip were Powell's wife, Emma; his sister Nellie; and Nellie's schoolmaster husband, Almon Harris Thompson—a bit of nepotism that would characterize much of Powell's later work. The sponsoring organizations were a handful of colleges and the new Illinois Natural History Museum, of which Powell himself was curator. Local railroads provided free travel as far as their tracks ran.

When Indian troubles blocked the road to the Dakotas, Powell quickly shifted to Colorado. After climbing Pikes Peak and Mount Lincoln, both above fourteen thousand feet high, the group went into camp at Hot Sulphur Springs, a resort located beside the headwaters of the Grand River and owned by William Byers, influential editor of Denver's *Rocky Mountain News*. Byers's brother-in-law, Jack Sumner, acted as the group's guide and one day took them to see Cedar Canyon, where the Grand River carves its thundering way through the Gore Range en route to the sea. It was there, in the fall of 1867, according to Powell's own reminiscences, that the idea of following the unknown river first came to him.[1]

Before returning to Illinois he announced that in the summer of 1868 he would lead another excursion to Colorado. He called it the Rocky Mountain Scientific Exploring Expedition and let it be known that in addition to collecting specimens the group would attempt the first ascent of Longs Peak. After the expedition had disbanded in the fall, he had further plans, which he kept to himself: He and Emma would winter in the plateau country of western Colorado with several mountaineers hired for him by Jack Sumner. In the

spring, having studied both the Grand and Green Rivers, he would go to
Washington with enough information to persuade the federal government to
back his explorations.[2]

The Rocky Mountain Scientific Exploring Expedition was launched on
meager grants from local institutions, Army rations obtained through the
good offices of Illinois congressmen, instruments loaned by the Smithsonian
Institution, and money out of Powell's own pocket. Emma Powell, Nellie
Thompson, and Almon Thompson were along again; with them they brought
Powell's moody, unpredictable brother Walter in the hope that the outdoors
would help restore his mental balance, shaken by ten months in a Confederate
prison. The group, which this year consisted of twenty-one persons, again set
up headquarters at Hot Sulphur Springs to begin high-altitude collecting.
Four tough, undisciplined mountaineers, all of whom had served as enlisted
men during the war and were congenitally suspicious of anyone with the title
Major, were hired as guides. One was Jack Sumner; another was a trapper
named Bill Dunn; a third was a fugitive from the law who had shortened his
name from Billy Rhodes Hawkins to plain Billy Rhodes. Also attached to the
expedition, evidently just for a lark, was Oramel G. Howland, who worked
on and off as a printer for the *Rocky Mountain News*. Tagging along with
Oramel was his younger brother Seneca, another Union Army veteran.

On August 20, the major and six others started up Longs Peak. They
passed shimmering Grand Lake, gathering-place of the river's crystalline
headwaters—Powell would remember the delicious taste of that water in time
to come—and spurred their horses into the chill shade of a dense forest of
spruce. They floundered through down timber and bogs, set up a base camp
at timberline, shifted to their own feet, lost their way in the immense piles
of gray talus, but at last, on August 23, gained the summit, 14,256 feet high,
which Indians almost surely had visited before in order to trap eagles. They
returned exhausted but triumphant.

Almost immediately thereafter Hot Sulphur Springs was visited by a
party of journalists, congressmen, governors, generals, and emancipated
women out to see and report on the postwar rush of settlers into the West.
To Samuel Bowles, one of the most influential editors in the nation, Powell
leaked word of his Colorado River plan. On returning to civilization Bowles
responded by extolling what Powell had achieved and pointing out the importance of studying "the central forces that formed the continent."[3]

After the visitors had left, Powell and a single companion attacked the
highest peak in the Gore Range, still unclimbed though it was seven hundred
feet lower than Longs. Oramel Howland, in a story to the *Rocky Mountain
News*, gave the no-longer-virgin summit the name Mount Powell, which it
still bears.

By then frost was whitening the meadow grass each morning. The

Thompsons and some of the party left for Illinois and the opening of school. The rest of the expedition, accompanied by the mountaineers Sumner, Dunn, and Hawkins, and by Oramel and Seneca Howland, worked a circuitous way west to a sheltered pocket beside the White River, one hundred miles or so above its junction with the Green. There the entire group threw together three rough cabins for the nine people who proposed to winter in the remote spot—Powell, his wife, his brother Walter, the three trappers, the Howland brothers, and a student named Sam Garman. The rest of the expedition, its chores completed, headed north and northwest toward the new tracks of the Union Pacific Railroad. The Major and Oramel Howland went along to sell the group's saddle animals and pack stock. On their return trip they would pick up winter supplies at Fort Bridger—free by virtue of their authorization to draw rations from Army camps.

Much of the way lay across vast, rolling, sagebrush hills laced by a labyrinth of dry arroyos. Blizzards shrieked, and they were fortunate to gain shelter in Brown's Hole, now Brown's Park. After the weather had moderated, they struck north to the railroad, saw their companions off, sold the excess stock, and detoured back by way of the fort. There it is quite possible that Powell encountered James White. Or quite possibly he didn't. We can't be sure. It is known that White had left the lower Colorado a few months earlier and had drifted north to a job cutting ties for the Union Pacific. Although Powell had certainly heard of him from Samuel Bowles, he never mentioned James White in print. There is one further bit of evidence, however. At Fort Bridger, Powell met a discontented soldier, George Bradley, who knew boats and who agreed to join an exploring expedition if the Major could get him out of the Army. Later, deep in the canyons, Bradley wrote in his diary that he doubted White's story and added, in an offhand way, that Powell had met the prospector. The fall of 1868 seems to be the only possible time and Fort Bridger the most likely place for the encounter.[4]

Their remaining mules loaded with rations, the Major and Howland made the difficult return trip to their winter camp. When weather allowed, various members of the party made long rides of exploration. They went south to the Grand, presumably in the vicinity of the oil shale cliffs between today's towns of Rifle and De Beque, Colorado. They jogged west to the Green and saw, far to the south, the canyon-cut bulk of Tavaputs Plateau. They went north to the Uinta Mountains, reached the deep yellow canyon of the Yampa, and possibly glimpsed the exit of the Green from Split Mountain. In between trips, Powell hobnobbed happily with a band of Ute Indians who wintered near his camp. He compiled a vocabulary of their tongue for the Smithsonian and swapped trinkets for native items he could take back to the Illinois Natural History Museum.

The winter's experiences shaped his inchoate plans. He decided not just to run the rivers but to stay in the canyons a full ten months, studying. So ambitious a program would entail taking along heavy loads of food; guns, ammunition, and traps for hunting; and tools for building winter shelters.[5] He spent hours in his rude cabin designing boats capable of carrying such cargo through boulder-strewn rapids. Three were to be twenty-one feet long, of oak, with waterproof bulkheads in either end to hold supplies and lend buoyancy. The fourth was to be smaller, lighter, and hence more maneuverable— sixteen feet long, of white pine. He planned to ride it downstream ahead of the others, scouting out danger spots. Because the new railroad gave freight easy access to the Green River in southern Wyoming, he decided to start down that stream, although he had originally intended to follow the Grand.

Each boat held space for three men. Two, one seated in front of the other, would row. Because the oarsmen would be facing backwards and the boat would need guidance in rapids, a third man was to stand in the stern, facing forward. He would bellow orders—*right, left, STEADY*—and in addition use a big sweep oar as a rudder. Years would pass before another Colorado river boatman, Nathaniel Galloway, demonstrated what canoists already knew: the best way to enter a rapid is to face forward. But for longer than memory ran, boats had been rowed backward because it was from that position that energy was transmitted most powerfully to the oar blades.

Three men in each of four boats added up to a crew of twelve, counting Powell, who, of course, could not row. During the winter he came to terms with seven—Bradley, Walter Powell, Sumner, Dunn, Hawkins, and the two Howlands. (Young Garman dropped out.) Big, strong, moody Walter Powell probably accepted whatever his brother told him. The others, Bradley excepted, were promised one thousand dollars each if Powell succeeded in winning a government appropriation funding the trip. Otherwise he would pay the workers twenty-five dollars a month for their ten months on the river. He would let them augment the pay by panning occasionally for gold and trapping for beaver during a specified number of days. Any gold they found would be theirs, and he would buy whatever pelts they produced at prices set forth in the contracts.[6]

In March a sudden thaw sent the White River out of its banks and into their cabins. As they fled to higher ground, they fell to quarreling. Cabin fever: it was time to separate for a while. After agreeing to meet the others in May at the town of Green River, Wyoming, the three Powells headed for the railroad by way of Fort Bridger, where they notified Bradley of the plans.

In Chicago, Powell gave orders for the boats to a professional boat-builder. Emma then went to Detroit to stay with her family until the adventure was completed. Her husband continued to Washington and made his pitch for funds; it was rejected.

He should not have been surprised. What claim to consideration did he have? He had led amateur field trips, not true investigations. He had seen only a small, unrepresentative fragment of a system that, if both the Green and Grand were included, extended for more than two thousand miles. Surprised or not, he met the rejection with the same stubbornness that had kept him in the front lines of the Civil War after losing his arm. From his friend President Grant he won an order allowing him to draw Army rations for twenty-five men. These he could commute into cash, a real boon. He obtained a discharge for George Bradley, and after hurrying to Illinois he wangled small sums from institutions that had supported him before. Finally, he prevailed on the Union Pacific to ship his boats and equipment to Green River, Wyoming, free of charge.

Strangely, he made no effort to fill the four vacant seats in his little fleet with experienced boatmen from the Great Lakes. But on May 11, after Walter and he had rejoined the rest of the party at Green River, he abruptly added two greenhorns to the crew. One was an eighteen-year-old bullwhacker, Andy Hall, whom Powell had seen sitting at the oars of a skiff near the railroad bridge. The other was a florid Englishman, Frank Goodman, who walked up out of nowhere and offered to go along for the excitement. The Major knew nothing about either's capabilities. Yet there was another volunteer whom he summarily rejected—Samuel "Steamboat" Adams. Though Adams was familiar with the lower river and with rafting on it, Powell must have sensed that Steamboat would try to take over the expedition. So he was turned away, and when the fleet nosed into the turbid stream on May 24, 1869, with most of Green River's citizens waving from the banks, two of the boats held empty seats.

The three large boats—*Kitty Clyde's Sister, Maid of the Canyons, No-Name* —were clinker-built, round-bottomed, double-ribbed with cured oak, and ponderous. Loaded, they responded sluggishly to the oars. Each carried in its watertight bulkheads two thousand pounds of supplies and equipment, cargo that by no means filled them to capacity. If the thought occurred to any of the group that six thousand pounds was hairline support for ten men for ten months, the doubt was shrugged aside; after all, wilderness hunting was generally good, and every crew member knew how to handle a gun.

The mountaineers, to whom Powell had given a bit of training during the winter, were also expected to act as scientific technicians. Bill Dunn was assigned the job of recording altitudes; he did this by taking barometric readings at a minimum of three different spots during each day's run. Oramel Howland collected data for a topographic map. Each time the boat he was traveling in rounded a point, he would note the compass direction to the next point and estimate the distance. Another man in a different boat also estimated distance. At camp that night an average was taken. Coordinated with Dunn's elevations, the figures produced a constantly descending baseline from which rough triangulations could be worked out for determining the height of the cliffs bordering the river.[7]

The river map that resulted then had to be placed on broader maps of the area. At fifty-mile intervals, or as near thereto as circumstances allowed, and at the mouths of major tributaries, Jack Sumner established "astronomical stations." Daylight shots of the sun with a sextant gave him raw material for calculating latitude; more complex stellar and lunar observations, carefully tied into the time revealed by Powell's expensive chronometer, gave him the longitude. Once a station had been firmly located, it was then possible for Powell to determine the direct distance from it to any other recorded spot— to Callville, say, which was the group's destination.

In addition to supervising the work, the Major jotted down observations of his own, not an easy routine for a one-armed man sitting on a rock while wind tugged at the paper. Between times his need for heights kept him scrambling up slits in the canyon walls; on reaching the top he could look over the surrounding country, its land patterns, its geology, its flora and fauna. His handicap considered, some of the climbs bordered on recklessness, the only situation in which he was not, at least in his men's opinion, unduly cautious.

In addition to the specialists were those who kept the specialists going —cook and camp-tender, wood-gatherers, hunters, fishermen, and those who repaired whatever needed fixing. Many of the camp chores were shared, of course. Powell was always ready to try his hand at baking biscuits. Everyone except Powell rowed; everyone, Powell included, helped on the portages, a backbreaking duty that before the run was over did much to drain away the spirits as well as the physical strength of the men.

For sixty miles the river, gray with spring mud, wound through dull gray hills capped by occasional freakish remnants of erosion. It dug into the Uinta Mountains as if to go straight through them, then swung west a short distance and looped east around a tight horseshoe curve. Rapids began to boil. After bucking through one or two of them the men were seized by standard river-running highs. "We plunge along singing, yelling like drunken soldiers . . .," Jack Sumner told his diary. (Only Powell was equipped with a life jacket.) "It is like sparking a black eyed girl—just dangerous enough to be exciting."[8]

The Major kept checking the exuberance. He dared not lose a single boat. Whenever ominous-looking froth appeared ahead, he stopped to reconnoiter —reading the water, boatmen say today. If the fall was steep and the channel had been littered by the wash of boulders out of side streams in times of flood, or with giant slabs fallen from the cliffs, he ordered the men to line through.

First, the party cleared a rough trail to the bottom of the rapids, unloaded the boats, and carried the cargo down bale by bale. Ropes were afixed to each craft's bow and stern. One by one the bowlines were taken as far as necessary downstream and secured to a rock or tree on the bank. Next, the boat to which it was affixed was let down foot by foot by men rearing back on the stern line. If conditions demanded, one man might stay inside the craft and use an oar to fend it away from rocks. Others armed with poles took up positions on the bank to keep the hull from being driven by waves onto protruding rocks or sharp corners. Sometimes two or three men had to jump into the water and boost the heavy craft over an obstruction or free it from a trap between two boulders. Tricky business, that. A sudden swirl might pull a man off his feet, or a misjudged step might drop him into a foaming hole.

As soon as the stern rope was played out, the men holding it let go. The boat leaped ahead, to be checked in its rush by the bowline and at last brought safely into the bank. Rough work, but at least the boat stayed in its proper habitat. Far more taxing was the need, when Powell judged a rapid too wild for lining, to lift the craft completely out of the stream and manhandle it down the portage trail to the end of white water.

They met their first rough water in the series of short, red-walled canyons that are strung like beads along the Green as it hews its way east by southeast through some of the ridges that buttress the north flank of the Uintas. Brown's Park brought respite, but then the Green jerked the boats around south into what Powell later wrote looked like "a black portal to a region of gloom." Noise! The men would learn to live with it, stretch after stretch, for days at a time—the constant, reverberating, deep-voiced roar of rock-torn water. Andy Hall, the young Scot that Powell had picked up at Green River town, remembered a poem from his childhood: How does the water come down at Lodore?

> Advancing and prancing and glancing and dancing,
> Recoiling, turmoiling, and toiling, and boiling. . . .
> All at once and o'er, with mighty uproar—
> And this way the water comes down at Lodore.

So Lodore was the name they gave the twenty-mile canyon. But Sumner was offended: Why go to European trash bins to find labels for new discoveries in America?

A scant five miles inside the portal, Powell, scouting ahead in the *Emma Dean* with Jack Sumner and Bill Dunn, heard and then saw a two-step rapid down which the water dropped thirty-five feet in little more than half a mile. He turned the boat into the bank, told Sumner and Dunn to signal a warning to the others, and walked ahead to study the turmoil.

The next two boats swung after the *Emma Dean* in good order. Not the *No-Name*, dragging in the rear with the Howland brothers and Frank Goodman. They had shipped considerable water while bobbing through a riffle a little farther back and may have kept bailing a trifle too long. In any event, when they bent to the oars in response to Sumner's signal, the boat hesitated leadenly and the current took over, hurling it, tilted precariously, into the churning waves. It burst through the first wall of froth but then smacked into a nest of boulders that wrenched the oars from their locks and tumbled the passengers overboard. Flailing, they caught the gunwales and pulled themselves back in as the boat, righting itself, roller-coasted through the first step. Swung broadside by the tailwaves, it careened against a huge red boulder at the top of the second step and broke in half.

Just below the red boulder was a spiny island of rocks. At the instant of impact Oramel Howland freed himself from the boat with a great leap onto the upper part of the island. Providentially he found a long, water-whitened pole of driftwood and reached it out to Goodman, who was clinging desperately to a foam-washed rock in the middle of the maelstrom. Now there were two perched on the slippery island. Then Seneca Howland, sorely bruised, crawled out onto the island's lower end. Three accounted for.

Working frantically, the rest of the party unloaded the *Emma Dean* and lined it down to the top of the second step. Alone at the oars, Sumner skimmed the lightened boat like a water ouzel to the island and effected a rescue. "We were as glad to shake hands with them," Powell wrote afterwards, "as though they had been on a voyage around the world and wrecked on a distant coast." Sumner, though, recalled the conclusion differently. In reminiscences given Robert Brewster Stanton years afterwards (but not in the diary of the first part of the voyage that he wrote for publication in the *Missouri Democrat*), he stated bluntly that the Major's first words were a blistering criticism of Howland for not landing as signaled. It was the beginning, Sumner added, of frictions between Powell and the three touchiest members, the Howland brothers and Dunn, that would grow steadily more disruptive as their situation deteriorated.[9]

They recognized the seriousness of the crash in the name they gave the rapid, Disaster Falls. Though they retrieved from the shattered *No-Name* a few precious barometers and a keg of contraband whiskey—Powell wisely held his temper about the smuggling—they had lost a third of the expedition's supplies and nearly all of the personal gear of the boat's three crewmen.

They had been on the river sixteen days, 5 percent of the projected total. Because of frequent stops to tinker with equipment and climb canyon walls for views, they had traveled only 126 miles, an average of six miles a day. How many more river miles separated them from Callville they did not know (it was about 875), but obviously adjustments had to be made. Their great hope was the new Ute Agency in the Uinta Valley; surely it would have stores on hand.

They needed hope. Spray and occasional rain showers dashed in their faces. They sat in water, waded in water. Their buckskin clothing stretched out of shape. When the sun poured down through breaks in the clouds and glanced off the canyon walls and the tossing current, it burned their exposed skins, a torture increased by the river's load of abrasive silt. Yet though *they* were wet, the brush along the river banks was tinder dry, and one day the embers of their campfire set it ablaze. In escaping from the inferno, they lost some of their clothing and most of their mess kit, an exasperating inconvenience.

Slave labor: making trail, toting cargo, lining boats. Trying to sleep, Bradley groused, on rock piles where a dog wouldn't lie down. Moments of heart-stopping fear: giant whirlpools spinning them dizzily; the *Maid of the Canyon* tearing its ropes from their hands, diving out of control, and then veering unharmed into an eddy.

And at last the benison of quiet. The river flattened out and coiled with the softest of whispers beside a long knife blade of yellow-pink Weber Sandstone seven hundred feet high. The Yampa River, discolored with silt, slid in through a rounding pocket from the east. Sunlight shimmered on the trembling leaves of box elders and cottonwoods. The very silence made them call out, so that they could listen to the syllables roll mellowly back from the cliff, a phenomenon that led them to name the spot Echo Park, now the heart of Dinosaur National Monument.

They halted to dry out and write letters that could be mailed at the Ute Agency. Most of those letters, they knew, would be printed in hometown newspapers, and as they reviewed their accomplishments, their spirits picked up. A strenuous trip, Howland told the *News*, but exciting. "Just let white foam show itself ahead and everything is as jolly and full of life as an Irish 'wake.' " Powell, the romanticist, grew literary. In spite of the din and labors of Lodore, "its walls and cliffs, its peaks and crags, its amphitheaters and alcoves, tell a story of beauty and grandeur that I hear yet—and shall hear." To a private correspondent who predictably trotted the letter down to the St. Louis *Missouri Democrat* he added, " . . . never before did I live in such ecstacy for an entire month."[10]

In that frame of mind they scooted through the rapids below Echo Park and emerged onto the north edge of the Colorado Plateau. Ahead was the broad, barren Uinta Valley. After toiling sixty-odd miles along the now torpid river, they reached the mouth of the Uinta (now Duchesne) River. There they camped, thirty-seven days and a meager 224 miles out of Green River. While the Powells, Andy Hall, and Frank Goodman trudged forty miles to the Agency, located near the remnants of Antoine Robidoux's old fur-trading post, the others gorged on wild fowl and fish, patched the boats, and endured, with no great patience, dense swarms of mosquitoes. A full week passed before the Powells and Andy Hall reappeared, riding rented Ute horses and accompanied by hired Ute Indians driving two pack animals loaded with three hundred pounds of flour and replacements for the mess kit. Three hundred pounds to replace almost two thousand? Powell shrugged. He had been short of cash, the Agency short of supplies. They'd have to make do. Anyway, there was one less mouth to feed. Deciding that he'd had enough, Goodman had dropped out.

On they went into a curving canyon of deep amphitheaters, its soil so pale and devoid of vegetation that they named it Desolation. Again and again Powell slowed them down by climbing for the skyline and more views. Bradley had to use his long underwear to hoist the one-armed Major from one untenable ledge. The boats continued to be unpredictable. The *Emma Dean* rolled over in one rapid; though there was no injury to Powell or his companions, more food and equipment were destroyed.

On July 13 they broke out of the pallid canyons past the great lighthouse rock of Gunnison Butte, crossed the Old Spanish Trail without noting it, and edged between a new set of walls—bright Navajo sandstone this time, its redness stained with sheets and streamers of desert varnish. Because of its windings they called the gorge Labyrinth Canyon. In time it gave way to Stillwater Canyon, where the riverbed dropped one foot a mile and the water seemed to stand dead quiet. Fiery heat on the rocks. Bend and pull, bend and pull. But the cliffs were stately, topped with vast, bare domes and tall pinnacles, and enlivened with huge blind arches. A feast for the eyes, though it is possible to grow weary of too much seeing.

Late in the afternoon of June 16 they ran anticlimatically into the confluence of the Green with the Grand, beside whose crystal headwaters they had been camped less than a year before. By Powell's estimate they had come 538 miles from Green River, Wyoming. (Later surveys would shrink the distance to approximately 480 miles.) Since leaving the Uinta Valley they had averaged nearly thirty miles a day, and perhaps that increase, combining with his insatiable curiosity, impelled the Major to lay over at the river junction for four days he could ill afford to spare.

He climbed, of course, once with Bradley, another time with his brother. Scrambling up talus slopes, crawling along ledges, squeezing into cracks, boosting and pulling each other, they emerged finally into "a wilderness of rock . . . ten thousand strangely carved forms in every direction, and beyond them mountains blending with the clouds"[11]—the heart today of Canyonlands National Park.

They also quarreled. The food situation was growing desperate. Though they had killed two beaver at the junction, fish and game in general were scarce. Heat had turned their bacon rancid. Heavy pounding in the rapids had caused the "watertight" bulkheads to leak. Wet flour had either molded or solidified into lumps like concrete. To salvage what they could, they strained the mess through mosquito netting and ended up discarding two hundred pounds. As Sumner later recalled the episode, the shrinkage led Howland to snap at the Major for getting so little food at the Agency—his revenge, in part, for Powell's constant picking at him for falling behind in his mapwork. Though such tensions in the bottom of an abyss were understandable, they did not bode well for the future.[12]

Four miles below the junction, the Colorado, as the combined streams were then known, resumed its rush—Cataract Canyon, sixty-four rapids in fifty miles, perhaps the greatest sustained length of white water in North America.[13] A warning of its potentials came with sledgehammer immediacy. On the first day in Cataract, the *Emma Dean* flipped again. There were no losses except for oars, and new ones could be carved from driftwood. But the accident intensified Powell's caution. For the next twelve days, soaking wet, shouting at each other above the constant reverberations, the men portaged their dwindling cargo around one rough spot after another, and then lined the boats through; or, if the water seemed hopelessly rough to the Major, they shoved and skidded them along improvised trails. They climbed cliffs to reach pine trees from which they could collect resin for staunching leaks. They marveled at driftwood lodged forty, fifty, sixty, or more feet above their heads. "God help the poor wretch that is caught in this canyon during high water," Sumner told his journal.

They crept into side canyons to see the sights; they rejoiced at the lucky killing of two young mountain sheep—"a Godsend to us," Bradley wrote, "as sour bread and rotten beans is a poor diet for as hard work as we do." It was such hard work that danger became preferable; they exulted when portages were impossible and Powell let them run the river, half exhilarated and half terrified by the thought of what might lie ahead.

They swept around a stupendous fin of stone crested with pinnacles—Mille Crag Bend they called the majestic curve—and the water quieted. It was also thick with mud from a cloudburst and so when they saw a side stream coming in from the right, they made eagerly for it—only to recoil from its stink. A new name for the map: Dirty Devil River. Yet it proved to be an introduction to a desert paradise—smooth red cliffs beautifully curved and carved, topped with domes called baldheads and girt with riverine glades so idyllic that after toying with the names Mound and Monument for the 149-mile stretch, Powell settled on Glen Canyon. It is lost now forever under the waters of a reservoir named, ironically, Lake Powell.

Marble Canyon, its walls of polished gray limestone (not marble) stained deep red by water oozing down from oxidized formations above, rushed them once more into turmoil. Waves slammed back at them from the curving walls. The sun broiled them until sudden cloudbursts sent liquid mud pouring over the rims. Another stinking stream, the Little Colorado, came in from the left.

There Powell called another halt to take observations and collect geologic specimens. Grumblings became open then, forcing him on into what he called "the great Unknown," which was a pretty fair description of what they had already been through. At the mouth of the Little Colorado, however, they were at the edge of their endurance, and when Powell remembered the scene years later he could not help dramatizing it. "We have but a month's rations remaining. . . . We are three-quarters of a mile in the depths of the earth . . . pygmies running up and down the sands or lost among the boulders. . . . What falls there are we know not; what rocks beset the channels, we know not. . . ."[14]

Then the Grand Canyon. On the 1869 trip Powell made the name official. No attempt to match the descriptiveness of Lodore, Desolation, Cataract, or Glen. Just Grand. There was nothing more to say.

As Powell quickly noted, the nature of the river changed with the nature of the rock. In the soft sandstone below the Little Colorado, the banded, highly colored walls spread apart, and rapids became infrequent and routine. But whenever the river cut down into dark, ancient granites, the furies returned. More swampings, more lost oars. More rain coming miserably at night. More pain for their eyes from sun glare, more for their ears and nerves from the unremitting roar. The bacon turned so revolting that they threw it away. They spilled their soda and had to be satisfied thereafter with unleavened bread. And the boats were splintering.

Underfed, burned, frightened—*when did it end?* According to the map they had, if they traveled a direct line, the Mormon settlements were not far away. But the river curved and curved and curved. They opened the last sack of flour. For the first time Powell spoke of the canyon as a prison—the same term that Padre Francisco Garcés had used ninety-three years before, though Garcés had never penetrated deeper than the bottom of Havasu Canyon.

On August 25, they portaged without great difficulty past raging Lava Falls, created by remnants of a huge igneous flow that a million years ago poured over the canyon wall, damming the river and backing it up, one estimate suggests, for 180 miles. Powell's imagination leaped. "What a conflict of water and fire. . . . What a seething and boiling. . . . What clouds of steam rolled into the heavens!" But he was also very much aware of his own progress. "Thirty-five miles today," he wrote. "Hurrah!"[15]

The exultation soon faded. On August 27 they faced a rapid, since named Separation, that looked to some of them, in their emaciated condition, utterly hopeless—impossible to run because of the wildness of the water, impossible to skirt because for scores of feet the cliffs pressed tight against the current.

No use, Howland told the Major. Their only chance was to climb out through the side canyon that drove into the river from Shivwits Plateau on the right and hike from there to the Mormon towns. Impossible, Powell replied. They might be boxed into the canyon by unscalable cliffs. If they did top out, they would find themselves in a waterless desert. The river was preferable. The end could not be far away.

A night of pondering brought no reconciliation of views. If there were bitter exchanges, no surviving diary records them. They simply decided to split up, the two Howlands and Dunn walking, the others—Sumner, Bradley, Hawkins, Andy Hall, and Walter Powell—following the Major. They baked the last of the flour and divided the biscuits, ammunition, and guns. Each group carried a set of notes. The defectors helped get two of the boats into position for running the rapids (lacking manpower for the *Emma Dean,* they abandoned it) and then climbed onto a high ledge to watch the run. The boaters shot through, wet, triumphant, and out of sight of their comrades. For a while they waited, hoping that the others would change their minds and come through in the *Emma Dean.* They did not.

Six miles farther on, the boaters encountered another maelstrom. While they were preparing to line it, a stern rope attached to one of the boats broke with Bradley still aboard. Frantically plying the sweep oar, he kept the bow pointed downstream into a smother of spray. Walter Powell and Sumner scrambled after him over the rocks on the bank. Hawkins, Hall, and the Major, losing their wits with excitement, took off in the other boat and were dumped for their pains. In that rapid, only thirty miles above the point where the river leaves the canyon at Grand Wash Cliffs, John Wesley Powell came as close to drowning as he ever would. But Bradley, who had made the run successfully, fished the battered trio out, and in effect the adventure was over. Three days later, on August 30, they reached the mouth of the Virgin, where four Mormons, one of them a boy, were seining fish and gathering driftwood for fuel to be used at Callville.

For a day they rested, ate, and contemplated what they had done. They had made the impossible run! And yet the men with the Powells soon felt their elation give way to disgruntlement. When they had agreed to join him, they had expected to be on the river for ten months, spending much of the time panning for gold and trapping beaver in uncrowded spots. Instead, they had been in the canyons for only fourteen weeks, laboring incessantly just to keep moving. Hardships had caused four of their original party to break away, and for all they knew the Howlands and Dunn, unlike Frank Goodman, would not survive. In that case some of the information they had worked so hard to gather for the Major would also be lost, for on striking overland the defectors had carried not only the duplicate set of notes Powell had entrusted to them but, by mistake, some of the originals as well.

A poor showing, in truth. Now what?—except to let inertia drag them on down the Colorado to its end. At least it would be something to talk about when at last they came to rest wherever the winds of chance landed them.

Powell saw things differently. The trip had fired his imagination. Like Joseph Ives before him, he had glimpsed in the stratified walls of the canyons the awesome record of a billion years of earth-building. Like John Strong Newberry, he had sensed the denuding power of water on that layered land. He felt in his bones the dynamics of time. The entire Colorado Plateau, he believed, was still being slowly uplifted, as indeed it is, though men still do not agree about the causes. As it rose, the river and its tributaries kept gnawing deeper into its heart, creating a unique landscape that demanded strenuous adaptations from all living things.

How could settlers—more and more of them were pouring west now that the Civil War was over—best fit themselves and their social institutions to those strange conditions? Was not the federal government the best sponsor of the expensive search for answers?

With such thoughts a ferment in him, Powell had no interest in navigating the final six hundred miles of the river. He gave Sumner, Bradley, Hawkins, and Hall what little money he could spare—it amounted to less than the twenty-five dollars a month he had promised them—and added the two hard-used boats, which might have some resale value downstream. In one of those boats Hawkins and Hall went all the way to salt water. Sumner and Bradley dropped out sooner, at Fort Yuma, where Sumner wrote in his journal: "After two years [dating from the summer of 1867] I find myself penniless and disgusted with the whole thing, sitting under a Mesquite bush in the sand."

Almon H. Thompson, J.W. Powell's brother-in-law, in Utah

11

Measuring the Land

On September 7, 1869, the new telegraph line between St. George and Salt Lake City carried a report of the killing of three white men, as yet unidentified, who had recently emerged from the canyon. They were said to have come upon a Shivwits woman gathering seeds, and to have raped and then murdered her. Men from her band had killed them in retaliation.

According to the *Deseret News*, any number of prospectors had been roaming the breaks of the canyon at the time. So Powell clung to the hope that Dunn and the Howlands were still alive—until word came that articles identifying the trio had been found among the Shivwits. Even then the Major refused to believe that they had committed the outrage.[1] And the nation took him at his word.

Powell had become a public figure, and he made the most of it. He consented to interviews and dashed off an article about the trip for the second edition of William Bell's popular *New Tracks in North America*. He lectured widely during the winter, and on July 12, 1870, Congress responded to his lobbying by voting him ten thousand dollars for a "Geographical and Topo-

graphical Survey of the Colorado River of the West" under the general
direction of the Smithsonian Institution.

Already he had shaped new plans.[2] Personnel first. He invited Jack
Sumner by letter to join the second run and take charge of whatever boatmen
were hired. As astronomer, head geographer, and second-in-command he
chose his own brother-in-law, Almon Thompson. A school superintendent
who had been with Powell in Colorado in 1867 and 1868 as an entomologist,
Thompson had had no training as a topographer, but he was good-natured
and resourceful. Powell told him to start learning his new trade by compiling,
as a dry run for the future, a base map of the river from such records of the
first expedition as had survived.

Instead of trying to stay on the river for a solid ten months, as he had
hoped to do the first time, Powell now planned to divide the venture into
segments. The expedition would leave Green River, Wyoming, about May
1, 1871, and spend the summer and fall floating to the mouth of the Paria River
in Arizona, climbing the canyon walls at frequent intervals in order to survey
the bordering countryside. In October or November a pack train would meet
the party near the mouth of the Paria and take it to winter quarters somewhere
in southern Utah. From that base the group would map the plateaus along the
northern fringes of the Grand Canyon. Then, on about May 1, 1872, the men
would descend again to the river to spend eight weeks studying its majestic
gorge.

Before the expedition began, Powell would have to visit the Shivwits
Indians, not only to learn the facts about the killing of Dunn and the Howland
brothers but also to placate the tribe so that small parties of his surveyors could
move unmolested through their country. To hold off the threat of starvation
in the canyons, he would have to cache supplies along the way. That in turn
entailed finding trails through the sandstone wilderness into the gorges, a
chore he hoped to turn over to Mormon scouts—if he could find suitable ones.

The two men he picked to go with him on his preliminary reconnaissance into Utah were practically next-door neighbors. One was Frank Bishop,
a twenty-eight-year-old veteran of the Civil War who had been a pupil of
Powell's at Illinois Wesleyan and who had gone to Colorado with him in the
summer of 1867. The other was Walter Graves, a seventeen-year-old freshman
at Illinois Wesleyan and a cousin of the slain Howland brothers. The three
reached Salt Lake City on August 19. Seeking advice about a guide to the
southern canyons, Powell called on Brigham Young, who recommended
Jacob Hamblin, adding that he and a dozen Mormon dignitaries were about
to ride south to consecrate the reoccupied town of Kanab, Utah. He suggested
that Powell's group come along.

Frank Bishop and Walter Graves did not accompany the caravan on the
last part of its trip. The main party took a shortcut through the High Plateaus

to Kanab. Bishop and Graves followed the older route via Ash Creek and the Arizona Strip. Powell wanted them to pick up supplies in Dixie and also evaluate the longer approach to the canyon country.

In Parowan the travelers picked up thirty-eight more persons, including Jacob Hamblin. Powell promptly hired him as guide at fifty dollars a month. Another addition to the party was John D. Lee, one of the leaders of the notorious Mountain Meadows massacre. He had been indicted for his part in the thirteen-year-old affair, along with several others, none of whom had so far been arrested because the Mormons refused to cooperate with federal officials. But the Church was accused of obstructing justice, and many Saints were openly resentful of all Mormondom's being blackened by the wrongs of a few. Young had already suggested that Lee sell his holdings in New Harmony and drop out of sight in some mountain fastness. During the trip, the suggestion would turn into an order.[3]

At Kanab, sixty or so whites and one hundred or more Paiute allies welcomed Young on September 10. Powell was fascinated. Through their church the Mormons had devised the call as a new way of promoting settlement. By reconciling individual acquisitiveness with the communal need for sharing resources, they had worked out new methods of distributing land and water. In time, when Powell, too, would be advocating changes in some of America's social and legal institutions, he would base much of what he proposed on ideas gained in Kanab and similar Mormon towns.[4]

Powell decided to make the town his headquarters while surveying north of the Grand Canyon during the winter of 1871–72, and after a two-day stay, the entire group continued south and west to Pipe Spring, where Young proposed to base a ranch for grazing cattle the Church had received as tithings. There Frank Bishop and Walter Graves appeared with a pack train, and Powell bade farewell to Brigham Young and John D. Lee.

From Pipe Spring Powell's group, guided by Hamblin and two Kaibab Paiutes, rode down among the shaggy mountains that dominated the southern section of the Uinkaret Plateau—mountains whose massive discharges of lava into the Grand Canyon had amazed Powell the year before. There they met and calmed several timid Indians of the Uinkaret band of Southern Paiutes, and prevailed on some of them to carry a message to the Shivwits band farther west. Would the Shivwits meet in council with Jacob Hamblin and other whites beside the water holes where the party was currently camped? There would be gifts and important talk about the future.

Powell decided that while awaiting the Indians he would hunt for a trail down which supplies could be carried into the gorge. The Uinkarets said there was a way. Actually, there are several; all we can tell from Powell's romanticized account of the adventure is that the party's wizened, bleary-eyed Uinkaret guide did not choose to show them the easiest. Only with great difficulty were they able to work their horses through jumbles of lava to the broad terrace, now called the Esplanade, that lies atop the deep red Supai escarpment in the western reaches of the Grand Canyon.

A little below the Esplanade's rim the trail petered out among "shelves and steps and piles of broken rock." While Powell and some of the men led the animals back to safety, Bishop worked his way on foot down among huge boulders into a knife-thin side gulch. Despite the lateness of the day, Powell and the rest followed as soon as the horses were provided for. When dark caught them, they lit torches of piñon pine and grass tufts, "one clinging to another's hand until we can get footing, then supporting the other on his shoulders; thus we make our passage." Bishop lit a bonfire of driftwood as a guide, strapped a huge torch to his shoulders, and climbed to meet them. "He looks like a fiend, waving his brands and lighting the fires of hell." But he got them down, and they spent the night where Powell listened again to the roar of desert water.[5] His river. Perhaps Indians could pack down supplies on which his surveyors could subsist while examining this stretch of the canyon, one hundred river miles above its ending at Grand Wash Cliffs. But unless there were better supply routes on the long upper reaches of the stream, he would be in trouble.

Back they climbed for the Indian council. Gradually the circumstances of the killings emerged. The slain woman had been a Hualapai, not a Shivwits; her violators had been prospectors; the outrage had taken place on the far side of the river.

Then why had the Indians killed Powell's men?

A mistake. Shortly after the death of the woman, a group from her band had chanced to cross the Colorado on a raft to visit their Shivwits friends. On hearing of three whites in the area, they had urged the Shivwits to kill them all, since undoubtedly they, too, were prospectors and "if they find mines in [Shivwits] country it would bring great evil among them. The three men were then followed and killed when asleep." A very bad mistake. But no such thing would happen again.

Powell and, presumably, young Graves accepted the story, though not everyone since then has done so.[6] After all, what the Major wanted most was assurance that others of his men would not be attacked in similar fashion. On gaining that promise he let the matter drop and shifted his attention to what had become a matter of consuming interest: the adaptation of the Indians to the desert. He dug deeply for as many details about Shivwits myths and customs as time allowed. Meanwhile his mind raced ahead. What could he learn by comparing what he was gathering from them with the culture of a more advanced tribe, the Hopis? Would Hamblin take him across the river?

Hamblin would. The Mormon scout suggested further that after visiting the Hopis they continue to Fort Defiance, where the Navajos would be assembling early in November to collect their annuities. Aided by Powell as a representative of the United States Government and by the Navajos' agent, perhaps he could at last persuade the Indians to end their raids on the Mormons in return for promises of beneficial trade.

Powell jumped at the suggestion. Two new tribes to study. Peace for the Mormons—and for his own men. During the ride to Fort Defiance, moreover, he could discuss with Hamblin the best means of taking supplies to various spots farther up the river.

The trip to Fort Defiance began September 24. Bishop and Graves again had charge of the pack train, some of its animals loaded with trade goods for the Indians and some with lumber so that the travelers could build a boat for crossing the Colorado at the mouth of the Paria. As the mules followed the dim trail to the ferry site, Powell and Hamblin rode south through the firs and aspens of the Kaibab Plateau to gain another view of the Grand Canyon. Tourists fortunate enough to have followed the high-centered dirt road to Point Sublime on the North Rim can appreciate what hit them. Even John Wesley Powell ran out of words: "The landscape is too vast, too complex, too grand for verbal description."

The whole trip produced one exhilaration after another. He spent two wondrous weeks among the Hopi. At Fort Defiance, speaking eloquently to the leading men of a gathering of six thousand Navajos, he helped Hamblin establish a tentative peace. And he arranged with the Mormon scout to take pack-train loads of supplies for the river runners of 1871 to the banks of the Colorado at two different points: the mouth of the Dirty Devil River, which no white had yet visited by land, and the Crossing of the Fathers—or, as the Mormons called it, Ute Crossing.

On Powell's return east from the reconnaissance, Emma became pregnant after nine years of marriage. This meant that if Powell stuck to his plans, the child would be born while the father was deep in the canyons. Since of course he meant to stick to his plans, he proposed finding lodgings for Emma and her sister-in-law, Nellie Powell Thompson, in Salt Lake City. After the birth the two women and the child would join the surveyors at their winter quarters in Kanab.

Meanwhile he assembled his crew. At the last minute Jack Sumner was snowed in at Hot Sulphur Springs at the headwaters of the Grand and could not join the party. This meant that every member except Powell was as ignorant of boating as the first group had been. The technical work would be headed by Powell, Thompson, and Stephen Vandiveer Jones, schoolteacher and relative of Thompson's from Wisconsin. Their assistants were Frank Bishop and John F. Steward, an amateur geologist with whom Powell had whiled away time during the siege of Vicksburg by collecting fossils.

In order to make the canyons more believable than words alone could do, Powell hired a professional photographer, E. O. Beaman. He came cheap. According to his agreement with Powell, along the way Beaman would take stereopticon views, which were popular at the time; Powell would sell them; and they would split the income. This was Beaman's only recompense. He would have twenty-one-year-old Clem Powell, an orphaned cousin of the Major's, as an assistant in the canyons. A seventeen-year-old self-taught artist, Frederick Dellenbaugh, was to sketch a running profile of the river's left wall. The laborers were Frank Richardson, a friend of the Powell family, and Jack Hillers, a teamster Powell hired in Salt Lake City to replace Jack Sumner. The cook was Andy Hatton, who had served under Powell as an enlisted man. Inasmuch as Powell by then could have had his pick of top-flight scientists from many disciplines, it was a strange crew indeed.

The expedition had three boats, all manufactured in Chicago and tested on Lake Michigan. The "flagship" was again named *Emma Dean*. The second boat was called the *Nellie Powell*, the third *Cañonita*. All were slightly larger than the biggest of the 1869 boats and correspondingly heavier. Each contained an extra watertight compartment amidships between the cockpits of the two oarsmen. A third man worked each craft's big sweep oar. Powell bolted a wooden armchair onto the top of the *Emma Dean*'s middle compartment. His notion was that while enthroned there he could peer ahead, read the water, and give signals to the boats following. According to later critics, the arrangement must have increased the *Dean*'s tendency to roll, but Powell insisted that it worked well.

To relieve the tedium of long stretches of sluggish water, and also to build a stronger feeling of camaraderie than had prevailed on the first trip, Powell sometimes lashed the boats together and let them drift quietly along while, seated in his armchair, he read aloud from poets he enjoyed—Scott, Tennyson, Whittier, Longfellow. Music helped. Richardson had a flute and Dellenbaugh a harmonica, which Steward frequently borrowed. Hillers proved to have a rollicking Irish tenor and led the singing of familiar tunes.

Better meals and happier evenings did not mean that the work was less trying. The river was lower, exposing many rocks. The men were everlastingly in the water wrestling the boats among and over boulders, lining them, portaging the cargo, and, at the worst of the rapids, lifting the craft from the water and boosting them along crudely prepared skidways.

And then there was Beaman's camera, "the terror of the party," as Dellenbaugh remembered it. Before the photographer resigned early in 1872, hoping to beat Powell to publication, he took approximately 350 views. Again and again the outfit had to be manhandled into position, sometimes up cliffs a thousand feet high—the big camera in its fortified box, the glass plates, the chemicals, the tent that served as a darkroom. At the desired location, the tent was set up, the plates prepared on the spot, exposed wet, and immediately developed and washed before being stowed carefully in a special container for transportation back down the precipices or through the side chasms to the boats.

As had happened in '69, the river quickly warned them of its power. While passing through one of the first of the gorges, Thompson misread Powell's signals. The *Nell* smashed against the left wall and turned turtle. Luckily Bishop was able to claw ashore with the boat's bowline and snub it to a tree. That was enough for Frank Richardson. Like Goodman in '69, he wanted no more such dunkings. In Brown's Park he quit and, taking his flute with him, rode back to the railroad with cattlemen who had wintered their herd in the Park.

The rest moved slowly on through Lodore, struggling with the rapids, climbing the slopes, taking observations, and, on reaching the Yampa, dragging the *Emma Dean* twelve miles up between the tributary's pale, curving walls. Voluminous records accumulated, yet Powell grew restless. A day or two below the junction of the Green and Yampa, he suddenly ordered his crew—Bishop, Hillers, Jones—to spurt eighty-five miles ahead to the Duchesne, leaving Thompson in charge of further observations. His intent was to walk with his crewmen up the Uinta Valley to the Ute Indian Agency. There he hoped to find a wagonload of supplies, and letters from Emma telling him how things were.

The message that awaited him said that she was sick. Beside himself with worry, Powell decided to ride to Salt Lake City to see her. Meanwhile, his boatmen were to take the supplies to the river, along with saddle animals so that Thompson and Beamen could utilize the wait to advantage by riding to the Agency and collecting Indian materials.

In Salt Lake City he found Emma well but received a new jolt from Jacob Hamblin, who was in town conferring with Brigham Young.[7] The scout had failed twice in his efforts to carry supplies through the slickrock wastes to the mouth of the Dirty Devil. He could not try again because he had been appointed United States Indian Agent for southern Utah and faced a full schedule. But Powell needn't worry. Hamblin had hired Captain Pardon Dodds, a former Union Army officer and a good desert traveler, to take the vital materials from Kanab to the Dirty Devil rendezvous.

As Powell rode back to the Uinta Reservation he did worry. How could he be sure Dodds would succeed where a man like Old Jacob had failed? Shouldn't he, John Wesley Powell, be the one to make the crucial effort?

And if he failed? Thompson asked.

Then he would work his way back out of the rock jungles with the supplies and meet the others at John Gunnison's old crossing of the Green River just south of the tan cliffs marking the southern border of Tavaputs Plateau.

When could the boatmen expect him?

Powell pulled a date out of the air: September 3 (it was then July 26). If he did not show up at Gunnison's crossing by then, it would mean that he had reached the Dirty Devil and that his brother-in-law should take the boats on through Cataract Canyon to join him, surveying as he went.

In his diary Thompson boiled over. From the mouth of the Duchesne to the Gunnison Crossing was 115 miles. Thirty-nine days for that? The dawdling would be bad for morale. And if Powell did not appear, killed perhaps, they would have to hit the terrifying Cataract without his guidance, unsure whether supplies would be waiting when they finally emerged—if they ever did. Obviously Thompson was afraid of the responsibility. He may also have been resentful. His wife was in Salt Lake City, too. But was Powell giving him any chance to see her?

The other diaries suggest that, in spite of plagues of mosquitoes, the crew did not mind dawdling as much as Thompson had predicted. They took exploratory hikes, hunted, gossiped with the Indians who drifted by, made moccasins to supplement their deteriorating shoes, worked on their maps, cut a chessboard out of a rubber poncho, and on August 5 started a leisurely run through Desolation Canyon. Some good climbs in there, some rugged white water. There were worse ways to pass a summer month.

Powell meanwhile visited Salt Lake City again. Afterwards (the records are unclear) he may have tried to ride through the San Rafael Swell to the Dirty Devil. In any event, he swung back across the mountains to the hamlet of Manti, 150 miles south of Salt Lake City.[8] There he met two men who had come in search of him—Old Jacob's younger brother Fred Hamblin and son Lyman. They told him that although Dodds had reached the head of the Dirty Devil, he had not been able to force a way down it to the river. Thus the Gunnison Crossing became the only point above Ute Ford where supplies could be brought to the boatmen.

Though Powell knew how long the stretch was, he grew strangely penurious about food—or else adequate supplies were not available at Manti. He bought three hundred pounds of flour, twenty of sugar, and some jerky. To that he added new clothing and shoes for the crew. Loading the purchases and the men's mail on four pack horses, he and Fred and Lyman Hamblin struck east along the Old Spanish Trail to the Gunnison Crossing.

They joined the waiting boatmen on August 29. Silently the nine rivermen matched the sustenance their leader had provided with the weeks that lay ahead. They had eaten freely—too freely—while dawdling, and now they found themselves, like the men of '69, facing famine. Well, there was nothing for it now but to go ahead to the Ute Ford, or, as Powell persistently called the place, *El Vado de Los Padres,* the Crossing of the Fathers. The Hamblins were to tell Pardon Dodds to meet them there on September 25 with fresh supplies, which by then they would badly need.

Under a blazing sun they curved along the swooping meanders of Stillwater and Labyrinth canyons, skirted bright-green riverine oases and soft sand beaches, heard their voices return to them from the grand alcoves in the red walls. On September 7, and again on the eighth, cloudbursts sluiced the land. Floods of syrupy mud studded with boulders and driftwood roared down the side gulches. Higher up, cascades rushed across the naked earth to leap over the gorge's purplish rim. Soon hundreds of fountains were plunging from ledge to ledge, disintegrating on impact to fill the canyon with vapor.

After a three-day pause at the junction of the Grand and Green, Powell at last grew alarmed about the rate at which food was dwindling. Beaman, moreover, was running out of photographic supplies. No more dawdling—but how was it possible to hurry through Cataract? The rocks there, Bishop later wrote in a letter to the Bloomington *Pantagraph*, "are huge masses of ragged, angular limestone that lash the immense volume of water . . . into a perfect fury, making the very walls tremble." Some days they succeeded in carrying the boats ahead no more than a half mile or so, "and then it would be *stop for repairs.*" Once the *Nellie* tore loose from restraining hands and bucked ahead among the slabs. "Visions of wrecks and short rations danced before us," wrote Clem Powell, but an eddy caught the boat and held it, spinning slowly, long enough for two men to swim out and retrieve it. And the men were as hard used as the boats. " 'Tis a wonder some of us has not had a leg or two broken. All of us wear horrible scars from our knees downward."

The solution, Powell decided, was to use up the remaining film without restraint, then cache the *Cañonita* at the mouth of the Dirty Devil and push ahead as fast as possible with the remaining boats. The following spring an overland party would retrieve the *Cañonita* and take it to the mouth of the Paria, completing the photographic record of Glen Canyon along the way. At the Paria it would rejoin the rest of the fleet for the concluding run through the Grand.

The abandonment overcrowded the remaining boats, but at least there was one less awkward burden to boost over the sandbars of Glen Canyon. Powell, though, could always be tempted to pile on more tasks. As they neared the mouth of the San Juan, he kept staring ahead at the erosion-lacerated sides of a 10,300-foot laccolith he called Mt. Seneca Howland. (The name didn't stick; today the handsome dome is known as Navajo Mountain.) A passion to climb it seized him, but the men protested, as their predecessors had done when he had paused too long with his cliff-scaling at the mouth of the Little Colorado. Couldn't he see their hunger, their exhaustion? Reluctantly he gave in.

It was well that they did not stop. Though the rendezvous with Pardon Dodds at *El Vado* had been set for September 25, the boat party did not arrive until October 6, just as Dodds and his two helpers were on the point of leaving.

Thankfully they feasted on fresh food and devoured stacks of mail. Powell exulted over his letters. At 10:00 P.M. on September 8, he learned, Emma had borne their first child, a girl, and mother and daughter were both well—which was more than could be said of some of his crew. Steward was so drained that he could scarcely rise from the bed of soft willow branches that had been prepared for him. Jones hobbled on an injured leg and could not sleep because of old war wounds. The cook, Andy Hattan, was drawn and pale from the sting of a scorpion. Yet there was still work to do—notes and maps to complete, fossils and rock specimens to arrange so that Dodds could pack them out.

There was also a hint of the future to wonder about. The men with Dodds—their names were George Riley and John Bonnemort—were prospectors and had volunteered to help Dodds so that on reaching the river they could test its gravels for placer gold. Straight out of the Rockies most of that water came, and it stood to reason, they argued, that metal washing down from the auriferous peaks would lodge in the bars. Powell's mountaineers of '69 had been motivated by that same logic, but their desperate run had allowed scant time for prospecting. Riley and Bonnemort, however, had spent nearly two weeks poking around the nearby bars. They had found enough dustings of gold to excite not only themselves but Dodds, who declared that he wanted to spend the next year examining as many parts of the stream as he could reach.

Meanwhile the others hurried through their paperwork. They were settling down to write loved ones when Powell announced that he was leaving at once for Salt Lake City. Tempers flared. He could at least wait until they had finished their letters, couldn't he? Thompson stepped in, Powell backed down with grace, and the group became a unit once more.

The Major then laid out the order of events. In Salt Lake City he would gather equipment for a winter's surveying and bring it to Kanab. Meanwhile the boaters were to drift thirty-five miles to the mouth of the Paria, where they were to cache the boats and river materials for use in the Grand Canyon the following summer. In due time a pack train would come to them with food, horses, and directions for the future. And off the Major rode to see his daughter. With him went Hillers, Dodds, and the two prospectors.

Not until December 7 did the entire group reassemble at winter headquarters, a few miles outside Kanab. Emma Powell was there, her three-month-old daughter nestled in a clothes-basket. So was Nellie Thompson, accompanied by a small dog named Fuzz. The prospectors, George Riley and John Bonnemort, were hired as assistants. Housing consisted of stove-warmed tents. Whenever the weather allowed, Andy Hattan cooked outside and served the meals on canvas spread on the ground. "Homelike," Dellenbaugh said. He liked the camp, the nearby town, so orderly and clean, and the beginnings of a new kind of work. From it would grow, though none could have known it at the time, the present United States Geological Survey.

On the flats south of Kanab they measured, with carefully prepared rods placed on trestles, a north–south base line nine miles long. By means of astronomical observations they determined where each end of the line lay. Triangulation then began. Tall poles bearing red-and-white flags were erected on a number of high promontories, forty miles or so from the base line. Telescopic sightings on each flag revealed two angles of a triangle, of which the flag was one point. By trigonometric calculations the topographers next determined the length of the other two sides of the triangle. Once those lengths were known, each could be used as a new base line for new sets of triangles—triangles within triangles within triangles if the terrain were so complex that many observations were needed.

Reaching appropriate flag points, building stone pyramids, and setting up poles was trying work. Off the crews went on horseback, many times through deep snow. Because their pack animals were loaded with axes, shovels, and scientific instruments, they had little room for food and tents. They cooked their own spartan meals under overhanging rocks or arching tree branches; they drank quantities of strong coffee; they wasted hours each day searching for strayed animals and also, when there was no snow to melt, for water holes. They scaled many cliffs on foot, and took many sightings from wind-buffeted perches high in pine trees.

At all key points they established their elevation above sea level by a series of barometric readings. Distances and altitudes having been determined, contour lines between points were judged visually. Field data and drawings were then transferred to the map that was being prepared inside a large tent located within the town of Kanab.[9] Measurements taken earlier along the river would be coordinated with those charts, and in that manner a large block of hitherto largely unknown land would be tied with scientific exactness to the rest of the United States.

Powell did not like field work of that sort. He turned his attention instead to locating a supply point for the concluding run through the Grand Canyon. In late December he, with Pardon Dodds, the prospector George Riley, and one of the sons of the Bishop of Kanab, managed to push horses through the boulder falls in narrow Kanab Canyon to the river. Serendipitously prospector Riley found traces of gold on a gravel bar there. After the party had returned with great difficulty to Kanab in early January, 1872, word of the discovery was sent out over the new telegraph line, along with a statement that the metal was as fine as dust and hard to recover. Ignoring the warning, miners swarmed in, floundered down the side canyon, found nothing profitable, and came back cursing the country instead of themselves. Behind them they left a rough trail they had scratched out for their pack stock, an improvement Powell's suppliers would find welcome when the time came.

Normal attrition took its toll of surveyors. Bishop and Steward resigned and were replaced with local residents. More serious was the defection of the photographer. Deciding to strike out on his own rather than split revenues any longer with Powell, Beaman made preparations to cross the river and photograph the Hopis before the Major could get there with another picture-maker.

For a time Beaman's erstwhile assistant, Clem Powell, tried to fill the photographer's shoes, but he could not get the hang of things. Though Clem and Thompson were sure the failure was the result of Beaman's maliciously doctoring the expedition's chemicals before departing, Powell was inclined to blame his cousin's ineptitude.[10] In Salt Lake City, on his way to Washington to woo Congress into extending his survey's appropriation (Emma and the baby went with him), he hired a frail twenty-three-year-old cameramen, James Fennemore, to take over. Clem, intensely mortified, became a mere roustabout. But he still kept the sprightliest journal of anyone in the group.

As the snow melted off the high country late in May, Thompson, leaving his wife in a tent in a corner of Hamblin's yard, started with his crew north and northeast across the rainbow-hued lands below the High Plateaus to retrieve the *Cañonita*. The men triangulated roughly and rapidly as they went, and thus were prepared to locate on their map an entire drainage system that had never before been properly recognized. Thompson named it Escalante. An embarrassed Pardon Dodds realized then why he had failed to reach the mouth of the Dirty Devil with supplies the year before. Lost in the red-and-white wastelands of the Escalante, he had been nowhere near his goal.

To avoid the Escalante's impassable upper canyons, Thompson's group toiled along narrow hogbacks to the lovely aspen forests on Boulder Mountain and then, zigzagging lower again, worked out a way through an extraordinary rock cock's-comb that Thompson called—for the pools of moisture that collected in its potholes—Waterpocket Fold. After climbing the principal peaks of the hitherto unscaled Henry Mountains (Thompson named one Mt. Ellen for his wife), they found a tributary gulch that took them to the Dirty Devil. At its mouth lay the *Cañonita*, just as they had left it.

Hillers, Dellenbaugh, Will Johnson of Kanab, and the new photographer, James Fennemore, were delegated to take the boat to the mouth of the Paria while the others returned overland, adding more triangles to their records as they went. Because the river, by Dellenbaugh's estimate, was fifteen feet higher than it had been the year before, they were able to speed through Glen Canyon without trouble, reaching their destination on July 13. There they saw what they had heard about earlier. Near the tall red cliffs a few hundred yards back from the main river, on a piece of flat ground partially embraced by a broad curve of the Paria, was a cabin that had been built by John D. Lee. A fugitive now, he shared the desolate spot with his seventeenth wife, Emma Batchelder. They had been married in 1858, when he was forty-five and she twenty-one.

Obedient to orders, after separating from Powell and Brigham Young in September, 1870, Lee had sold his New Harmony real estate, loaded his remaining possessions into wagons, and, with some of his grown sons and sons-in-law driving his cattle, had moved into the timbered hills back of Kanab. He had begun running a sawmill there when he received word that he had been excommunicated by the Church without a hearing. Federal officers were looking for him because of his polygamy as well as his alleged involvement in the Mountain Meadows Massacre. On November 16, 1871, Jacob Hamblin had told him that the Church's plans for pushing colonies south into Arizona were still alive and that someday soon a camping place and ferry would be needed where the Paria flowed into the Colorado. If Lee would pioneer the area, Hamblin would do some hauling for him and contribute seed and fruit trees in exchange for a share in the ranch. "So if you have a woman who has faith enough to go with you, take her along and some cows."[11]

Lee had decided to take not one but three wives—Caroline, Rachel, and Emma. They and their children were to drive wagons to the new homestead by way of the Kaibab Plateau. The route wouldn't do for his cattle, however —at least Hamblin said it wouldn't—because of shortages of grass and water in House Rock Valley. Accordingly he determined to tackle Paria Creek instead. As helpers he enlisted two men and his small son Ralph.

They started December 3 with fifty-seven head. To anyone who has backpacked through the slit the stream has hewn through Paria Plateau (today's Paria Primitive Area) the tale strains credulity. The fifty-mile trip (thirty miles of it in the canyon) took eight days, in Lee's words, "through brush, water, ice & quicksand & some time passing through narrow chasms with perpendicular Bluffs on both sides, some three thousand feet high & without seeing the sun for forty-eight hours, & every day some of our animals down & had to shoot one cow & leave her there, that we could not get out, & I My Self was under water, Mud & Ice every day."[12] They ran out of provisions, and for four days their only food was strips of beef they had the foresight to slash off an exposed flank of the mired cow they shot.

No wives were waiting at the junction of the streams. Anxiously Lee

hurried back along the rough way he supposed their wagons would have had
to take. In time he learned that the heavily loaded vehicles had stalled and the
occupants had scattered. Caroline, pregnant, had made her way to Kanab to
await the birth of her child. Emma had rejoined friends at the old sawmill site.
Rachel, the oldest (Lee had married her in 1845, when she was twenty and he
thirty-three) had kept struggling ahead and with several of her children had
reached the mouth of the Paria after missing her husband in the gulches along
the way. They were snugly ensconced in tents when Lee showed up after
desperate toil of his own with Emma and three groaning wagons.

Quickly realizing that he could control most of House Rock Valley by
establishing squatter's rights to its few waterholes, Lee settled Rachel and her
children twenty miles away from the Paria, at a spring called Jacob's Pool near
the blazing Vermilion Cliffs, in an octagonal hutch made of interlaced willow
withes plastered with mud. Their duty: the care of forty or so cows. Emma
stayed at the Paria. Her domain was a one-room log cabin with a brush-roofed
verandah along one side. She broke the sun's glare by hanging a blanket from
the verandah's outer edge, and on days when the thermometer reached 105
degrees or more she found relief by sprinkling water on the earthen floor. She
called the place Lonely Dell. Hamblin did not provide as much help as he had
promised. So Lee, who would be sixty on September 6, 1872, was on the road
much of the time, bringing in necessities from Kanab, plowing, planting,
ditching, fencing, and trying to keep two women content on primitive ran-
ches twenty miles apart.

As usual, Powell was late, and the four men who had brought the *Cañonita*
to Lonely Dell found time heavy on their hands. They spruced up the two
boats they would use—the *Nellie Powell*, they discovered, was no longer
serviceable—read, wrote, played cards, and helped Lee work on his dam and
hoe his garden. In return Emma nursed Fennemore, who had fallen ill during
the trip, until he was able to ride out to Kanab, at which point Hillers, who
had been hanging around the photographic equipment since joining the
expedition, became the cameraman—a good one. They feasted with the Lees
on the Mormons' principal holiday, July 24, and listened to Lee's account of
the massacre. He insisted that he had done all he could to stop the bloodlet-
ting, but added that nothing would ever make him point a finger at those who
were guilty.

On August 17 the last part of the run down the canyon began. Powell
climbed into his armchair on the *Emma Dean;* Jones, Hillers, and Dellenbaugh were his crew. Thompson, Andy Hattan, and Clem Powell handled
the *Cañonita.* Water was high for that season of the year (though it never
approached the flood stages of spring), and from the beginning they had
trouble with the headlong velocities.

Cold rains beginning August 28 and lasting for five days intensified their difficulties. Cooking meals with soggy wood under a tarpaulin was almost impossible, sleeping on granite in wet blankets a torment. The silt-thick river kept rising; whirlpools spun the boats helplessly; the need for repairs was constant. At one camp, trapped in a cove by rising water, they had to climb to a high shelf and hoist the boats up with ropes until they were hanging against the cliff like dead chickens in a market.

The closest call came when the Major's chair unbalanced the *Dean* (so Dellenbaugh thought), and the boat turned over. An oar smashed Hillers painfully and "down, down I went," he told his diary later. Lungs bursting, "the Major and I came up in the same boile." Though only the Major wore a life preserver, both men reached the boat, to which Dellenbaugh and Jones were clinging. All squirmed up onto its bottom, reached over, grabbed the opposite rim, and, rearing back, pulled the craft right side up.[13]

Swampings, bruisings, more narrow escapes, exhausting portages, halts for repairs: they spent twenty-two days going the 144 miles from Lonely Dell to the mouth of Kanab Canyon. Three men were waiting there with supplies —and with two saddle horses, sent by Mrs. Thompson in case her husband and the Major decided to leave the river there.

The horses may have turned the tables. Because of the unexpected turmoil of the river, the surveyors had collected relatively little data and could not anticipate doing more in the granite inner gorges that lay ahead. Making their measurements from the rims, Thompson argued, would be more productive. Besides, the packers had brought word from Jacob Hamblin that Indians along both sides of the river below them had been aroused by prospectors invading their lands; a party forced to abandon its boats and strike across country might become victims of their anger.

Or perhaps the men were afraid of the kind of water they were meeting. Anyway, after discussing alternatives throughout Sunday, September 8, Thompson and Powell called the trip off.

"Everybody," Hillers wrote in his journal, "felt like praising God."

Powell was more reticent. When he finally put together an account of his adventures for popular consumption, he confined his descriptions of river-running to the pioneer dash of 1869, its drama heightened by the deaths of the men who had forsaken him on the threshold of success. He tacked onto that tale material he had prepared for *Scribner's Magazine* about visiting the Uinkaret and Shivwits Paiutes in order to learn the truth about the slaying. Into that travelogue he tucked an account of a daring foot trip he had made in 1872 (not 1870, as he said) with one Mormon and one Indian through fantastic Parunaweap Canyon on the East Fork of the Virgin River. He then closed the book with a description of his journey to the Hopis and Navajos.

It was good copy, and he did not reduce suspense by including redundant or anticlimactic digressions about the supply-plagued 1871 run from Green River, Wyoming, to the mouth of the Paria or about the aborted 1872 attack on the Grand Canyon. The omissions, of course, shrank the contributions of those crewmen to nothingness. And once he had confined himself to the years 1869–70 he was obliged to misdate the Parunaweap saga in order to include it.

But is a flair for dramatic wholeness the entire reason for the manipulations? I suspect not. Powell put together his belated account at a time when civilian scientists in the employ of the Department of the Interior were warring among themselves and with the Army for control of the Western surveys. A principal Army opponent was the ambitious Lieutenant George M. Wheeler, in charge of the War Department's Geographical Surveys West of the One Hundredth Meridian.

Wheeler had first invaded Powell's field in 1871 by using Mojave Indian laborers to drag three boats up the rough water of the lower Grand Canyon as far as Diamond Creek. During subsequent years he had prowled around the Virgin River drainage, and in 1873, under Almon Thompson's nose, he had even named some of the western tributaries of Glen Canyon. Later on, Powell realized, as feuds over the surveys heated up, the matter of timing might be important. And so he nailed down priorities by emphasizing his 1869 run and shifting the date of the Parunaweap adventure from 1872 to 1870. *He* was the first to evaluate the canyons, the plateaus, the Indians.

By the end of 1872, the year he moved his home from Illinois to Washington, his position was secure and his survey was developing into a highly competent operation. Thompson became a first-class geographer, Hillers a photographer unsurpassed in the western field. New men lured away from other surveys lent additional luster: the geologists Grove Gilbert and Clarence Dutton, the artists Thomas Moran and William Henry Holmes.

Powell would soon be director both of the United States Geological Survey, into which all other federal surveys were finally consolidated, and of the Bureau of Ethnology as well. Meanwhile he was insisting, in his 1878 *Report on the Lands of the Arid Regions of the United States, with a More Detailed Account of the Lands of Utah*, that the country should seek innovations in its policies governing settlement. Before the land was opened to indiscriminate homesteading, he said, it should be classified according to its primary values —irrigable cropland, pasturage, timber, coal, or whatever. Ownership patterns should be determined by the nature of the terrain, not by the arbitrary gridwork patterns that prevailed. No one should be permitted to monopolize water. Nine or more farmers should be allowed to band together, form irrigation districts, acquire joint title to the land, and develop its water communally. Grazing homesteads should embrace 2,560 acres, twenty of those acres irrigable for raising supplementary feed, so that a single family could run enough cattle on the sparse grasses of the plateaus to support itself.[14]

He was too radical. Just as it took time to acquire "the meaning and spirit of that marvelous scenery which characterizes the Plateau Country" (in Dutton's words[15]), so it took time and study to comprehend the economic and social needs of the region. The slow and still-incomplete emergence of a new ethic would have to await the stirrings of a new century.

Aerial view of Lee's Ferry

12

Searching for New Oases

On December 26, 1872, John D. Lee wrote in his diary: "There is doubtless a storm gathering. The Message of President Grant indicates it."[1]

What he meant was the latest of the president's repeated requests that Congress put teeth into the anti-bigamy law it had passed in 1862. There had been increasingly strident criticism of Mormon practices from gentiles living in Utah—the railroad workers, miners, federal officials, and merchants who constituted about 15 percent of the territory's population and were concentrated for the most part along the Wasatch Front between Ogden and Provo. Aside from the matter of polygamy, there was the open flouting of authority typified by the Mountain Meadows Massacre. None of the participants had been brought to trial, although the names of several were known—one of them being John D. Lee.[2]

Meanwhile, most of the arable land in Utah had already been settled. John Wesley Powell had estimated that only 3 percent of the entire area could be cultivated; the actual figure was even lower. If the Mormons were to remain isolated and self-sufficient, as they intended, they would have to expand into whatever oases might still remain—and quickly. Casting about for safe retreats, Church officials took account of a wide belief that bigamists who had been married in Utah could not be tried in Arizona. The latter territory also had a three-year statute of limitations that could probably be used to advantage.³ And the ferry Lee ran at Lonely Dell would serve as a link between the colonists and their Utah homeland.

Accordingly, a call went out late in 1872 for more than one hundred colonists to take possession of the unredeemed lands of the Little Colorado in east-central Arizona. Simultaneously a messenger brought word to John D. Lee, according to his diary, that "The Ferry Boat must be in & the Road Made preparitority for the Emergency."⁴

Wagons loaded with lumber and other materials for boat-building soon followed. Carpenters arrived from St. George, along with several of Lee's children, raising Lonely Dell's population to twenty-two. Saturday, January 11, 1873, saw the launching of a skiff, the *Pahreah,* and a twenty-six-foot ferryboat, the *Colorado.* The workers celebrated with a picnic and what Lee called a "Pleasure Ride" twice across the river and back. To deal with the problem of getting wagons up the south side, twenty-five construction workers appeared on April 3 and spent two weeks scratching out a long, rough, frightening road that led diagonally up the precipices on the far side of the river, in order to reach a gully that opened a way along the rumpled base of Echo Cliffs toward the Little Colorado. As the men were beginning their work, Lee was asked by a Church representative whether he would provide the crew with beef in exchange for produce at Kanab. His reply was that he would furnish the meat as a part of the tithing he owed the Church—or, if tithings were not acceptable from one who had been excommunicated, he would make a contribution.⁵

The meat was accepted as a contribution rather than a tithing. But Lee's point had been made. The Church had forced him to sell his holdings at New Harmony, had excommunicated him, and had finally exiled him here lest his arrest lead to embarrassment; nevertheless he had remained loyal. He worked hard through April and May, ferrying colonists across the river, and was disgusted when many of them, appalled by the bleak lands beyond the river, turned back. He ferried them north, chiding them for their lack of faith and predicting that more replacements would soon be found—as indeed the Church set about doing. But then a gale toppled a huge cottonwood tree into the river. It gathered a mass of floating driftwood with its branches and struck the *Colorado* like a battering ram, tearing it from its moorings, sending the wreckage plunging into Marble Canyon, and leaving the route south impassable to colonists.

Nine days later, on June 25, a report came that troops were marching south with orders to capture Lee and hang him on the spot. In fact the report was false; the troops were on their way to another destination, two hundred miles away. But Lee panicked. Tying a saddle horse behind the skiff *Pahreah*, he rowed across to the south bank and fled into the Arizona desert. Sixty miles of hard riding brought him to the new Hopi settlement of Moenkopi, which the Mormons hoped to utilize as a rest stop on the way to the Little Colorado. Some gentiles had also settled there along with the Indians. Chief Tuba made the frightened Lee welcome, and he found a new hideout at Moenave, eight miles away—a place of green cottonwoods and red bluffs. There his wife Rachel joined him, driving their cattle with her.

Lee settled down to farming, hauling rocks, and building a house. Several gold-hunters passed his place that fall, bound for the San Juan Mountains in the southwestern part of Colorado Territory. Hoping that he would guide them along the rugged trail, they spoke of fertile soil, prime grazing grounds, and good markets at the foot of the Rockies. But he was not to be lured out of Mormon country. Back at Lonely Dell, his wife Emma was pregnant again, with the baby due in late October. Mormon custom allowed no male except the father to attend a childbirth. Lee had asked Jacob Hamblin to take a midwife to the Dell on his next visit. In the end, however, he risked going back himself and found a new baby girl, who had been delivered by Emma and her six-year-old twin daughters. Hamblin, according to Lee's journal, had not only failed to summon a midwife but had mocked Emma for bringing into the world the children of a man whom God and the Church had spurned.[6] The episode caused an irreparable break between the two men.

A new crew of boat-builders now arrived to construct a replacement for the shattered ferryboat, so that colonization of the Little Colorado could be resumed in the spring of 1874. But the project had to be abandoned after gentile outlaws killed three Navajos near Panguitch. A fourth Indian had been wounded but had somehow reached the Colorado at Ute Ford, crossed, and carried word to his tribesmen that the slayers were Mormons. When the Navajos began talking war, Chief Tuba of the Hopis sent a warning to Lee, who had returned to Moenavi with one of his sons. The two of them rode through the night of January 15, 1874, back to Lonely Dell, whence others of Lee's sons transmitted the warning to Kanab.

By then it was known in the southern settlements that no Mormons had been involved, and Jacob Hamblin was sent to make peace with the Navajos. But they stayed angry and forced the abandonment of Moenkopi. Lee himself returned to Lonely Dell, and talked of moving to the San Juan Valley in southeastern Utah. But a letter from Brigham Young confirming his ownership of the ferry, which had at last been rebuilt, and a meeting with Young himself at St. George in April, perhaps made him overconfident. When he went to Panguitch that autumn to visit his wife Caroline, he was arrested and charged with participating in the murders at Mountain Meadows.

Lee's trial in July, 1875, resulted in a hung jury—eight Mormons holding out for acquittal against four non-Mormons. He was free on bail for a time, but rejected suggestions that he might flee. When his new trial began in September, 1876, it was obvious that the Church was now ready to use Lee as a scapegoat. Witnesses who had supported the accused during the first trial changed their testimony. Others who had not been summoned before came to the stand with incriminating details. One eloquent accuser was Jacob Hamblin.

After less than four hours of deliberation an all-Mormon jury found Lee guilty. On March 23, 1877, he was taken to Mountain Meadows for execution by a firing squad as he sat on his coffin. Just beforehand he was photographed by James Fennemore, who had worked briefly for Powell. In his final statement Lee declared, "I feel as calm as a summer morn, and I have done nothing intentionally wrong." Though he was bitter in private about having been singled out for punishment, he never tried to soften his fate or drag others down with him by revealing their names.[7]

His body was delivered to his sons for burial at Panguitch. Ownership of the ferry passed to Emma, as he had wished. She managed it with the help of an assistant until March 16, 1879. By that time the Navajos had been pacified, and the occupation of the upper reaches of the Little Colorado River was once again vigorously under way. The Church bought Emma out for three thousand dollars, payable mostly in cattle. Her assistant, Warren M. Johnson, and his sons continued as managers for the next several years, ferrying Indians on their way to Kanab to trade, as well as colonists bound for the Little Colorado. From then on the Dell was a busy place. Travelers went on using the crossing until 1929, when a bridge was opened to traffic six miles downstream. Today, to the thousands of boaters who each year start the run through the Grand Canyon at the mouth of the Paria, the spot is known as Lee's Ferry.

In 1961, largely because of the carefully detailed work of a Mormon historian, Juanita Brooks, Lee's excommunication was revoked and he was reinstated, eighty-two years after his execution, in the congregation of the Church of Jesus Christ of Latter-Day Saints.

As it turned out, there was less arable land along the upper Little Colorado watershed than the colonists had been led to expect. Moreover, several gentiles had arrived ahead of them and had dotted the valleys with pre-emption claims.[8] So some of the Mormons placed their tiny communities closer to the new White River Apache Reservation than their gentile rivals were willing to go. Others scraped together enough money to buy out the latter. As a result, many of the new towns provided no more than one lot per family inside the village and a meager twenty acres outside. Cattle, mostly milk cows and work oxen, were grazed in a common herd on public land beyond the periphery of each settlement. By 1880 close to a dozen small towns had taken shape. Though missionaries worked diligently to make friends of the Apaches the Indians drove off, in 1880–82, scores of their horses, butchered many of their cattle, and killed one man. As a result, most of the people lived clustered in forts—a number of small cabins built side by side around a dusty central square.

Cloudbursts were another hazard. Again and again waves of flood water burst through their dams of stone, sand, logs, and brush—or else the unstable streams changed course and left these laboriously built waterworks useless. Topping off the troubles came the mismanagement of a promising opportunity. When the Atlantic & Pacific Railroad began building west from Albuquerque in 1880, John W. Young, a son of Brigham Young, used his father's influence to obtain grading and tie-cutting contracts for one hundred miles of the line to the north of the Little Colorado enclave. He filled as many jobs as he could with local Saints and asked that more missionaries be sent from Utah—a program that also helped keep gentile laborers out of the district. He allowed the local people, who had just passed through a starving winter, to draw advances against their wages in the form of supplies for their families. That, it turned out, was all they were ever to receive. The railroad was short of funds, and Young had been inveigled into bidding too low on his contracts.

The Atlantic & Pacific was land-grant railroad. That is, Congress had authorized giving the company forty alternate sections—each section containing 640 acres—of land from the public domain for each mile of track it built in New Mexico and Arizona. The remaining sections were to stay in the public domain and to be available to settlers in 160-acre parcels at $2.50 an acre. The reason for alternating the mile-square sections in this checkerboard fashion was to prevent speculators from buying up huge chunks of the grant and then keeping the area closed to settlement until prices rose.

But in 1884 the railroad was forced by a financial crisis of its own to sell 1,059,560 acres of its grant in the Little Colorado River area to a syndicate of New York financiers and Texas cattlemen incorporated as the Aztec Land and Cattle Company—at a price of fifty cents an acre. The purchasers of course had no intention of separating their 1,650-odd mile-square pieces from the same number of public-domain sections with which they were mixed. If no fences existed, the buyers' cattle—the syndicate promptly imported forty thousand head—could wander at will over both public and private sections. Thus the Aztec Land and Cattle Company obtained for its fifty cents an acre the use of two million acres—actually more, for the railroad still held some unsold, unfenced sections scattered around the area.

The Mormons were stunned. They had known that at least some of their settlements were located within the forty-mile-wide ribbon of land on which the Atlantic & Pacific proposed to lay down a railroad. But no one would know until surveys were completed where railroad sections and public-domain sections lay. Unwilling to delay their occupation that long—others might beat them to choice locations—the Saints had purchased from gentiles or had filed for homesteads on whatever ground had pleased them most, assuming that necessary adjustments with the railroad could be made when the time came. But the Aztec deal almost literally cut the ground from under their feet. When they appealed to the Atlantic & Pacific for a hearing, its agent loftily disclaimed responsibility.

The Aztec Land and Cattle Company then began to use threats, backed up with beatings and barn-burnings, as their cowboys set about clearing every farmer, small rancher, and sheepman out of the district, regardless of the nature of his claim. Complicating the problem for the Mormons was a new drive against polygamy in Arizona: in 1882 five Mormons, including three bishops, were disenfranchised, fined five hundred dollars each, and imprisoned. Others then went into hiding, some in Old Mexico, and those who remained were increasingly demoralized.[9]

In the chaos, outlaws were soon rustling cattle from Aztec as well as from the Mormon farmers. After vigilantes hanged three horse thieves and drove four of the syndicate's leading bully boys out of the country, Apache County officials belatedly sent law-enforcement posses into the region. And in the East a special agent of the federal government's General Land Office warned the Aztec Company to put its house in order.

The upshot of prolonged negotiations was that the railroad and the cattle company agreed to sell to the settlers the homesteads they thought they had already purchased or earned by their labors—the railroad at a flinty $8.00 an acre, Aztec at $4.50 an acre in parcels of 640 acres each. To save about one thousand acres of cultivated land that fell within Aztec holdings, the colonists had to buy a total of 4,480 acres. Though the excess land could be used for grazing, it was a costly venture. But as the Utah historian Charles Peterson makes eloquently clear, the great toll was in human demoralization. Most of the colonists lived out the turbulent years in abject poverty. They had been uprooted from Utah to come here in the first place, only to have natural disasters and human cussedness cut them loose again and again. A few became compulsive wanderers, drifting down into Old Mexico, back to Utah, and to the Little Colorado once more, their animals bony, their wagons decrepit, their wives and children blank-eyed with hopelessness.

These private tragedies were symptomatic of a general collapse. How splendid the agrarian ideal had sounded as Thomas Jefferson had voiced it more than a half a century earlier: "Cultivators of the earth are the most valuable citizens . . . the most vigorous, the most independent, the most virtuous." But a new industrial society, energized by huge accumulations of capital hungry for dividends, would not tolerate the necessary isolation. Agrarian Mormonism, having reached the limits of its physical expansion, had either to perish or come to terms with the outside world. Those who could not do that became the drifters. Others, however, reached eventually an accommodation on the Little Colorado and also on the San Juan.

In 1879, after the summer's heat was over, approximately 250 men, women, and children were called by the Church to forsake their homes in the towns of southwestern Utah—St. George, Cedar City, New Harmony, and Parowan —and move in a body to the San Juan watershed, in the southeastern part of the state, traveling in eighty-three wagons, and taking nearly a thousand head of livestock with them.

Before they set out, there was the question of which route to follow. The direct line from Parowan, which the maps showed to be about two hundred miles, was interrupted by the Colorado River's Glen Canyon. It was generally believed that a wagon train would have to skirt the gorge far to the north, fording the Green at the base of the Book Cliffs and the Grand at Spanish Valley, where Moab now stands, or else circle south and use the ferry at Lonely Dell. By the southern route the distance was estimated to be 350 miles. From Kanab to Moenkopi, the land was parched and seamed with rough gullies. Then came sandhills, Navajos, and more desert. But West Coast miners bound for the San Juan Mountains in Colorado were known to have gotten through somehow.

The northern route was well known, except for its last leg, but the distance that way seemed from the maps to be as much as 450 miles. For a wagon caravan the difference could be important, especially for people starting in the fall. So in the preceding spring a scouting party was sent ahead to examine the southern route—a total of twenty-six men, two women, and eight children traveling in a dozen wagons and driving somewhere between two hundred and three hundred horses and cattle. They left Paragonah— which was to be the rendezvous point for the main caravan and which was a few miles north of Parowan—on April 14, 1879. On June 18 they pushed through the pink bluffs bordering the San Juan at a point midway between Montezuma and McElmo creeks, which flow into the river from the north. They had averaged a bit more than five miles a day, and were unanimous in their belief that a large party would have a difficult time of it.[10]

Having found one Mormon family and a handful of gentiles already in the area, they were fearful that other non-Mormons might appear before the main colony did, and strung out protective claim stakes along the sandy valley floor. They built shelters for those of their group who were delegated to remain behind, worked on a dam, and listened to tales of hardship. Crops that had been planted earlier in the year were not doing well, and the settlers already in the valley feared that their supplies would not last through the winter. Hoping to keep the shortages from being a drain on their own mission, four of the scouting party rode 250 miles to the railhead of the narrow-gauge Denver & Rio Grande at Alamosa in the San Luis Valley of Colorado. They returned with several pack animals loaded with supplies.

On August 19 those who were returning to Paragonah started north. They were far behind schedule, but they traveled light and reached their destination in mid-September. They had, they proudly pointed out, covered the longer northern road in half the time the southern one had taken.

But by then everyone was talking about a recent report of a direct route straight across the canyons. It could be done. Just two hundred miles. By going that way they could be on the San Juan, have shelters up, and their fall planting done before the onset of snow.

Apostle George A. Smith, one of the most influential Church officials in southern Utah, was at least partly responsible for the excitement.[11] He refused to believe that there was no place between the Green River ford and the Lonely Dell ferry where a wagon could cross. In pursuit of his hunch, he had written two prominent residents of the new town of Escalante, Bishop Andrew Schow and Constable Reuben Collett, and had asked them to take a look. The two had improvised a boat out of a seven-foot wagon box and lashed it onto the running gears of a two-wheeled cart. Heading southeast out of Escalante, they rattled and banged along the wide, rough platform that lay between the Kapairowits Plateau on their right and the deeply entrenched meanders of Escalante Creek on their left. About seventy miles of rough travel brought them to the row of pink mounds that top the western wall of Glen Canyon. Between two of these they had found a cleft formed by an ancient fault line. It sloped straight as the arm of a T-square down to the dull red river, three-quarters of a mile away, dropping in that distance one thousand feet. Although the top part of the crack was too narrow for their cart and the first forty-five feet of the drop were almost perpendicular, the crevice widened below the cliff, and the slope grew steadily less steep, like the basal part of a letter U, as it approached the stream's edge.

Schow and Collett debated whether the sides of the crack could be blasted out wide enough to admit a wagon, and whether the bottom could be trenched back into the sandstone at an angle not too steep for horses to keep their footing—in other words, whether the top of the long crevice could be turned into a chute. The conclusion was a tentative yes, provided the workers were given plenty of blasting powder.

In order to gain a look at the other side of the canyon, the explorers drove their cart north along the west rim to a smooth slope less steep than the cliffs that bracketed it. There they unloaded the boat, tied ropes to its stern, slid it down the slope from ledge to ledge and finally to the river, and paddled to the far bank. Climbing a 250-foot bluff, they came to a broad bench, hiked across it, and were stopped by convolutions of slickrock as round and smooth as a bin of apples. Though these could not be penetrated, the two men did peer into the spectacular gorge that encased the San Juan River as it flowed into the Colorado. So at least they were on the right track.

They crossed the High Plateaus to Paragonah with this information, arriving just ahead of the scouting party from the San Juan. There was scarcely any debate. A new rendezvous was set for Forty-Mile Spring, so named because of its distance beyond Escalante, and the first wagons began to roll. Although late starters had trouble with early snow in the mountains, they were confident of reaching the San Juan before winter really took hold. The ground at Escalante was bare, and by early December, 1879, all eighty-three wagons and about one thousand head of livestock had reached Forty-Mile Spring.

Worried faces met the last arrivals. Several of their own people, guided by Schow and Collett, had crossed the river in a new boat for a second look at the land beyond. Now they were back, and the majority said that the maze of hummocks and gulches east of the river was impassable. Yet it might be too late for the company to return to Paragonah and a different trail. Their livestock, famished already because of the sparse grazing along the way, might not be able to break through the deepening snowdrifts that already heralded what was to be one of the harshest winters ever recorded in Utah. Thus a great deal hung on the opinion of a minority of the party that had explored the land to the east. Their report was delivered by George Hobbs, who had accompanied the first scouting group through Moenkopi and was regarded as knowledgeable.

Supported by Schow and Collett, Hobbs said that with faith, powder, and plenty of sharp tools, the migrants could carve a way through. Trust the Lord. After discussing the alternatives in private, the leaders of the colonists called a mass meeting and asked for discussion. The final vote, by voice, favored going ahead. Spontaneously a hymn arose, and the work of organization began.

The president of the mission, Silas Smith, and a select escort mounted on strong horses spurred toward Salt Lake City to ask the Church and the state legislature to send in supplies, no matter what the obstacles. Roadbuilders charged with smoothing out the last twenty miles to the canyon rim established a camp at Forty-Mile Spring which also served as a center for stock-tenders, mostly boys, who ranged the company's animals far and wide in search of food. A non-Mormon cattleman, Tom Box, complicated the grazing problem. Hearing that a wagon train was bound for the supposedly empty ranges of southeastern Utah, he pushed several hundred cattle along its tracks, hoping to benefit from the pioneering. The strain of the additional animals on the sparse grass was serious—but Box's hands turned to with a will to help build the road through the cleft.

A camp for the blasters was established near the canyon's rim. During the early stages of the work the men were lowered in half barrels suspended from ropes into what from the beginning was called the Hole-in-the-Rock. Fortunately, the sandstone was friable, and soon a steeply pitching chute led down through the topmost band of the cliff. Below that band, engineering problems forced the road-builders out of the bottom of the crevice onto its northern side. For a short stretch the slope was so steep that the builders could not dig a roadway into it. Instead they set stakes into holes drilled into the plunging wall. Against those stakes they laid a cribwork of driftwood lugged up from the river banks and filled the space between crib and wall with rubble, thus creating a narrow, rail-less roadway protruding like a shelf from the sloping rock.

Meanwhile an Escalante carpenter, Charles Hall, came in with a disman-tled ferryboat. After lowering the materials with ropes down the same slope that Schow and Collett had used, he put the craft together and transported workers and supplies to the east side of the stream so that road-building could be pushed ahead there as well as within the notch. Hoping to speed travel from camp to camp and also open new grazing areas in the canyon bottom, trail-builders scratched a precarious path into the same sandstone slope the boatmen had used. Of the first animals that tried it, nine fell to their deaths.

To learn how best to reach the embryo settlements on the San Juan, George Hobbs and three companions were sent on a new scouting mission. On December 17 they edged two pack animals (one a donkey) and two riding animals down the trail to the river bottom. Twelve hungry, storm-swept days of alternate riding and walking brought them to their destination. They started back after resting and eating ravenously for just one day. The weather was now even worse, and when they reached the Colorado on January 8, 1880, it was running thick with ice. But they had found the key passes the company would need—once by following mountain sheep (Hobbs called them llamas) out of what at first had seemed a hopeless cul-de-sac.

Inspirited by the discoveries and by the arrival of an additional ton of giant powder from the Church, the men redoubled their efforts. The first wagon started down through the Hole-in-the-Rock chute a little after dawn on January 26. Chains wrapped around its two rear wheels kept them from turning. Gangs of men holding onto ropes attached to the wagon's rear end acted as additional stabilizers. Down it skidded without a bobble, and with the chains removed from the wheels, on over the shelf. Twenty-five more fol-lowed that day, and all were ferried safely across the river through channels broken in ice that reached from both banks almost to the middle of the stream.

After the wagons were all across, the reluctant cattle came, nearly two thousand head split into manageable segments. At the water's icy edges, and in it, they balked. Some of the herders swam their horses back and forth through the slush more times than they remembered to count, whipping at the cantankerous beasts with doubled lariat ropes. They all made it.

Now the maze. More dugways slanting across steep hillsides. More chutes. Up, down. Foot by foot. A blizzard roared across Gray Mesa, shutting out the stupendous view of the converging canyons of the San Juan and Colorado Rivers. A baby was born on the mesa while the wind howled. It was the third birthing of the trip—one stillborn at Escalante, a girl named Deseret at the camp near the Hole-in-the-Rock rim, and now this one, a boy. To name him Saint John for the San Juan River would burden him too much, so his parents, the Larsons, called him simply John Rio Larson.

The travelers had one bit of luck. Windblown sand and debris from floods had created a natural dam across a canyon (today's Lake Canyon) that otherwise might have been impassable. Behind the dam was Lake Pagahrit, as the pioneers called it, half a mile long and as clear as a winter morning. For once the weather was good. Rejoicing, the women did their laundry, and then the train rolled on across the dam. (Years later, in 1915, the dam would collapse, and now there is no lake in Lake Canyon.)

Pack trains occasionally overtook them with supplies, so that they were able at one point to send George Hobbs ahead to the San Juan to relieve the starving settlement there. But most of the time they were caged in misery—storms and bitter cold followed by a swift thaw that turned Clay Hills into a mass of mulberry-colored mud. They had to go scores of miles out of their way to skirt the chasm of Grand Gulch, and they spent weeks chopping a passage through the thick piñon forest that barred the approach to Comb Wash.

On the far side of the wash a sawtoothed reef cut at the sky. Unable to find a way to surmount its cliffs, they crawled down the wash's gravelly bottom to the San Juan River. There they found that projecting cliffs prevented their driving along the river bank to their goal. So they made a sharp U-turn around the pointed end of the reef and, dead tired, faced the most devastating part of the journey, building yet another dugway so that they could climb onto the plateau behind the barrier.

When completed, the route made a shallow S-curve up through tilted, scabby strata. They put as many as seven span of horses onto a single wagon, and the men walked beside the animals, whipping relentlessly. Some horses went into spasms from exhaustion. Others fell to their knees, scraping the hide from their forelegs as they struggled to stand again. But always enough were on their feet at one time, lunging ahead, to keep the wheels turning. There were now eighty-two wagons, one having been abandoned on Gray Mesa. Well before Theodore Roosevelt rode off to Cuba, the pioneers named that part of the road San Juan Hill. Trying to tell about it afterwards, Lemuel Redd, leader of one of the units, always choked up and wept.[12]

They came gently off the mesa into a valley green with April. In six months they had come two hundred miles. Montezuma, their original destination, was a mere eighteen miles farther, but now they stopped. They would put their town here. They called it Bluff, for the fluted, dull red cliffs that rose two hundred to three hundred feet above the pinched bottomland.

As time passed, pride in what they had done along the road replaced the bitter awareness that by using routes their own scouts had explored, they could have avoided the ordeal. The mystique grew. Today a big white sign, "Hole-in-the-Rock," sways on a buoy in Lake Powell above the old crossing and points to the cleft in the rim. Now and then passing boatmen throttle down a moment and marvel, envisioning the pioneers as they had come to see themselves. Tough old birds, those Mormons. Who else would try to take wagons down there?

Just as on the Little Colorado, the colonists at Bluff and Montezuma watched floods sweep away their dams and carve arroyos through their fields.[13] Now and then outlaws raided their herds. Navajos, Paiutes, and southern Utes were frequent visitors, sometimes trading and doing odd jobs, more often begging and pilfering. Navajos killed a trader at Rincon, ten miles from Bluff, and Paiutes at least two prospectors in Monument Valley, not much farther away. Among the soaring crimson buttes of Castle Valley at the foot of the La Sal Mountains, Ute horse thieves ambushed and shot down a dozen members of a pursuing posse: the Pinhook Massacre. Whenever such things happened, alarm rippled throughout the sparsely settled, ill-defended countryside. Too often many men were away, hauling in supplies from the new Denver & Rio Grande Western Railroad, 130 miles to the north, or working at the Colorado mines for cash enough to get through the next winter. What if some truculent band took advantage of their absence to attack the colony itself?

Twice the settlers—those who just didn't give up and leave on their own —asked to be freed from their mission. The Church was reluctant.

Even before the founding of Bluff, a few pioneering Mormon stockmen had drifted into two sets of tall mountains north of the river—the Abajos (local people called them the Blues), fifty miles to the north, and the triple-peaked La Sals, near the crossing of the Grand River at Moab. Both massifs offered fine summer ranges—perennial streams, cool pine forests high up, juniper and Gambel oaks interspersed with sage and grama grass lower down. Best of all, markets were near. Animals that could not be sold in the Colorado mining camps could be taken to the railroad and shipped outside.

These advantages attracted too much attention. In the early 1880's, three big non-Mormon outfits from the East bought out the local people. The first to come was the LC outfit of the widow Lacey from New Mexico. While trailing a big herd west in search of new range, her husband, I. W. Lacey, and one of his cowboys had been killed in a brawl at Fort Lewis near Durango, Colorado. His widow had hurried in to bury him. Then, helped by her brothers, she had gone on moving the herd west, settling finally beside Recapture Creek on White Mesa, not twenty miles north of Bluff, where velvety sagebrush flats begin sloping up toward the blue-green, pyramidal summits of the Abajos.

Not far from White Mesa, where the North Fork of Montezuma Creek coils down the eastern flank of the Abajos, was the headquarters camp of the Kansas and New Mexico Land and Cattle Company, managed by Edmond and Harold Carlisle. In Bluff they were thought to be Englishmen, and the record shows that they raised three-quarters of a million dollars by selling shares to investors in London and Edinburgh. After locating suitable winter range in the San Juan Valley of northwestern New Mexico, they scouted the high country of southeastern Utah for summer range. There, for $210,000, they picked up seven thousand head of Mormon cattle and the "right" to run the animals in the same country as the previous owners. No legal titles changed hands. A "right" was simply a privilege stock-raisers thought they acquired by being first on any part of the public domain.

Then came the Pittsburg Cattle Company, which wintered its cattle in the Uncompahgre Valley of Colorado and summered on the southern slopes of Utah's La Sal Mountains. Together, the three outfits—Pittsburg, Carlisle, Lacey—controlled fifty thousand or more cattle and a swath of land sixty miles long, reaching from the vicinity of the Grand River almost to the San Juan. That control became visible each spring when they trailed back out of the low country to summer range. The school in the little town of Mancos, Colorado, was closed for three days while the Carlisle herds trooped along Main Street on their way to Utah—mile-long herds, one Bluff youngster remembered, of "yellow cattle, white, black, brindle, all of them starving and hollow from the long trail. And horns! such a river of horns as you might see in a nightmare—horns reaching up and out, out and up again in fantastic corkscrews."[14]

If enough gentile voters followed those tracks, they might well gain political control of newly formed San Juan County—such a thing as had never yet occurred in Utah Territory. To prevent it, Church leaders envisioned three colonies, to be placed in a 180-degree arc around the eastern flank of the Abajo Mountains. The southernmost was to be on White Mesa as a challenge to the LC outfit, the middle one beside North Montezuma Creek, close to the Carlisles, and the third at Indian Creek, on the mountain's northeast side. All Mormons along the San Juan were to join in a cooperative cattle company to be known as the Bluff Pool, which would invade the west end of the Abajos in order to keep outside ranchers from advancing in that direction.

But only five new families arrived in 1886, and only one more in 1887. So the Blue Mountain Mission, as it was called, had to be limited to a single spot —North Montezuma Creek, half a dozen miles from the Carlisles' Double Cabin headquarters. Twenty men were brought in from Moab, Mancos, and Bluff in the summer of 1888 to work on ditches, corrals, and fences—improvements that lured in more families in 1889. They named their town Monticello, in direct reference to Thomas Jefferson and his vision of a nation of yeomen owning the land they tilled.

The Carlisles' Kansas and New Mexico Land and Cattle Company, which neither owned nor tilled a foot of earth in Utah, did not welcome them. There is a legend that the cowboys, taking umbrage at the cows of the homesteaders—what is a clearer sign of a sodbuster than a belled milch cow? —stole the bells so that the settlers could not find the animals at milking time. When the owners padlocked the bells to straps, the cowboys cut the straps. The settlers—or so the story goes—then substituted chains, whereupon their opponents cut off the heads of the cows to get the bells—as many as three hundred decapitated animals, one old-timer averred. Then there was the famous evening in 1890 when the boys at Double Cabin got liquored up and came into town looking for fun. The bell on the new schoolhouse gave them a chance to ring chimes with their sixshooters. What a clatter! There were seventy-five bell-ringers, one woman declared. She knew because she counted them by the flashes of their guns.[15]

Other reminiscences center on the death of a woman bystander, killed when two Carlisle cowboys fell into a squabble at a Mormon dance and began shooting at each other. That killing, however, was an accident, not harassment. In fact, the Carlisle brothers seem to have been desirous of avoiding the kind of trouble that had beset them in 1886, when their men killed three Mexican sheepherders in the San Juan Basin of northwestern New Mexico. Besides, the settlers had one decided advantage. Bluff was the county seat; the sheriff, tax assessor, probate judge, and water commissioners were Mormons.

In the early 1890's, under pressure from Colorado ranchers and miners, the federal government opened hearings concerning the advisability of buying the land the Southern Utes still held in Colorado and relocating the Indians on a two-million-acre reservation that sprawled all the way across San Juan County. Thinking discussion was tantamount to decision, nine hundred Utes—men, women, and children—moved across the state line into the Monticello district with their horses, cattle, sheep, goats, and innumerable dogs, and set up camp on the choicest meadows and beside the best springs. From mission towns and ranch houses, an irregular army of settlers and cowboys gathered to repel the invasion. After the Utah militia sent them arms and ammunition, federal mediators rushed to the scene.

Fortunately the mediators prevailed, the Utes withdrew, and the idea of relocation fell through. In the meantime, however, the Carlisles, already pinched by the depression of 1893, decided they'd had enough. Their departure, the ending of their long water quarrel with the people of Monticello, and the quieting of the Indians at last produced the influx the Church had been hoping for. Monticello replaced Bluff as county seat; dry farmers and small sheep- and cattle-ranchers spread eastward across the great Sage Plain into Colorado. The colony that had been projected for White Mesa took shape in 1905 and was named Blanding. The third proposed site, Indian Creek, was occupied by David Goudelock and another unemployed Carlisle rider who had fallen in love with the country. In time their Dugout Ranch would become, under different owners, one of the fabled cow camps of the nation. Tourists following Utah State Highway 211 toward Canyonlands National Park can still see its rambling buildings, only slightly changed, crouched in the shade of rustling cottonwoods planted long ago at the foot of Shay Mesa's stunning red prow.

While the Monticello colonists were busy resisting the Carlisles, the communal cattle-owners of the Bluff Pool, guided at first by Indians, set about laying claim to the southwestern and western flanks of the Abajo Mountains. It was easy to see why most of that land lay open. Caught between the converging arms of the San Juan and Colorado rivers, the earth collapsed into a welter of pinnacles, monuments, and buttes. Mesas ended as abruptly as if chopped off by a cleaver, the ribbons of colored cliffs that bound them winding away toward a horizon made misty by windblown sand. Everywhere in between twisting gorges rushed to join the main canyons. One awesome example is Dark Canyon, plunging nearly five thousand feet on its way to Cataract Canyon, only twenty-five miles to the west.

Southward, a dense black forest of piñon and juniper covered an elongated hummock that geologists named the Monument Upwarp. Dotted by occasional openings where an edible plant called cow alfalfa grew, riven by canyons (the Grand Gulch Primitive Area embraces the most spectacular of them), it was, in the cowboy cliché, a hell of a place to lose a cow. And it wasn't the only bewildering maze. At lower elevations near both main rivers, creased, scoured, and skimmed by eons of cloudbursts, the land looked hopelessly sterile. But life is persistent. A ranch woman wrote about a pack trip across similar country west of the Green one May: "This is the most exciting country—you look out over a land of rocks and guess that it is all slickrock and not fit for anything and then come out into one little grassy valley after another and the feed was a foot high and bright green and lots of it."[16]

They were small valleys, quickly grazed out. That was one problem. The cattle had to be run in small bunches and moved every so often across hair-raising trails from one pocket to another, generally several miles away.

The second difficulty was water. Cows could lick winter's thin scuffs of snow as long as they lasted, and summer rains temporarily filled the potholes in the slickrock. Otherwise there wasn't much to drink, and horror tales abound of cattle smelling moisture in some canyon, getting rimrocked while trying to reach it, and dying of thirst within sight of water.

One way of overcoming the hazard was to find springs that sweated through the contact cracks between different layers of sandstone or welled up in a gulch bottom and trickled a short distance before disappearing again into the sand. Such dribbles could be made usable by collecting the water in troughs. Or earthen dams could be stretched across shallow draws to catch the runoff of rainstorms—provided it did not come in too big a rush. Sometimes men had to use the same water cattle had been standing in, belly deep, for hours under a 100-degree sun. Just brace yourself and bite it off, they said.

Another way of making water available was to build trails, stairways sometimes, down cliffsides to a running stream, generally where a widening of the bottomlands added a bonus of grass. There were dozens of these trails in Stillwater and Labyrinth canyons along the Green and in Glen Canyon along the Colorado, and driving the cattle back up them could be taxing. Under the hot sun the animals grew tired and tried to turn back. Balling up, they often crowded a few head off the trail into places from which they could not escape. One cowman operating in what is now Canyonlands National Park told of cutting the throats of twenty-nine animals that he could not retrieve and that otherwise would have died slowly of thirst and injuries.[17]

High Plains methods of raising cattle did not work in such country. There was no home ranch. The Mormons still preferred living in villages near churches, schools, and stores, and riding out to their work, even though the stay might last six weeks, with only a three- or four-day break between tours. They established base camps in deep recesses under overhanging cliffs. Over the years simple household goods collected there—homemade wooden benches, tables, and cupboards; Dutch ovens, frying pans, tin cutlery; horse equipment; occasionally, a battered mattress. Dry food and grain for horses were stored in holes dug in the loose, fine sand of the cave floor—so loose that it slid back faster than rodents could burrow into it. (One such cowboy cave is preserved as a historic artifact in Canyonlands National Park.) Nearby box canyons were fenced off for holding extra saddle horses.

During the late 1880's and early 1890's, a few outsiders, generally called Texans though they might have been from anywhere, did drift small bunches of cattle into the region but seldom mastered it well enough to succeed. The Bluff Pool fell apart more because of the low prices of the nineties than because of ineptitude. In time the dominant figures of the area came to be the Scorup brothers—Jim, the elder, and John Albert, the pioneer.

In 1891, Al Scorup, then aged nineteen, came into the region from Salina, in central Utah. Working for the owner of a small herd convinced him that the region could be turned into a cow range. So he swam his horse back over the Colorado River at Dandy Crossing near the mouth of White Canyon and, on reaching Salina, persuaded his brother to join him. They began small, herding other men's cattle for a share of the calves and literally living with the animals as they moved them from one rock-bound pocket to another. When they needed cash for supplies, Al, the more gregarious of the two, went outside for odd jobs, sometimes as a rider for the fading Carlisles. They roped wild steers that had escaped from other men's herds, cut off their horns, tied the animals to trees, and let them fight the ropes until their bellies were empty and their heads sore. The bewildered steers could then be put with gentler animals and turned into income instead of being wasters of scarce grass.

They sold and bought, swapped, dickered, and—in connection with their friends, Andrew and Snuffy Somerville—formed the Scorup-Somerville Cattle Company. In 1917 they acquired David Goudelock's Indian Creek outfit and made it their headquarters. Though Jim Scorup died shortly thereafter, the company pressed vigorously ahead, bringing new partners into the organization and thus extending their range for 150 miles along the east breaks of the Colorado River to the San Juan, up that to the huge chasm of Grand Gulch, and back across the western Abajos—more than two million acres of torn, twisted public-domain land controlled by the ownership of twenty-five thousand acres embracing every bit of living water, except the two main rivers, in the entire area.[18]

Though all the partners were Mormons, the ranch was not a Mormon commune. Al Scorup and his companies succeeded because they learned to integrate their cattle enterprises with those of the rest of the United States and to use the corporate methods of organization and capital accumulation that had become the mainstay of America's entire economy.

They were not alone, of course. Preston Nutter, a gentile freighter and one-time member of the Colorado legislature who moved into Utah in 1881, operated for a time between Greenriver town and the red canyon of the Grand at Cisco. On learning that the Ute Indian reservation was to be opened to leasing in 1893, he put together a company of New York investors that made a successful bid on upwards of six hundred thousand acres. Immediately thereafter Nutter went to western Arizona to collect five thousand cows for stocking the new range. In September, 1893, his riders swam the herd across the Colorado River just below the mouth of the Grand Canyon without losing an animal. Punishing heat followed by early snows made it impossible for him to reach his destination that year. Backtracking in search of wintering grounds, he "discovered" the Shivwits Plateau south of St. George. A season there convinced him that its hundreds of thousands of acres would make a nice calving ground for the reservation lease. Adroitly he secured every spring in the region, under the noses of Mormons who, depending on squatter's rights, had been using the water for years without obtaining title. Their lapse let Preston Nutter, corporate rancher, straddle the state, one huge unit in Utah's southwest corner, the other in the northeast.[19]

In the early 1880's Ora Haley moved the main part of his enormous herds out of the crowded Laramie Plains of eastern Wyoming, across the Continental Divide, into the Yampa Valley of northwestern Colorado. Cantankerous and arrogant, he crowded out the region's small ranchers, defied the grazing regulations laid down by the new United States Forest Service, lied to the tax assessor about the number of cattle he owned, and was widely believed to have hired the killer of two Brown's Park rustlers who were bothering him. But his real notoriety arose from what he probably considered a routine act of self-defense. Charging that "Queen" Ann Bassett Bernard, also of Brown's Park, and her paramour, Tom Yarberry, had butchered one of his thousands of heifers, he had the pair dragged into court in the county seat in Craig in 1911.[20]

After the first trial ended in a hung jury, Yarberry skipped bail. Ann Bernard's husband, who had once been Haley's foreman, divorced her, and she faced her second trial alone. She was equal to it. Years before, her father, Herbert Bassett, a former federal employee who had gone to Brown's Park for relief from asthma, had used his Civil War pension to send his harum-scarum daughter first to a convent in Salt Lake City and then to Miss Porter's exclusive finishing school in Boston. The airs she picked up there, without ever forgetting the ways of the bunkhouse, brought her the nickname Queen. At the time of her second trial—she was thirty-seven, five feet two inches tall, and beautiful still—she remembered those days of decorum. She came into court the epitome of demure innocence. While she sat with downcast eyes, her attorney skillfully veered away from the charge against her. To the spectators' delight, he called Haley to the witness stand and in effect put *him* on trial for his sins.

The evening after the trial closed the jury acquitted her. At the local theater, the showing of a motion picture was interrupted to flash on the screen, amid thunderous cheers, the image of a hand-lettered card reading "HURRAH FOR VICTORY! Long live the Queen." Ann Bassett Bernard took a second husband, a respectable rancher named Willis, settled down, and grew fat and sedate. And Haley's fifteen thousand or more cattle, their handling from birth to shipping financed by eastern capital, continued to range undisturbed from the White River Forest Reserve past Craig a hundred miles down the Yampa and around Douglas Mountain to winter range on the Green.

So it went, from the cold steppes of the upper Green to the windings of the Gila in southern Arizona—pure alchemy: four-legged machines rhythmically transforming ordinary vegetation into money. The only cost was soil.

Intense erosion, as has been noted, has been a characteristic of the Colorado River Basin since the elevation of the Rockies and the Colorado Plateau. Storm water roars down steep hills checked only slightly by the sparse vegetation. Recurrent drought that reduces vegetation still more, together with shifts in precipitation patterns from a preponderance of winter snows to rare but violent summer deluges, regularly quickened the stripping away of the soil. But eventually the pendulum swung back and the land healed. Not until man began pushing it around did nature prove unable, between cyclical swings, to restore the balance.

The worst of many grievous results, from the time of the prehistoric Indians to the present, has been deep gullying in areas where trees have been destroyed for lumber, native plants to make room for irrigated field crops, and grass to feed livestock. The deepening of arroyos lowers water tables. Either nothing grows and sandstorms swirl, or hardy, uneconomic mesquite, juniper, sagebrush, thistles, and cactus take over. When rain falls, the unprotected, irreplaceable topsoil sweeps in torrents of mud down the San Juan, from whose basin comes one-quarter of the silt in the Colorado River system. One-sixth of the total originates in the Little Colorado, much from the trampling of ravenous Navajo sheep, goats, and horses. The total load has been estimated at 180 million tons a year.

Grazing lands are turning into what are wryly called 10-by-80 ranges: a steer has to have a mouth ten feet wide and be able to run eighty miles an hour from one grass clump to the next to get enough to eat. Stock ponds that ranchers build to water their animals sometimes fill with slime within a decade or two. Lake Mead, Lake Powell, and dozens of other Bureau of Reclamation and Corps of Engineer dams will take somewhat longer, but inevitably they too will fill with the products of erosion. How much longer will depend in part on what those concerned learn about managing the land in accordance with the inevitabilities of nature. So far, the prospects are not encouraging.

Railroad surveyors

13

Exploitation Begins

Early in 1889, a prospector named S. S. Harper, who was in Denver trying to sell some mining claims, let slip to a real-estate speculator, Frank M. Brown, the notion of a railway line along the snow-free water-level grade that the Colorado River had carved through Arizona. Brown sat straight up. Right away a starting point popped into his mind—Grand Junction, a small farming town located where the Gunnison River joined the Grand in western Colorado. The Denver & Rio Grande Railroad had already built tracks into Grand Junction, and so bringing construction equipment to the head of the canyon line would pose no problem. Moreover, there were enormous deposits of coal in the Book Cliff fields near the Grand River north of Grand Junction and in the Gunnison's North Fork and Slate River tributaries. Coal could be stockpiled at Grand Junction and then all but coasted through the Colorado canyons to the lower desert for a short land haul to southern California, which at the time was importing most of its coal from Australia and British Columbia. Finally, there would be the attraction of the Grand Canyon's already famous scenery. On the strength of such reasoning, Brown and a few cronies incorporated, on March 25, 1889, the Denver, Colorado Canyon, and Pacific

Railroad Company. Frank M. Brown was elected president. As a reward for his ideas and to forestall suits he might instigate if he were left out, S. S. Harper was named to the board of directors.[1]

The day after the incorporation, Brown hired a thirty-six-year-old mining engineer, Frank C. Kendrick, provided him with an assistant, Thomas Rigney, and went with them by train to Grand Junction. Disembarking at 3:45 A.M. on March 28, they groped through the darkness to the river bank, where they drove a symbolic stake in the mud. The Denver, Colorado Canyon, and Pacific had been launched. For the benefit of a newspaper reporter or two on the scene he repeated his instructions. Kendrick and Rigney were to survey a railroad gradient down the Grand to its meeting with the Green. Then they were to swing back up the Green to the town of Blake (today's Green River, Utah) in order to estimate the resources of that area as well. Those publicity gestures completed, Brown then hurried East to tell potential investors that he already had a survey crew in the field.

Kendrick and Rigney spent a day hiring three workers and filling with supplies a fifteen-foot dory, the *Black Betty*.[2] Over the next five weeks and three days, they surveyed 160 miles of grade down the Grand to the Green, dodging the only rapid of consequence (today's Westwater, then called Hades) by running a twelve-mile cord across the great red arc in which it lay. The *Black Betty* meanwhile covered those same twelve miles of sagebrush in a farmer's wagon.

The hard part was the 117-mile ascent of the Green. Most of the way the surveyors had to tow the boat against the sluggish current and over the sandbars. Cold rains lashed them until their shoes disintegrated; Kendrick had to tie his together with wire. They ran out of food, as early river parties so often did, and would have suffered acutely had not a rancher several miles below the railroad station at Blake come to their aid.

Dead tired, Kendrick and Rigney reached Denver at 7:00 A.M. on May 17, and reported straightaway to Brown. The promoter barely listened to them but instead talked until three o'clock that afternoon about what *he* had been doing. Boats especially. Having read of Powell's difficulties in portaging his heavy craft around the worst rapids, Brown had decided to use lighter boats constructed of thin, pliant red cedar and only fifteen feet long. To add maneuverability (so he supposed), he had them built with narrow beams and round bottoms. There were five of them, each equipped with an extra set of oars and two hundred feet of rope for lining through rough water. Because Kendrick had surveyed the Grand as far as the confluence, the main party would save time by taking a train directly to Green River and embark from there, after adding Kendrick's *Black Betty*, renamed *Brown Betty*, to the fleet. It had not occurred to the company president to buy life preservers for anyone.

There would be sixteen men in the party: Brown and two wealthy friends traveling as guests; six surveyors, counting the photographer, Franklin Nims, who would use his camera to corroborate the engineers' written reports; five boatmen, including Rigney, who agreed to go along and lend his experience; and two black cooks, George Gibson and Henry Richards, long-time servants of Robert Brewster Stanton, the chief engineer, whose left arm had been crippled in a childhood accident; like John Wesley Powell, he could neither row nor swim well.

Sixteen men, their equipment, and food for seventy-five days—enough to see the party to Lee's Ferry—would not fit into six boats. Accordingly Brown had stowed the overflow in several big, watertight boxes of zinc encased in pine. They would be tied together and towed along behind the cook boat, the *Brown Betty*.

Powell had made his first run exactly twenty years before, and no party had gone through since. When Brown invited Kendrick to join the party, the weary engineer declined. He wrote in his diary afterwards, "I have given up going back as I think a mans place is near home & those he loves rather than far away even if he does not make so much money or gain as much glory."

It may have been the wisest decision he ever made.

Brown's party rowed easily to the confluence of the rivers and on May 31 coasted on another three miles to the first of Cataract Canyon's notorious rapids. Warned by its roar, the little fleet turned toward land, intending to look the situation over. Confusion developed, and the cooks' boat, the *Brown Betty*, swung around too slowly. The accelerating current caught the bundle of zinc boxes they were towing and whipped it past the *Betty* into a tumult of white water.

To save themselves, the men cut the tow rope and managed to get the unburdened *Betty* ashore. The boxes, however, disappeared toward the Gulf —an omen of misadventure to follow. Late on June 4 Brown's boat, the *Mary*, flipped upside down, pitching him and his two guests into the torrent. They managed to cling to it, however, and were dragged a mile and a half before the *Mary* lodged against a cliff. They managed to climb out onto a ledge, where they shivered out the night waiting for help. Three days later the *Brown Betty* jammed under a rock in such a way that it could not be moved. With just five boats remaining, repairs had become so frequent that they were obliged to break up the *Mary*, the most battered craft of the fleet, for patching material. "The thought of it," Brown wrote in his diary, "made me very unhappy as she was named after my wife. I finally broke down completely and had to leave the men."

Now that they were down to four boats, each upset meant critical losses. On June 13 Brown estimated that although they had left Green River with provisions enough to feed sixteen men for seventy-five days, accidents had cost them all but a ten-day supply. Meanwhile, travel conditions were deteriorating. The annual spring rise had reached Cataract. The waves in the rapids grew gigantic; the thunder of the river hammered night and day. Portaging around the most alarming stretch of water they had seen yet—known today as Big Drop, it ends in the howling Satan's Gut—brought matters to a crisis. The men declared their intention to drive ahead as fast as possible, without surveying, to the placer mining camps in Glen Canyon, some thirty miles below, and then quit the river. No railroad would ever run here.

As Brown wavered, Stanton stepped in, saying that if he were given one boat and enough volunteers to handle the instruments he'd finish the survey on his own. His chief assistant, John Hislop, stepped to his side, prompting Stanton's servants and one other man to follow. The remaining eleven elected to push ahead in three boats. Brown promised that if food were available at the mines, some of them would return to the surveyors with it.

On June 17 they divided their provisions into sixteen tiny portions—a little bread, coffee, condensed milk, sugar, and syrup for each man. Nims, the photographer, who went ahead with the large group, wrote that at lunchtime "We poured the syrup in a hole in a rock and every man dipped his bread in it." Stanton recorded that for six days his group went without a noon meal. Breakfast was a slice of bread and a cup of coffee with condensed milk in it; at night the menu was repeated, with the addition of three cubes of sugar for each man—enough to keep them going until they reached the placid waters of Glen Canyon, where provisions awaited them.

At Glen Canyon, Brown had been welcomed by Cass Hite, an entrepreneur as glibly optimistic as he was. Hite and many of his neighbors believed that the ancient ruins which abounded in the canyon and its tributaries had once housed Indian slaves who had worked the river's placer bars for the Spanish. Somewhere there were lode mines, too—for instance, Pish-la-ki, from which the Navajos supposedly extracted the silver they used for making their jewelry. Cass Hite, after making friends in Monument Valley with a local chief, Hoskanini, and learning the Navajo language, had spent two years looking for it. He never found it. Finally, however, Hoskanini did tell him that if he crossed the San Juan River and traveled north to a certain valley—now known as White Canyon—he would reach a place where the Colorado River's red walls broke down for a short distance into low terraces and rolling hills. There he would find gold in the sand.[3] The Mormons had not known the place was there, though it was the only spot between Moab and Lee's Ferry, a distance of 271 miles, that gave easy access to wagons from either side. In mockery of Hole-in-the-Rock and of Hall's Crossing, another ford occasionally used by the Mormons of southeast Utah, Cass Hite had at first called his discovery Dandy Crossing.

And just as Hoskanini had said he would, he had found gold there—tiny dots of it glistening in his pan. As word spread, a little community grew up on the west bank, opposite the mouth of White Canyon. He named it Hite. Soon wagons were coming in from the railroad at Green River, by way of Hanksville and Trachyte Canyon.*

Frank Brown, bouncing back quickly from his ordeal in Cataract Canyon, took it all in: accessibility for his railroad builders, plus enormous amounts of gold—dusted in minute grains throughout gravel terraces rising from fifty to two hundred feet above the river and in sandbars that lay in the stream itself and were exposed only during low water—from one end of Glen Canyon to the other, a distance of two hundred miles.[4] Also, according to a local rancher named Charles Sanford, 200,000 head of beef animals and more than that many sheep were already ranging along a forty-mile strip of land bordering the river. More would come if a railroad appeared to facilitate transportation. There was also talk of timber in the mountains, irrigated fields at the headwaters of nearby creeks, and petroleum seeps here and there, especially along the San Juan.

Brown, having heard all this, decided to let five men continue the survey in Glen Canyon while he pushed ahead with Stanton and the rest on a quick reconnaissance of the Grand. Three men now dropped out, but Brown was able to replace one of them with an able, buckskin-clad miner and carpenter, Harry McDonald.

On July 1 this advance group, traveling in three boats (the fourth remained with the surveyors), reached Lee's Ferry. There they paused for a week, patching the battered craft while Brown rode a borrowed horse to Kanab to buy a wagonload of fresh provisions. Early on July 9 they started into Marble Canyon.

On the first day they portaged around the reef of boulders that had been washed out of Badger Creek by floods, and continued part of the way past the bellowing head of Soap Creek rapids. Deciding the next morning that Soap's tail waves could be run, Brown took off in the lead. McDonald was at the oars, his back to the prow, standard rowboat technique. Seeing rough water ahead, Brown, acting as steersman, ordered his companion to pull to the bank for an investigation.

The current was running at ten or fifteen miles an hour. Between its edges and the bank a powerful eddy thrust upstream. When the unstable,

*After floods made Trachyte impassable, the road was shifted to North Wash, approximately the route followed today by Highway 95 from Hanksville to the Hite marina, at the head of Lake Powell.

round-bottomed boat cut across the line between the opposing currents, the torque rolled it over. McDonald swam out easily, but not Brown. Possibly— as his companions believed—a whirlpool caught him, or perhaps he had a seizure of some sort. The party spent the rest of the day watching the river and searching the banks. They found the overturned boat a mile and a half away, but saw no trace of Brown—who, incidentally, had been carrying all the money the party had.[5]

Five days later and twenty miles farther down into Marble Canyon, the current drove a boat carrying Peter Hansbrough and Henry Richards, one of Stanton's servants, against a cliff. They tried to push off with oars and hands. The rounded bottom failed them as it had Brown, the boat rolled, and both men drowned. With life preservers they might not have. Again, the boat was recovered, but no bodies.

Though the crew was badly shaken, Stanton remained resolute. He was convinced by now that a railway could be built in the canyons and that as Brown's heir apparent he was the one to do it. In order to finish the survey, however, he would need more men and a better outfit. So he led the group another ten miles downstream to a gash in the north wall. They climbed out in the midst of a deluge, each man carrying a single blanket and a small supply of food. A rancher picked them out of the mud of House Rock Valley and took them to Kanab. There Stanton borrowed six hundred dollars from the Mormon bishop—enough to pay off the crew and get him to Denver, where he arrived late in July.

The company backed his request to be allowed to continue. Working rapidly, he and Harry McDonald designed three new double-seated, flat-bottomed, very heavy boats—*Water Lily, Bonnie Jean, Sweet Marie*—and had them hauled to Hite from the Green River railroad station by wagon. With them were eleven crewmen and surveyors, only three of whom—McDonald, John Hislop, and the photographer Franklin Nims—had been on the first trip. They took to the water on December 10, 1889. Every man was equipped with a cork life jacket. On Christmas Day they feasted at Lee's Ferry with the ferryman, Warren Johnson, and his family. Then they dived, surely with some trepidation, into Marble Canyon.

The first trouble came New Year's Day, 1890. Franklin Nims fell twenty feet from a rock onto which he had climbed for a picture. He broke his jaw and one leg, and suffered a concussion that left him unconscious, blood oozing from his ears and mouth. Stanton and McDonald performed first aid and then strapped him tight to a stretcher made of extra oars and canvas, with spreaders of driftwood. On January 2 the party made a wild run through water that normally would have called for lining the boats, and reached a side canyon that sliced down from the north rim—a different canyon and more difficult to scale, as events proved, than the one the first party had used the preceding summer. While Stanton went ahead to fetch help from Lee's Ferry, the other men took turns boosting Nims, who remained unconscious most of the time, up ledges and over chockstones, sometimes swinging the stretcher on ropes around rough spots where, one of them wrote later, "a fall would have hurled him several hundred feet."[6]

They reached the rim at dusk. Snow was falling. Throughout the night, after wrapping Nims in all the blankets they had, they took turns pulling up dry weeds and sagebrush to feed a small fire. Stanton appeared the next morning with Johnson, the ferryman, and a wagon—a hard trip, thirty-five miles each way. Johnson carried the injured man back to the ferry and made a bed for him on the floor of the cookhouse. There he lay unconcious until January 12. Finally some passing Mormons agreed to take him, for a fee of eighty-five dollars, 185 miles south to the Santa Fe railroad station at Winslow, a nine-day trip. All but unbelievably, he survived.

Stanton took over as photographer (by then roll film had replaced the bulky glass plates that required immediate developing) and the surveyors went on. They found Peter Hansbrough's skeleton, recognizable from the remaining shreds of his clothing, and buried it. Low water made portaging difficult. Then a rare winter flood swept out of the Little Colorado, caught the boats, and tossed them like chips. The center section of one of the heavy craft was stove in so badly that Harry McDonald, acting as head carpenter, cut out the middle five feet and pulled the ends together into a stubby makeshift. A little later, in the granite gorge below Bright Angel Creek, the *Sweet Marie* was turned loose in a torrent around which they could not portage. The hope was to catch it at the bottom, but it smashed to pieces and had to be abandoned. At that McDonald quit and started alone up a tributary canyon. In spite of a laborious tussle with snow on Kaibab Plateau, he, too, survived.

Packed uncomfortably into the remaining one and a half boats, the others continued slowly for approximately 125 miles to Diamond Creek. There, twenty-three miles from the Santa Fe whistle stop of Peach Springs, they saw in the sand what they took to be the print of a woman's boot. One of them fell to his knees and kissed it before beginning a hike to Peach Springs to replenish their stock of food.

To relieve the overcrowding, Stanton released the crew of the *Sweet Marie* at the railroad. Loyally the rest dragged on. During the running of Separation Canyon, where during Powell's first expedition the Howland brothers and Dunn had split away, Stanton was thrown from the lead boat, spun deep into a whirlpool, and spewed back up in time to be jerked "mercilessly"—his word—into the following boat. Yet he was able to write repeatedly in his journal of the enchantment of the canyon's colors and contrasts, the play of light and shadow—a glorious work of nature that, above all, was

158COLORADO RIVER COUNTRY

"a living, moving being"—through which he was ready, nevertheless, to drive an endless succession of coal-burning locomotives.

On April 9 they feasted on roast beef at Fort Mojave. On the twenty-sixth they reached tidewater, abandoned the boats, and found a rancher who agreed to take them in a wagon back to the Southern Pacific Railway at Yuma. Equipped with sheaves of drawings, engineering calculations, cost-and-profit estimates, and eleven hundred photographs to prove that a railroad was feasible, Stanton went to New York to see his backers. They were cool, in part because of the poor profit record of other Pacific railroads but also because extensive discoveries of oil in California had reduced the need for Colorado and Utah coal. Though Stanton never raised enough money to build a single foot of the line, he remained a captive of the river. In one way or another it would absorb his energies for the rest of his life. By the spring of 1897 he had developed the notion of generating electricity from water impounded behind dams in the lower sections of Cataract Canyon and in tributaries to Glen Canyon, for the purpose of dredging gold from the floor of Glen Canyon.

It was then that he wrote Cass Hite for his opinion of the prospects. Hite assured him that Glen Canyon did contain gold from end to end, and that dredges, which were just then beginning to be used in mining, probably offered the best means available for scooping up the sandbars in the river bottom. By October, 1897, Stanton had found enough money to start work. Accompanied by one of his backers, he hauled two boats from the railroad to Glen Canyon on wagons. There they set up claim notices to water rights, surveyed reservoir sites and rights of way for power lines, pipe lines, and canals. On December 11 they set out to file a series of mining claims along the canyon. The winter was unusually cold and the river exceptionally low. When they weren't overboard in the current boosting the boats over sandbars, they were either breaking channels through the ice or hauling the craft along the frozen surface.

On January 12, 1898, a little below the mouth of the San Juan, they encountered, working a bar with a few associates, the semiliterate jack-of-all-trades named Nathaniel Galloway, who was the originator of whitewater techniques that led to the development of river running as it exists today.

Galloway had begun life at Lehi, Utah, in 1855. By 1891 he had moved to Vernal, near the point where the Green breaks out of the Uinta Mountains, and had become a trapper. Until his time, so far as is known, every oarsman had rowed with his back toward his destination. Galloway's credo of river running was a simple reversal: Face the danger! The technique of rowing stern-first enabled him to dispense with a steersman and to thrust ahead for speed or hold back as the situation demanded, pulling or pushing now on one oar, now on the other, maneuvering between rocks or spinning away from the holes that yawn where water billows over a boulder and falls with a crash on the downstream side.

With the danger of slamming into rocks minimized, he found he could use light boats, no more than sixteen feet long. He learned, too, that flat-bottomed craft, comparable to today's flat-bottomed "rubber" rafts, were more stable than the round-bottomed ones that Powell, Brown, and Stanton had used. He built such a craft out of wood and would later experiment with canvas, taking long journeys through canyons that had seldom been trapped. The adventure of it excited him as much as the furs. In the fall of 1896 he and William Richmond had shoved off north of the Uinta Mountains, run stern-first through Lodore, Desolation, Cataract, and the Grand Canyon, and landed at Needles in February, 1897. How many rapids they lined through or portaged around is no longer known.[7]

Stanton, who had heard of Galloway's feat from the miners, hired him on the spot to improve the road from Hanksville to the Colorado, bring in a big Keystone drill, and eventually load it onto a scow so as to move it from place to place for testing the river bottom. The engineer, his partner, and their boatmen, staking claims as they went, then struggled on through the ice to Lee's Ferry, stored their equipment, and left for the East by way of Flagstaff. There, on March 28, 1898, the Hoskaninni Company, authorized capital $300,000, came into being. (Cass Hite's tale obviously accounted for the title, though the chief's name is generally spelled with one *n*.) Julius Stone of Ohio, a wealthy manufacturer of fire engines, was president; Stanton became vice-president, engineer, and superintendent.

Hired crews finished staking the 145 claims needed to control the canyon bottom. Galloway brought in ten tons of drill parts, assembled them, and loaded them onto the scow he had built. Stone, Stanton, and a company director named Knox arrived to oversee the drilling of eighteen test holes between Hite and a pleasant terrace twelve miles away, to which Hite himself had given the name Ticaboo. The results enthralled them. The gravel ran deep, and its gold content averaged twenty-five cents a yard. In the prospectus he was preparing for the company's first stock offering, Stanton estimated the amount of available gravel at half a billion cubic yards—enough, he predicted, to keep twenty electric dredges working for forty-five years at an annual net return to the company of $1.2 million—perhaps $12 million in today's terms.

Of course, pilot operations should precede the building of dams and generating plants. Stanton proposed launching the work with a gasoline-powered dredge—a floating, flat-bottomed gold-recovery plant 105 feet long, 36 feet wide, and two stories tall. An endless chain of forty-six steel scoop buckets would feed its self-contained mill.

Preparations consumed more than a year. Finally, in the early summer of 1900, the parts for the giant machine, which had been manufactured in Wisconsin, were loaded onto two special trains for transportation to Green River. There the material was transferred to relays of high-wheeled freight wagons, many of them pulled by from sixteen to twenty horses each. The road to the river, much of it specially built, was 125 miles long. Camps, cook shacks, barns, and corrals were established along the way, wherever water was available.

There is no record of what led Stanton to select the place he did for launching the work.* Cliffs prevented wagons from reaching the exact spot he wanted to excavate, and the nature of the river above and below precluded assembling the 180-ton dredge elsewhere and floating or towing it to its destination. Of necessity he had to find ways of bringing the pieces to a flat on the west bank opposite the bar he had chosen and do the assembly work there.

The road-builders found a side canyon that enabled wagons to reach the river about a mile and a half below the assembly point. Heroic expedients had to be undertaken. Because the drop into the side canyon was too steep for horses, they were unhitched at the brink. Iron shoes were placed on all four wheels, which were then locked to prevent their turning. A cable that acted as a brake was fastened to the rear end of the wagon and it was skidded down the near-precipice in ruts carved a foot deep into the stone. Teams led over a narrow, zigzag trail into the gulch's bottom finished the short pull to the river. After each wagon had been unloaded, it was hauled back up the slick-rock precipice by a horse-powered pulley.

The parts were next loaded onto an array of scows, barges, and power launches, and taken, sometimes with the aid of winches set into the bordering cliffs, to the ways at the launching site. Camp Stone, as the place was called, was equipped with several big tent houses warmed by rock fireplaces, a mess hall, a blacksmith shop, and an ice plant. A battery-powered telephone connected its office with the camp at the end of the road.

The completed machine was skidded into the river in February, 1901. By March the buckets were chewing into the sand twenty hours a day—two ten-hour shifts. The company's top officials arrived in April and stood around watching Stanton like vultures as he cleaned the amalgamating plates to present them with the first returns. The little button of gold he showed them was worth $30.15. Three more weeks of frantic effort produced $36.80.

In time the reason became clear. Separating gold from sand by sluicing depends on the metal's high specific gravity; it drops first to the bottom of the apparatus, where it is captured by a variety of devices, while the rest of

*It lay on the west bank, about two miles above today's Bullfrog Marina—some 107 miles above Glen Canyon Dam—and is now lost to sight beneath the reservoir's waters.

the material washes on through the sluices. Water, however, has a surface tension that supports tiny objects that might otherwise sink; every farm child has seen the property demonstrated by long-legged water-striders skittering across the surface of a still pond. Glen Canyon's gold flakes were just as light. Most floated instead of dropping—more than would have done so in a prospector's modest sluice box, though the latter didn't work very well either.

Stanton's plea that he be allowed to make adjustments was refused. The company went into bankruptcy, and he was appointed receiver. His fee came to $750. He sold the horse herd for a small profit, but the dredge brought in only one bid—two hundred dollars. By February 15, 1902, his work was finished.

Still, the river held him. He spent several years gathering and setting down all the stories he could unearth about it, along with his own experiences. The manuscript came to eleven hundred pages. Only parts of the work were ever published, some not until after his death.

Grand Canyon's
Lava Falls

14

Selling the Scenery

On December 18, 1888, Richard Wetherill and his brother-in-law, Charley Mason, turned their horses up a hazardous Indian trail onto the top of Mesa Verde, in southwestern Colorado.[1] The Wetherill family's headquarters ranch was two days' ride away, on a cottonwood-shaded meadow beside the Mancos River, a few miles below the town of the same name. This winter range, which they shared with a few neighbors, lay at a lower altitude between the protective tan walls of Mancos Canyon. Both it and the adjacent mesa were within the Southern Ute Reservation, but few Indians lived in the area and the trespass by the white cattlemen went unchallenged.

The night before, the two young men, who were hunting strays, had camped with a group of cowboys near the head of Cliff Canyon, a narrow tributary of the Mancos. That morning a thin snow was falling as they rode out onto the rim. It was then that they saw, just under the cap-rock of the opposite wall, a cave that made them halt in astonishment. It was enormous —more than 120 yards long and ninety feet deep, and in it were the ruins of a village. Familiar as they were with the Anasazi dwellings scattered elsewhere in the region, they had never seen anything like this: at least two hundred rooms arranged in terraces and dominated by a number of square and round towers.[2]

When work on the ranch was slow, they had often prowled through nearby ruins, collecting artifacts to sell to tourists who occasionally wandered in from the railroad town of Durango, thirty miles away. Now, after circling the head of Cliff Canyon, they tied their lariat ropes to a tree and lowered themselves into the cave. Prowling around the silent chambers, they noted that loot was readily available. They named the place Cliff Palace. That afternoon, wondering whether other ruins were nearby, they searched the next gulch to the west and found a smaller but better preserved ruin which they named Spruce Tree House. They spent the night in the snow without food or bedding, and the next morning they discovered, a few miles away in Navajo Canyon, a third big ruin—Square Tower House. The three, all found within a twenty-four hour period, are still Mesa Verde's best-known cliff dwellings.

Returning to their canyon camp they blurted what they had seen to the cowboys there. A small stampede ensued. When they piled their gleanings together at the Alamo Ranch several days later, there were hundreds of objects: turkey-feather robes, fabric sandals, handsome gray pottery decorated with black lines, skeletons, bows and arrows—far more of them than they could dispose of to chance tourists. They set up an exhibit in Durango, which drew next to nobody. Nor was the town of Pueblo any more lucrative. Eventually, however, the Denver Historical Society bought the entire collection for three thousand dollars. Heartened, the Wetherill family, during the next fifteen months, explored 250 miles of Mesa Verde's canyons, discovered 182 ruins, and collected so many treasures that they had to build a museum on the ranch to house them.

The Alamo became a dude center, and the five Wetherill brothers began acting as guides. In June, 1891, they took a young Swedish nobleman, Baron Gustaf Eric Adolf Nordenskiöld, to the cliff dwellings. Twelve weeks of watching the precision with which the baron and his hired laborers exhumed the mummified corpses and black-and-white pottery converted Richard Wetherill from a thoughtless looter into a serious if inadequately educated archeologist. After helping Nordenskiöld collect six hundred artifacts, the brothers packed them off the mesa on donkeys and hauled them in wagons to the railroad at Durango for shipment to Sweden. To their astonishment a Durango lawman, acting at the behest of the town's newly formed archeological society, impounded the goods.

Nordenskiöld promptly telegraphed the Swedish consul in Washington, where lawyers pored over statute books but found no edicts dealing with prehistoric relics. The material was released with apologies, and the baron returned to Sweden. In 1893 he published *The Cliff Dwellers of Mesa Verde*, a book that drew acclaim throughout Europe and the United States—and also increased the determination of Colorado preservationists to retain their treasures. Even before the book appeared, the State of Colorado had built a display, intended for the Chicago Columbian Exposition of 1893, around the relics that the Wetherills had discovered and that were now owned by the Denver Historical Society (soon to become the Colorado Historical Society). The brothers were asked to add more items by skimming Mesa Verde again. Then Richard went with the collection to the fair, to stand beside the display and answer whatever questions visitors asked. He proved to be a good publicity agent for the state.

Until 1893, Mesa Verde had been pretty much the private preserve of the Wetherills. Following the Chicago Exposition, however, they went to work in other areas. Grave-robbers were soon picking up marketable curios in the region they had discovered—littering the ground, destroying with their carelessness more objects than they recovered, and leaving the plundered sites so disarranged that later study became impossible.

To combat the vandalism, Virginia Donaghe McClurg, a Colorado Springs clubwoman, in 1895 formed the Cliff-Dwellers Association and began a campaign to establish Mesa Verde as a national park.[3] At the time there were only three national parks in the United States, two of them in California.[4] Mesa Verde did not meet the criteria for which they had been set aside— unusual formations, monumental scenery, inaccessibility, and ruggedness making the area worthless for commercial development. The ruins were man-made, not natural. And the region, though dry, was not useless.

The Cliff-Dwellers Association began their attack by leasing Mesa Verde from the Southern Utes—on whose reservation it was—for ten years, at three hundred dollars a year, and posting guards at strategic sites. Eight years later, in 1903, the Association decided to buy the land outright and to present it to the government. First, however, the Utes had to agree. Virginia McClurg and two companions hired guides and horses, and met Chief Ignacio and some of his tribal leaders at Navajo Springs. The Indians accepted their terms, but the federal Bureau of Indian Affairs rejected the contract.

A drive spearheaded by Representative John Lacey of Iowa led to the passage of the Antiquities Act, which Theodore Roosevelt signed in June, 1906. The president promptly set aside four national monuments in various parts of the West. One was Mesa Verde. There were no teeth in the law, however, and later in the year Congress, prodded by the Cliff-Dwellers Association, elevated Mesa Verde to the safer status of a national park—the eighth in the nation and the first in the Colorado River Basin.

A year later, Roosevelt added to the growing list of monuments the ruins of Chaco Canyon, where in the winter of 1895–96 Richard Wetherill had begun his work as an archeological field superintendent for an exploring expedition whose goal was to gather artifacts for the American Museum of Natural History. Sponsors of the project had been a pair of wealthy young dilettantes, Talbot and Fred Hyde, whom Wetherill had met at the Chicago Exposition. After combing Grand Gulch and Keet Seel with the Hydes, Richard had come to the surface ruins in Chaco Wash, some of which were five stories tall. Since excavating the numerous complexes would require years of work, he had built, in the spring of 1898, a three-room stone house for himself and his new wife, Marietta—a squatter's claim that he would turn into a 160-acre homestead two years later, aligning the boundaries so that they embraced the greatest of the ruins, Pueblo Bonito, and two satellite groups.

While building the cabin he had hired about a hundred Navajo laborers to work on the excavations. They, their families, and visiting friends had created a market for supplies. Often they paid for the purchases, Navajo-style, with wool, some of it woven into rugs. Inevitably the new house became a trading post as well as a home. Pleased to have a little money coming in, Fred Hyde had decided impulsively during a visit late in 1898 to put the Hyde Exploring Expedition into the mercantile business. Soon long wagon trains of merchandise were supplying, in addition to Chaco Canyon, eleven other posts scattered along both sides of the Arizona–New Mexico border. Meanwhile the company had opened retail outlets for Navajo blankets and Hopi basketry in the East, no small factor in developing American awareness of native Southwestern crafts, and even operated a fruit-processing plant in the new town of Farmington, New Mexico.

Richard had done his best to keep on top of this sprawling operation. The Alamo Ranch by then had failed, and he had hired his brothers to help run the trading posts, while he did what he could to keep excavation continuing on schedule. But the ground was crumbling. In 1902, Talbot Hyde, appalled by the debts incurred during the Expedition's rapid mercantile expansion, sold out to a syndicate, which then dispensed with Richard's services. The Santa Fe Archeological Society, which had close ties to powerful New Mexico political figures in Washington, objected to Chaco's being exploited by untutored men. Digging was ordered stopped, and in 1907, when the ruins were designated a national monument, the temporary restraint became permanent. Without asking for recompense—though he might have gotten something—Richard surrendered to the government his own title to the forty-seven acres on which Pueblo Bonito stood.

From then on he tried to get along as a cattle rancher and small-time trader. He had trouble collecting debts from some of the Indians, and he was constantly harassed—he felt—by politically appointed Indian agents who wanted him out of their bailiwick. On June 22, 1910, a Navajo confronted him as he was preparing to move some cattle out of the canyon onto a mesa-top. The trader contemptuously jerked the man's rifle from him and smashed its stock on a fence post. Stung by this public humiliation, the Navajo borrowed another gun from a watching friend, slipped off through the brush, and killed Wetherill as he moved along the road with his cattle.

The discovery on Mesa Verde had been followed by others, notably in the thinly settled regions of the Colorado Plateau. In 1903, the rancher Jim Scorup led Horace Long, caretaker of Stanton's recently sold Hoskaninni gold dredge, to the massive stone bridges of White Canyon. An Indian told of an even greater bridge, curved like a rainbow over a pink canyon at the northern foot of Navajo Mountain. In 1909, competing parties, one assisted by John Wetherill, undertook to find it. En route they discovered in one of Tsegi Canyon's tributaries the awesome ruins of Betatakin, twin of Keet Seel. The combined groups reached Rainbow Bridge on August 14, 1909. Far to the north, meanwhile, Earl Douglass, following cowboy clues through the bleak, pastel-colored hills where the Green River breaks out of Split Mountain, found and began digging up the fossilized bones of an eighty-foot-long prehistoric monster called brontosaurus.

The White Canyon spans became Natural Bridges National Monument in 1908; Keet Seel, Betatakin, and nearby Inscription House were lumped together as Navajo National Monument in 1909; Rainbow followed in 1910, Dinosaur in 1915. Theodore Roosevelt designated the Grand Canyon as a monument in 1906. President Taft set aside "The Yosemite of the Desert," Mukuntuweap Canyon, in 1909; it is now known as Zion National Park.

Although the Santa Fe Railroad's precursor, the Atlantic & Pacific, had "opened" northern Arizona during 1882–83, a tourist had to have more help than the railroad offered if he wanted to see the Grand Canyon.[5] So from tiny Peach Springs, on the Hualapai Reservation, at the point where the tracks came closest to the chasm, J. H. Farlee in 1884 scraped a rough twenty-mile road to Diamond Creek, where Lieutenant Ives and Baron Möllhausen had camped nearly thirty years earlier. There he built a small shack with a kitchen and dining room on the lower floor and two bedrooms above. Travelers who had made arrangements to be picked up at Peach Springs disembarked in the dark (both east- and west-bound trains went through between 2:00 and 3:00 A.M.), ate breakfast at the station restaurant, and then were rattled in a wagon down to the resort.

From Farlee's hotel they could reach the booming river by either hiking or riding horseback over a rugged, boulder-strewn, two-mile trail between somber walls two thousand feet high. At the river they learned, as Ives had, that the banks were passable for only a few hundred yards. The novelty soon faded, and Grand Canyon tourist traffic shifted one hundred miles upstream to the high South Rim, with its exhilarating vistas of what naturalist John Burroughs called "the Divine Abyss."

Prospectors quickly offered to serve them. A basis for the work already existed—dizzy trails into the gorge to reach copper and asbestos mines, and rough wagon tracks leading to the railroad at Flagstaff, Williams, or Ashfork, depending on the distance. Shortly after 1885 John Hance built a small log hotel and a few tent houses at Grandview Point, sixty miles or so from Flagstaff. Far to the west of Grandview, at Havasupai Point, seventy-plus miles north of Ashfork, William Wallace Bass erected a similar hostelry with double attractions; daring guests could either follow him down to his cable crossing of the main river or drop leftward into Cataract Canyon to visit the Havasupai Indians. A third entrepreneur was Ralph Cameron, who with two partners decided to launch a dude business sixty miles north of Williams. Their lure was an old Indian trail that dropped along an ancient geologic fault line in the south cliffs.

A tiny stream, Garden Creek, flowed along the fault. In prehistoric times it had provided water for Indian farms located where the cliffs leveled off briefly at a terrace called the Tonto Platform. The fault then continued across the canyon and broke a line far back into the north wall. A creek flowed over there, too. Much larger than the trickle on the south side, it had been named Bright Angel by Powell.

A good name. The partners used it when obtaining a franchise from Coconino County to operate, on the south side of the canyon, what they called the Bright Angel Toll Road. "Road" was an overstatement. They simply widened the Indian trail a bit and eased the most precipitous of its grades. They built a hotel at the head of the trail and a camp at the abandoned farms which they called Indian Gardens. Later they extended the trail to the river, but they never did touch Bright Angel Creek. Business flourished, partly because of the names and partly because their "road" was the least rugged of the pioneer trails.

Traffic to the South Rim resorts expanded enough so that Edward Ripley, the Santa Fe's new president, decided to put the railroad into the tourist business. His wedge was a branch line that the Santa Fe had helped finance as far as the Anita Copper Mine, thirty-five miles north of Williams. The Anita was located in a shallow valley that overlay a southward extension of the same fault that the Bright Angel Toll Road followed to Indian Gardens. Up on the flats the depression provided an almost perfect railroad grade. So when the Anita's owners failed to meet their mortgage payments in 1900, the Santa Fe foreclosed and next year stretched the line onto the rim. The Fred Harvey Company, which ran sumptuous hotels and restaurants beside the railroad's principal depots, then erected a luxurious, one-hundred-room log resort named El Tovar, building it of imported Oregon fir since the Arizona ponderosa pine that grew nearby was deemed aesthetically unsatisfactory. Next door rose the huge Hopi House, an adobe curio shop enlivened by Indian artisans making jewelry and weaving rugs in full public view. Finally, the painter Thomas Moran was brought to the canyon; lithographs of his romantic paintings were then struck and distributed throughout the country.[6]

In 1919 the Grand Canyon became a national park and was placed under the jurisdiction of the newly organized National Park Service. In 1928 Cameron surrendered his toll road to the government, which had already built a competing trail of its own—the Kaibab, from Yaki Point to Bright Angel Creek—and the man who had once boasted that he owned the Grand Canyon moved to Philadelphia.[7]

The Canyon's high North Rim lay more than two hundred miles from the nearest railroad stop at Marysvale, and people would not suffer that far in stagecoaches or wagons just to see scenery. The lesson was learned first by John W. Young, the son of Brigham Young who had worked unsuccessfully for the Atlantic & Pacific in the Little Colorado River Basin. He purchased holdings on the east side of the Kaibab Plateau with the thought of making it into a hunting preserve. In 1891 Buffalo Bill Cody helped him lure in a few British noblemen as potential investors. The dusty wagon ride from Flagstaff to the South Rim, which the Santa Fe had not yet reached, then through the Painted Desert and across Lee's Ferry, did not entice them, and Young let the mortgaged ranch go.[8]

The picture changed with the arrival of the Santa Fe at the South Rim in 1901, followed in 1902 by a successful traverse of Bright Angel Canyon, long thought impassable, by the great mapper of the central part of the Grand, François Émile Matthes of the U.S. Geological Survey. After talking to Matthes, a Utah rancher, E. D. Woolley, conceived the notion of building a trail down Bright Angel Creek and swinging a cable across the river to link up with Cameron's Bright Angel Toll Road. (Whereas the road via Lee's Ferry was close to 250 miles long, the cable would bring the rims within twenty trail miles of each other.) And some thrill-seekers, the promoters believed, on arriving on the South Rim via the Santa Fe would surely ride across the great abyss to a lodge perched on the edge of the Kaibab Plateau. The North Rim's fame would spread, roads to the railroad at Marysvale would be improved, and tourism would take hold. In 1903, Woolley and a few Kanab friends put together the Grand Canyon Transportation Company and went to work. Things moved slowly. The land was rugged, materials expensive, money short. In 1906 Woolley's son-in-law, David D. Rust, took over as supervisor and freed the older man to generate publicity. The trail and a cableway across the river were completed in 1907—and used, among other things, for transporting—on donkey-back—a live, tightly bound, and very angry mountain lion from the North Rim to the South. Motion pictures of the feat were distributed throughout the country.

In 1909, Woolley and a few friends strung caches of gasoline and lubricating oil from Utah's southernmost service station at Marysvale down through Kanab to the North Rim. At a cost of nine shredded tires they then bulled two automobiles from Salt Lake City to the edge of the Grand Canyon. The accomplishment gave impetus to Utah's own "See America First" program; the Union Pacific took an interest, and by the early 1920's the Utah Parks Company (a Union Pacific subsidiary) had launched its "Celestial Tour"—a ten-day bus ride that began at the Escalante Hotel, in Cedar City, and took in Zion National Park, the North Rim, Bryce Canyon National Park, and Cedar Breaks National Monument. Meanwhile, automobile traffic to the South Rim was growing rapidly; after 1926 more tourists arrived there each year by car than by train.

Also in 1909, Julius Stone, who had helped finance Robert Stanton's gold dredge, became the first person ever to hire a guide to take him down the river just for the sport of it. The man he chose was Nathaniel Galloway, with whom he had become well acquainted in Glen Canyon during the work with the dredge.[9]

The party was to consist of four men—Stone; his brother-in-law, Raymond Cogswell, who was to act as trip photographer; a friend, C. C. Sharp; and the guide. Each was to handle his own boat, built to specifications provided by Galloway: weight, 243 pounds; length, sixteen feet four inches; beam, four feet. Watertight compartments were placed fore and aft for carrying supplies and lending buoyancy; a canvas splash-shield would protect the occupant of the cockpit when he was running rapids.

When the party gathered at Green River, Wyoming, on September 12, Galloway added a dog—the first for a long canyon run—and a friend, Seymour Sylvester Dubendorff, who soon became known to his companions as Dubie. Although inexperienced with fast water, Dubie took charge of one of the boats with Cogswell as passenger, sitting on the deck with his feet in the cockpit. Galloway trapped beaver on and off throughout the run. He supplemented the larder by shooting mountain sheep and ducks and by hiking up side streams of the Green to catch trout; Jones Creek, which runs into the river six or seven miles below the junction of the Green and Yampa, provided him with ninety-eight fat rainbows.

The group learned fast and were soon running every rapid that Galloway said did not have to be portaged or lined. At such places Cogswell had to either lie flat on the deck clutching the rope that ran around the gunwales or skirt the white water by walking along the bank. Wherever possible he chose the latter method. The big drops of Cataract Canyon satisfied Sharp's yearning for adventure: he left the party at Hite. After abandoning his boat—Cogswell declined to take it over—the others rowed on through Glen Canyon as swiftly as low water and sandbars allowed. Stone was ecstatic as he brought his diary up to date one moonlit night in the upper part of Marble Canyon: "I have reached," he wrote, "the land where dreams come true."

On November 3, they climbed the Bright Angel Trail to El Tovar to have exposed film developed and to order fresh supplies of food packed down to the river. On November 15, they broke out of the Canyon at Grand Wash Cliffs, "Highley Elated," Galloway wrote in his journal, "over our Speedy and Successful trip."

News of the run swept through the Canyon Country, and in 1911 Ellsworth and Emery Kolb decided to duplicate it in order to take the first motion pictures of a canyon traverse. The two had come to the South Rim in 1901 and had perched a small photographic studio at Grand Canyon Village, on the brink of the cliffs at the head of the Bright Angel Toll Trail. Their windows opened onto a magnificent view of the canyon's maze of color-banded buttes, promontories, and zigzagging fissures. Their main income was derived from taking souvenir pictures of tourists gingerly starting on rented mules down the trail toward Indian Gardens. Although the brothers had climbed extensively around the cliffs and had rowed back and forth across the river at a few of its crossings, they were totally lacking in white-water experience.

They left Green River, Wyoming, on September 8, 1911. Ellsworth characteristically named his boat *Defiance;* Emery called his *Edith,* after his daughter.[10] With them was a twenty-one-year-old helper, James Fagin. The miseries of running heavy water flat on the deck, as Cogswell had done, and the labors of portaging where rapids could not be run soon disenchanted him. He left the expedition at Echo Park, where the Green and Yampa join, rented a horse at a nearby ranch, and rode away. Undeterred, the brothers pushed on through Desolation, climbed to the rim at the junction of the Green and Colorado to photograph the meeting-place from above, and then, much more proficient than they had been when starting the trip, dived into Cataract. Jungles of rock studded the low water. Soaked, deafened by the constant roar, their eyes filled with jumbled visions of cracked, towering walls and leaping waves, they lined their boats more often than the Stone–Galloway party had. For the sake of their movies they also took more chances. At one point they lashed the boats together in tandem and ran a medium-sized rapid, Ellsworth rowing the first craft and Emery sitting on the deck of the second as he cranked away in the hope of capturing a sense of how a boat heaves in rough water. Later, at Soap Creek Rapid, near the spot where Frank Brown had died, Emery crawled onto a promontory to film Ellsworth turning turtle in the *Defiance*, if he did. The *Defiance* obliged. So did the *Edith* when Ellsworth tried to run it through the same rapid a little later. They spent the next two days reassembling boats and gear that had been strewn for more than a mile along both banks of the river.

They paused for a month at their studio on the South Rim. On December 19, they returned to the river with a new helper, Bert Lauzon, and an idea for a motion picture of a cops-and-robbers chase through the rapids. During the filming, workers at Bass's riverside camp served as extras and lifeguards, heaving cork preservers to actors floundering in the ice-cold stream. Unfortunately, water got into the camera and spoiled the sequence.

Enough film was left to last as far as Needles. After it was added to earlier footage stored at their South Rim studio, Emery toured the East with what turned out to be a highly popular documentary about canyon scenery, camp life, and river-running. Ellsworth meanwhile decided to finish the run to the Gulf. He caught a train back to Needles, arriving in May, 1913, when the Colorado was approaching its spring high. Undeterred by the power of the brown torrent, he bought a boat from a Mojave Indian for eighteen dollars and headed alone toward the Gulf.

He had the river to himself. Steamboat traffic had been dwindling since the railroads had begun bringing passengers and freight to Arizona at cheaper rates than they could be carried through the Gulf of California. The final blow came in 1909 when the United States Reclamation Service completed the first dam to stretch entirely across the main stem of the Colorado. Named Laguna, it was located thirteen miles above Yuma, Arizona. Intended as a diversion dam only, it consisted of parallel walls of concrete forty-three feet high. The space between the walls was filled with rock and gravel, and the whole was capped with a gently rounded concrete arch so that floods could pour over the top. A ragged pile of boulders and concrete slabs lined the base of the downstream wall to keep the cataract from back-cutting into the barrier as it fell over the arch, creating with its surge a deafening maelstrom.

Although Ellsworth Kolb knew of the obstruction, the flood rushed him toward it faster than he anticipated, and only desperate rowing got him into the safety of a canal a moment ahead of disaster. From there on, the journey was easy. He picked up a companion in Yuma, and the two of them sped down the newest channel the river had created for itself. They passed miles of huge levees erected to keep water out of the Imperial Valley, entered the shallow expanses of Volcano Lake in Mexico, threaded a watery jungle, emerged onto mudflats, and saw at last the sheen of the Gulf ahead of them.

For Ellsworth it was the completion of a sixteen-hundred-mile journey (by his figures) from Wyoming. Exuberant, he dashed off a book which was published in 1914 under the curious title *Through the Grand Canyon from*

Wyoming to Mexico, as though the great gorge filled the whole distance. The volume remains a classic of Colorado River literature. And, together with the movies they had taken, it helped bring both brothers back to the river a few years later, this time as guides for reclamation engineers seeking sites for still more dams.

Steamboat Explorer *near*
Mohave Canyon

15

Claiming the Water

The Hispanic peoples of New Mexico and southern Arizona, the Mormons of Utah, and cooperative colonies in Colorado and California all appeared to give visible proof that irrigation worked. Western railroads with land to sell and empty freight cars to fill, and canal corporations seeking customers for their water, added assurance: dry lands were better than humid for farming, for there were few clouds to check growth, and stream water laden with natural fertilizing elements could be applied in proper amounts when needed rather than when storms dictated.

Inspired by floods of brochures, thousands of would-be farmers trooped into barren valleys whose rivers, born in distant mountains, seemed to give promise of agricultural prosperity. A series of alternate droughts and flash floods during the late 1880's and early 1890's brought them the belated realization that they could not maintain their farms unless they stabilized their water supplies by building larger reservoirs and stronger dams and canals than those they had attained so far through private effort. At the same time, developers were becoming convinced that a systematic attack on aridity was vital if they were to continue selling land. In 1888, Congress responded to pressure from western congressmen, led by Senator William Stewart of Nevada and Henry Teller of Colorado, with a cautious appropriation of one hundred thousand dollars. With this sum the U.S. Geological Survey, then headed by John Wesley Powell, was to start determining where irrigable lands lay amid the mountains and deserts, where reservoirs fortifying those lands could be built, and where the water to fill the storage basins was to come from.

In 1889, the appropriation was increased to $250,000. Although inadequate still for the detailed topographical and hydrological land-classification study Powell envisioned, the figure struck his opponents as outrageous. States' rights philosophers objected to the federal government invading a field where it had no business being. Midwest farmers said the money was being used to subsidize competition. Many eastern taxpayers resented paying for an apparent boondoggle that would benefit only a small number of westerners.[1]

Yet it was in the West that fatal hostility arose. Powell, it was charged, could not finish the surveys for decades. Worse, he had persuaded Congress to close the entire arid part of the nation west of the 110th meridian—about 850 million acres—to settlement under the country's homestead laws until the president decreed that parts of it could be re-opened. The purpose was to keep speculators from grabbing irrigable sections of the domain as fast as they were identified. Powell's western opponents, however, read the message differently. They saw the restriction on their freedom as one more maneuver to tighten federal control over the public domain.

The protestors won. In August, 1890, public lands were re-opened to settlement, and the survey's scope was confined to the finding and mapping of reservoir sites alone. Agrarians were stunned. Then the Populist fervor of the times caught them up, and they returned to the attack with a series of interstate irrigation congresses designed to pressure the government into doing even more than Powell had attempted.[2]

They began with a breathless proposal: Let the nation cede to the states and territories of the West all the newly opened public lands within their borders. The states would sell those lands, no more than 320 acres per buyer, and earmark the proceeds for irrigation projects.

The vision intoxicated many westerners. When orators at the second irrigation congress, in October, 1893, spoke of remaking the deserts, Powell, who had been invited to address the gathering, cast aside his prepared speech and said bluntly that there was not enough water in the West to irrigate the amount of land they were talking about. He was booed for his pains, and the next year he was squeezed out of his job as director of the Geological Survey.

Under the Carey Act, passed in 1894, the seven driest states, but no territories, could apply for up to a million acres of arid land each, provided that the state engineer oversaw the distribution of water to bona fide settlers on 160-acre tracts.

The economic depression of the 1890's crippled the enterprise, and of the seven million acres that might have been appropriated, only 1.2 million had been applied for by 1900, and title was perfected to only a fraction of those. Then the conservation-minded Theodore Roosevelt was elected president, and in 1902 he helped browbeat through Congress a reclamation bill that put the federal government in the water business.

The first federal reclamation project in the Colorado River Basin, and one of the first in the nation, was the Yuma Project, designed to salvage existing homesteads rather than to open new ones—although it did some of that as well. Back in 1897, Eugene Ives, grandson of the explorer Joseph Christmas Ives, had sought to weave a network of irrigation canals across 160,000 acres of fertile Arizona river-bank land. He had gone broke within a year. In 1903, after two more private companies had also failed, the area's farmers formed a quasi-public corporation, the Yuma Water Users Association, legally empowered to enter into contracts with the new federal Reclamation Service. To pay for the Service's work, the association issued bonds supported by assessments levied on its members—arrangements that were the financial heart of all Reclamation Service projects.

The Service's solution for the Yuma irrigation problems was Laguna Dam, which diverted 1,060 cubic feet of water per second from the Colorado River into a canal on the California side of the stream.[3] About 12 percent of that flow was used to irrigate roughly 15,500 acres—seven thousand owned by private individuals and companies, and seventy-five hundred by the Fort Yuma Indian Reservation. (Rather than farm the land themselves, the Indians leased it to whites.) The remaining 88 percent of the diverted water flowed on to the Colorado River below Yuma and dived into an inverted siphon that carried it underneath the stream to the Arizona side. There it was picked up by three distribution canals and a labyrinth of laterals that moved it to approximately fifty-three thousand acres stretching south to the Mexican border—a considerable shrinkage from the 160,000 that had originally been proposed by Eugene Ives. The discrepancy is indicative of the sort of unrealistic plans Powell was trying to restrain when he lost his job.

Even more drastic was the shrinkage of the Uncompahgre Project, in western Colorado. Farmers hurrying into the area during the 1880's had estimated that the valley contained 200,000 somewhat scattered acres of irrigable land. The canals and ditches they had built, however, had reached only forty thousand acres—and during the drought of the late 1890's orchards had died and homes had been abandoned. Whereas the farmers of the Yuma Project had sought to divert a river that ran past their doorsteps, those of the Uncompahgre had to seek out a distant stream—the Gunnison. A far bigger river than the Uncompahgre and roughly parallel to it, the Gunnison had carved a jagged canyon through the high tableland that formed the northeast boundary of the dry valley. The gorge, about fifty miles long, is called the Black Canyon because of its dark schists and granites. The almost perpendicular couloirs that crease the steep walls are filled with rubble in which evergreens have taken precarious root. In places the cliffs are streaked with zigzagging bands of intrusive pegmatite; one striking façade is called the Painted Wall. The narrowest part of the canyon bottom is forty-four feet wide. The floor of the deepest section is twenty-seven hundred feet below the canyon rim.

In 1881–82, workers of the Denver & Rio Grande Railway had blasted a narrow-gauge roadbed through the first fifteen miles of the canyon and then had led the tracks out of the gorge by way of a side stream. During the next eighteen years an occasional adventurer had climbed from the rim into the lower canyon and back again, but no one had traversed the final thirty-five miles. In 1900, however, dryness provided a motive, and five men from Montrose, the Uncompahgre Valley's principal town, decided to check elevations to learn whether a gravity tunnel was feasible. They shipped wooden boats to the river by train, spent twenty-one days dragging the heavily loaded craft through fourteen miles of rock-torn water, and then, abandoning their equipment, climbed out, convinced that the canyon was impassable. They had learned, however, that a tunnel would work.

In order to collect more data, Abraham Lincoln Fellows, head of the U.S. Geological Survey's hydrographic section in Colorado, decided to backpack through the gorge. If he and the volunteer he hoped to find were forced into the water by protruding cliffs, they would swim, dragging their instruments, blanket rolls, and a minimum amount of food along on a light rubber raft. During June, Fellows searched the canyon rim for breaks down which additional rations could be brought to the river. After finding three places that looked possible from above, he ransacked Montrose for assistants. A man named A. D. Dillon agreed to act as a human elevator, carrying food into the gorge and bringing out notes and film. William Torrence, a husky member of the first five-man party, signed on as assistant surveyor.[4]

Fellows and Torrence started their trip on August 12, 1901. Only occasionally did they find a gravel bar along which they could walk for more than a few steps. The frequent rapids again and again made swimming the stream impossible. The alternative was to scale the blockading precipices until they found narrow ledges that let them inch ahead high above the torrent—without their raft, which they soon abandoned. They did swim through the narrows—in his reminiscences Fellows called that stretch the jaws of the canyon—and on the far side they ran into huge piles of water-polished boulders whose tops rose a hundred feet above the water that surged through the crevices beneath. Sometimes they climbed the barricades, one standing on the other's shoulders to reach a necessary handhold. Sometimes they swam through the channels, fighting eddies that threatened to suck them into deep caverns. There is a legend that at one point they deliberately jumped into the stream and let it rush them underneath a rock-fall they could not surmount. Fellows does not mention such an adventure in his account, though he does tell of surprising two mountain sheep asleep in a cranny thirty or forty feet above the stream. One was so startled that in its leap to escape it fell to the rocks below, crippled beyond escape—a godsend, for the men had just consumed the last of their second relay of provisions.

One day they ran into a cul-de-sac, retreated, and camped for the night directly across the river from the point where they had eaten breakfast that morning. On another day they spent six hours advancing less than a quarter of a mile. Altogether they swam the river seventy-six times. The key to winning was Dillon, who met them on schedule at the base of three different razor-thin couloirs. Revived periodically, they finished the thirty-five-mile traverse in ten days. Each lost fifteen pounds in the process. They not only confirmed the possibility of the tunnel but also found a pocket, approachable by a corkscrewing road across the intervening mesa, that would do as a construction site.

The story of Laguna Dam was then repeated. The first contractor to undertake the tunneling went broke. An Uncompahgre Water Users Association was formed, and at its behest the Reclamation Service took over the work in 1905, fighting unexpected inflows of boiling water and carbon dioxide gas that necessitated the drilling of additional ventilating and drainage shafts. In 1909, President Taft arrived in the valley to open what was then the longest irrigation tunnel in the world—just under six miles. Before long, 439 miles of canals and laterals were carrying water not to 146,000 acres, as irrigation optimists had once predicted, but to about half that amount. Still, the valley had been salvaged, though the full cost of the project has not, at this writing, been entirely amortized.

By the opening of the twentieth century, twelve companies of various sorts were trying to draw reliable supplies of water from Arizona's Salt River, and not one was succeeding. Some of the firms built timber cribs across the river, filled the hollows with rocks, and faced the dams with planks. Some were content to pile up thick mats of brush and stone. All told, they were responsible for wetting about 120,000 acres—a smaller area than the Hohokam Indians had been irrigating eight centuries earlier.[5]

The Salt and its principal tributaries drain a watershed in the Arizona Highlands as big as Massachusetts and Connecticut combined. Precipitation is erratic. Of the fourteen years from 1890 through 1904, eleven were dry. During the other three, flash floods thundering out of the mountains destroyed every one of the twelve dams. Each time the settlers rebuilt, they encountered more drought. Toward the end of the century, armed patrols were riding the canal banks to make sure no one was stealing water.

The answer seemed to be building a big storage and flood-control dam in a canyon just below the point where Tonto Creek flows into the Salt. Financing seemed hopeless, however, until the passage of the Reclamation Act, which allowed the area's farmers to form the Salt River Valley Water Users Association and enter into contracts with the Reclamation Service for the building of Roosevelt Dam—key element in the Service's first large storage project. (Laguna Dam was for diversion, not storage.) Because Roosevelt Dam combined water storage and flood control, it was also the Reclamation Service's first multiple-purpose structure. Built of stone blocks, it was 184 feet thick at its base and 280 feet high—still the highest masonry dam in the world. Each rock in it had to be individually shaped, transported, and cemented into place. To reduce costs, the contractor, Louis Hill, decided to generate electric power on the site for mixing cement and tramming and hoisting the stones. So when Arthur Powell Davis, a nephew of John Wesley Powell and assistant chief engineer of the new Service, was running surveys for the dam, he also ran a line for a canal that would pick up water from the river thirteen miles away and then drop it down a penstock into a power plant built in the canyon at one end of the dam site. Then the question arose: What should be done with the power after the dam had been completed? The obvious answer: Why not sell it, preferably to a public agency to keep private utility companies from howling about government competition, and apply the revenues to the cost of the project? And so power generation became a permanent function of multiple-purpose dams.

There were troubles. Floods like those that had destroyed the river's first diversions tore out the coffer dams at Roosevelt and set work back by years. The road that supplied the dam, called the Apache Trail after the workers who built it, was much longer and fully as terrifying as the one that serviced the Gunnison Tunnel. But by the time the structure was finished and dedicated by Theodore Roosevelt himself, on March 18, 1911, the cocky young men who ran the Reclamation Service felt capable of producing any kind of dam, however huge, that was needed anywhere in the land. And at that point they ran into a problem to which they had given little heed before—the bizarre water laws of the West.

In spite of the emphasis placed by government dam-builders on the term "multiple-purpose," more than 80 percent of all water diverted from the Colorado system is still used for irrigation. Some of this water, often highly charged with undesirable saline compounds leached from the soil, seeps back into the stream channel and is reused. The rest vanishes, mostly by transpiration through the leaves of the plants it nourishes.

The common law of England and of the eastern United States had no provisions for dealing with such disappearances. Agriculture in those regions did not need irrigation. Rivers were used primarily for transportation and turning mill wheels. Persons who took water from a stream were legally obliged to return it with its quantity and quality substantially undiminished. If a city wished to degrade the supply in any way, it requested special permits. Water, in short, was supposed to flow as nature intended. Laws covering that situation were called riparian.

Laws in arid lands were different.[6] There water had always been physically seized and moved from where it was to where it was wanted; the Romans, for instance, were building giant aqueducts hundreds of years ago. Despite those precedents, however, American law was slow to recognize aridity. It long ignored the Mormons, who began diverting water under Church supervision in 1847, and the Spanish settlers, who had done the same thing even earlier. California miners were the ones who, in 1866, finally forced the custom onto the nation's statute books, where it is known as the doctrine of prior appropriation.

The miners' reasoning was simple. A man found a good placer bar in the Sierra foothills, say, and promptly turned part of the closest stream through his sluice box in order to wash out the gold in the gravel. During the spring, when quantities of snow melt poured out of the mountains, the claimant and his neighbors got along. In the fall, when there was no longer water enough to go around, quarrels arose.

Dividing what little was available into equal shares would mean that no one got enough. So it became a custom in California's largely self-governing mining districts to rule that the person, or the corporation, who *first* filed a claim could continue using the entire amount appropriated as long as desired without hindrance from anyone else. After the first claimant had taken his allotment, the second could move in, then the third, and so on. The water to which a person was entitled was called his water right. Since appropriated water could be used anywhere one liked, the right could be sold separately from the land. Water thus became what it never was in the East—namely, private property.

There were certain restraints. A claimant was supposed to put his water to beneficial use, which in the early days was defined as any activity that was potentially profitable. He was not supposed to claim more than his project needed and he was to begin his use within a specified time. Obviously, endless record-keeping and adjudication were necessary.

Miners carried the rule of prior appropriation to Colorado. There, on the grounds that the states, not the federal government, own the unappropriated waters within their borders, the doctrine was for the first time incorporated into a state constitution. (California still mingles riparian and appropriation law.) Known as the Colorado doctrine, the law spread throughout the West, generally with modifications. Differing circumstances have resulted in so many variations, and the federal government has thrown in so many shockers (when the government established Indian reservations and National Forests, did it, by implication, "reserve" enough water to meet the needs of those entities?) that eastern lawyers throw up their hands in despair. Their favorite adjective for western water law is "Byzantine." Nevertheless its basic premise —"first in time is first in right"—is starkly simple, as the Reclamation Service was forced to realize when it began talking of even bigger structures than Roosevelt Dam.

In the spring of 1891, a higher rise than usual caused the Colorado River to spill off the elevated ribbon of silt along which it meandered in the vicinity of the border between the United States and Mexico. Some of the escaped water flowed southwest along what was called New River, to shallow Volcano Lake, in Mexico. From there, part drained into the Gulf; the rest turned north across the featureless land into the Salton Sink in California, where it puddled into a lake. Simultaneously, a second break in the river bank carried water through Mexico into the same Sink by way of an ancient and much shorter overflow channel, the Alamo Barranca.

One person who watched the brief filling and fading of the lake in the desert—the flood that year soon receded—was Charles Rockwood, a civil engineer connected with the Southern Pacific Railroad. From the event rose an idea that had occurred to others: Why not divert the Colorado through the Alamo Barranca to irrigate the long, fertile, below-sea-level Sink? After a few years of reflection he came up with a feasible plan.

The first step, taken in 1896, was the incorporation, in New Jersey, of a firm that he and his associates called the California Development Company. Four more years were spent raising capital. Ready at last in 1900, they posted a claim for twenty thousand acre-feet of Colorado River water, bought an old dredge, and, under the direction of a renowned real-estate plunger named George Chaffey, began opening a canal near Pilot Knob, less than a mile north of the border.[7] (It would have been easier to cut through the bank in Mexico, as the river had, but the company decide to limit its claim to the United States.) After traveling four miles between the river and the sand dunes west of Yuma, the new canal dipped into the Alamo Barranca, which had been cleared of brush and smoothed up a bit here and there. The Barranca served as a waterway for the next fifty miles before veering north into the United States, where control gates for distribution canals were located. The first water arrived in June, 1901—but only after a Mexican corporation had absorbed half of the flow in exchange for transit rights across its land.

Settlers lured by advertising brochures were waiting in the American part of the Sink—and so was the Imperial Land Company, controlled by the same men who ran the California Development Company. (One of George Chaffey's inspirations had been changing the name of the Salton Sink to Imperial Valley.) The Imperial Land Company helped settlers to locate and file claims on suitable government land and generously arranged mortgages so that the farmers could buy water from the Development Company. It then took over the acreage of those who failed to meet their payments and resold it to latecomers on a rising market.

The success of the venture was phenomenal. The Southern Pacific built a branch line into the area. By 1904, nearly one hundred thousand acres were in production, population had jumped from zero to seven thousand, and the Imperial Land Company was thriving. A group of settlers actually tarred and feathered a government representative who tried to talk a mass meeting into supporting the Reclamation Service's plan for a coordinated development of the entire lower Colorado River.

Although the Imperial Land Company was prospering, the California Development Company, on which water delivery depended, was not. There were animosities among the directors, Chaffey was ejected, and Rockwood sold the water firm's assets to the Southern Pacific Railroad for two hundred thousand dollars. He then stepped into Chaffey's shoes as chief engineer of the delivery system.

He had stepped into a precarious position. The river's heavy loads of silt had clogged the intake of the original canal within a year. When dredges and suction pumps failed to clear the obstruction, the company moved down the stream a short distance and cut another opening, then another. Neither solved the problem, and early in 1905 Rockwood broke still another canal through the bank, this time well inside Mexico. Like Chaffey before him, he did not install a headgate for shutting off the flow into the canal. The problem, as he saw it, was keeping the channel open, not closing it.

Having seen the relatively minor flood of 1891, he should have known better. Just after his newest cut was made, both the Colorado and Gila rampaged, not once but several times. By August 1905, the breach in the river bank was more than half a mile wide, and the entire Colorado River was roaring down the Alamo Barranca. On reaching the valley it spread out into a series of streams, gashing thousands of acres beyond redemption and washing away parts of the twin towns of Mexicali and Calexico before finally coming to rest in what is now the Salton Sea.

In spite of the flood, many farms were unscarred, and the operators managed to get enough water to mature their cotton, cantelopes, and alfalfa.

Prices were fine, but how much longer could the valley hang on? The elevation of the break in the river bank was about 110 feet above sea level; the bottom of the Salton Sink was 232 feet below that level—enough tilt that the flood began gouging its channels deeper and at the same time eroded backwards. Thus the immediate threat was not the slow rise of the Salton Sea—though it inundated some arable land, buried a salt works under forty feet of water, and forced the Southern Pacific to move its tracks to higher ground—but the deepening of the Alamo beyond the point where the valley's irrigating system could reach it. And what if headward erosion also deepened the river breach beyond hope of closure?

Meanwhile, both the development company and the parent Southern Pacific were struggling to close the gap. The first efforts involved building wing dams of pilings and thick mats of brush whose tangled twigs and stems would catch and hold enough sediment to deflect the current from the break. The river slapped them aside. Next, during low water in the summer of 1906, the Southern Pacific built a trestle across the gap and dumped in three thousand carloads of clay, gravel, and rock. In November the gap was closed. A month later a new surge of high water began dissolving the barrier and it had to be rebuilt. Final victory over the two-year flood did not come until February 10, 1907.

Optimistic once more, the residents of Imperial County voted to break away from San Diego County and take destiny into their own hands. Four years later, in 1911, the farmers of the new county banded together as the Imperial Irrigation District and shortly afterward purchased the water system that served them. Yet growth remained shackled. When winter crops were being planted late in the season, water was short, partly because half of the flow through the Alamo canal had to go to farmlands in Mexico. Meantime the river had completed its shift from the east side of its silt bed to the west. Dozens of miles of levees, the most critical of them near Volcano Lake in Mexico, had to be built and constantly raised to keep spring floods from encroaching again—a work handicapped by revolutions in Mexico and by the demands of various generals that customs duties and taxes be paid on materials taken across the border for use in flood-control projects.

The many problems led to increasing agitation for an All-American canal that would avoid touching Mexico and the construction, somewhere in the river's lower canyons, of a dam large enough to reduce silt loads, provide storage, and check floods. Rich though Imperial's agricultural lands were— perhaps, acre for acre, the richest in the world—the District could not finance a project of such magnitude by itself. Accordingly the farmers chose to forget the tar-and-feathering they had administered to an early lobbyist for the Reclamation Service and sought a reconciliation.

The Service was willing. But could Congress be persuaded that a massive pouring of money into one small section of a relatively small river basin was a justifiable tax on the rest of the nation?

At that point another ally appeared, brainchild of San Diego boosters who believed that the growth of their city would be quickened if it were tied to a coordinated program for the development of the entire Southwest. Accordingly they persuaded delegates from California, Arizona, New Mexico, Nevada, Utah, Colorado, Texas, and Oklahoma to meet in their city in November, 1917, and form a League of the Southwest for promoting mutual interests.

It was soon clear that mutuality did not extend to the last two states. The League's third meeting, held at Los Angeles in April, 1920, closed with a declaration that "the development of the resources of the Colorado River fundamentally underlies the progress and prosperity of the Southwest."[8] Finding themselves superfluous, Texas and Oklahoma withdrew. Wyoming, which was hardly a Southwestern state but did contain the headwaters of the Green, then joined, making the League a Colorado River institution. Its next meeting was set for Denver in August, 1920.

The Colorado River: Congressman Edward Taylor, who represented all twenty of the sparsely populated counties of the State of Colorado that lay west of the Continental Divide, brooded about that name. In 1920, according to every map in existence, the Colorado River began where the Green River of Wyoming and the Grand River of Colorado met, fifty miles inside Utah. An outrage, the congressman decided, though the situation had existed since Spanish times. Surely the state that had been named for the river should contain its headwaters. He proposed, therefore, to rename the Grand River the Colorado, even though the shift would make orphans out of Grand County, Utah; Grand County, Colorado; and such other Colorado landmarks as Grand Lake, at the edge of Rocky Mountain National Park, Grand Valley, towering Grand Mesa, and the town of Grand Junction, where the Grand River picks up its principal tributary, the Gunnison.

His motives in proposing this geographic adjustment seem clear. Western water law, to which all of the Basin states subscribed, was based on antagonistic principles. One, as we have seen, decreed that water went to whomever claimed it first for beneficial use—or, as water lawyers sometimes cyinically remarked, water flowed toward money. Because of the alliance joining the Imperial Valley, San Diego, the utility companies in Los Angeles, and the Reclamation Service, the flow in 1920 was plainly away from the State of Colorado.

But according to another declared principle, each western state owned all the unappropriated water within its borders. If that were so, then prior appropriation would not hold between citizens of *different* states. In 1920

Colorado and Wyoming were engaged in a marathon suit—it had been instituted in 1911—before the U.S. Supreme Court over that point. Colorado contended that it owned and hence controlled all of the water originating in the Laramie River east of the Continental Divide, while Wyoming maintained that prior appropriations of Laramie water by Wyoming residents were legal no matter where the stream originated. A decision was not likely in the immediate future, however, and in any case it might be limited to the quarrel over the Laramie. Congressman Taylor decided, accordingly, to change the name of the Grand River and thus make a point to the League of the Southwest about the origins of the Colorado. Shortly after the Los Angeles meeting passed its resolution about the river, he asked the United States Board of Geographic Names to change the stream's designation. His request was declined, on the grounds that usages had been established. Taylor then introduced a bill into Congress to effect the alteration. Hearings began in February, 1921, after the League had adjourned its Denver meeting. Taylor himself offered most of the testimony. The adjective *Grand*, he told his bored listeners, was overworked and flabby. By contrast, *Colorado* meant "the heart of the Golden West, the top of the world." Yes, the Green River was 700 miles long compared to the Grand's 340 miles. The Green did drain 45,000 square miles compared to 26,500 for the Grand. But recent hydrological measurements by the U.S. Geological Survey showed that the Grand carried more water than the Green. Furthermore, the Green's principal tributaries, the Yampa and the White, originated in Colorado. Finally, there was the San Juan, born in southwestern Colorado. All told, the state of Colorado produced 70 percent of the river's flow. Was it not entitled to claim the heritage of its name?[9] (And, by implication, could it not claim the water that it, and no other state, produced?)

On July 5, 1921, a congressional bill mandating the change in names became operative. Since then the world's atlases have all said that the Colorado River rises in Rocky Mountain National Park, on the western slope of the Colorado Rockies.

Taylor was triumphant. But for Delph Carpenter, a Greeley, Colorado, water lawyer, the victory was irrelevant. At the League's Denver meeting in August, 1920, he had suggested that the Basin states forget both the doctrines of origin and prior appropriation as far as the Colorado River was concerned and settle the problems of water allocation by means of treaty, or compact. The seven governors concerned were in favor of the idea. Their legislatures and the national Congress voted the necessary authority, and in January, 1922, President Harding authorized Secretary of Commerce Herbert Hoover to serve as a federal representative on what was named the Colorado River Commission.

Aided by their advisers, the commissioners appointed by the several governors—Delph Carpenter was Colorado's representative—tried to determine what the annual flow of the river would be if nothing were taken out of it anywhere, for of course an equitable division would have to be based on what the negotiators called virgin flow. They worked from what they knew, plus many assumptions. They knew approximately how many acres were being irrigated by Colorado Basin water in each state. As water experts, they were able to guess how much of that water seeped back into the river system as "return flow," available for re-use. They had figures on what was already being diverted over the Rockies into eastern Colorado and over the Wasatches into central Utah. They collected gauging records that had been kept near or at the site of Laguna Dam since 1899. Finally, they assumed that whatever water was lost to evaporation between Lee's Ferry and Laguna Dam was replaced by the creeks that boil down the sides of the Grand Canyon and by the Bill Williams River of central Arizona. What they did not consider was the possibility that records dating from 1899 through 1921 might be an inadequate base for determining long-range fluctuations in the river's volume.

After adding the records together, they decided that they could conservatively set the river's mean annual virgin flow at 16.4 million acre-feet.[10] That amount, then, was to be divided among seven states of greatly differing aspirations (New Mexico and Nevada could hardly hope to be allotted very much), with some left over in case the United States entered into a water treaty with Mexico or demanded an apportionment for the streamside Indian reservations, for which the federal government was trustee.

In 1922, not one of the states was using anywhere near a million acre-feet of water a year from the Colorado River. But when they saw in black and white how much water was available, their aspirations grew enormously. Whenever a formula of apportionment was offered, it was immediately attacked as favoring one state or group of states over the others. The Supreme Court's decision in the case of *Wyoming* v. *Colorado*, rendered on June 5, 1922, made matters worse by stating that in contests between states subscribing to the same code of water laws, the doctrine of prior appropriation has precedence over that of state ownership. Californians, who had several huge projects waiting for development, rejoiced; under the court's new ruling they could appropriate all the water they wanted before the other states could launch counterclaims—if federal money was available. It might not be. Congressmen of the other states, who held seats on key Interior committees, were sure to block any reclamation bill offered on California's behalf, unless formulas for division were agreed on.

For nine months the squabbling negotiators zigzagged across the Southwest, holding public hearings in Phoenix, Los Angeles, Salt Lake City, Grand Junction, Denver, and Cheyenne—and getting nowhere. With their final meeting scheduled to begin at Santa Fe on November 9, 1922, Carpenter

returned to an idea that he and several others had tentatively suggested earlier:
Why not divide the water between an Upper and Lower Basin, and let the
states within each basin decide on further apportionments among themselves?[11]

The weary negotiators agreed. Unanimously they selected Lee's Ferry,
Arizona, as the dividing point between the basins. (The ferry was still operating, but on a cable arrangement rather than with the big sweep oars John D.
Lee and his successors had used until 1896.) As one of the conferees remarked,
the mouth of the big red pocket was like a gigantic funnel. By the time water
reached it, every major tributary except the Gila had contributed its portion.
The pocket, moreover, gave the only ready access to the river between Hite
and the lower end of the Grand Canyon, and access would be vital to the
enforcement of whatever allotments the conferees decided on.*

Apportioning the 16.4 million acre-feet of water thought to be available
led to further controversy. W. S. Norviel, commissioner for Arizona, refused
to let the Gila–Salt River system be counted as part of his state's share, for
that would reduce by about three million acre-feet (his bargaining figure) the
amount of water the Lower Basin could demand from the Upper. In the end
he forced a compromise. Each Basin was granted by Article III(b) of the
compact "the exclusive use of 7,500,000 acre-feet of water per annum." Since
the erratic river would rarely send exactly that amount past the Lee Ferry
gauging station in any one year, actual deliveries were to be calculated over
a ten-year period. That is, the Upper Basin was *required* to dispatch seventy-
five million acre-feet to the Lower Division states each decade; thus a skimpy
flow in one year could be balanced off by a good one later on, but the annual
average could not fall below 7.5 million.

Now for the Gila. Since the division was being made by basins, Arizona
could not be singled out for preferential treatment. Accordingly, the commissioners yielded to Norviel in terms so imprecise that they were bound to cause
trouble later. Article III(b): "In addition to the apportionment in paragraph
(a) the Lower Basin is hereby granted the right to increase its beneficial use
of such water by one million acre-feet per annum." Arguments over the exact
meaning of that clause would eventually result in the longest case ever taken
before the Supreme Court. Submitted in 1952, it was decided in 1963—and

*The negotiators called the dividing point Lee Ferry because the National Board of Geographic
Names frowned on using possessives as place names. Only official water documents ever use the
form Lee Ferry, however. Its precise location is on the left bank, one mile below the mouth of
the Paria River and two miles below the actual ferry site. The Upper Basin states are Wyoming,
Colorado, Utah, and New Mexico, although a little water from northeastern Arizona does drain
into the San Juan and thence into the upper Colorado. The Lower Basin states are Nevada,
Arizona, and California, though some Utah water drains through the Virgin into the river, far
below Lee's Ferry. As most rafters know, river miles in the Grand Canyon are measured
downstream from the Lee Ferry gauging station.

Arizona won. Except for a token amount of water assigned to New Mexico, where the Gila heads, the river was entirely Arizona's. No other Basin state, not even Colorado with its renamed Grand, has maintained that much control over one of the main river's tributaries.

Having decided, as they supposed, how much water existed, the commissioners then had to decree where it could be used. Their tampering with geographic terms was even more cavalier than Congressman Taylor's.

Article II of the Colorado River Compact states: "The term 'Colorado River Basin' means all of the drainage area of the Colorado River system and [here comes the eyebrow-raising part] all other territory within the United States to which water of the Colorado River System shall be beneficially applied."

Upon approval of those words by the governmental bodies concerned, the Rocky Mountains on the east side of the Basin, and the Wasatch and Peninsular Mountains on the west side, disappeared so far as water law was concerned. Farmers as far from the river as the western borders of Kansas and Nebraska, Hispanos in Albuquerque as well as in Tucson, factory workers in Denver and Salt Lake City, patrons of resorts in Colorado Springs, and residents of the five thousand square miles of the Metropolitan Water District of Southern California (San Diego included) were members of the same plumbing complex as the land developers in Phoenix and the uranium miners in Green River, Utah. Some sixteen million people, most of them living outside the Basin's topographic boundaries, became water residents of it, entitled to draw at least part of their well-being—jobs, food, recreation, and outdoor inspiration—from its thin bounties.

Or they would become so entitled once the legislatures of the seven Basin states ratified the compact. Arizona refused. The doctrine of prior appropriation still held in each basin, and circumstances favored California. A big flood-control dam scheduled for either Black or Boulder Canyon, the All-American canal for the Imperial and Coachella Valleys, aqueducts for the Metropolitan Water District of Southern California, electricity for Los Angeles—all would confer instant water rights on the coast state and nothing on Arizona, which was not yet ready to undertake any major diversion. Whenever talks were initiated about apportioning water within the Lower Basin, they collapsed because of what Arizona considered California's hoggishness.

Finally Congress broke the impasse by decreeing that if California limited its take to 4.4 million acre-feet a year, leaving 2.8 million to Arizona, not counting the Gila, and 300,000 to Nevada, and if six states ratified the original full-basin compact, work on the big dam could begin. The terms were accepted, and in 1931, in the depths of America's most severe economic depression, high-scalers set off the first preparatory dynamite blasts in Black Canyon.

Its location notwithstanding, the structure was called Boulder Dam until 1947, when its name was officially changed to Hoover.

The sleek, white concrete of Hoover Dam, curving gently upstream on a carefully calculated line, contrasts vividly with the rough, scaly, dark-gray and rust-colored cliffs to which it is anchored. It is 660 feet thick at its base, 726.4 feet high, and 1,244 feet long at its crest. A hum lives inside it. The power plant at the downstream base of the structure purrs throatily to the spin of giant turbines. The huge pipes leading from the penstocks tremble with the rush of water whose energy will soon be transformed into electricity. When we emerge from the dam's cool interior into the intense sunlight and see the cables leaping from the powerhouse to steel towers canted over the rim of the canyon, we sense in our nerve ends the rush of the current upward to be dispersed throughout the Southwest.

The dam soon became a symbol. This was the era of Art Deco, designed originally to give homage to technology. The concrete exclamation marks that punctuate the downstream rim of the crest between the dam's elevator towers reflect that homage. So does the artistic style of the cameos on the bronze plaques set in those towers. Some portray the Indians of the region; some show the benefits conferred by water. One, near the Arizona abutment, pays honor to the men who died during the dam's construction. And close to the abutment on the Nevada side, seated at either end of a curving wall of black diorite, are two monumental figures, thirty feet high, arms extended overhead. Rising from the figures' massive rib cages and attached to the uplifted arms are wings. Midway between the two Winged Figures of the Republic, as they are called, is a flagpole 142 feet tall. Flooring the area is a circular star map, gold lines on black, contrived so that by studying the chart at any future time, no matter how remote, astronomers can determine the day —September 30, 1935—on which Franklin Delano Roosevelt dedicated the dam.[12] The whole display is an engineer's boast, a statement to the ages that with the completion of what was then the world's largest dam, the Colorado River had ceased to be a free-flowing stream. Technology had triumphed over nature.

Even before the compact of November, 1922, had made the imprisoning of the Colorado politically possible, members of the water lobby had started surveying the river for other feasible dam sites. From 1921 through 1923, boat expeditions, jointly financed and manned by the Reclamation Service, the Southern California Edison Company, and the Utah Power and Light Company, had combed the major canyons of the Green, San Juan, and Colorado Rivers, in Galloway-type boats and guided through some of the gorges by Ellsworth and Emery Kolb.[13] The results of the surveys declared that sites for dams abounded—high on the Colorado River near Rocky Mountain

National Park; in Cataract, Glen, Marble, and Grand Canyons; and in the big tributaries, the Green, Gunnison, and San Juan. The first to receive attention was the Colorado–Big Thompson project, whose intricate system of reservoirs and whose 13.1-mile tunnel under Rocky Mountain Park provided hydroelectric power for Denver and supplemental irrigation water for 615,000 acres of farmlands stretching along the South Platte River from the foothills of the Front Range to Nebraska. Because of delays caused by World War II, construction, begun in 1938, was not completed until the mid-1950's, and the project's cost exceeded that of Hoover Dam.

In 1946, a thick, blue-covered volume entitled *The Colorado River: A Comprehensive Report of Its Water Resources . . . for Irrigation, Power Production, and Other Beneficial Uses,* published by the Bureau of Reclamation, declared that there was not enough water in the river to justify every proposal that had been outlined.* Just what dams were to be built in the Upper Basin would not be decided until the states of that region had agreed among themselves on allotments. (The division of the Lower Basin's share of the river had been suggested by Congress before the building of Hoover Dam.)

A fundamental problem was finally out in the open. The mean flow of the river since the signing of the compact had not been 16.4 million acre-feet, as the commissioners had calculated, but was closer to 13.8 million.** In 1944, moreover, the United States had agreed by international treaty to let 1.5 million acre-feet flow down the river to Mexico each year. Half of this amount, or 750,000 feet, was to come from the Upper Basin's share. Delph Carpenter and his associates had committed the Upper Basin to deliver an average of 7.5 million acre-feet at Lee's Ferry each year. Subtract that and the 750,000 feet due Mexico each year from a flow of 13.8 million feet, and the Upper Basin ends up—not counting evaporation or what may yet be allotted to Indian reservations—[15] with a maximum of 5.6, not 7.5, million acre-feet to call its own.

Wiser from experience than Carpenter and his fellow negotiators had been, the Upper Basin commissioners of 1947–48 split the water by percentages, not flat figures. Colorado was to receive 51.75 percent; Utah, 23 percent; Wyoming, 14; New Mexico, 11.25. Then they went after the dams that the Bureau of Reclamation had said could be built. They did not get all that were

*The Reclamation Service was renamed Bureau of Reclamation in 1923. In 1979 the title was again changed, to Water and Power Resources Service. This created such an identity crisis that in 1981 the Reagan administration restored the title Bureau of Reclamation.
**Careful records kept from 1922 through 1978 confirm an average annual flow of 13.8 million acre-feet. The commissioners missed this mark because the records they worked with dated from 1899 through 1921—the wettest years, according to tree-ring studies covering four centuries, in the history of the Colorado River. The decade 1931–40 was one of the driest periods, producing an average annual flow of only 11.8 million acre-feet.[14]

proposed in the original versions of the Colorado River Storage Project Act of 1956 and the Colorado River Basin Project Act of 1968, the latter authorizing —among other things—the big Central Arizona Project.*

A coalition of environmental groups, led by David Brower of the Sierra Club, kept two major dams out of Dinosaur National Monument, one out of Marble Canyon (which is now part of Grand Canyon National Park), and another out of the lower Grand. But they could not keep a dam almost as big as Hoover from drowning 186 miles of the scenic wonders of Glen Canyon and backing up under the splendid arch of Rainbow Bridge. The upper Green is plugged by Flaming Gorge Reservoir, which extends from Utah into Wyoming. Three dams, part of the single Curecanti Unit, have filled the upper part of the Black Canyon of the Gunnison. Navajo Dam has closed off the San Juan a little below the Colorado–New Mexico border. At all of them except Navajo, power plants turn out electricity whose sale will pay for relatively small "participating projects" located where they will satisfy the wishes of local people. Power to replace the electricity lost by the dams that weren't built is generated by substitute coal-burning plants that already haze the air for hundreds of miles, and more such plants are in prospect.

To date, the Upper Basin states have not yet diverted all their entitlements from the stream. The mammoth Central Arizona Project has not yet come on flow. The wet years at the end of the 1970's filled the river system's main storage reservoirs with 56.2 million acre-feet of water. (Space for another 5.4 million acre-feet is reserved for flood control.) The United States has agreed with the Basin states that meeting the demands of the Mexican Treaty is a national obligation. So far the federal government has not had to produce that water, for the Basin has been able to provide the 1.5 million acre-feet called for—very silty water, to be sure, to which the Mexican government objects strenuously. But when the entitlements are all utilized and shortages begin to develop, then what? There are plans, but as yet none seems politically or financially feasible. And even if they are instituted, for how long will they keep the plumbing at work?

Walk from the winged figures at Hoover Dam across the star map that was prepared for scholars of future ages, and at the far side of the highway, lean on the fence and look down. Here and there on the steep, otherwise barren rock of the cliffs are low, gray-green clumps of brittle brush. In April, a burst of bright yellow flowers tells of roots that have worked their way into small cracks in the stone, where they find their own tiny sources of water and nutrients. As the plants grow and insects and perhaps a rodent or two take up residence in each of these cracks, pressure from the roots loosens tiny flakes of rock that tumble down the slope and eventually reach the water.

*Arizona had finally ratified the 1922 compact in 1944.

Throughout the 244,000 square miles of the Colorado River Basin the process is being repeated by billions of many kinds of plants. From that and other sources of disintegration come loads of silt that in time the river picks up. It has been calculated that before the dams were built the delta received between 150 million and 180 million tons of fragmented limestone, sandstone, shale, granite, and gneiss *each year.*

These materials now go into reservoirs. Each new structure on the upper reaches of the streams traps additional amounts and thus prolongs the lives of Hoover and Glen Canyon dams. But no sediment trap can last forever; no river like the Colorado can be completely killed. Not at a rate of 150 million tons a year.

Yet nowhere on the plaques at Hoover Dam nor anywhere near the Winged Figures of the Republic is there a representation of the small yellow flower that forecasts the ultimate victory.

Appendix:
The Geology of the Colorado Basin

Water in the form of glaciers accounts for most of the scenic rock carving in the high peaks of Wyoming and Colorado. During a sequence of cold spells that occurred many thousands of years ago, ice accumulated to great depth in drainage courses already creasing the upper slopes of the mountains. As the glacial deposits began to move in response to gravity, they scoured away the surrounding rock (mostly granite) not only downward but laterally and even backward, creating open-ended gouges called cirque basins. Given time, a vigorous glacier could break down a side wall or the back wall of its cirque and merge with a neighboring basin. Before the Ice Ages ended about ten thousand years ago, many Colorado peaks had been transformed into what geologists call "subdued" mountains, characterized by broad, rolling tops and great rounded slopes where soil clings and short-stemmed alpine flowers meet summer with a blaze of color. Farther north, above timber-line in the Wind River Mountains, many adjoining cirque basins are still separated by thin walls of granite crowned with splintered crags.

Each spring as temperatures rise, melting snow streaks the cliffs. Transparent trickles of water run together, squirm under talus boulders, then cascade into lakes half blue with sky reflection, half gray with sludge ice. Water escapes from the lakes to form creeks and small waterfalls which in turn are fed by the saturated humus of the forested slopes until the word *river* becomes appropriate.

As elevation drops, the look of the land changes. After flowing northwest through the heavily forested foothills of the Wind River Range, the Green swings abruptly into an open valley and begins its long journey south. Gradually the snow-covered mountains slip out of sight to the southeast, making way for a vast, rolling plain of gray-green sagebrush. Except for narrow bands of willows and cottonwoods along the stream banks and around occasional ranch-houses, there are no trees. The Uinta Mountains, running roughly parallel to the Wyoming-Utah border, form the southern border of the sage country. Beyond them lies the Colorado Plateau—or, more properly, the Colorado Plateaus, for within the master unit are many smaller plateaus and mesas. Shaped like a lopsided pear, its small end toward the north, the region is about 150,000 square miles in size. Its maximum length from north to south is 450 miles, its maximum width, about 400 miles. On the east the streams cascading out of the Colorado Rockies are bordered by flat-topped mesas whose escarpments often plunge downward as abruptly as if they had been sheared by a trowel. A stone dropped from Land's End on Grand Mesa between the Gunnison and Colorado Rivers (the Colorado River used to be called the Grand) will fall and roll almost a mile from moist forest country onto talus slopes as dry as bones.

Northwest of Grand Mesa and on beyond the Colorado River is Tavaputs Plateau; its bulk, in places high enough to support bunch grass and aspens, fills most of the northern part of the pear. On the west side of the pear are the High Plateaus of south-central Utah—lava-topped Aquarius, 11,600 feet in altitude; Paunsaugunt, almost as high, its pink rim supporting the preposterous carvings of Bryce Canyon National Park; and Markagunt, the grassy, spruce-clad source of the Virgin River, sculptor of Zion Canyon. From the southern tips of all three plateaus a giant stone staircase, each broad step outlined by a pink, gray, white, or vermilion cliff, drops down toward the Grand Canyon.

The central province also contains several handsome mountains that once were active volcanoes or laccoliths. (Laccoliths, "cisterns of lava," result when magma from deep in the earth intrudes into sedimentary rock, spreads out in sheets, and raises the overlying layers into a dome.) The La Sals, a laccolithic formation near the Colorado–Utah border, approachs 13,000 feet in elevation; the volcanic San Francisco Peaks near Flagstaff, Arizona, surpass 13,000 feet. Denuded volcanic plugs like stately Shiprock in New Mexico and cinder cones like Sunset Crater east of the San Francisco Peaks are other remnants of the Basin's fiery interludes. Some of the area's lava flows have been extensive; about a million years ago one poured red hot over the north rim of the Grand Canyon into the Colorado River and created what must have been a fantastic caldron.

Vegetation changes with altitude. Below the spruce and firs and aspens of the high peaks and plateaus come majestic groves of ponderosa pine, the trees widely spaced so as not to compete for water. Lower down are thickets of Gambel oaks, sweeping forests of twisted junipers, and nut-bearing pinon-pines. Sagebrush takes over the broad flats that lie at elevations of between 5,500 and 7,500 feet. Mingled with it, near the lower part of its range, is desert scrub: saltbrush, shadscale, greasewood; and rabbitbrush, the last flaunting feathery yellow branch-tips in autumn. Also included in the mix are prickly-pear cactus, yucca, and many varieties of grass, including grama, gallatea, and the delicate filagrees of Indian rice-grass.

In places, even desert scrub disappears. The lower sections of the Colorado Plateau Province receive less than ten inches of moisture a year. Soil forms slowly, and the roots of the scattered plants do little to anchor the thin mat. As a result sheet erosion from occasional cloudbursts has peeled the covering from large patches of ground. This is especially noticeable near the deep canyons of southeastern Utah and northwestern Arizona, leaving the pink, white, and red sandstone naked to the sky. Creased, domed, and dimpled, hewn into pinnacles and fins that are sometimes pierced with archlike openings, this is the fabled "slickrock" country of the Canyonlands desert.

Extensive exposures of different layers of rock in cliffs and canyon walls, many of them rich in marine fossils, show that at least seven times in the past, during the epochs when the formations that would later be uplifted as the Colorado Plateaus were submerged under oceans, streams draining from the landmasses along their shores carried billions of tons of sediment to the submerged lands. Coarse grains settled near the shore; finer material was deposited farther out. As ages passed, the deposits thickened and settled deeper into the ooze of the ocean bed. The waters receded, then returned to receive new deposits of different makeup. Tremendous pressures indurated sand into sandstone, silt into siltstone, clay into shale, all bound together by cement made of the earth's own chemicals.

Limestone, whose principal constituent is calcium carbonate, was formed differently. Under certain situations, soluble carbonate materials are carried in immense quantities into lakes and seas. If the receiving water becomes supersaturated, the lime precipitates on grains of sand and settles. Oceans and some lakes add a constant snowstorm of tiny calcite shells discarded by multitudes of dying aquatic creatures. Under pressure these mingled carbonate compounds compressed into limestone. Of the several exposed layers in the Plateau Province, the most noticeable is the huge Redwall formation of the Grand Canyon. Dating back 330 years to what is called the Early Mississippian period, it is hundreds of miles long, five hundred or more feet thick, and stained deep red by iron oxide carried across it by water seeping down from overlaid bands of crimson rock.

Evaporites are another product of the sea. Stretching two hundred miles from southeastern Utah into southwestern Colorado is an ancient depression now called Paradox Basin. When the oceans covering the area retreated, the water left in the basin slowly evaporated. Successive fillings and evaporations left behind accumulations of salt three thousand feet thick. Under pressure the salt became plastic and pushed, in elongated cores, into weak sections of the surrounding strata. Further compressions created bulges known as anticlines. When seeping water dissolved the topmost salt in such a formation, the anticline collapsed. In some places spectacular valleys have resulted—flat-bottomed, red-walled Paradox Valley in Colorado is one. In other places, notably Devil's Garden, Arches National Park, Utah, erosion has slashed the anticline's ruined walls lengthwise into a bewildering—and strikingly beautiful—series of parallel fins.[1]

Wind, too, has helped shape the Plateaus. Many millions of years ago the continental plate on which North America sits was closer to the Equator than it is now. The climate was like that of the Sahara today. Whenever the land that is now the western United States was above water, winds howled across it, rearranging loose sand into towering dunes. Under pressure, and with the addition of cementing material carried by groundwater, these dunes, too, coalesced into rock. Prime example of many in the Plateau region is Navajo sandstone, a principal constituent of Rainbow Natural Bridge, the walls of Glen Canyon, and the two-thousand-foot precipices of Zion National Park.

Each time the land was elevated and exposed to erosion, accumulations of strata that had been gathering for eons were stripped away. Then, as the land was submerged and deposition took place again, young layers of rock came to rest on formations much older than the ones that had vanished. Geologists called the dividing surfaces an unconformity and designate them on their maps with a thin, wavering line. Grand Canyon maps show at least five unconformities.[2] Near the bottom, where brownish-red, horizontal layers of Tapeats sandstone rest directly on the tilted "Grand Canyon series" of rocks, the wavery line represents eight hundred million years of lost geologic history. In other places the dividing line between Tapeats sandstone and the Vishnu schist below indicates 1.2 billion years of vanished stone. Since the Cenozoic period in which we are living is a time of intense erosion, the great landmarks that now stir our imaginations will eventually disappear and our own lost geologic history (if anyone is left to map it) will show as just another hairlike line.

Each erosional period began, in a sense, when tectonic shifts in the earth's crust produced multitudes of thin cracks, both vertical and horizontal, in deeply buried layers of rock. When this rock was exposed by the weathering of overlying stone, the release of pressure caused the cracks—or joints, as they are called—to widen. Expansion and contractions brought about by the day's heat and the night's chill further weakened the gaps. Seeping water helped dissolve binding chemicals. Plant roots intruded. Chunks broke off, huge ones sometimes, when seeps and creeks cut away soft layers of stone that had been supporting burdens of harder rock.

Various kinds of rock react differently to erosional forces. Shales and soft sandstones weather into slopes. Harder sandstones and limestone form cliffs, or, if the soft material covering them is swept away, they lie exposed as the flat mesa tops and terraces that give the Colorado Plateau its predominantly horizontal cast. In cliffs made up of alternating soft and hard strata, lateral weathering proceeds more rapidly than does downcutting by streams. Hence canyons hewn into varied kinds of stone are wider than they are deep, as the Grand Canyon magnificently demonstrates. (Slit canyons only a few yards wide and a thousand or more feet deep almost invariably occur in homogenous rock, generally Navajo sandstone.) Curiously, as walls retreat, they maintain the same profile they always had; a million years from now a perpendicular escarpment will appear from the front much as it does today. But when both sides of a mesa or promontory retreat simultaneously, the narrowing division between them finally breaks apart into spectacular cock's-combs, fences of pinnacles, isolated buttes, or monuments, their lines starkly apparent because of the region's lack of vegetation.

Color is everywhere, the result of the oxidation of minute amounts of iron coating the otherwise colorless grains of sedimentary rock. Hematite produces a rusty red. A touch of ferrous oxide gives a greenish cast to the Bright Angel shale of the Grand Canyon. Limonite produces buff and brownish tints. And there is also the phenomenon known as desert varnish, which appears on red cliff faces as purple splotches, or on lighter-colored rock as streamers and tapestries of black and brown.

The cutting and transporting powers of the Colorado River and its main tributaries owe much to their precipitous descent. In going from the high Rockies to the sea, they fall a vertical distance of two and a half miles. (The Mississippi, which travels farther, falls a third of a mile.) The loads of silt the rivers carry add tremendously to their abrasive power. As the Colorado Plateaus began rising under streams already in place, the speed of the currents quickened and the rivers were able to maintain their original courses by cutting downward as fast as the land lifted, a phenomenon given vivid illustration by the deeply entrenched meanders—called Goosenecks—of the San Juan River near Bluff, Utah. Recent geologic investigations, however, have shown that in some places great blocks of elevated land came into existence *before* the present rivers were in place, and yet the streams have cut through them anyway. To explain this apparent impossibility, which is particularly evident in the Uinta Mountains and in the Kaibab Plateau of northern Arizona, two revolutionary theories of stream capture have been advanced.

The Uinta Mountains run mysteriously east and west in a land where all other major mountain ranges are oriented roughly north and south. It is now believed that when the Rocky Mountains were first being thrust upward, sixty-five or seventy million years ago, the Continental Divide followed the crest of the Uintas from what we call Colorado west to the range's end before veering north again close to today's Idaho-Wyoming border. The Wind River Mountains to the east were then within the Mississippi drainage system. After pouring off the western slope of the mountains, the Green River, blocked by the Uintas from going south, curled east around the toes of the Wind River Range and—theory says—joined the ancestral North Platte, which carried its waters on to the Missouri and, eventually, to the Mississippi.

About twenty million years ago, during Miocene times, the pattern changed. Mountains that had been eroded almost to peneplains lifted again. The Continental Divide slowly shifted its course eastward until it reached the Wind River mountains, where it has remained ever since. Late in this period of change, the eastern end of the rejuvenated Uinta Range collapsed, creating a rough trough, or graben, that ran completely through the range from north to south. Below the trough on the south slope was a small, swift stream. Slowly but relentlessly its headwaters eroded backwards, as headwaters will. Entering the trough, they continued chewing backwards through the range and eventually tapped, on the north slope, a tributary that was flowing east to join the Green. Baffled by the rising of the Continental Divide in its new position, the river yielded to capture by the south-flowing stream. Reversing direction, the whole pirated system poured south through the graben. From the carving that followed came Lodore Canyon, beloved by river runners as one of the most beautiful and exciting gorges in the upper Colorado River Basin.[3]

Many geologists believe that the Grand Canyon was created in similar fashion. The speculation was triggered by the discovery, in the 1940's, that on leaving the Grand Canyon the Colorado River flows over certain deposits that were laid down no more than ten million years ago. It followed that the Grand Canyon had to be younger than that, at least in its lower reaches. Yet the Kaibab Plateau, nine thousand feet high, through which the Grand Canyon runs, and the Kaibab's southern extensions, the Coconino and Hualapai Plateaus, have been in place for thirty million years. How had this massive uplift, its western components lumped together under the label Hualapai Drainage, been breached millions of years after its formation?

One theory has it that ten million years or so ago, when the Colorado River was a smaller stream than it is today, it traveled south along what is now Marble Canyon, east of and roughly parallel to the Kaibab Plateau. On reaching the bed now occupied by the Little Colorado River, the stream turned *down* that to a huge, ancient inland sea, Lake Bidahochi, in northeastern Arizona. Meanwhile, small, vigorous streams were pouring west off the far side of the Hualapai Plateau. Because the drop was great, the headward erosion of those streams was vigorous. One of them nibbled backward through the entire Kaibab-Hualapai system and intercepted a stream draining into the south-flowing Colorado. A tug-of-war ensued. The west-flowing stream won, and the

Colorado turned into the small canyon its captor had sliced through the Kaibab Plateau. The captive Green, roaring down from the north, added its weight, and thus —the conjecture goes—the Grand Canyon as it exists today came into being, some seven million years ago.[4] Whether or not the theory is correct, we may never know. Some romantics prefer it that way. To them the Grand Canyon is too stupendous to be belittled by explanation.

Notes

1. THE LAND

General accounts of geology that provided useful background material for this chapter are George (1977), Harris (1976), Hunt (1967), Menard (1974), and Shelton (1966). Stokes (1969) gives a good if somewhat simplified overview of erosional processes.

Of the many accounts that concentrate on the Colorado Plateaus or sections thereof (see Appendix), I drew most on Baars (1972); Eliot Blackwelder, "Geologic Exhibit," in Stegner, ed. (1955); Hansen (1969); Hunt (1956); and Lohman (1974, 1975). River runners interested in geology will benefit from the four guidebooks published by the Powell Society of Denver in honor of the Powell centennial of 1969. They are Hayes and Simmons, Mutschler (2), and Simmons and Gaskill. (These pamphlets do not contain publication dates.) Baars, ed. (1973) gives a brief geologic overview of the San Juan River.

Several technical papers on the Grand Canyon are in W. J. Breed and Roat, eds. (1976). More easily handled material includes Beal (1967), Collins (1980), and McKee (1931 and many subsequent editions). A book of extraordinary visual impact that uses the Grand Canyon to explain the formation of the earth and the origins of life thereon is Redfern (1980).

Four other handsomely presented books, one on the Canyonlands area, one on Arches National Park, and two on the Grand Canyon, that contain some geology are Crampton (1964, 1972), Hoffman (1981), and Wallace (1973). Two of the river's major tributaries, the Green and the San Juan, are well covered by a discerning and sensitive naturalist, Zwinger (1975, 1978).

2. THE ANCIENT ONES

A staggering amount of southwestern archeological material is available. I have relied on all or parts of the following: Breternitz and Smith (1972), Ceram (1971), Farb (1978), Fowler, Euler and Fowler (1969), Glassow (1980), Haury (1976), Haury, Baldwin and Nusbaum (1950), Hirst (1976), Jennings (1957, 1960, 1964, 1966), Jennings and Sharrock (1965), Josephy (1968), Martin and Plog (1973), Rippeteau (1979), and Schaafsma (1980). Although the work of Carl O. Sauer is outdated in some respects and no longer appears in anthropological and ecological discussions as often as it used to, I find much of it challenging. For a useful compendium of his writings, see Leighly (1965).

1. A handsomely illustrated introduction to the varied techniques and styles of southwestern rock art is Schaafsma (1980).

2. The persistence until modern times of Desert Culture traits among the Southern Paiutes of southwestern Nevada and southeastern Utah is one of the reasons anthropologists can reconstruct post-pluvial prehistoric cultural patterns in as much detail as they do. See Euler (1966) and Farb (1978), Chapter II.

3. Archeologists first supposed that the Hohokam were descendants of the Desert Cochise, who had evolved their own patterns of horticulture after picking up seed from neighbors in Mexico. Current theory holds that the Hohokam themselves brought the fully developed skills with them when they arrived as invaders. Dates are controversial. Such respected Arizona archeologists as Charles Di Peso and Harold Gladwin believe that the invasion occurred sometime between 700 and 900 A.D. Emil Haury (1976), pp. 247, 351–353, thinks that the first waves of outsiders arrived about 300 B.C.

4. Breternitz and Smith (1972), pp. 65, 75; Jennings (1966), p. 45; Glassow (1980), pp. 51–53

5. Powell's conjecture, made during a lecture in Salt Lake City, was reported in the *Deseret Evening News*, Salt Lake City, Sept. 17, 1869, reprinted in *Utah Historical Quarterly*, Vol. 15, 1974, pp. 146–147. Powell soon realized his error.

6. Robert C. Euler, George G. Gumerman, Thor N.V. Karlstrom, Jeffrey S. Dean, and Richard Hovley, writing in *Science*, Vol. 205, Sept. 14, 1979, pp. 1089–1099, divided Anasazi culture into three main traditions. (In this connection it should be noted that although the Anasazi were bound together by cultural ties, different groups probably spoke different languages, as their descendants, the modern Pueblos of New Mexico and Arizona, still do.) The main traditions:

    (1) *Kayenta*. These were the most aggressive colonizers in terms of cultural dissemination. At its maximum their range was bounded on the east by Monument Valley, on the north by the Henry Mountains of Utah, on the west by the lower Grand Canyon, on the south by the Little Colorado River. Subprovinces of the Kayenta, in the minds of Euler *et al.*, were the *Winslow* group south of the Black Mesa in Arizona and the *Virgin River* group in Nevada. Curiously, the Virgin River people did not adopt the kiva, which played so important a part in the lives of the other Anasazis. (2) *Mesa Verde*. Talented dry farmers and energetic traders, this cultural group spread throughout southwestern Colorado and into the triangle formed by the converging San Juan and Colorado Rivers. For a time they also occupied a section of the west bank of Glen Canyon. (3) *Chaco*. Trade was perhaps the main forte of this branch of the Anasazi. Their industrious commerce may have led to the building of the populous clusters whose remnants still loom so boldly from the now desolate soil of Chaco Canyon National Monument, New Mexico. From the canyon the group spread throughout northwestern New Mexico and spilled over into contiguous parts of Arizona.

    To the west and northwest of the Mesa Verde Anasazi were the *Fremont* people. Once considered backward "country cousins" of the Anasazi, the Fremont have since attained separate status. They are best known for their striking rock art depictions of square-shouldered, triangular-bodied, shield-carrying men and horn-bedecked anthropomorphs representing no one knows what. They also built unidentifiable rock shelters (little forts or look-out stations perhaps) on many hard-to-reach pinnacles and jutting promontories. Indifferent farmers and careless artisans but skilled foragers, the Fremonts ranged from central Utah into northwestern Colorado.

Other neighbors of the Anasazi and much influenced by them were the Cohonina, a Yuman-speaking group who in the years following 600 A.D. moved from west-central Arizona to the Hualapai and Coconino plateaus bordering the south rim of the Grand Canyon. Although archeologists once thought the Cohonina became extint during the years that saw the dispersal of the Virgin River Anasazi, 1100–1150, it now appears that some of them found refuge in the steeply plunging south-side tributaries of the Grand Canyon. There, perhaps in conjunction with the Cerbats from farther southwest, they became the ancestors of the modern, closely related Hualapai and Havasupai tribes. (Hirst, 1976, pp. 41–43.) When Spanish explorers first reached the Hopi pueblos, they heard of the Havasupais under the name Cosnina, most probably a corruption of Cohonina.

7. Breternitz and Smith (1972), p. 75.
8. The Tsegi experience has been reconstructed in Dean (1969).

3. THE SPANISH *ENTRADAS*

1. Bolton (1949), p. 27. My account of Coronado's expedition rests primarily on that work and Hammond and Rey (1940). Bannon (1974) presents a useful survey of all Spanish frontier activities in northern Mexico.
2. Apologists for Marcos suggest that he saw Háwikuh early one morning, when a flood of golden sunlight made the town look more impressive than it was. Detractors point out that inasmuch as he was back in Mexico City by midsummer, he did not have time enough to reach that far north. There are other discrepancies. Marcos said that all but three of Esteban's escort of three hundred persons were killed; Pedro de Castañeda, who accompanied Coronado's army, said the black man's escort consisted of sixty people and that none except Esteban died. The road that Marcos described as excellent was actually abominable. The sea was not one day distant, as he reported, but fifteen. And so on. An introduction to the controversy can be found in articles by Henry Wagner and Carl O. Sauer in the *New Mexico Historical Review*, issues of April, 1934, July, 1937, July, 1941.
3. Tidal bores—or, as the Mexicans called them, "burro waves"—occur when an incoming tide encounters, in a confined space, the outflow of a considerable river. The bores in the delta of the Colorado reputedly were exceeded in violence only by those that sweep into the Ch'ien-t'ang River, in China. The geographer Godfrey Sykes has described watching an ordinary Colorado River bore take shape in pre-dam times. As ebb tide ended, patches of tossing water formed into a roller advancing at a right angle to the shore. Simultaneously the level of the water rose rapidly—ten feet in five minutes—while the wave itself, traveling on top of this rising water, reached a height of three feet within the course of a mile. As pressures increased and the channel narrowed, the wave climbed to a height

of seven feet, with more rollers churning and roaring behind it. Sykes (1937), pp. 49–50.

4. Bolton (1949) p. 169, has Díaz slant northwest out of Sonora along the Camino del Diablo to the Colorado River. But why would Díaz start looking for Alarcón's ocean-going vessels on a river? (He knew from Ulloa's explorations that the Gulf ended up in that direction.) A still untranslated account, *Crónica Miscelánea*, by Antonio Tello (1590), is more logical in having him go directly west to the Gulf and then follow the coast northward on his search. The matter is thrashed out in Jack D. Forbes, "Melchior Díaz and the Discovery of Alta California," *Pacific Historical Review,"* Nov., 1958, pp. 351–359.

5. Most historians follow Bolton (1949, p. 174) in suggesting that Díaz went no higher than present-day Yuma before swinging west and south into the Imperial Valley. Forbes argues that he went at least as far upriver as Blythe, and possibly as high as Parker, and then cut southwest to the vicinity of today's Salton Sea.

   Forbes also believes that Díaz "evidently" had been ordered to find out where the river sighted by Cárdenas reached the sea. But although the narratives are obscure about the date of Díaz's departure from Háwikuh, it seems probable that he left before Tovar returned from the Hopi towns with rumors of a river in the west. Certainly he departed well before Cárdenas reported on the Grand Canyon. It appears unlikely, therefore, that he knew of Cárdenas's river but simply, like a good explorer, asked questions of the Indians until he learned the general course of the stream he was on. Later writers, notably Pedro de Castañeda, then stitched the disparate bits of evidence together and deduced a single stream, our Colorado.

6. For Espejo, see Hammond and Rey (1929).

7. Hammond, (1926–27.) Oñate, incidentally, called the Hopi "Mohoqui," a name he probably picked up in one of the Rio Grande pueblos. In time this became "Moqui," a term the Hopis resent, for in their language it means "dead." The term persisted well into the American period. There is one curious offshoot: oldtime cowboys in southwestern Colorado and southeastern Utah, to whom such terms as "Anasazi" and "Fremont" do not come easily, still call Indian ruins "Moqui houses."

8. Spicer (1962, pp. 190–195) summarizes Hopi obstinacy.

9. Bolton (1936) is the standard biography of Kino. An appraisal of Kino's work is Spicer, pp. 118–128, 314–318.

10. Activities in southern Arizona following Kino's death are covered in John A. Donohue, *After Kino* (St. Louis: Jesuit Historical Institute, 1969); Peter Dunne, ed., *Jacobo Sedelmayr* (Tucson: Arizona Pioneers Historical Society, 1955); John L. Kessel, *Friars, Soldiers, and Reformers* (Tucson: University of Arizona Press, 1975).

11. E. B. Adams (1976), p. 47n.

12. The standard, heavily annotated account of Garcés's explorations—one that attempts to follow his journeys in geographical detail—is Coues (1900). A more readily available, handsomely presented translation, without notes, is John Galvin, *A Record of Travels in Arizona and California, 1775–1776* (San Francisco: John Howell Books, 1965).

13. Coues, p. 408
14. For Domíngues-Escalante, see Bolton (1950), fortified by Adams and Chavez (1956), and the introductory material in Chavez and Warner (1975).
15. Wheat (1957), Vol. I, p. 102.
16. The route by which the explorers escaped from the Lee's Ferry area is described in Rusho and Crampton, pp. 11–12, 100–101. See especially the photograph, p. 101.

4. THE AMERICANS ARRIVE

Data on the fur trade of the Upper Colorado River Basin were drawn principally from Berry (1972), DeVoto (1947), Morgan (1953, 1964), and Morgan and Harris (1967). On the fur trade of the Lower Basin, see Camp (1966), Clelland (1950), Hafen and Hafen (1954), Kroeber (1964), Marshall (1916), Pattie (1962), M. Smith (1972), and Weber (1971).

1. Biographical data on Ashley are from Morgan (1964), pp. xv–xxvii. On Provost, see Morgan and Harris (1967), pp. 343–351.

2. The British were not the first whites to see the Green. Wilson Price Hunt, taking a party to the Columbia River for John Jacob Astor, crossed the stream near its headwaters in 1810. In the fall of 1812, Robert Stewart and two companions, carrying messages back to Astor, followed the same river for a few miles while making for South Pass. There is no evidence that Smith knew of those predecessors.

3. The mistakes inherited from Miera caused American fur trappers trouble for years. Concerning Robinson's plagiarisms, see Morgan (1953), p. 163.

4. Morgan (1964), p. 99, reprints two pertinent letters from traders located near Fort Atkinson.

5. Many reasons have been advanced to explain Ashley's motives in making his pioneering run down the Green. He naturally wanted to know whether he was on the supposed San Buenaventura or the Colorado, and he wanted to examine beaver prospects. But beyond that was the temptation to penetrate Mexican markets by way of the back door, a point that, as far as I know, has hitherto been overlooked. Yet to omit the possibility is to slight several bits of otherwise inexplicable data.

6. Ashley's diary entry, May 14, 1825 in Morgan (1964), p. 111.

7. Quoted in Zwinger (1975), p. 151. Zwinger, describing her own run through the canyon, speaks of "the oppression of the bloody [colored] rock walls of Lodore" (p. 161). Such reactions are common among river runners preparing to dive into Lodore for the first time. The name "Lodore," incidentally, was not attached to the canyon until 1869, when one of Powell's men, inspired by a highly alliterative poem of Robert Southey's, suggested it.

8. Morgan (1953), pp. 121, 145–147.

9. Morgan (1964), p. 279, notes 152, 153.

10. Morgan (1953) p. 195, and (1964), p. 279, says that three or four men escaped with Provost. Weber (1971), p. 76, reduces the number to one.

11. Morgan (1964), p. 248, note 183.

12. Weber (1971), p. 95. Young Pattie's claim that he was granted a license as a reward for saving the luscious daughter of a former governor from Comanches is more of ghost-writer Timothy Flint's embroidery.

13. Marshall (1916); Weber (1971), pp. 125ff.

14. Hill, Joseph J., "New Light on Pattie and the Southwestern Fur Trade," *Southwestern Historical Quarterly*, Vol. 26, No. 4 (1923).

15. Pattie (1962), p. 93, repeats Pike's mistake about the Yellowstone, Columbia, Platte, Arkansas, Rio Grande, and Colorado all rising in the same area—hence the compression. See also Goetzmann (1966), pp. 73–74. Conventional theory has Pattie following the south rim of the Grand Canyon. But see Camp (1966), pp. 256–258; M. Smith (1972), pp. 112–115; and the map in Kroeber (1964) for varying degrees of support for the north-rim thesis.

16. Camp (1966, p. 45) states that both parties went to the delta, but Pattie (1962), pp. 11, 124ff., never mentions the southward cast of Yount's group after the separation at the mouth of the Gila.

17. Morgan and Harris (1967), pp. 266–267.

5. REDISCOVERY

1. Emory (1848), pp. 98–99.

2. Cooke's report forms the first part of Bieber (1938).

3. Forbes Parkhill wrote a biography of Antoine Leroux, *The Blazed Trail of Antoine Leroux* (Los Angeles: Westernlore Press, 1965), which he later summarized for Hafen, (1969), Vol. 4, pp. 173–184.

4. Goetzmann (1959), pp. 153–157.

5. A close student of the Yuma Indians, Forbes (1965), pp. 297ff., estimates that six to nine thousand Americans and six to fifteen thousand Mexicans crossed the lower Colorado in 1849. Colonel Carrasco, Couts's Mexican counterpart, estimated twelve thousand, the figure I use. The last chapter in Forbes (1965); the early pages of Woodward (1955); and Wagoner (1975), pp. 299–311, give useful compendiums of early affairs at the Yuma crossing.

6. Wagoner (1975), p. 306; Woodward (1955), p. 29.

7. "Hardy's Colorado" later became a term of mockery, implying that the Briton had either been stupid in charting the Gila, or was a liar and had not ascended the stream as far as he claimed. The unjust denigration originated with later navigators, not with Derby. In addition to Hardy (1826) and Faulk's editing of Derby's report (1969), see George Stewart's 1937 biography of Derby and an evaluation by the geographer Godfrey Sykes (1937).

8. For supply and Indian problems, see Woodward (1955), pp. 46ff.; Forbes (1965), pp. 315ff.; Lingenfelter (1978), pp. 8–12; and Wagoner (1975), pp. 309–310.

9. Arthur Woodward has written a biography of Sarah Bowman (one of her many aliases), *The Great Western: Amazon of the Army* (San Francisco: John & Seeger, 1961).

10. For Aubry, see Bieber (1938), pp. 353–383; and Donald Chaput, "Babes in Arms," *Journal of Arizona History*, Vol. 13, No. 3 (Autumn, 1972) pp 197–204. Aubry was

called the "Skimmer of the Plains" for his speed in traveling the Santa Fe Trail. In 1848, he led three caravans from Missouri to New Mexico, an accomplishment made possible by his swift returns to Missouri to gather new outfits. In May, he covered the eight hundred miles in eight days despite being held captive by Indians for one day, going without food for three, and walking forty miles after a horse had collapsed under him. On returning again to Independence, Missouri, in September for his third caravan, he covered the distance, aided by prearranged relays of horses, in five days and sixteen hours. For a brief biography see Walker Wyman, *New Mexico Historical Review*, Vol. 7, No. 1 (January, 1932).

11.   M. Smith (1972), pp. 192–194, struggles with the vexing problem of Aubry's exact route.

12.   For Whipple, see Foreman (1941).

13.   Goetzmann (1959) pp. 295–337, and (1964), pp. 303–331, evaluates the work of the engineers and their accompanying scientists.

6. THE MYTHIC RIVER

1.   I assume Green River town because Manly (1949, p. 95) later speaks of gaining "the regular trail from Santa Fe to Los Angeles." Since the trail ran south of Tavaputs Plateau, the boaters evidently coursed not only Lodore but Desolation and Gray as well, an extraordinary journey for wooden dugouts (pp. 52–89).

2.   McNitt (1964) has reproduced Simpson's journal. For the lieutenant's road suggestion, see pp. 160–161 and 215, note.

3.   Sitgreaves's almost perfunctory *Report of an Exploration Down the Zuñi and Colorado Rivers*, first published in 1853 as 3rd Congress, 2nd Session, Senate Executive Document 59, was reissued in 1962 by the Rio Grande Press, Chicago. More notable than the lieutenant's prose are the drawings by the expedition's artist, Richard Kern.

4.   Quoted in Peterson (1973), p. 12.

5.   Furniss (1960), pp. 40–42.

6.   For Mowry, see Sacks (1964); L. Bailey (1965); and letters from Mowry to Edward Bicknall in Mulder and Mortensen (1958), pp. 272–278.

7.   Furniss (1960), p. 37; Alter (1962), pp. 244ff.; and Trenholm and Carley (1964), pp. 142–149.

8.   L. Bailey (1965), p. 345.

9.   Sacks (1964), p. 17.

10.   Data on the jockeying for command of the survey are from Woodward (1955), pp. 61–69; Goetzmann (1959), pp. 378–379; Miller (1972), p. 8 and p. 24, note 16; and Lingenfelter (1978), p. 16.

7. THE BIG ONE

This chapter depends primarily on Ives (1861), Woodward (1955), and David H. Miller's (1972) synopsis of Möllhausen's diary of Ives's lower Colorado River trip in 1858, a diary whose German title translates as *Journeys into the Rocky Mountains of*

North America as Far as the High Plateaus of New Mexico . . . , Arizona then being part of New Mexico.

1. Brooks (1962), pp. 15–19. For a general survey of the Utah war, see Furniss (1960).
2. Billington (1957), p. 207; Morgan (1947), pp. 266–267.
3. Woodward (1955), p. 76; Ives (1861), p. 44.
4. Neither Ives nor Lieutenant J. L. White, commander of Johnson's escort, deigns to mention the other party in his report. Möllhausen, however, describes the amiable meeting. Miller (1972), p. 12.
5. The story of the camel experiment, including Beale's report, is in Lewis B. Leslie, *Uncle Sam's Camels* (Cambridge, Mass.: Harvard University Press, 1929).
6. Miller (1972), p. 20; Ives (1861), pp. 90–91.
7. Miller (1972), p. 178.
8. *Ibid.*, pp. 183–186. Cf. Ives (1861), pp. 98–100.
9. Newberry, Part II, pp. 45–46 of Ives (1861).
10. *Ibid.*, p. 59.
11. Hirst (1976), p. 52. The trail to the ladder can no longer be used by outsiders. Of the sixteen ways, some difficult, that lead into Havasu (Cataract) Canyon, whites can travel only two: the one starting down at Hualapai Hilltop and the longer, drier route from Topacoba.
12. The errors show clearly on the Egloffstein map that accompanies the Ives report. See also Wheat (1960), Vol. 5, pp. 98–100.
13. Because of the interruption of the Civil War, publication of Macomb's report was delayed until 1876. Meanwhile, William H. Jackson of the Hayden Survey had seen and photographed some of the Mesa Verde ruins in 1874. The impact of those pictures on the public was such that Macomb's earlier notices were overlooked.
14. Newberry's contribution forms Part II of Macomb (1876); see especially pp. 94–97. The spires that the explorers were looking at from the top of the butte are stunning features of the Canyonlands area now called the Needles. Composed of Cedar Mesa sandstone, the Needles look like huge red-and-white gendarmes petrified while deployed erratically across an almost level plain. For a geologist's view, see Lohman (1974), pp. 73–83, especially the photographs.

8. UTAH'S DIXIE

1. Brooks (1962), pp. 34–35
2. Hamblin biographies include Little (1881), which draws uncritically on Hamblin's oral reminiscences; Corbett (1952), which inclines toward adulation; Bailey (1948); and Creer (1958).
3. Data on Mormon town-founding and work among the Indians are scattered throughout Arrington (1966), Nelson (1925), and three solid works by Peterson (1971, 1973, 1976). See also Brooks (1944); Gregory (1945); and Stegner (1942), pp. 25–71 *passim.*
4. Peterson (1973), p. 215.
5. *Ibid.*, p. 169.
6. Brooks (1944), pp. 6–7, 15. Some of the adopted Indians, both male and female,

did grow up to marry whites. The situation was seldom easy, however; most Mormons held the nation's common prejudices against Indians (indeed, against all dark skins), and interracial marriages were scorned, no matter what the Church may have said.

7. Brooks (1962), p. 61. This thorough account by a Mormon of the Mountain Meadows massacre is the best one available. Where it differs from the tales told in Little (1881) and Corbett (1952), I follow Brooks.

8. Forney's report, *Senate Executive Document 42*, 36th Congress, 1st Session, reprinted in Brooks (1962), p. 259.

9. Brooks (1962), pp. 118–126, discusses Hamblin's probable complicity in the cattle raid.

10. *Ibid.*, 101–103, 171–172; and Forney's report (see note 8, above).

11. Corbett (1952), pp. 147–148; Peterson (1971), pp. 194–196, (1975), p. 181.

12. Robert C. Euler and Henry Dobyns, *The Hopi People* (Phoenix, Ariz.: Indian Tribal Series, 1972), p. 54, estimates a 60-percent population drop from 1853 to 1861. I am simply guessing that the shrinkage amounted to 50 percent by the end of 1858.

13. Brooks (1962), pp. 101–103.

14. Peterson (1971), pp. 185–186.

15. Brooks (1944), pp. 42–43, discusses the Indian wives, a sticky point because the family denies their existence. Corbett (1952), p. 187 and p. 512, note 7, states that although neither of the women on the 1860 venture was wed to Hamblin, he later married one of them.

16. Corbett (1952), p. 183, says that George, Jr., was fifteen. Reilly (1978) says eighteen.

17. Woodbury (1950), p. 151. Other useful summaries of early Dixie are Larson (1947), pp. 189–190; Gregory (1952); and Arrington (1956).

18. M. Smith (1972), p. 377–378; Corbett (1952), pp. 206ff.; and Peterson (1971) are the principal sources for Hamblin's south-side trips to the Moquis.

19. Little (1881) p. 90; Hirst (1976), pp. 52–53.

20. Arrington (1966), pp. 217–218; M. Smith (1972), pp. 265–266.

21. Quoted in Corbett (1952), p. 239. Indian troubles between 1865 and 1869 are summarized in Woodbury (1950), pp. 167–177, and Crampton (1964a), pp. 92–95.

22. Crampton (1964b), p. 156.

23. Because Adams later flooded Congress with arguments designed to win recompense for meritorious national service in developing the river, there is no dearth of material about him. The problem is what to believe. Sources include (1871) *House Miscellaneous Document 12*, 41st Congress. 3d Session: Samuel Adams, "The Exploration of the Colorado River and Its Tributaries"; and (1875) *Senate Report 662*, 43rd Congress, 2nd Session: "Report Submitted by Mr. Washburn for the Committee of Claims." See also Stegner (1954), pp. 50–53. Additional data connecting activities on the river to Dixie's transportation problems are in M. Smith (1972), pp. 261–301; Arrington (1956); Faulk (1964); and Lingenfelter (1978), pp. 41–49.

24. M. Smith (1972), pp. 160–162.

25. Melvin Smith, "Mormon Explorations in the Lower Colorado River Area," in Jackson (1978), pp. 36–41.
26. M. Smith (1972), pp. 291–295.
27. The maneuverings are outlined *ibid.*, pp. 349–351; and in Lingenfelter (1978), pp. 48–49.
28. Marcy (1866), pp. 278–282.
29. M. Smith (1972), pp. 167, 352–353.

9. FIRST MAN THROUGH?

1. Basic materials for the White story are Bell (1871), which is largely a transcription of Parry's report as published in the *Transactions of the Academy of Science of St. Louis* in 1868; Stanton (1932), pp. 3–93, and (1919); Dawson (1917); Lingenfelter (1958); and Bulger (1961). Masses of other data of varying degrees of usefulness are in the three James White file boxes of the Marston Collection, Huntington Library.
2. Eloquent support of the contention that White began his river run in Glen Canyon and reached Callville in fourteen days is in Collins and Nash (1978), pp. 191–193.
3. Among the proponents of an entry to the river via Diamond Creek or Spencer Canyon, twenty miles downstream from Diamond, are Corle (1946); and P. T. Reilly, letter to Otis Marston, Jan. 11, 1958, White file box 1, Marston Collection, Huntington Library. Henry Dobyns and Robert Euler object to the supposition (in a review of Lingenfelter's *First Through the Grand Canyon* in *Arizona and the West*, Autumn, 1959), on the grounds that the Hualapai Indians, who had strongholds in both canyons, were so hostile in 1867 that white men could not have passed them.
4. M. Smith (1972), p. 164.
5. Stanton (1919). Like Stanton, Otis Marston argues for an entry below the Grand Wash Cliffs, but believes murder was involved: "Early Travel on the Green and Colorado Rivers," in *The Smoke Signal* (Tucson: Westerner's Brand Books, 1969), pp. 233–234.

10. TESTING THE RIVER

Biographies of Powell are Darrah (1951) and Stegner (1954). Source material for Powell's Rocky Mountain ventures is Watson (1954). For the 1869 trip, see Darrah's (1947) editing of the Bradley and Sumner journals and related documents.

As is well known by now, Powell's own work presents problems (for a discussion, see Stegner [1954], pp. 147–152). I have used Powell (1895), a compendium of his "official" *Exploration of the Colorado River of the West and Its Tributaries* (Washington, D.C.: Government Printing Office, 1875) and of various magazine articles. The flaws in the *Exploration* account are Powell's inventions of exciting episodes for dramatic effect; his use, as though they had happened in 1869, of events and place names taken from the 1871–72 run down the river without so much as a mention of the second venture or its personnel; and his implication that his explorations of Zion Canyon took place in 1870, though that trip was made in 1872. These manipulations, however, do not impair the validity of his descriptive passages and scientific observations, handily collected in the 1895 volume and its 1962 reprint, both illustrated with a wealth of fascinating woodcuts.

For sometimes ill-natured criticism of Powell, see Stanton (1932), pp. 135–232. Otis Marston, Colorado River veteran, also gives Powell low marks as a white-water explorer, whatever he may have been as a scientist, administrator, and social innovator.

1. Dellenbaugh (1908), p. 117. Sumner disagreed and claimed the idea of the canyon run was his. (Sumner to Robert Brewster Stanton, quoted in Anderson [1979], pp. 392–393.) As Stegner indicates (1954, pp. 374, 377), Sumner's belated and embittered recollections have to be read with a large grain of salt. But, then, so do some of Powell's.

2. I reconstruct the course of Powell's planning from a story in the *Rocky Mountain News* of November 6, 1867, which stated that he planned to return to the Grand River in 1868 and follow it to the Green. Yet once he was back in Illinois, late in 1867, he had so little to say about the project that his own brother-in-law, Almon Thompson, recalled no mention of it until 1868 was well under way. (Anderson [1979], p. 391.)

3. Samuel Bowles, *Our New West* (Hartford, Conn.: Hartford Publishing Company, 1869), p. 503; Stegner (1954), pp. 31–32.

4. The Arizona Pioneers Historical Society documents White's tie-cutting for the Union Pacific in 1868 (Society to Richard Lingenfelter, copy in White file box 1, Marston Collection, Huntington Library). Bradley's diary entry is August 14, 1869, *Utah Historical Quarterly*, Vol. 15, 1947. For Powell's meeting with Bradley, see Stegner (1954), pp. 39, 46.

5. Powell (1895), p. 119.

6. The contracts with Sumner, Dunn, and O. G. Howland have survived. Presumably Hawkins and Seneca Howland received similar terms. (Anderson [1979], pp. 394, 396.)

7. Anderson (1979), p. 394, lists the assignments. Powell (1874) gives methods.

8. Marston (1969), p. 177.

9. Powell (1895), p. 156; Anderson (1979), p. 397; and Dellenbaugh (1908), p. 38. See also Stanton (1932).

10. Powell (1895), p. 165. "Ecstacy" is quoted in Anderson (1979), p. 399. Howland's letter appeared in the *Rocky Mountain News*, July 17, 1869.

11. Powell (1895), p. 212–215, gives his version of the pause.

12. Anderson (1979), p. 400. Sumner's story of the quarrel is a belated reminiscence. Dissension is not mentioned in journals kept at the time, which does not necessarily mean that peace prevailed.

13. Statistics from Mutschler (1969?). Counters of rapids seldom agree. In a quick sequence of rapids, where does one end, another begin? High water can also blur distinctions.

14. Powell (1895), p. 247.

15. *Ibid.*, p. 274; Collins and Nash (1978), p. 183.

II. MEASURING THE LAND

Main sources for Powell's 1870–72 trips are Powell (1895), pp. 299–364; Dellenbaugh (1908); and the following journals published in Volumes 7, 15, and combined 16–17 of the *Utah Historical Quarterly*: Herbert E. Gregory (1937, 1948–49), editor of diaries by Thompson and Jones; Charles Kelley (1946, 1948–49), editor of diaries by Bishop and W. C. Powell; W. C. Darrah (1948–49), editor of a diary by Steward. An additional diary, that of Jack Hillers, has been edited by Don D. Fowler (1972).

The work of the Powell survey is summarized in Stegner (1954), pp. 155–191; Darrah (*loc. cit.*), pp. 204–220; Bartlett (1962), pp. 313–329; and Goetzmann (1966), pp. 566–578. Dutton (1882) should be at least skimmed for its aesthetic sensibilities and vivid descriptions, as well as for its geology.

Material on John D. Lee comes primarily from Brooks (1962), pp. 288–370; and Cleland and Brooks (1955), Vol. 2, *passim*. Adonis Findlay Robinson (1970), pp. 49–52, adds useful data about Kanab during its formative years.

1. Darrah (1947), p. 148.
2. J. W. Powell left no record of his plans. My reconstruction is based on an undated letter by his cousin Clem Powell, printed in the *Chicago Tribune*, July 17, 1871. See the *Utah Historical Quarterly*, Vol. 16–17, 1948–49, p. 401.
3. Brooks (1962), pp. 277–290.
4. For Powell's thinking, see Darrah (1969). See also Stegner (1954), pp. 219–231, for an analysis of the background of Powell's *Report on the Lands of the Arid Region*.
5. Data about the journey across the plateaus is from Powell (1895), pp. 299–325, with addenda from Bishop's diary, *Utah Historical Quarterly*, Vol. 15, 1946, pp. 159–161.
6. For the Indians' story, see Powell (1895), pp. 321–323; and Little (1881), p. 97. Dellenbaugh (1908), p. 243, speculates that the Indians had no prompting from outside but killed the trio for their guns, knives, and clothing. Michael Belshaw, a close student of the area, agrees, in "The Dunn-Howland Killings: A Reconstruction," *Journal of Arizona History*, Winter, 1979. Belshaw's account prompted the anthropologists Henry Dobyns and Robert C. Euler, close students of the Pai people, to retort, in "The Dunn-Howland Killings: Additional Insights," *Journal of Arizona History*, Spring, 1980, with arguments supporting the Shivwits version. The controversy is not likely to be resolved.

One added note: Graves's interest in the affair surely was significant, but Powell never mentions the youth's blood relationship with the Howlands. Powell's dramas almost always center on Powell. "That night," he wrote after the council, "I slept in peace, although the murderers of my men . . . were sleeping not five hundred yards away." Well, so did Walter Graves, unmentioned, though he was a cousin of the murdered men.
7. Corbett (1952), pp. 311–316, says that Hamblin was in Salt Lake City in late July. Powell was also there at the time, and surely they looked each other up.
8. Did Powell make a serious effort to reach the Dirty Devil? Thompson (diary entry, August 29, 1871) says that he doubts it. Dellenbaugh (1908), p. 99, in discussing his boss's wanderings, makes no mention of any attempt—a significant omission. Still, the possibility does exist that Powell and Jacob or others of the

Hamblin tribe did start toward the junction but turned back on seeing the upheaved wastes ahead of them.

9. Descriptions of the surveying process can be found in Powell (1874), pp. 136–137; Harvey De Motte, in Watson (1954), pp. 104–113; and Olson (1969), pp. 262–267.

10. Kelley (1948–49), pp. 387–400 *passim*.

11. Cleland and Brooks (1962), Vol. 2, pp. 175–176. Lee's own running account of his troubles with the Church occupies pp. 142–210. See also Brooks (1955), pp. 290–315.

12. Cleland and Brooks (1962), Vol. 2, p. 178.

13. Descriptions of the run are from appropriate pages of the diaries of Almon Thompson (*Utah Historical Quarterly*, 1939); Clem Powell and S. V. Jones (*ibid.*, 1948–49); Jack Hillers (ed. Fowler, 1977); and Dellenbaugh (1908).

14. Stegner (1954), pp. 219–235, and Darrah (1969) analyze Powell's report on the arid lands.

15. Dutton (1882), p. 141.

12. SEARCHING FOR NEW OASES

1. Cleland and Brooks (1955), Vol. 2, p. 217.

2. Sources for the Mormon-Gentile impasse during the 1870's are Howard Lamar, *The Far Southwest, 1846–1912* (New York: W. W. Norton, 1970), pp. 365–388; and Gustive O. Larson (1971), pp. 1–89, *passim*.

3. Peterson (1973), pp. 5–6, 46–47, 232.

4. Data for the section on Lee are drawn primarily from his diaries and from Brooks's biography (1950); Rusho and Crampton (1975), pp. 32–49; and Reilly (1971).

5. Cleland and Brooks (1955), Vol. 2, p. 242.

6. *Ibid.*, pp. 306–307.

7. Detailed analyses of the trials are in the concluding chapters of Brooks's studies of Lee (1950, 1962).

8. Peterson (1973) is a thorough account of the Little Colorado settlements.

9. Larson (1971), pp. 111–112.

10. The trip by the scouts is covered in Miller (1959), pp. 17–35; and Perkins *et al.* (1957), pp. 28–32, 88–89.

11. Principal sources for the Hole-in-the-Rock trip are Miller (1959); Perkins *et al.* (1957); Redd (1950); and my tracing of the trail in 1960 and 1961, much of the way with descendants of the pioneers.

12. Redd (1950), pp. 23–24.

13. Peterson (1975), another fine work, touches on Bluff's early years (pp. 37–53). See also Perkins *et al.* (1957), pp. 59–87; Lyman (1962), *passim*. References to the entire drainage area are scattered throughout Gregory (1938).

14. Albert Lyman, quoted in Walker (1964b), p. 269.

15. For early Monticello, see Peterson (1975), pp. 72–88; and Perkins *et al.*, pp. 87–119. The cowbell story is in Perkins *et al.*, p. 106; the gun-flashes in Walker (1964b), p. 282.

16. Hazel Ekker, describing an experience of May, 1969, to Otis Marston (Ekker file, Marston Collection, Huntington Library).

17. Sheire (1972) Pearl Baker (1963, 1965), contain material on canyonland ranching. Crampton (1959, 1962) locates many of the stock trails that drop from both sides of the river into Glen Canyon. Young (1964) and Lavender (1940) described hunting wild cattle.

18. My recollections of Al Scorup appear in Lavender (1943), pp. 159–203. See also his sister's biography, Scorup (1944); and Lambert (1964).

19. For Nutter, see his daughter's account; Price and Darby (1964); Whipple (1961); and Belshaw (1977), Vol. 2, pp. 35–44.

20. Many references to Haley and Queen Ann Bassett are scattered throughout Burroughs (1962); and Dunham and Dunham (1977); consult the indexes. Queen Ann's own laundered recollections are in Willis (1952).

13. EXPLOITATION BEGINS

1. Data on Brown, the railroad proposal, and the surveys are from Brown's diary and field notes (1889); Stanton (1892 and 1964); Dwight Smith (1960 and 1962b); Nims (1967); and Marston (1969b).

2. Kendrick's diary has been edited by Stiles (1964).

3. It is unlikely that Hoskanini would have known that flour-fine gold, detectable only after thorough washing by experienced miners, existed in Glen Canyon. Still, getting rid of unwelcome guests by telling of gold somewhere else was a standard Indian ploy, and Hoskanini may have used it to remove Hite.

4. Brown (1889), n.p.

5. Whirlpools are linked to Brown's death in Stanton (1965), pp. 78–81, and in two stories Stanton gave Denver newspapers, one by telegraph from Kanab (*Denver Times,* July 22, 1890) and one in a direct interview (*Rocky Mountain News,* July 30, 1890). P. T. Reilly, who found the exact eddy, says (1969) that it is not troublesome and blames the construction of the boats for the accident. The implication is that Brown died from something other than whirlpools.

6. Nims's diary (1967), pp. 60–67; and Stanton (1965), pp. 120ff.

7. Marston (1955) p. 68, and (1960), pp. 292–293.

14. SELLING THE SCENERY

1. Frank McNitt (1966) has written a biography of Richard Wetherill. Frances Gillmor and Louisa Wade Wetherill (John's wife) have performed a similar service for John Wetherill. Although these accounts refrain from mentioning the matter, Charles Mason was probably the Wetherills' cousin as well as their brother-in-law.

2. Mason's account of the discovery, written after Richard's death but attested to by four other Wetherills, is in McNitt (1966), pp. 323–329.

3. Short references to Mrs. McClurg are in Francis Kinder's *Evenings with Colorado*

Poets (Denver: World Press, 1926), p. 258; Le Roy Hafen's *History of Colorado* (Denver: Linderman Co., 1924), p. 1243; Ira S. Freeman's *History of Montezuma County* (Boulder, Colo.: Johnson Publishing Co., 1958), p. 169; Edmund Rogers's article "Notes on the Establishment of Mesa Verde National Park," *Colorado Magazine*, January, 1952; and Duane A. Smith, *Rocky Mountain Boom Town: A History of Durango* (Albuquerque: University of New Mexico Press, 1980).

4. Yosemite and Sequoia in California; Yellowstone, mostly in Wyoming.
5. Accounts of early tourist development at the Grand Canyon are Verkamp (1940), Watkins (1969), Strong (1969), Crampton (1972), and Hughes (1978).
6. Bryant (1974), pp. 116–120.
7. Woodbury (1950), pp. 190–191.
8. North Rim promotions have received sketchy treatment at best; see Woodbury (1950), pp. 191–194; Robinson (1970), pp. 101–104; Crampton (1972), pp. 203–209; and Hughes (1978), pp. 76–77.
9. Data from Galloway's diary (1909); Sharp's diary (1909); Stone (1932); and a letter from Stone to Freeman, January 12, 1923, concerning the early history of the Colorado River (Marston Collection, Huntington Library).
10. Ellsworth Kolb (1914) writes well of the adventure.

15. CLAIMING THE WATER

Background material for this chapter came primarily from James (1917), LaRue (1925), Olson (1926), Force (1936), U.S. Bureau of Reclamation (1946), Golze (1961), Warne (1972), Hundley (1975), Johnson (1977), Colorado River Board of California (1978), Goslin (1978), Kahrl (1978), and Robinson (1979). I am also indebted to Rockwell Hereford for giving me access to a thesis he prepared at the Massachusetts Institute of Technology (1924).

1. Powell's irrigation survey is discussed in Sterling (1940); Darrah (1951), pp. 299–314; Stegner (1954), pp. 299–328; and Alexander (1968, 1969).
2. Smythe (1900) gives a somewhat self-serving view of the irrigation congresses. More objective summaries are in Carlson (1968); Taylor (1970); and Lee (1972).
3. Lingenfelter (1978), pp. 135–136; and an undated fact sheet prepared by the Lower Colorado Region of the (then) Water and Power Resources Service.
4. Fellows (n.d.). I am indebted to Fellows's daughter, Ella Jane Settles, for a copy of his reminiscences.
5. A wealth of material on the Salt River Project is available, notably James (1917), pp. 67–78; C. Smith (1972), pp. 9–13; Meredith (1968); *Arizona* (1972), pp. 121–124; Lowe (1978); and an undated, technical handout, "Salt River Project," by the former Water and Power Resources Service. The statistics given by the different authorities do not always agree.
6. A small start toward expounding the intricacies of western water law is provided by Breitenstein (1950); Gopalakrishnan (1973); and Null (1974).
7. Lingenfelter (1978), p. 139. Fine summaries of the Imperial troubles are Hosmer

(1966); and Hundley (1975), pp. 17–30. See also Kerschner (1953) on Chaffey; and Morrison (1962) on Rockford. Woodbury (1941) is "novelized."

8. Hundley (1975), p. 93. pp. 53–101 summarize the League's work and influence.
9. Hearings on "Renaming the Grand River," Committee on Interstate and Foreign Commerce, 66th Congress, 3rd Session, Feb. 18, 1921.
10. Hundley (1975), p. 193.
11. Most of the books listed at the beginning of this section of notes discuss the compact. The document itself is reprinted in Hundley (1975), pp. 337–343.
12. O. J. W. Hansen (1978). Hansen was the sculptor of most of the artwork at the dam.
13. Data on the survey trips are from Kolb (1921); LaRue (1921 and 1925); Freeman (1923 and 1924); Birdseye and Moore (1924); and Miser (1924); as well as masses of notes in folders for the years 1921, 1922, 1923, Marston Collection, Huntington Library.
14. Colorado River Board of California (1979), p. 15.
15. Peter McDonald, chairman of the Navajo Tribal Council, even stated in 1978 that the Navajos have a right to *all* the water in the Colorado River (*ibid.*, p. 19).

APPENDIX

1. Hoffman (1981), pp 12–15.
2. See chart in Simmons and Gaskill (n.d.), pp. 28–29.
3. Hansen (1965), pp. 58–64
4. Recent literature about the formation of the Grand Canyon includes McKee *et al.* (1967); and C. Breed (1969, 1970). In addition, see summaries in Baars (1972), pp. 218–221; Rahm (1974), pp. 142–146; and Redfern (1980), Chapter II. Objections to the theory are in Charles Hunt, "Grand Canyon and the Colorado River: Their Geologic History," in Breed and Roat, eds. (1974). Gerald Thompson, "A Brief Geologic History of the Grand Canyon," in Euler *et al.* (1980), summarizes yet another theory.

Bibliography

ABBEY, EDWARD. 1968. *Desert Solitaire.* New York: McGraw-Hill.

———. 1971. *Slickrock.* San Francisco: Sierra Club Books,

ADAMS, ELEANOR B. 1976. "Fray Francisco Atanasio Domínguez and Fray Silvestre de Escalante." *Utah Historical Quarterly,* Vol. 44 (Winter).

ADAMS, WILLIAM Y. 1960. *Ninety Years of Glen Canyon Archaeology, 1869–1959.* Flagstaff: Museum of Northern Arizona, Bulletin 33.

ALEXANDER, THOMAS G. 1968. "The Powell Irrigation Survey and the People of the Mountain West." *Journal of the West,* Vol. 7 (January).

———. 1969. "John Wesley Powell, the Irrigation Survey, and the Inauguration of the Second Phase of Irrigation Development in Utah." *Utah Historical Quarterly,* Vol. 37 (Spring).

ALTER, J. CECIL. 1962. *James Bridger: A Historical Narrative.* Norman: University of Oklahoma Press.

ANDERSON, MARTIN J. 1979. "First Through the Canyon: Powell's Lucky Voyage in 1969." *Journal of Arizona History,* Vol. 20 (Winter).

Arizona: Its People and Resources. 1972. Tucson: University of Arizona Press.

ARRINGTON, LEONARD J. 1956. "The Mormon Cotton Mission in Southern Utah." *Pacific Historical Review,* Vol. 25, No. 3.

———. 1966a. *Great Basin Kingdom.* Lincoln: University of Nebraska Press,

———. 1966b. "Inland to Zion." *Arizona and the West,* Vol. 8, No. 3 (Autumn).

BAARS, DONALD L. 1972. *Red Rock Country: The Geologic History of the Colorado Plateau.* New York: Doubleday/Natural History Press.

BAILEY, LYNN. 1965. "Lt. Sylvester Mowry's Report on His March in 1855 from Salt Lake City to Fort Tejon, California." *Arizona and the West,* Vol. 7, No. 4 (Winter).

———. 1966. *Indian Slave Trade in the Southwest.* Los Angeles: Westernlore Press.

BAILEY, PAUL. 1948. *Jacob Hamblin, Buckskin Apostle.* Los Angeles: Westernlore Press.

BALDWIN, GORDON C. 1950. "Archeological Survey of the Lake Mead Area." In Reed and King, eds., *For the Dean. . . .* Santa Fe, N. M.: Hohokam Museum Association and Southwestern Monument Association.

BANNON, JOHN FRANCIS. 1974. *The Spanish Borderlands Frontier, 1513–1821.* Reprint, Albuquerque: University of New Mexico Press.

BARTLETT, RICHARD A. 1962. *Great Surveys of the American West.* Norman: University of Oklahoma Press.

BEALL, MERRILL D., JR. 1967. *Grand Canyon: The Story Behind the Scenery.* Flagstaff, Ariz.: KC Publications.

BELKNAP, BILL, and BUZZ BELKNAP. 1974. *Canyonlands River Guide.* . . . Boulder City, Nev.: Westwater Books.

BELKNAP, BUZZ. 1969. *Grand Canyon River Guide.* Boulder City, Nev.: Westwater Books.

BELL, WILLIAM. 1871. *New Tracks in North America.* New York: Scribner, Willard.

BELSHAW, MICHAEL. n.d. "Historic Resources Study, Lake Mead Recreational Area." Manuscript at Lake Mead Recreation Offices, Boulder City, Nev.

———. "High, Dry, and Lonesome: The Arizona Strip." *The Journal of Arizona History,* Vol. 19 (Winter, 1978).

BERNHEIMER, CHARLES L. 1929. *Rainbow Bridge.* New York: Doubleday, Doran.

BERRY, DON. 1961. *A Majority of Scoundrels.* New York: Harper and Brothers.

BIEBER, RALPH P., ed. 1938. *Exploring Southwestern Trails, 1846–1854.* Glendale, Calif.: Arthur C. Clark.

BILLINGTON, RAY A. 1974. *The Far Western Frontier, 1830–1860.* New York: Macmillan.

BIRDSEYE, CLAUDE H., and RAYMOND MOORE. 1924. "A Boat Voyage Through the Grand Canyon of the Colorado." *Geographical Review,* April.

BLACKWELDER, ELIOT. 1955. "Geologic Exhibit." In Wallace Stegner, ed., *This Is Dinosaur.* New York: Alfred A. Knopf.

BLEAK, JAMES G. n.d. "Annals of the Southern Utah Mission," Books A and B. Dixie College Library, St. George, Utah (typescripts of original copies).

BOLTON, H. E. 1936. *Rim of Chistendom.* New York: Macmillan.

———. 1949. *Coronado, Knight of Pueblo and Plains.* New York and Albuquerque: Whittlesey House and University of New Mexico Press.

———. 1950. *Pageant in the Wilderness.* Salt Lake City: Utah Historical Society.

BRANDON, WILLIAM. 1966. *The American Heritage Book of Indians.* New York: American Heritage.

BREED, CAROL S. 1969. "A Century of Conjecture on the Colorado River in Grand Canyon. "In D. L. Baars, ed., *Geology and Natural History of the Grand Canyon Region.* Four Corners Geologic Society, 5th Field Conference.

———. 1970. "Two Hypotheses of the Origin and Geologic History of the Colorado River." In *Guidebook to the Central Rocky Mountain Region.* Cedar City, Utah.

BREED, W.J., and EVELYN ROAT, eds. 1974. *Geology of the Grand Canyon.* Flagstaff, Ariz.: Museum of New Mexico and the Grand Canyon Natural History Association.

BREITENSTEIN, JEAN. 1950. "Some Elements of Colorado Water Law." *Rocky Mountain Law Review,* Vol. 20, pp. 343–356.

BRETERNITZ, DAVID, and JACK E. SMITH. 1972. *Mesa Verde and Rocky Mountain National Parks.* Casper, Wyo.: World-Wide Research and Publishing.

BROOKS, JUANITA. 1944. "Indian Relations on the Mormon Frontier." *Utah Historical Quarterly,* Vol. 12 (January–April).

———. 1962. *The Mountain Meadows Massacre.* Reprint. Norman: University of Oklahoma Press.

———. 1962. *John Doyle Lee: Zealot, Pioneer-Builder, Scapegoat.* Glendale, Calif.: Arthur H. Clark.

BROWN, FRANK M. 1889. "Diary and Field Notes." Copy of original manuscript in the Marston Collection, Huntington Library, San Marino, Calif.

BRYANT, KEITH L. 1974. *History of the Atchison, Topeka and Santa Fe Railroad.* New York: Macmillan.

BULGER, HAROLD A. 1961. "First Man Through the Grand Canyon." *Bulletin of the Missouri Historical Society,* Vol. 17 (July).

BURROUGHS, JOHN R. 1962. *Where the Old West Stayed Young.* New York: William Morrow.

CAMP, CHARLES, ed. 1966. *George C. Yount and His Chronicles of the West.* Denver: Old West Publishing.

CARLSON, MARTIN. 1968. "William E. Smythe: Irrigation Crusader." *Journal of the West,* Vol. 7 (January).

CARR, RALPH. 1944. "Delph Carpenter and River Compacts Between Western States." *Colorado Magazine,* Vol. 21 (January).

CERAM, C. W. 1971. *The First American: A Study of North American Archeology.* New York: Harcourt Brace Jovanovich.

CHÁVEZ, FRAY ANGÉLICO, trans., and TED WARNER, ed. 1976. *The Domínguez-Escalante Journal.* Provo, Utah: Brigham Young University.

CLELAND, ROBERT GLASS. 1950. *This Reckless Breed of Men.* New York: Alfred A. Knopf.

———, and JUANITA BROOKS. 1955. *A Mormon Chronicle: The Journals of John D. Lee.* 2 vols. San Marino, Calif.: The Huntington Library.

COLLINS, ROBERT, and RODERICK NASH. 1978. *The Big Drops.* San Francisco: Sierra Club Books.

COLORADO RIVER BOARD OF CALIFORNIA. 1978. *California's Stake in the Colorado River.* Los Angeles: Colorado River Association.

CORBETT, PEARSON H. 1952. *Jacob Hamblin, the Peacemaker.* Salt Lake City: Deseret.

CORLE, EDWIN. 1961. *Listen, Bright Angel.* Reprint. Lincoln: University of Nebraska Press.

COUES, ELLIOTT. 1900. *On the Trail of a Spanish Pioneer: The Diary and Itinerary of Francisco Garcés.* 2 vols. New York: Francis P. Harper.

CRAMPTON, C. GREGORY. 1952. "The Discovery of the Green River." *Utah Historical Quarterly,* Vol. 20. (October).

———. 1959. *Outline History of the Glen Canyon Region, 1776–1927.* University of Utah Anthropological Papers, Glen Canyon Series, No. 9. Salt Lake City: University of Utah Press.

———. 1962. *Historical Sites in Glen Canyon.* University of Utah Anthropological Paper No. 61. Salt Lake City: University of Utah Press.

———. 1964a. *Standing Up Country: The Canyonlands of Utah and Arizona.* New York: Alfred A. Knopf and the University of Utah Press, in Association with the Amon Carter Museum of Western Art.

———. 1964b. "A Military Reconnaissance in Southern Utah." *Utah Historical Quarterly,* Vol. 32 (Spring).

———. 1965. *Mormon Colonization in Southern Utah and in Adjacent Parts of Arizona and Nevada, 1851–1900.* United States National Park Service.

——. 1972. *Land of Living Rock: The Grand Canyon and High Plateaus.* New York: Alfred A. Knopf.

CREER, LELAND H. 1958. *The Adventures of Jacob Hamblin in the Vicinity of the Colorado.* University of Utah Anthropological Papers, No. 33. Salt Lake City: University of Utah Press.

DARRAH, WILLIAM C., ed. 1947. "The Exploration of the Colorado River in 1869." Includes Bradley and Summer journals, and related documents. *Utah Historical Quarterly,* Vol. 15.

——, ed. 1948–49. "The Exploration of the Colorado River and the High Plateaus of Utah in 1871–72." Includes journal of John W. Steward and related documents. *Utah Historical Quarterly,* Vols. 16–17.

——. 1951. *Powell of the Colorado.* Princeton, N.J.: Princeton University Press,

——. 1969. "John Wesley Powell and an Understanding of the West." *Utah Historical Quarterly,* Vol. 37 (Spring).

DAWSON, THOMAS F. 1917. *The Grand Canyon.* Senate Executive Document 42, 65th Congress, 1st Session.

DEAN, JEFFREY S. 1969. *Chronological Analysis of the Tsegi Sites in Northeastern Arizona.* Tucson: University of Arizona Press.

DELLENBAUGH, FREDERICK S. 1902. *The Romance of the Colorado River.* New York: G. P. Putnam's Sons.

——. 1908. *A Canyon Voyage.* New York: G. P. Putnam's Sons. 1908.

DEVOTO, BERNARD. 1943. *The Year of Decision: 1846.* Boston: Little, Brown.

——. 1947. *Across the Wide Missouri.* Boston: Houghton Mifflin.

DUNHAM, DICK, and VIVIAN DUNHAM. 1977. *Flaming Gorge Country.* Denver: Eastwood Printing and Publishing.

DURRENBERGER, ROBERT. 1972. "The Colorado Plateau." *Annals of the Association of American Geographers,* Vol. 62 (June).

DUTTON, CLARENCE E. 1882. *Tertiary History of the Grand Canyon District, with Atlas.* Washington, D.C.: Government Printing Office.

EMORY, WILLIAM H. 1848. *Notes of a Military Reconnaissance from Fort Leavenworth, in Missouri, to San Diego, in California.* 30th Congress, 1st Session. Senate Executive Document No. 7. Washington, D.C.: Wendell and Benthuysen.

EULER, ROBERT C. 1966. *Southern Paiute Ethno-History.* University of Utah Anthropological Papers, No. 78. Salt Lake City: University of Utah Press.

——. 1967. "The Canyon Dwellers." *The American West,* Vol. 4 (May).

EVANS, LAURA, and BUZZ BELKNAP. 1974. *Desolation River Guide.* Boulder City, Nev.: Westwater Books.

FARB, PETER. 1978. *Man's Rise to Civilization: The Cultural Ascent of the Indians of North America.* New York: E. P. Dutton.

FAULK, ODIE B. 1964. "The Steamboat War That Opened Arizona." *Arizoniana,* Vol. 4 (Winter).

——. 1969. *Derby's Report on the Opening of the Colorado.* Albuquerque: University of New Mexico Press.

FELLOWS, ABRAHAM L. n.d. "The Exploration of the Grand Canyon of the Gunnison."

Unpublished reminiscence in possession of Ella Jane Settle.

FENNEMAN, NEVIN M. 1931. *Physiography of Western United States.* New York: McGraw-Hill.

FORBES, JACK D. 1958. "Melchior Díaz and the Discovery of Alta California." *Pacific Historical Review,* November.

———. 1965. *Warriors of the Colorado.* Norman: University of Oklahoma Press.

FORCE, E. T. 1936. "The Use of the Colorado River in the United States, 1850–1933." Ph.D. dissertation, University of California, Berkeley.

FOREMAN, GRANT, ed. 1941. *A Pathfinder in the Southwest: The Itinerary of Lieutenant A. K. Whipple . . . 1853–1854.* Norman: University of Oklahoma Press.

FOWLER, DON D., ed. 1977. *Photographed All the Best Scenery: J. K. Hillers' Diary.* Salt Lake City: University of Utah Press.

———, ROBERT C. EULER, and CATHERINE S. FOWLER. 1969. *John Wesley Powell and the Anthropology of the Canyon Country.* U.S. Geological Survey Professional Paper 670. Washington, D.C.: Government Printing Office.

FRADKIN, PHILIP L. 1981. *A River No More.* New York: Alfred A. Knopf.

FURNISS, NORMAN F. 1960. *The Morman Conflict.* New Haven: Yale University Press.

GALLOWAY, NATHANIEL. 1909. Ms. diary of trip with Julius Stone. Aleson Collection, B-187. Utah Historical Society, Salt Lake City.

GARCÉS, FRANCISCO. 1950. *A Record of Travels in Arizona and California.* Translated by John Galvin. San Francisco: John Howell—Books.

GEORGE, UWE. 1977. *In the Deserts of This Earth.* New York: Harcourt Brace Jovanovich.

GILLMOR, FRANCES, and LOUISA WADE WETHERILL. 1953. *Traders to the Navajos: The Story of the Wetherills of Kayenta.* Albuquerque: University of New Mexico Press.

GLASSOW, MICHAEL. 1980. *Prehistoric Agricultural Development in the Northern Southwest.* Socorro, N.M.: Ballena Press.

GOETZMANN, WILLIAM H. 1959. *Army Exploration in the American West.* New Haven: Yale University Press.

———. 1966. *Exploration and Empire.* New York: Alfred A. Knopf.

GOLZE, ALFRED R. 1961. *Reclamation in the United States.* Caldwell, Idaho: Caxton Press.

GOPALAKRISHNAN, CHENNAL. 1973. "The Doctrine of Prior Appropriation and Its Impact on Water Development." *American Journal of Economics and Sociology,* Vol. 32 (January).

GOSLIN, IVAL. 1977. "Interstate River Compacts: Impact on Colorado." In *Denver* [University] *Journal of International Law and Politics,* Vol. 6 (Special Issue).

———. 1978. "Colorado River Development." In Dean F. Peterson and A. Barry Crawford, eds., *Value and Choice in the Development of the Colorado River."* Tucson: University of Arizona Press.

GREGORY, HERBERT E. 1938. *The San Juan Country: A Geographic and Geologic Reconnaissance of Southeastern Utah.* USGS Professional Paper 188. Washington, D.C.: Government Printing Office.

———, ed. 1939. "Diary of Almon Harris Thompson . . . 1871–1875." *Utah Historical Quarterly,* Vol. 7 (January–July).

———. 1945. "Population of Southern Utah." *Economic Geography,* Vol. 21 (January).

———, ed. 1948–49. "Journal of Stephen V. Jones." *Utah Historical Quarterly*, Vols. 16–17.

HAFEN, LEROY R., ed. 1965–1972. *The Mountain Men and the Fur Trade of the Far West.* 10 vols. Glendale, Calif.: Arthur H. Clark.

——— and ANN W. HAFEN. 1954. *Old Spanish Trail, Santa Fe to Los Angeles.* Glendale, Calif.: Arthur H. Clark.

HAMBLIN, W. KENNETH, and JOSEPH R. MURPHEY. 1969. *Grand Canyon Perspectives.* Provo, Utah: H & M Distributors.

HAMMOND, GEORGE P. "Don Juan de Oñate and the Founding of New Mexico." *New Mexico Historical Review*, Vols. 1, 2 (1926–27).

———, and AGAPITO REY, eds. 1940. *Narratives of the Coronado Expedition.* Albuquerque: University of New Mexico Press.

———. 1953. *Don Juan de Oñate: Colonizer of New Mexico, 1595–1628.* 2 vols. Albuquerque: University of New Mexico Press.

HANSEN, OSKAR J. W. 1978. *Sculptures at Hoover Dam.* Washington, D.C.: Government Printing Office.

HANSEN, WALLACE R. 1969. *The Geologic Story of the Uinta Mountains.* U.S. Geologic Survey Bulletin 1291. Washington, D.C.: Government Printing Office.

HARRIS, DAVID V. 1976. *The Geologic Story of the National Parks and Monuments.* Fort Collins: Colorado State University Foundation Papers.

HAURY, EMIL W. 1976. *The Hohokam, Desert Farmers and Craftsmen.* Tucson: University of Arizona Press.

———, GORDON BALDWIN, and JESSE NUSBAUM. 1950. "Prehistoric Man." In *A Survey of the Recreation Resources of the Colorado River Basin.* U.S. Department of the Interior. Washington, D.C.: Government Printing Office.

HAYES, PHILIP T., and GEORGE C. SIMMONS. 1973. *River Runners' Guide to Dinosaur National Monument and Vicinity, with Emphasis on Geologic Features.* Denver: Powell Society.

HEREFORD, ROCKWELL. 1924. "The Colorado River Development." M.A. thesis, Massachusetts Institute of Technology.

HILL, JOSEPH J. 1923. "New Light on Pattie and the Southwestern Fur Trade." *Southwestern Historical Quarterly*, Vol. 26.

HIRST, STEPHEN. 1976. *Life in a Narrow Place: The Havasupai of the Grand Canyon.* New York: David McKay.

HOFFMAN, JOHN F. 1977. *Grand Canyon National Park.* Casper, Wyo.: World-Wide Research and Publishing.

———. 1981. *Arches National Park.* San Diego: Western Recreational Publications.

HOSMER, HELEN 1969. "Triumph and Failure in the Imperial Valley." In T. H. Watkins, ed., *The Grand Colorado.* Palo Alto, Calif.: American West Publishing.

HUGHES, J. DONALD. 1978. *In the House of Stone and Light: A Human History of the Grand Canyon.* Grand Canyon, Ariz.: Grand Canyon Natural History Association.

HUNDLEY, NORRIS, JR. 1975. *Water and the West.* Berkeley: University of California Press.

HUNT, CHARLES B. 1956. *Cenozoic Geology of the Colorado Plateau.* U.S. Geological Survey Paper 279. Washington, D.C.: Government Printing Office.

———. 1969. "Geologic History of the Colorado River." In *The Colorado River Region and John Wesley Powell.* U.S. Geological Survey Paper 669. Washington, D.C.: Government Printing Office.

INGRAM, HELEN. 1978. "The Politics of Water Allocation." In Dean F. Peterson and A. Berry Crawford, eds., *Value and Choice in the Development of the Colorado River Basin.* Tucson: University of Arizona Press.

IVES, LT. JOSEPH C. 1861. *Report upon the Colorado River of the West.* House Executive Document 90, 36th Congress, 1st Session. Washington, D.C.: Government Printing Office.

JACKSON, RICHARD. 1978. *The Mormon Role in the Settlement of the West.* Provo, Utah: Brigham Young University Press.

JAMES, GEORGE. 1917. *Reclaiming the Arid West: The Story of the United States Reclamation Service.* New York: Dodd Mead.

JENNINGS, JESSE D. 1957. *Danger Cave.* University of Utah Anthropological Paper No. 27. Salt Lake City: University of Utah Press.

———. 1960a. "Early Man in Utah." *Utah Historical Quarterly,* Vol. 28 (January).

———. 1960b. "The Aboriginal People." *Utah Historical Quarterly,*" Vol. 28 (July).

———. 1964. "The Desert West." In Jesse D. Jennings and Edward Norbeck, eds., *Prehistoric Man in the New World.* Chicago: University of Chicago Press.

———. 1966. *Glen Canyon: A Summary.* University of Utah Anthropological Paper No. 81. Salt Lake City: University of Utah Press.

———, and FLOYD W. SHARROCK. 1965. "The Glen Canyon; A Multi-Discipline Project." *Utah Historical Quarterly,* Vol. 33 (January).

JOHNSON, DAVID M. 1977. "Our Changing Climate—Its Impact on the Availability of Water." Unpublished paper presented to the 73rd Annual Meeting of the Association of American Geographers. Salt Lake City, April 25, 1977.

JOHNSON, RICH. 1977. *The Central Arizona Project.* Tucson: University of Arizona Press.

JOSEPHY, ALVIN M., JR. 1968. *The Indian Heritage of America.* New York: Alfred A. Knopf.

KAHRL, WILLIAM H. 1978. *The California Water Atlas.* Sacramento: Office of Planning and Research.

KELLEY, CHARLES, ed. 1947. "Journal of Francis M. Bishop." *Utah Historical Quarterly,* Vol. 15.

———, ed. 1948–49. "Journal of Walter Clement Powell. *Utah Historical Quarterly,* Vols. 16–17.

———. 1953. "Chief Hoskanini." *Utah Historical Quarterly,* Vol. 22 (July).

KERSHNER, FREDERICK, JR. 1953. "George Chaffey and the Irrigation Frontier." *Agricultural History.* Vol. 27 (October).

KLUCKHOHN, CLYDE, and DOROTHEA LEIGHTON. 1974. *The Navajo.* Revised edition. Cambridge, Mass.: Harvard University Press.

KOLB, ELLSWORTH L. 1914. *Through the Grand Canyon from Wyoming to Mexico.* New York: Macmillan.

KROEBER, CLINTON. 1964. "The Route of James O. Pattie on the Colorado in 1826, with . . . Comments." *Arizona and the West,* Vol. 1, pp. 119–136.

KRUTCH, JOSEPH WOOD. 1958. *Grand Canyon and All Its Yesterdays.* New York. William Sloane.

———. 1967. "The Eye of the Beholder." *The American West,* Vol. 4 (May).

LAMBERT, NEAL. 1964. "Al Scorup, Cattleman of the Canyons." *Utah Historical Quarterly,* Vol. 32 (Summer).

LARSEN, GUSTIVE O. 1947. *Prelude to the Kingdom.* Francestown, N.H.: Marshall James.

———. 1971. *The "Americanization" of Utah for Statehood.* San Marino, Calif.: The Huntington Library.

LARSON, ANDREW K. 1961. *I Was Called to Dixie: The Virgin River Basin.* Salt Lake City: Deseret News Press.

LARUE, EUGENE C. 1916. "*Colorado River and Its Utilization.* U.S. Geological Water-Supply Paper 395. Washington, D.C.: Government Printing Office.

———. 1925. *Water Power and Flood Control of Colorado River Below Green River, Utah.* U.S. Geological Survey Water-Supply Paper 556. Washington, D.C.: Government Printing Office.

LAVENDER, DAVID. 1940 "Take Down Your Rope." *Esquire,* August.

———. 1943. *One Man's West.* Garden City, N.Y.: Doubleday, Doran.

LEE, LAWRENCE B. 1972. "William Ellsworth Smythe and the Irrigation Movement: A Reconsideration." *Pacific Historical Review,* Vol. 41, No. 3 (August).

LEIGHLY, JOHN, ed. 1965. *Land and Life: A Selection from the Writings of Carl Ortwin Sauer.* Berkeley: University of California Press.

LINGENFELTER, RICHARD E. 1958. *First Man Through the Grand Canyon.* Los Angeles: Glen Dawson.

———. 1978. *Steamboats on the Colorado, 1852–1916.* Tucson: University of Arizona Press.

LITTLE, JAMES A. 1881. *Jacob Hamblin: A Narrative of His Personal Experience.* . . . Salt Lake City: Juvenile Instructor's Office.

LOHMAN, S. W. 1974. *The Geologic Story of Canyonlands National Park.* Geological Survey Bulletin 1327. Washington, D.C.: Government Printing Office.

———. 1975. *The Geologic Story of Arches National Park.* Geological Survey Bulletin 1393. Washington, D.C.: Government Printing Office.

LOWE, CHARLES W. 1964. *Arizona's Natural Environment: Landscapes and Habitats.* Tucson: University of Arizona Press.

MCKEE, EDWIN D. 1931, revised 1966. *Ancient Landscapes of the Grand Canyon.* Flagstaff, Ariz.: Northland Press.

———, et al. 1967. *Evolution of the Colorado River in Arizona.* Flagstaff: Museum of Northern Arizona.

———. 1969. "Stratified Rocks of the Grand Canyon." In *The Colorado River Region and John Wesley Powell.* U.S. Geological Survey Professional Paper 669. Washington, D.C.: Government Printing Office.

MCNITT, FRANK. 1964. *Navajo Expedition: Journal of a Military Reconnaissance . . . in 1849 by Lieutenant James A. Simpson.* Norman: University of Oklahoma Press.

————. 1966. *Richard Wetherill, Anasazi.* Albuquerque: University of New Mexico Press.

MCPHEE, JOHN. 1971. *Encounters with the Archdruid.* New York: Farrar, Straus & Giroux.

MACOMB, JOHN. 1876. *Report of the Exploration from Santa Fe New Mexico to the Junction of the Grand and Green Rivers . . . in 1859.* Washington, D.C.: Government Printing Office.

MANLY, WILLIAM LEWIS. 1949. *Death Valley in '49.* Reprint. Los Angeles: Borden Publishing.

MARSHALL, T.M. 1916. "St. Vrain's Expedition to the Gila in 1826." *The Southwest Historical Quarterly,* Vol. 19 (December).

MARSTON, OTIS. 1960. "River Runners: Fast Water Navigation." *Utah Historical Quarterly,* Vol. 28 (July).

————, ed. 1969. "The Lost Journal of John Colter Summer." *Utah Historical Quarterly,* Vol. 46 (Fall).

MARTIN, PAUL S., and FRED PLOG. 1973. *The Archaeology of Arizona.* Garden City, N.Y.: Doubleday.

MAXON, JAMES C. 1971. *Indians of the Lake Mead Country.* Globe, Ariz.: Southwest Parks and Monuments Association.

MEREDITH, H. L. 1968. "Reclamation of the Salt River Valley, 1902–1917." *Journal of the West,* Vol. 7 (January).

MERK, FREDERICK. 1978. *History of the Westward Movement.* New York: Alfred A. Knopf.

MILLER, DAVID E. 1955. "Discovery of Glen Canyon." *Utah Historical Quarterly,* Vol. 26 (July).

————. 1959. *Hole-in-the-Rock.* Salt Lake City: University of Utah Press.

MILLER, DAVID H. 1972. "The Ives Expedition Revisited: A Prussian's View." *Journal of Arizona History,* Vol. 13, pp. 1–25.

MORGAN, DALE L. 1953. *Jedediah Smith.* Indianapolis and New York: Bobbs-Merrill.

————. 1947. *The Great Salt Lake.* Indianapolis and New York: Bobbs-Merrill.

————. 1964. *The West of William Ashley.* Denver: Old West.

————, and ELEANOR T. HARRIS. 1967. *The Rocky Mountain Journals of William Marshall Anderson.* San Marino, Calif.: Huntington Library.

MORRISON, MARGARET D. 1962. "Charles Robinson Rockwood, Developer of the Imperial Valley." *Southern California Quarterly,* Vol. 44.

MULDER, WILLIAM, and A. RUSSELL MORTENSEN, eds. 1958. *Among the Mormons.* New York: Alfred A. Knopf.

MUTSCHLER, FELIX E. 1972. *River Runner's Guide to Desolation and Gray Canyons, with Emphasis on Geologic Features.* Denver: Powell Society.

————. 1977. *River Runner's Guide to Canyonlands National Park and Vicinity. . . .* Denver: Powell Society.

NASH, RODERICK. 1967. *Wilderness and the American Mind.* New Haven: Yale University Press.

————, ed. 1970. *The Grand Canyon of the Living Colorado.* New York: Sierra Club and Ballantine Books.

NATIONAL ACADEMY OF SCIENCES, COMMITTEE ON WATER. . . . 1968. *Water and Choice in the Colorado Basin.* Washington, D.C.; Government Printing Office.

NELSON, LOWRY. 1952. *The Mormon Village.* Salt Lake City: University of Utah Press.

NIMS, FRANKLIN A. 1967. *The Photographer and the River: The Colorado Canyon Diary of Franklin A. Nims.* Edited by Dwight L. Smith. Salt Lake City: Stagecoach Press.

NULL, JAMES A. 1974. "Water Use as a Property Right." *Colorado Quarterly,* Vol. 22.

OLSEN, ROBERT W. 1965. "Pipe Spring, Arizona, and Thereabouts." *Journal of Arizona History,* Vol. 6 (Spring).

———. 1969. "The Powell Survey's Kanab Base Line." *Utah Historical Quarterly,* Vol. 37 (Spring).

PATTIE, JAMES OHIO. 1962. *The Personal Narrative of James Ohio Pattie of Kentucky.* Edited by Timothy Flint. Reprint. New York: J. B. Lippincott.

PERKINS, CORNELIA, *et al.* 1957. *Saga of San Juan County, Utah.* San Juan County Daughters of Utah Pioneers.

PETERSON, CHARLES S. 1971. "The Hopis and the Mormons." *Utah Historical Quarterly,* Vol. 39 (Spring).

———. 1973. *Take Up Your Mission: Mormon Colonizing Along the Little Colorado River.* Tucson: University of Arizona Press.

———. 1975. *Look to the Mountains.* Provo, Utah: Brigham Young University Press.

———. 1976. *Utah: A Bicentennial History.* New York: W. W. Norton.

POGUE, JOSEPH E. 1911. "The Great Rainbow Natural Bridge of Southern Utah." *National Geographic Magazine,* Vol. 22 (November).

PORTER, ELIOT. 1963. *The Place No One Knew.* San Francisco: Sierra Club.

POWELL, JOHN WESLEY. 1874. "Preliminary Report to Professor Joseph Henry, Secretary of the Smithsonian Institution." Reprinted in *Utah Historical Quarterly,* Vol. 7 (1939).

———. 1895. *Canyons of the Colorado.* Meadville, Pa.: Flood & Vincent. Reprinted as *The Exploration of the Colorado River and Its Canyons.* New York: Dover, 1961.

PRICE, VIRGINIA NUTTER, and JOHN T. DARBY. 1964. "Preston Nutter, Utah Cattleman, 1886–1936." *Utah Historical Quarterly,* Vol. 33 (Summer).

PRUDDEN, T. MITCHELL. 1906. *On the Great American Plateau.* New York: G. P. Putnam's Sons.

PURDY, WILLIAM. 1960. "Green River: Main Stem of the Colorado." *Utah Historical Quarterly,* Vol. 28 (July).

RAHM, DAVID A. 1974. *Reading the Rocks: A Guide to the Geologic Secrets of the Canyons, Mesas, and Buttes of the American Southwest.* San Francisco: Sierra Club.

REDD, CHARLES. 1950. "Short Cut to the San Juan." *1949 Brand Book.* Denver: Denver Posse of the Westerners.

REDFERN, RON. 1980. *Corridors of Time.* New York: Quadrangle/New York Times.

REILLY, P. T. 1969. "How Deadly Is Big Red?" *Utah Historical Quarterly,* Vol. 37 (Spring).

———. 1971. "Warren Marshall Johnson, Forgotten Saint." *Utah Historical Quarterly,* Vol. 39 (Winter).

———. 1978. "Roads Across Buckskin Mountain." *Journal of Arizona History,* Vol. 19 (Spring).

RICHARDSON, ELMO. 1973. *Dams, Parks, and Politics.* Lexington: University of Kentucky Press.

RICKS, JOEL E. 1964. *Forms and Methods of Early Mormon Settlement in Utah.* . . . Logan: Utah State University Press.

RIPPETEAU, BRUCE E. 1979. *A Colorado Book of the Dead: The Prehistoric Era.* Denver: Colorado Historical Society.

ROBINSON, ADONIS FINDLAY, comp. and ed. 1970. *History of Kane County, Utah.* Salt Lake City: Utah Printing.

ROBINSON, MICHAEL C. 1979. *Water for the West: The Bureau of Reclamation, 1902–1977.* Chicago: Public Works Historical Society.

RUSHO, W. L., and C. GREGORY CRAMPTON. 1975. *Desert River Crossing: Historic Lee's Ferry on the Colorado River.* Salt Lake City and Santa Barbara: Peregrine Smith.

SACKS, B. 1964. "Sylvester Mowry." *The American West,* Vol. 1 (Summer).

SCHAAFSMA, POLLY. 1980. *Indian Rock Art of the Southwest.* Santa Fe and Albuquerque: School of American Research and University of New Mexico Press.

SCORUP, STENA. 1944. *J. A. Scorup: A Utah Cattleman.* Privately printed.

SHARP, C. C. 1909. "Notes of a Colorado River Trip." Manuscript, Marston Collection, Huntington Library, San Marino, Calif.

SHEIRE, JAMES. 1972. "Cattle Raising in the Canyons." Typescript, Canyonlands National Park Historic Resources Study, Denver Service Center.

SHELTON, JOHN. 1966. *Geology Illustrated.* San Francisco: W. H. Freeman.

SIMMONS, GEORGE C., and DAVID L. GASKILL . 1969. *The River Runner's Guide to Marble Gorge and Grand Canyon, with Emphasis on Geologic Features.* Denver: Powell Society.

SMITH, COURTLAND. 1972. *The Salt River Project.* Tucson: University of Arizona Press.

SMITH, DWIGHT L. 1960. "The Engineer and the Canyon." *Utah Historical Quarterly,* Vol. 28. (July).

———. 1962a. "Robert B. Stanton's Plans for the Far Southwest." *Arizona and the West,* Vol. 4 (Winter).

———. 1962b. "Hoskaninni: A Gold Mining Venture in Glen Canyon." In *Probing the American West.* Santa Fe: Museum of New Mexico Press.

SMITH, MELVIN. 1970. "Colorado River Exploration and the Mormon War." *Utah Historical Quarterly,* Vol. 38.

———. 1972. "The Colorado River: Its History in the Lower Canyon Area." Ph.D. dissertation, University of Utah.

SPICER, EDWARD H. 1962. *Cycles of Conquest.* Tucson: University of Arizona Press.

STAHLER, GERALD. 1976. "The Grand Canyon Dams Controversy." M.A. thesis, University of Toronto.

STANTON, ROBERT BREWSTER. 1892. "Availability of the Canyons of the Colorado River of the West for Railway Purposes." *Transactions of the American Society of Civil Engineers,* Vol. 26 (April).

———. 1919. "The Alleged Journey, and the Real Journey, of James White, on the Colorado River in 1861 [printer's error for 1867]." *The Trail* (Denver, September).

———. 1932. *Colorado River Controversies.* Edited by James Chalfant. New York: Dodd, Mead.

————. 1961. *The Hoskaninni Papers, Mining in Glen Canyon, 1897–1902.* Edited by C. Gregory Crampton and Dwight L. Smith. University of Utah Anthropological Papers, Glen Canyon Series, No. 15. Salt Lake City: University of Utah.

————. 1965. *Down the Colorado.* Edited by Dwight L. Smith. Norman: University of Oklahoma Press.

STEGNER, WALLACE. 1942. *Mormon Country.* New York: Duell, Sloan & Pearce.

————. 1949. "Jack Summer and John Wesley Powell." *Colorado Magazine,* Vol. 26 (January).

————. 1954. *Beyond the Hundredth Meridian.* Boston: Houghton Mifflin.

————, ed. 1955. *This Is Dinosaur.* New York: Alfred A. Knopf.

STERLING, EVERETT. 1940. "The Powell Irrigation Survey, 1888–1893." *The Mississippi Valley Historical Review,* Vol. 29 (December).

STEWART, GEORGE R. 1937. *John Phoenix, Esq., the Veritable Squibob.* New York: Henry Holt.

STILES, HELEN, ed. 1964. "Down the Colorado in 1889." *Colorado Magazine,* Vol. 41 (Summer).

STOFFLE, RICHARD W., and MICHAEL J. EVANS. 1978. *Kaibab Paiute History: The Early Years.* Kaibab Paiute Tribe.

STOKES, WILLIAM LEE. 1969. *Scenes of the Plateau Lands and How They Came to Be.* Salt Lake City: Publishers Press.

STONE, JULIUS. 1932. *Canyon Country: The Romance of a Drop of Water and a Grain of Sand.* New York: G. P. Putnam's Sons.

STRONG, DOUGLAS H. 1969. "The Man Who Owned Grand Canyon." *American West,* Vol. 6 (September).

SYKES, GORDON. 1926. "The Delta and Estuary of the Colorado River." *Geographical Review,* Vol. 16 (April).

————. 1937. *The Colorado Delta.* Washington, D.C.: American Geographical Society.

————. 1944. *A Westerly Trend.* Tucson: University of Arizona Press.

TANNER, FAUN MCCONKIE. 1976. *The Far Country.* Salt Lake City: Olympus.

TAYLOR, PAUL S. 1970. "Reclamation." *The American West,* Vol. 7 (July).

TILLOTSON, MINER RAYMOND. 1929. *Grand Canyon Country.* Stanford, Calif.: Stanford University Press.

TRENHOLM, VIRGINIA COLE, and MAURINE CARLEY. 1964. *The Shoshonis, Sentinels of the Rockies.* Norman: University of Oklahoma Press.

TRIMBLE, STEPHEN. 1979. *The Bright Edge: A Guide to the National Parks of the Colorado Plateau.* Flagstaff: Museum of Northern Arizona Press.

UDALL, STEWART L. 1963. *The Quiet Crisis.* New York: Holt, Rinehart Winston.

UNITED STATES BUREAU OF RECLAMATION. 1946. *The Colorado River, A Comprehensive Report on the Development of the Water Resources . . . for Irrigation, Power Production, and Other Beneficial Uses.* Washington, D.C.: Government Printing Office.

UNITED STATES CONGRESS. 1954. House Document 364, 83rd Congress, 2nd Session. *A Report on the Colorado River Storage Project and Participating Projects.* Washington, D.C.: Government Printing Office.

UNITED STATES DEPARTMENT OF THE INTERIOR. 1950. *A Survey of the Recreational Re-*

sources of the Colorado River Basin. Washington, D.C.: Government Printing Office.

UNITED STATES V. UTAH. 1931. Supreme Court of the United States, October Term, 1929.) *Abstract in Narrative Form.* . . . 2 vols. Washington, D.C.: Government Printing Office.

VANDENBUSCHE, DUANE. 1973. "Man Against the Black Canyon." *Colorado Magazine,* Vol. 50 (Spring).

————, and DUANE SMITH. 1981. *A Land Alone: Colorado's Western Slope.* Boulder, Colo.: Pruett Publishing.

VERKAMP, MARGARET M. 1940. "History of Grand Canyon National Park." M.A. thesis, University of Arizona.

WAGONER, JAY J. 1975. *Early Arizona: Prehistory to Civil War.* Tucson: University of Arizona Press.

WALKER, DON D. 1964a. "The Cattle Industry of Utah." *Utah Historical Quarterly,* Vol. 32 (Summer).

————. 1964b. "The Carlisles: Cattle Barons of the Upper Basin." *Utah Historical Quarterly,* Vol. 32 (Summer).

WALLACE, EDWARD S. 1955. *The Great Reconnaissance:* Boston: Little, Brown.

WALLACE, ROBERT. 1972. *The Grand Canyon.* New York: Time-Life Books.

WARNE, WILLIAM E. 1973. *The Bureau of Reclamation.* New York: Praeger.

WATERS, FRANK. 1946. *The Colorado.* Holt, Rinehart & Winston.

WATKINS, T. H., ed. 1969. *The Grand Colorado.* Palo Alto, Calif.: American West.

WATSON, ELMO S., ed. 1954. *The Professor Goes West.* Bloomington, Ill.: Illinois Wesleyan University Press.

WEBER, DAVID J. 1971. *The Taos Trappers.* Norman: University of Oklahoma Press.

WHEAT, CARL I. 1957–63. *Mapping the Transmississippi West.* 5 vols. San Francisco: Institute of Historical Cartography.

WILLIS, ANN BASSETT. 1952. "Queen Ann of Brown's Park." *Colorado Magazine,* Vol. 29 (four installments).

WINSHIP, GEORGE P. 1896. "The Coronado Expedition, 1540–1542." Bureau of Ethnology, *Fourteenth Annual Report.* pp. 339–613. Washington, D.C.: Government Printing Office.

WOODBURY, ANGUS M. revised ed. 1950. *A History of Southern Utah and Its National Parks.* Salt Lake City: Utah State Historical Society.

WOODWARD, ARTHUR. 1955. *Feud on the Colorado.* Los Angeles: Westernlore Press.

YOUNG, KARL. 1964. "Wild Cows of the San Juan." *Utah Historical Quarterly,* Vol. 32 (Summer).

ZWINGER, ANN. 1975. *Run, River, Run.* New York: Harper & Row.

————. 1978. *Wind in the Rock.* New York: Harper & Row.

Index